I0731303

MIAMI NIGHTS 3

THE CLIMAX

VICTOR L. MARTIN

WAHIDA CLARK
PRESENTS
INNOVATIVE PUBLISHING

This is a work of fiction. Names, characters, places, and incidents either are the product of the author's imagination or are used fictitiously, and any resemblance to actual persons, living or dead, business establishments, events, or locales are entirely coincidental.

Wahida Clark Presents Innovative Publishing
60 Evergreen Place
Suite 904
East Orange, New Jersey 07018
973-678-9982
PO Box 383
Fairburn, Georgia 30213
www.wclarkpublishing.com

Miami Nights 3 by Victor L. Martin
ISBN 13-digit: 978-1-954161-45-0 (Paperback)
ISBN 13-digit: 978-1-954161-46-7 (eBook)
Library of Congress Cataloging-In-Publication Data:
LCCN 2021916349

1. African American Contemporary Fiction 2. African American Urban Fiction 3. Alpha Male Crime Romance 4. Fast Paced Thrillers 5. Steamy Urban Romance 6. Steamy Fiction Reads
Cover design and layout by Nuance Art.*.
Book design by Nuance Art.*.
Proofreader Rosalind Hamilton
Sr. Editor Linda Wilson

Miami Nights 3
The Climax

A Novel by

VICTOR L. MARTIN

To my uncle, Donald McMillan & my cuzo, Shonda Dobbins...RIP, you'll be forever loved and missed.

ACKNOWLEDGMENTS

Here we are at the final scene of *Miami Nights 3*. I want to mention a few that inspired me to push this pen across these pages.

Michelle Lucas, you know how you played a part in this project, smile. Sophia Carlton, I can't pen enough words to describe the lasting impact you have in my life. Thank you for letting me make your heart smile.

Of course, I gotta mention a few ladies that are living the reality of what I've written, Yum Thee Boss, Victoria Cakes, Ivy Sherwood, Aryana Adin, Lola Marie, Layton Benton, Kira Nori, Cecilia Lion, Jasmine Webb, Cherokee D Ass, and, of course, Pinky. A special mention to Book Club Erotica. Your support is appreciated. Shardasia Jacobs, thank you for everything.

And once again, my readers on Facebook, Coddie Mclawhorn, Hope O'Neal, April O'Neal, Arletha Orr Allen, Author Robin Baskerville Hearon, Keisha McCormick, Janice Robinson, Martina Gainey, Anita Frazier, Ayee Lightskinn Ashley-Nicole, Pam Lunsford, and Keisha Cameron. And James Daye, stay true, bro.

Keep your eyes dry and your heart easy.

- VLM

WEB- VICTORLMARTIN.COM

FACEBOOK- Victor L Martin-Author

Instagram & Twitter- victorlmartin_

1

THE WHITE WAY

Coconut Grove, Florida
July 27th, Present Time

Trevon made no effort to hide the noticeable print of his penis from Chelsea as he joined her out by the pool. He lowered his shades over his eyes as she looked up from the script of their next film.

"Happy belated birthday, handsome!" Chelsea Kelliebrew sat up on a purple cushioned deck chair, flaunting her suntanned breasts. "I know I'm two days late and—"

"It's all good," he assured her as he stepped around the poolside table. "Better late than never." He grinned as the scent of her coconut sunscreen lotion lingered in the midday humid air.

"Glad to hear that," she replied softly as she lowered her light blue eyes from his face and down his body until she reached his crotch. She sucked her bottom lip between her teeth and placed the script aside. "How does it feel to be thirty-five?" she asked as she continued to leer at his arousing 6'4, 248-pound frame.

"You act like I turned fifty or something." He sat down on a matching deck chair beside her.

"You're an old man to me," she kidded. "I'm twenty-three, remember?"

"I gotcha old right here!" He grabbed his masterpiece through the black and green swimming trunks. "I betcha won't be sayin' I'm old when I'm beatin' your back out."

She blushed. "Hmm, that gives me an idea," she said. "The fence is high enough to give us some privacy," she added as a strand of her hair dangled over her mirror tinted shades.

"Privacy for what?" he asked as she twisted her blonde hair into a bun.

"I wanna give you some belated birthday head right out here." She stood and slid her hands down her topless body until she reached the tie-string of the white thong. "You'll always be special to me because you broke my virginity in porn." She slowly pulled the knot on her waist loose with lust, making its way from her eyes to her pussy. "Just lay back and let me make it feel good." She stood over him, willing to state his every desire. A melodious moan escaped her when he slid a hand up between her sun-warmed thighs. She stood motionless until his fingers teased the folds of her moist pussy lips. This is when she enjoyed the sex with him the most. There were no cameras and no director to stop the flow of the raw, sensual chemistry she had with him.

"Ooohhh. You know th-that's my spot," she cooed as his fingers pushed up inside her wetness. She cupped her breasts and squeezed them as he eased his fingers in and out of her.

"You got the sweetest pussy," he moaned. "It's so wet and tight!" He sat up and filled his other hand with her bare ass. He caressed it and made her shudder by sticking his tongue inside her coconut-scented navel.

She squirmed from his tongue, fingers and strong hand molding her ass. She would never delete the intense memory of her first time on film with him. Her mind and body surrendered without fail when it came to sex. Especially with Trevon.

He inhaled the fragrant scent of her pussy as he brushed his lips over her hairless mound. "Here's my belated birthday gift." He licked around her clitoris.

She moaned as he treated her pussy like a gift. He spread her lips apart and jabbed the tip of his tongue inside her. "Yesss!" She dropped her hands to his broad shoulders as he gently moved his tongue up and down the length of her wetness.

He slurped between her thin folds with his hands massaging the soft flesh of her ass. He was intimate with every part of her 5'4 38D-25-42 frame. With his eyes shut, he could navigate every curve of her seductive body.

She felt lightheaded when he pulled his lips from her velvety folds. Under the sweltering sun, she shamelessly fingered herself as he slid his swimming trunks off. They switched positions as he stood, and she sat on the deck chair. She immediately circled her hands around his fully erect penis and stroked it.

"How long has it been since you had those pretty lips wrapped around that right there?" he asked.

"Too long," she answered. "Mmm, it looks delicious," she cooed as she worked her grip back and forth. "Ready?"

He stared at his reflection in her designer shades as she sucked his penis into her mouth. "That's it right there." He put one hand on his waist and the other on her blonde mane. "Work it, baby! Mmm, your lips are so fucking soft!"

She released her hold on him and dug her blue fingernails into his ass. With her eyes closed, she affectionately sucked along the thick shaft of his penis. Her breasts joggled as her head bobbed at a steady pace. Her jaws stretched to accommodate his pulsating girth as she zoned out in her fluid pace. Sweat rolled down her spine and vanished at the split of her suntanned ass. He took in the erotic sight as her wet mouth lathered his dick with a glistening sheen. She moaned as her noisily slurps matched the impassioned effort she exerted.

"Work it baby," he groaned at the performance of her engulfing his protrusion. "Mmm, deepthroat it like I know you can. Yeah, that's it. Just suck it nice and s-slow."

She hummed around his ebony flesh as it slid in and out of her slippery mouth. His dirty talk encouraged her to swallow all of him. Or at least she tried.

"Mmm, I love this!" He gently rocked his hips as she slid a hand between his legs. "Suck it good! Aaahh, just like t-that."

She kept sucking as the sun bathed her from her shoulders to her waist. A thirst for him burned inside her, and only his climactic release would extinguish it. Her lips remained encircled on his long, veiny penis as sweat beaded on her forehead. She paused to lick and suck his tip free of precum that she twirled around her tongue. Her lips traveled up and down the underside of his flesh until her name quavered between his moans. She took him back inside her hands and licked the tip like a chocolate lollipop.

"Ch-Chelsea!" He threw his head back as she traced her pouty lips with the tip of his dick. As she pulled back, a gooey line of precum clung to her bottom lip.

"Mmmm. It's sweet," she whispered with her hands pumping his shaft. "I love your cock, Trevon!" She didn't wait for his reply as she twirled her tongue on the helmet-shaped head of his dick. A breath later, she lashed the tip with her tongue while stroking his shaft and fondling his scrotum.

"Ooohh, fuck!" He dropped his hands on her shoulders when she took him back between her lips. He rode the waves of the sensual pleasures that she was able to induce with her mouth. Spasms raced up and down his legs as the euphoric pleasure continued.

She sped up when he squeezed her shoulders. She sucked harder, knowing he was on the verge of reaching his pinnacle. "Cum for me!" she said excitedly after she whipped his dick from her mouth.

He grunted as he shot his load against her lips. She reacted like a seasoned porn star by opening her mouth and sticking out her tongue.

"Mmmm. That's sooo delicious." She smiled with remnants of his release oozing down her breasts.

"Damn, that was so fucking—"

She swallowed him and giggled while sucking gently on his penis.

"Ooohh, shit! You're killing me with that sweet mouth," he groaned and stood planted in her jaws until she had her way with him.

"THANKS FOR LETTING me spend the night," Chelsea said as she later stood in the shower with Trevon.

"You know you're welcome here anytime," he replied, staring at the sexy dimples above her voluptuous ass.

"And I'll keep that in mind." She handed him the soapy rag over her shoulder. "Can you wash my back?"

Trevon intentionally brushed his penis against her tempting ass as he took the rag. "Do you like the new script?" he asked as he washed her back.

She shrugged as she lifted her soapy breasts under the lukewarm water. "Jurnee could have written a hotter scene of us in the hot tub." *His dick feels so good against my ass! Just once, I want him raw inside me.*

"Send her an email about it."

"Maybe," she replied, wanting to back her ass up closer. "How do you like it?"

He slid the peach-scented rag down her spine and watched the suds run down the split of her ass. "Uh, as long as I'm balls deep inside you, it's all good." He grinned.

"Remember what you did in our first film?" she giggled.

"Yeah," he nodded. "I couldn't pull out of your ass because it felt too good."

"It seems like yesterday," she said dreamily. "You were the first to fuck me on film. And I was your first of the white way." She giggled again as the suds rinsed clear off her perky breasts. "Um, how are things with you and Kandi?"

Trevon sighed as he slid the rag down her spine. "She's going through one of her major mood swings again."

"Everyone thought you two were gonna be the power couple in porn when she had your baby."

"I did too. But I guess life had another idea."

"I know you still got feelings for her because I can hear it in your voice."

He didn't know what to say. "How are things with you and your manager?" He deliberately changed the topic off his issues with Kandi.

"She's cool. Last week she told me she's still working out my new contract with AEF. Vivid wants me to do a few films. But I'd like to work exclusively with AEF."

"What did Vivid offer?"

"A lot! But my heart is with AEF because of Janelle and Jurnee and of course I'm hooked on being with you."

He squeezed the rag at the nape of her neck. "Turn around."

She bit her bottom lip when she faced him. It seemed natural when she lowered her hands to his penis.

He closed his eyes and grabbed a handful of her ass. With sex being their foundation, they kept condoms on hand to maintain their insatiable needs. He lost count of the number of times he had sex with her off the set.

"Let's do it again before I leave." She danced her tongue in and out of his ear as she stood on the tips of her pedicured toes. "You know how I like it."

In a scramble, they got out of the shower and fed their unbridled desires at the bathroom sink.

"Tre-Trevon! Trevon! Ooohh, fuck!" Chelsea whined, bent over the sink with her breasts swaying beneath her. "Ooohh, you're going sooo deep!" she moaned as his thick shaft plunged in and out of her.

He kept a firm hold on her tiny waist until he pumped a climax inside the condom. She treated him like the only man in her life when she removed the condom with her mouth. He stood speechless as she turned the condom inside out and smeared his release all over her breasts. She pulled him back into the shower and washed him clean, spending extra TLC on his masculine torso and his masterpiece of a penis.

"I'LL CALL YOU TONIGHT!" Chelsea waved and blew a pouty kiss as she backed out of the driveway under the toasting sun. The royal blue mid-engine Chevy Corvette matched Chelsea's nature. Fast, beautiful, and sexy.

As she sped off with Taylor Swift pumping from the system, Trevon keyed the alarm on his Lamborghini Aventador SVJ Roadster. The midnight sapphire blue exotic vehicle glimmered under the sun as Trevon watched the driver's side door lift open. His lucrative career in porn allowed him to cover his body in the finest linen and add the Aventador beside his S580 in the driveway. He lived alone in the same house he once shared with LaToria. She filled his thoughts as he drove off toward the first gate with the tinted windows up. He revved the Lamborghini's powerful V-12 engine when he slowed for a speed bump near the front security gate. He grinned as he lowered the driver's side window as the on-duty security guard exited the air-conditioned booth and walked up to his ride.

"Good afternoon, Mr. Harrison," Vanessa Moore said with a cute smile.

He took his shades off and locked eyes with the plus-size, brown-eyed beauty. "Same to you." *She gotta be holding some triple D's under that uniform!*

"I just signed your guest out a moment ago. And I see she spent the night with you," she said with the knowledge and common sense that he had likely spent most of his moments in bed with Chelsea.

Trevon nodded and said. "We had to go over the script for our next film. But, um, when will you find the time to swing by and be my guest? What's stopping that from happening?"

She playfully rolled her eyes. "Because my boyfriend wouldn't like the idea of me being alone with you," she said. "And besides, why would you want my big ole butt when I know you enjoyed that small-waisted blonde you've been laid up with?"

"It's business."

"Business my ass!"

"And I bet it's a lovely sight."

"You're a mess, Tre- I mean, Mr. Harrison."

He licked his lips. "You still having to watch my films behind your boyfriend's back?"

"Unfortunately, yes. And it's all porn, not just your films. But I think he'll come around. He thinks it's wrong for me to lust over another man...even on TV."

"Uh, you be lusting over me?" he grinned.

Vanessa knew she was flirting too much with Trevon. She had *all* of his hardcore films. Behind her boyfriend's back she had reached plenty of orgasms with Trevon on TV and a vibrator buzzing between her full-figured thighs. For those reasons, she had jumped at the open position to be a security guard at Quovadis Estates, where the famous dick slanging Trevon Harrison lived. Before she could continue flirting with him, a Lexus SUV pulled up behind his Aventador SVJ.

"I'll talk to you later, Mr. Harrison." Vanessa *tried* to keep things professional, even with her budding infatuation toward Trevon intensifying beyond her control.

"Can you make that a promise?"

"Mr. Harrison," she said, struggling not to smile. "You can't hold up the gate like this. It'll take only one complaint and my ass is fired."

"Okay, you got it this time." He eased up toward the gate with his eyes undressing her. *I'ma get some of that pussy!*

Trevon left Quovadis Estates behind and wheeled his attention-grabbing roadster to Miami Beach. Along the way, he remembered an important task, and he made a stop at Walmart to buy some pull-up diapers for his thirteen-month-old firstborn baby girl, Victoria VaSandra Harrison. She and his eight-month-old son, Tayvon Leon Harrison, were the two joys in life.

When he reached the condominium, he dwelled on the depressing fact of being apart from LaToria and his child. If he had it his way, he would be with his family without any drama. He hoped LaToria wouldn't be in a bad mood as he entered the lavish suite she shared with Tahkiyah. As he adjusted the diapers under his arm, he wondered how LaToria would react to the news he wanted to share.

"LaToria!" he called out as he closed the door with his elbow. He took off his shades as he crossed the green carpeted living room floor. Just as he started to call LaToria again, he heard the shower running in her bedroom. He stared at the partially opened door and easily pictured LaToria nude under the pelting showerhead. This should be his home. That desire moved him to drop the diapers on the white leather sectional sofa. His steps carried him straight into LaToria's bedroom. The joy of the good times he shared with her stirred the emotions that remained a solid part of him. *Fuck this bullshit! I'm getting my woman back!* He barged into the strawberry-scented bathroom and right up to the purple frosted glass shower. In one motion, he slid the shower door open and stumbled back, speechless from the sight that filled his eyes. *Oh shit!*

2

MILF & PACIFIERS

Miami Beach, Florida
Monday, July 27th

Trevon struggled to find his composure as he stared at Tahkiyah. A flood of dormant lust rushed from his head to his penis as LaToria's mom turned the shower off. She smiled at him, as she didn't bother to cover her seductive nakedness.

"Can you hand me a towel?" she asked as her nipples stiffen in his unexpected presence.

"Uh." He blinked. "Where is—"

"LaToria took Victoria shopping with Jurnee and Tayvon."

"I thought they were gonna do that tomorrow?"

She shrugged. "She left about ten minutes ago."

He lowered his eyes to the floor. "I—Tell her I'll swing by later and—"

"Relax," she said as she stepped out of the shower. "What we did in that room is forever our secret and it will stay that way."

He nodded with his back against the wall, too stunned to speak.

"Just wait for me in the living room because I need to talk to you about something."

He looked at her with his heart drumming. There was no sense to ignore how strickling she looked, even at the seasoned age of fifty-six. She stood 5'4, with a seductive figure and unblemished light honey complexion. Her hazel eyes and sensuous body left him stuck in silence. His first impression of LaToria's mom was lust at first sight. He would never forget how she had sexually pleased him inside the room at the Mondrian Hotel. He knew the intense pleasure of her soft hands massaging his dick and how life-changing it felt to be inside her. Minutes later he sat up on the sofa when Tahkiyah breezed out of LaToria's bedroom in a pair of white leggings and a black halter top. He quickly averted his eyes from her nipple prints.

"Stop acting like you're afraid of me, Trevon." She sat beside him, smelling like a bowl of mixed fruit. "I really need to talk to you."

He sighed and settled back, hoping she would be quick with whatever she had to say. "Okay, what's up?"

"That's what I've been meaning to ask you." She turned in his direction. "Every time I try to be alone with you to talk, you find an excuse to run me, c'mon now."

"No, I don't."

"Yes, you do," she said. "But seriously, we never had the chance to talk about what happened between us. I know this is uncomfortable being that I'm LaToria's mom and you have to believe that I—"

"I've hurt LaToria enough, and if she knew about what we did, she—"

"I'm aware of all that, okay?" She slid a strand of wet hair behind her ear and continued. "I was actually sick to my stomach when I found out you were doing porn with my daughter. This isn't easy for me at all. I deal with this shit almost every night in bed. I still think about it."

He stared at the floor. "We have to leave it in the past, Tahkiyah, for all it's worth, I don't think any less of you because of what we did."

"That's not my point. Right now, I *really* want to talk about what we did. I need to get it off my conscience so I can move on with my life."

He looked at her and struggled to steer away from any lust driven ideas. "Okay, let's talk about it and after today, it's dead."

She nodded. "I agree."

A brief moment of silence sat between them until Tahkiyah spoke again.

"Do you tell all the women you've been with the same line?"

"And what would that be?"

"On that card you left with my rose, you wrote 'you're the best I've ever had'."

"Damn," he said, grinning. "You remember that?"

"I remember everything. Now answer my question. Was I really the best or was it a game?" She waited for his answer.

He slid a hand down his face. "You bugging."

"Just keep it real with me. Like you said, after today it's dead."

"You really wanna know?"

She nodded.

"Honestly...and all bullshit aside. When we had sex-"

"Fucked," she corrected him.

"Okay, when we fucked, it was different from any other moments I had. And, uh, yeah." He nodded. "You were the best."

She smiled. "And I assume I'm the oldest woman you've been with?"

"Yep." *And no need to mention that cougar I had sex with on the location of my debut film.*

"Well, for your information, I still daydream about how you felt inside me and how incredibly long your penis is when it's..."

"Whoa! You, uh—"

"I what?" She crossed her legs. "All I'm doing is speaking the truth. And if it wasn't for my daughter and grandbaby, I'd be on that dick right now. You can't sit there and tell me you didn't enjoy it."

"No, I can't. But we can't sit here and play with fire, Tahkiyah," he said, maintaining control of the awkward situation.

"I'm too grown to play *any* type of games with you," she replied. "We fucked, I took a shower with you, and I moaned *your* name as I came with your dick inside me. I have to live with that secret forever and it's an issue with me."

"How?"

She bit her upper lip. "I had a wet dream about you last week. And when I woke up, I prayed your name didn't run through my lips while I was dreaming. My fear was centered on LaToria hearing me. Anyway, the dream messed me up because it seemed so damn real."

"What's up with that dude you met last month?"

She rolled her hazel eyes and sucked her teeth. "He's too dull! And he isn't a fan of giving oral sex, so I had to dismiss him."

He laughed. "You crazy."

"Hey!" She touched his shoulder. "Let's play truth or dare!"

He wanted to leave, but he couldn't move himself to do so. *Shit. Ain't got nowhere else to go.* "Truth or dare? Yeah, we can do that."

She slid her hand down his arm and pulled away before she did something out of order. "I'll go first. Truth or dare?"

"Truth," he said.

She pondered for a few seconds to come up with a good question. "Um, if we could go back in time. Would you fuck me again?"

He shifted his position to conceal his erection. "Yeah. But it would have to be the same with me not knowing you're LaToria's mom."

"I can understand that. Now, your turn."

"Truth or dare?"

She took her glasses off and set them on the cocktail table. "Truth."

"What's on your mind right now?"

"Hmmm. That's a good question." She grinned. "Well, since I have to play fair, I'll tell the truth. Right now, or a moment ago, I was thinking about how good it felt when we fucked."

"You have any regrets about it?"

She licked her lips. "At first I did. But now, it's just something I have to live with. But if you really want to know my regrets, I'll tell you. To be blunt, I wish I could have wrapped my lips around that wonderful dick of yours. You'd like that, right?"

"Yeah, you're right about that." *Damn, this shit is crazy! Up in here talking freaky shit with my baby mama mom!*

"I feel so guilty to have this urge to be with you again," she admitted. "I know you love my daughter and I wouldn't dare cause any sort of drama between you and her. But every time I see you, my mind takes me back to that moment we shared. You—Trevon, fucked me so good that day. My mind, and especially my body, won't let me forget it."

"I understand," he answered. "And you're not the only one dealing with it. We both have this secret to keep and the urge to do it again. But it's different now, and you know it. LaToria loves you and she's been hurt too much by those that were supposed to protect her."

Tahkiyah respected Trevon and lusted for him in the same breath. "My daughter loves you, but she's afraid of so much. I got upset with her after that issue you two had a few days ago."

"Talking about my new film with Chelsea?"

"Yeah. LaToria keeps telling you she's okay with you doing porn and we both know it's a lie. It's killing her to keep seeing you with other women."

"Why won't she just tell me! I asked her before the baby was even born if she wanted me to stop doing porn."

"It's her pride, and you know how stubborn her ass is."

Trevon sighed and dropped his face in his hands. He had two kids to support, and he wasn't sure if LaToria was worth the risk to end his career. *What if I stop doing porn and we still continue to bump heads over petty shit? Then I'll be—*

"My birthday is on the eleventh of next month," Tahkiyah interrupted his troubled thoughts.

He looked up at her and forced a smile. "I guess I gotta cop you a gift since you got me one for my birthday. And thank you again for those dumbbells."

She laughed. "You were going to get me a gift, regardless. And you're welcome for the dumbbells." She glanced at his large arms, knowing the strength in them.

"Life is crazy," he said. "I keep thinking about all the bullshit I've been through since I've been outta prison."

"Anything you'd like to change?"

He sat back and closed his eyes. "No," he answered.

"What are you going to do about your career?"

"I gotta finish my contract." He opened his eyes and stared at the ceiling.

She battled her lust toward him with each breath she took. "I'll never forget what we have in secret between us."

He reached for her hand. "Don't feel guilty about it."

She squeezed his hand as her heart raced. Right now, for the moment, she was weak. Her body wanted the weight of him on top of her. She smiled at him, knowing she would welcome the whole of him inside her if he made an advance. *What am I thinking! This was my daughter's baby's father!*

Releasing her hand, he stood. "I'ma head on out."

Tahkiyah nodded, figuring it was pointless to speak what was on her mind. *No, I can't fuck him again, no matter how good it felt.* She felt alone and empty when he left her on the sofa.

~

TREVON LATER SLOWED his Aventador SVJ Roadster for a red light on Biscayne Boulevard. He had life on his mind. Everything that mattered to him seemed to be an issue. Having two kids by two women wasn't something to brag about in his honest belief. He tried to make things work with LaToria, but he was afraid to face the chance of their relationship being spoiled if they weren't meant to be. As he waited for the light to turn green, he received a text from Jurnee.

Hey Papi! Call me when u can.

"Hey, Siri, call Jurnee," Trevon spoke clearly to activate the hands-free calling system. The line connected after the third ring.

"Hey, Baby Daddy!" Jurnee's sexy, bubbly voice emitted from the speakers. "Didn't expect you to call me so fast. Whatcha doing with your handsome self?"

"Just riding around," he said as the light changed. "You still shopping with the kids with LaToria?"

"We're doing that tomorrow. Gosh, I just told you about it last night."

He frowned. "LaToria isn't with you?"

"Nope."

What the fuck? I know Tahkiyah ain't tell me a lie!

"Is something wrong?" Jurnee asked.

"Nah, I just got my days mixed up."

"Oh. Well, I just got an email from Chelsea's manager, and she wants me to rewrite the hot tub scene in your next film. You got any ideas?"

"Uh, not really. Chelsea said something about it this morning and I told her to get up with you. Just think of something, okay?" he replied with his mind on LaToria's whereabouts.

"How about this? I can write a new scene of you being a college professor, and Chelsea will be a student you're tutoring. That sound good?"

"Yeah, run with that and see what you come up with."

"I will, and I should have it done by the end of the week."

"How my son doing?"

"He's fine. Trying to crawl all over the house and losing pacifiers every single day," she said in good spirits.

"Use the ones I gave you with the string on 'em."

"Your son pulls that shit off like it ain't nothing."

"Need me to stop and get a new pack since I'm already out?"

"Si, por favor. And get some baby oil because I only have half a bottle left."

"Anything else?"

"Umm, can I get some dick tonight? I need it *real* bad. Like, I need you to spend the night up in it bad." At the age of forty-three, her sex drive was close to being insatiable.

"What time are you leaving?"

"Not sure, because I have to do a Zoom call with Janelle and Wahida Clark before I leave. The latest will be around eight, so I guess I'll text you when I'm about to leave."

"Alright. Just hit me up and yes, I'll spend the night with my Jennifer Lopez looking baby mama." He laughed.

"J-Lo ain't got shit on me and you know it. If anything, she looks like *me*!" Her soft laughter was music to his ears. "But seriously, don't forget the pacifiers and the baby oil. I have to get back to work. I'll see you tonight. Love ya!"

"Okay, sexy. Love ya back." Trevon sped through a green light with his mood twisted between Jurnee and LaToria. In truth, Jurnee was stress free and believed in free love. He realized now that LaToria lived with drama and today proved it. Instead of assuming where she was with his daughter, he chose the better option of calling her.

"Call LaToria," he said as he accelerated up the boulevard. Once. Twice. Three times the line rung before LaToria's voicemail clicked over.

"Hi! Sorry, I can't take your call right now. But if you feel important, leave a message. Bye."

Trevon waited for the tone. "Call me ASAP when you get this! And *call*, don't send me no text. Be safe and kiss Victoria for me.... Love you." When the line disconnected, he couldn't stop his mind from running with the reason why a lie was told. He believed Jurnee, so it turned his thoughts on Tahkiyah and LaToria. One or both were on some bullshit, and Trevon stood far from being in the mood for any such lies when it involved his daughter.

AT THE SAME time in West Palm Beach, Kandi turned heads as she returned to the outdoor restaurant table with Victoria on her wide hip. Her new body measurements were on full display under the figure-hugging oyster-white Gucci sundress. She looked deadly sexy in a matching color straw hat and tinted shades over her alluring green eyes. After giving birth to her firstborn, she whipped her figure back in shape and proudly advertised her 5'7, redbone 34DD-30-48 proportions. As she neared the table, she smiled as her guest jumped up from his chair to pull her seat back. For a white man, at the age of forty-one, she ranked his looks and sex appeal at a modest eight. She admired his refined looks and the trendy salt and pepper beard. His grey eyes and full head of black hair pushed lewd ideas of sex into Kandi's mind.

"So, where were we, Mr. Levinson?" Kandi asked as Victoria pulled her black and brown hair extensions. "Stop pulling mommy's hair," Kandi said endearingly.

"You can call me Sean." He took his seat at the table. "As I mentioned, my film company will be fair *and* pay you more than what you made at AEF. The deal will start with two films and both will be interracial."

"And the theme?" She stayed focused on business, with Victoria squirming on her lap.

"One will be a gangbang with four of my actors and the second will be with me."

Motherfucker just wants some black pussy! "Will you also cover my living expenses while I'm in California?"

"Absolutely! We'll cover everything, food, transportation, clothes, entertainment. All you have to do is—"

"Fuck you and your friends on film," Kandi blurted. "And that's the only time I'll do it. On film."

3

LIKE MOTHER, LIKE DAUGHTER

Miami Beach, Florida
Monday, July 27th

Tahkiyah turned from the stove when LaToria and Victoria entered the condominium.

"Hey, ma! Whatcha cooking?" Kandi asked as she lowered Victoria to the floor.

"Chicken and rice," Tahkiyah smiled as Victoria -already walking at 13 months- made a beeline toward her with tiny arms held up. "You leave your bags in the truck?" She picked up Victoria and kissed her mahogany cheek.

"Uh, yeah." Kandi lied. "Did the maintenance crew fix the drain in your bathroom yet?"

Kandi flopped down on the sofa and removed her stylish stilettoes.

"Not yet and yes, I sent another email about it." Tahkiyah bounced Victoria in her arms.

Kandi sighed. "Trevon drop these diapers off?" She stared at the bag across the living room.

"Of course, he did, and you need to call him."

Kandi rolled her eyes. "Want me to finish cooking because Victoria needs to be changed."

Tahkiyah sniffed at Victoria's belly, causing a fit of giggles from the little one. "Yeah, and don't put too much salt in it this time."

Kandi waited until her mom stepped into the bathroom with Victoria, until she called Trevon. The line sounded with one of his frequently changing ringtones as she stirred the chicken and rice with the wooden spoon.

"Hey, what's up?" Trevon answered after the second loop of a current song by Lucci.

"Nothing much. I got your voicemail, and you didn't have to be so demanding."

"Where you at?"

"Home and thank you for the diapers."

Trevon sighed. "Will you stop acting like I'm going out of my way to take care of my little one? You don't have to thank me for anything I do to support Victoria."

"Whatever!" *Ain't got time for this shit!*

"Where you been?"

She smacked her lips. "Boy, you can miss me with that bullshit 'cause you ain't got no ring on my finger to be checking me!"

"I do when you dragging Victoria with you!"

"She's *my* daughter too, and I can take her anywhere without getting your permission! I'm the one that's taking care of her while yo' ass is running the streets slanging dick!"

"You still tripping on the bullshit you started? LaToria, you're the one that kicked me out for the second time!"

"That's because I got tired of you coming to bed smelling like other bitches!" She slammed the spoon on the counter.

"It's my job, LaToria!" He lowered his tone. "The same job you said you didn't have a problem with me doing.

"No!" she shouted. "I said I didn't care!" *But I do.*

"LaToria—Please stop this shit. I *hate* how things are between us and—"

"I don't wanna hear it, okay? You're doing what makes you

happy, and that's being the man you are. There will never be an us and we—"

"You really believe what you're saying?"

She fought to keep her tears at bay. "Just do what makes you happy," she said morosely, with her lips quivering. "Even if it's not with me!" She closed her eyes and turned the phone off before he could reply. She wiped her wet eyes as she dealt with the heartache of her issues with Trevon. *Love ain't shit but a fucking fantasy!* She snatched the spoon off the counter and broke a nail. "Shit!" She took her mood out on the chicken and rice since she didn't know how to sort out the matters of her heart.

~

TAHKIYAH WAITED until Victoria took a nap before she asked LaToria to join her at the dining room table.

Kandi picked at her food until the silence got under her skin. "What's wrong, ma?" She laid the fork down. "You've been giving me that *look* since we started eating."

"Why are you afraid to be real with yourself?" Tahkiyah asked from across the glass-topped table.

Kandi frowned. "Ma, if this is about Trevon—"

"It's about you and your future, LaToria! I'm tired of you acting like you don't love that man!"

"Ma, please," Kandi shook her head. "I appreciate your concern, but whatever problems I have with Trevon, is my business."

"Really?" Tahkiyah replied tersely.

"Yes, *really*!" Kandi snapped. "Don't sit there and treat me like a kid because I'm not! I've been through hell and back and look at me now!"

"But are you happy?" Tahkiyah asked. "All this material shit doesn't mean nothing, LaToria. I hear how you cry yourself to sleep at night, and we both know why."

"You don't know me!" Kandi jumped to her feet. "You gave up

on me, remember! Now you want to waltz into my life? I don't need you or nobody else to tell me how to live my fucking life!"

Tahkiyah saw the fire in LaToria's eyes. "I can't argue on the past," Tahkiyah said without matching LaToria's tone.

"I know damn well you can't!"

"Where is all this anger coming from?"

"I'm just tired of all this drama, okay?" Kandi shouted. "I wish I never met Trevon and I wish I never had his baby—" *No, I don't mean that!* Kandi gasped and covered her face in shame.

Tahkiyah snatched her glasses off. "Now you listen to me! I know I'll never get the best mom in the world award. However... I will not let you end up like me! Victoria needs you to get your act together and stop all this foolishness!"

"But—"

"No! You need to shut up and listen to me!" Tahkiyah stood and saw herself across the table in her daughter. "I won't let you run from your daughter like I did when I had you. Life isn't meant to be easy, and being a mother sure as hell ain't. You have to figure out what you want out of life, and no matter what that is Victoria comes first!"

"I d-didn't mean it," Kandi said with tears in her eyes. "I just hate m-my life."

Tahkiyah sat back down and stared at the table. I *hate my life too.*

"I'm sorry about the things I said," Kandi whispered.

"It's okay. Stop crying before your eyeliner starts to run."

Kandi wiped her eyes and glanced at the time on her phone. "Can you watch Victoria for me?" She held up her chipped fingernail. "I need to go to the nail shop before it closes."

"Go ahead," Tahkiyah replied, as she slid her glasses back on. "Just make sure you don't bring that sour attitude back with you."

"Thanks," Kandi said as she pulled her emotions in check. Ten minutes later, she sat behind the wheel of her brand-new obsidian black BMW X7 SUV down in the parking garage. She checked her eyeliner and mascara before she lowered her shades over her eyes.

Flawless. With her mind made up, she left the garage and hit the streets of Miami with a purpose.

KANDI LATER EXITED the nail shop at 5:35p.m. with a new pink and white Cuban manicure. Like always, her figure and model looks drew attention everywhere she went. She flirted with a tall and handsome brown-skinned police officer that pulled her over for doing 68 in a 55-mph zone. The deep neckline of her sundress gave the cop a free display of the inner swells of her breasts. She got off with a simple warning *after* she typed his name and number into her phone.

As she pulled from the curb, she used the hands-free calling system to call her mom.

"Hello?" Tahkiyah answered, with Victoria laughing and screaming in the background.

"I hear Lil Mamma is up. What is she doing making all that noise?"

"Splashing water *out* of the tub and getting me wet. She's going straight to bed after I get her tail out."

Kandi giggled. "Now you see why I take baths with her because you'll end up wet, just like her little butt."

"Put that rag down and stop putting it in your mouth! That's nasty, Victoria."

"Did she use the potty today?"

"Yes, and no. She did her little pee pee on time, but we had a late call with stinky. She'll get it. We have to be patient with her. You get your nails fixed?"

"Yeah and I'm on my way home."

"How about you stay out for a little longer to unwind," Tahkiyah suggested. "You haven't had any time to yourself since Victoria was born. Go to a bar or something."

"You sure?"

"Yes. But call me if you plan to stay out late," Tahkiyah said.

"Look, let me get off this phone because this girl is a handful. Now she's trying to let the water out the tub!"

Kandi laughed. "I doubt I'll stay out late. Thanks for this."

"Just unwind and get your mind right. And have some fun."

"I will. And one more thing."

"Yeah?"

"I love you."

"I love you too, baby."

Kandi ended the call with a new sense of relief. *Have some fun.* She smiled. *What I need is a face between my legs!* She thought of a few male porn stars she could call, but she didn't think they could keep her business off social media. Her pussy throbbed at a feverish level that changed the shape of her nipples. At a red light in downtown Miami, she spread her legs and touched herself through the white thong. A warm wetness met her fingers. "Damn!" She bit her bottom lip in heat and in need of some sexual attention. The thong absorbed the juices that seeped from her throbbing furrow. She fought the urge to slide it aside and touch herself as she drove. With lust compelling her, she made the choice to do something spontaneous and freaky.

KANDI'S X7 ended up in the driveway of a gated, modest size home in Coral Gables. She was met at the front door by a former porn star by the name of Heather Cocks. "Kandi!" Heather hugged her old friend, mashing her fake 30GG breasts against her. "What are you doing here? Come in, girl! Gosh, ya look fabulous! How's the baby?"

"She's fine," she replied.

"Good! Good!" Heather nodded as she guided Kandi into the smoky, dim-lit living room. "I can't believe you're here! Do you wanna catch a live peep show?" She winked.

Kandi came to a stop when she saw a suited, blindfolded white man in the corner with his pants around his feet. Seated in front of him was a topless redhead slurping back and forth on his average-length penis. "I see business is good?" Kandi nodded in the direction of the redhead.

Heather smiled and adjusted her lopsided titties. "HOP, House of Pleasure. Where your sexual fantasy can *cum* a reality."

Kandi was well aware of the sexual deeds that happened under the roof at HOP. Heather staged live sex acts for a fee and she employed four women and three men to cater to her customer's sexual request. To be blunt about it, HOP was a brothel and House of Prostitution seemed a better title for the establishment in Kandi's view. "What's the special tonight?" Kandi asked as she stepped around the "C" shaped sofa to get to a side view of the redhead at work.

"I got three of my girls taking on one man in a few minutes. And later I'll let a few guys titty fuck me in the hot tub. You just missed the orgy. Mmm, cum was flying all over the place."

Kandi studied the skinny redhead. *She don't know how to suck dick.* "Who's she?" Kandi softly whispered.

Heather frowned. "She's new and the worst at giving head."

"Can't tell him that," Kandi noticed the slacked jaw of the man as he enjoyed the feeling of being in the redhead's mouth.

"Guess who's here?" Heather danced on her toes. "You won't believe it!"

"Who?" Kandi asked as the man moaned across the room.

"The guy that had the honor of licking your pussy in your debut film with AEF!"

Kandi gasped. "Conda! Conda is here?" *Ain't seen his ass in... three years!*

Heather nodded. "He's lined up to use his *special* talent on one of my loyal clients later on tonight. I know he'll be shocked to see you!" she gushed.

Kandi felt a chill dance up and down her spine at the sound of Conda's name. When she did her debut film for AEF, Conda was at the height of his porn career. All the ladies wanted a piece of Conda, including Janelle. Conda's downfall was his heavy drug use of heroin and opioids. “Where is he?” *Mmm! I gots to see him!*

“Follow me.” Heather reached for Kandi’s hand.

Heather took Kandi down the hall with an idea spinning in her head. *Conda’s Kandi* was one of AEF’s top-selling films, and Heather knew why Kandi was so giddy to see her former costar.

CONDA DROPPED an unlit cigarette when a knock sounded on the door behind him. “Yeah, who is it?” he asked with his face twisted. He assumed it was his next session. *Bitch early as hell!* The knock rapped again. Conda sighed and strolled to the door shirtless with a mock smile. His entire mood and posture perked up when he opened the door.

“Surprise!” Kandi greeted him.

“What the hell! Kandi, what are you- wow, you look-” Conda motioned her inside and closed the door a little too quick for her comfort.

OMG, he looks like he’s sixty, and we’re the same age! “Long time no see!” She hugged him. “What in the hell are you doing up in here?” *I already know. But I wanna hear it from him.*

Conda shrugged his bony shoulders and sat at the foot of the bed. “Making a living the best way I can,” he replied spiritlessly, with his head down.

“I last heard you were trying to make a comeback in Los Angeles. What happened?”

“Couldn’t kick my habit.” He took a sweeping glance at the baddest bitch in the porn industry, in his opinion. “What’s been up with you?”

“I’m retired,” she replied.

“Bullshit!”

She nodded. “My last film was last year.”

“Why? I mean—you’re the best in the biz! Can’t nobody fuck with—”

"I had a baby, Conda," she interrupted his praise of her.

"By who? Damn! Sure, wish I coulda hit dat sweet ass raw." Kandi shifted her feet and noticed the lecherous looks in Conda's beady eyes. "Ever heard of Trevon Harrison?"

He shook his bald head. "Nah. I've been out of the porn loop because of my trips in and out of rehab," he explained. "And I don't do the social media."

"So, what brings you back to Miami, of all places?"

"Familiarity, I guess. I just got here three weeks ago after Heather reached out to me."

"And you like it here?" She frowned with a disgusted expression.

He sighed. "It's a roof over my head and money in my pocket, so I won't bitch about it. I let a lot people down that tried to help me back in the day."

Kandi recalled how she once paid off one of Conda's drug debts to a notorious drug dealer in Liberty City. "Are you still using drugs?"

"Just weed. I've been off the strong stuff for ten months," he told her as he tried to imagine how her new figure looked under the sundress. "Enough about me. What are you doing in this dump? And don't tell Heather I said that," he said with a lopsided grin.

She cleared her throat. "I'm just passing through and I thought about dropping in on Heather to see how she was doing."

"She's still the same. Earning a living with sex."

"Looks like she's using your talents, huh? But this isn't AEF."

"Those were the days."

She cracked a smile. "Did you ever have that operation?"

He shook his bold, acorn-shaped head. "I'm still the same."

Kandi glanced at the door, and then she reached for the hem of her sundress. "Can I see it?"

"Only if I can use it."

She nodded and tugged up the hem of her sundress as he opened his mouth. Slowly, he extended his abnormally long tongue. It lolled past his chin before he flicked the tip in a manner that reminded her of its thrilling pleasure. She acted on pure lust for his tongue in her pussy. She pulled the sundress up over her luscious ass and hips until it circled her waist. He snapped her thong off and held the soaked fabric to his nose. He inhaled her raw scent as she lay back on the bed with her legs spread. He lowered his face to her center, straightened his tongue and slowly pushed it between the slick flaps of her sweet juiciness.

"Oohh! Sh-shit!" she moaned as he slithered his tongue in and out of her. "Mmm, I love it! Yasss! Just keep doing whatcha doing!" she hissed in rapture and was oblivious to the redhead quietly entering the room.

4

KANDI SO SWEET

Coral Gables, Florida
Monday, July 27th

"C-cummin' again!" Kandi's high-pitched moans bounced off the walls as she lowered and lifted herself on Conda's stiff tongue. Her thick thighs straddled his face as she lost herself in total absorption to reach her third orgasm. "Almost th-there!" She rode his tongue like an erection, clapping her ass against him. Stark nude, her big breasts bounced between her outstretched arms that were braced against the headboard.

Conda slapped her juicy ass as the flavorful nectar of her pussy oozed down his throat. He wanted her to cum again and again until he drowned in her release. His tongue had this effect over every female he tasted. They became addicted and acted compulsively in need of his tongue. Kandi was no different as she howled above him. Conda felt whole again with her on his face and the redhead sucking impassioned on his less than average size dick.

Kandi shivered in the clutch of her third orgasm. Sweat rolled down her heavy breasts as she gyrated on his face. Unlike a dick, his tongue stayed forever rigid inside her. Her heart thudded as he removed his tongue from her pussy and wormed it deep in the split of her sweaty, succulent ass.

"Awww! Yass!," she whined. "I can't take it no more," she said, winded as she rolled off his rope of a tongue while the redhead continued to tend to Conda's penis. *His tongue is longer than his dick,* Kandi thought as she reached for the redhead's wrist and guided it between Conda's legs. "Rub his balls while you suck." She gave the redhead a pointer before she slid off the bed.

Conda propped up on his elbows and stared at Kandi as she started to put her clothes back on. His bond with Kandi wasn't what it used to be. He made no move to stop her as she got dressed. Instead, he simply closed his eyes as his own climax gradually rose between his legs.

Kandi shimmied the taut sundress down her hips, ass, and thick thighs as Conda released a low throaty moan in the midst of his climax. She left her thong on the floor as she turned her back on Conda and the redhead. Her exit was made without any words and she surely wasn't down to stay in touch with Conda. As she reached the living room, she glanced at her watch. *Shit! It's five minutes to seven! Don't seem like I've been here almost an hour.* Her steps came to a sudden halt when she reached the front door. Heather's white, nude body was on full exhibit atop a sturdy wooden table in the middle of the candlelit living room. She lay on her back, servicing four Asian men at the same time. The tallest of the four men hammered away at Heather with her legs hooked over his arms. His pale ass moved rapidly as he frantically had his way with the worn-out porn star. Asians two and three stood on Heather's left and right, moaning as she stroked their lubricious erections. Asian four had his head tilted back as he pumped his penis in and out of Heather's experienced mouth. Seated around the live show were four more Asian men sharing a hookah. The sight didn't turn Kandi on. She took it as a warning that she needed to get her life together.

I gotta get the fuck up out of here! Kandi rushed out of the house and jumped into her X7 with no thought of ever returning. She drove undirected through the streets of Miami. When her eyes blurred with tears, she left them unchecked. At a red light, she glanced up at the rearview mirror and noticed her eye shadow had turned her tears black. She left the streaks on her face as she dealt with her heartache over Trevon. Conda's world-class tongue had Kandi feeling impure. *I'm tired of this shit.* She blinked her eyes clear as she drove mile after mile with the weight of her stress crushing the life out of her. The thought of being alone shook the fight out of Kandi. She knew the difference between her wants and needs, and the truth filled her with the want of loving Trevon. Deeper, she needed him like a bird needed wings. She had the fortitude to exist on the ground, on her own two feet. But with Trevon, her wings, she flew high and with him there were no rules that defined her love for him. She shoved the stupid idea of going to California to fuck white men on film out of her mind. She wanted to make Trevon choke on a pill of jealousy so he could know the feeling of her suffering. Finally, she wiped her eyes, hopefully for the last time, due to the strain in her heart. *I know what I have to do. Please God, don't let me make a fool of myself.* As she cruised toward the green light at the intersection ahead, she never saw the dump truck speeding in for a violent collision with the driver's side door of her BMW X7.

~

"You need to hurry and get over here, Papi," Jurnee's sultry voice came through the speaker of Trevon's phone on the bathroom sink.

"Yeah, hurry up!" Ariana chimed in the background. "We so horny."

He turned the shower off and reached for a towel. "Patience is a virtue, ladies. And good thangs come to those that wait."

"Damn that!" Jurnee remarked. "The only thang I want to *cum* is that dick of yours. It's nine o'clock and you're late," she whined. "My pussy is throbbing for that dick!"

"Mine too!" Ariana added whimsically.

"And when you get over here," Jurnee continued. "I want you to beat it real good from the back."

He smiled. "With the lights on?"

"Uh huh. And Ariana said she wants to ride you again." Jurnee giggled.

"What's funny?" he asked as he dried his arms off.

"Ariana and her silly ass. She is doing a bunch of stretching because she knows how you like to bend her ass up. Hell, I'm missing half a leg and I still throw this pussy good!"

Trevon chuckled as Rex poked his head in the bathroom. "Y'all crazy."

"No, we ain't," Jurnee said. "We horny for some dick that you need to bring to us ASAP. Oh, don't forget to bring the-"

"Pacifiers and baby oil. I got'em, baby."

"Thanks, baby daddy," Jurnee cooed amorously.

He shook his head. *She's just like LaToria. Thanking me for shit I'm supposed to do for my seed.* "When is Janelle coming back from maternity leave?"

"Not sure. I spoke to her a little after that zoom videoconference and she isn't in any rush to return to work."

"I guess not, since she gave you a big promotion and left you in charge. Damn, my baby mama is the VP of the company!"

"And my baby daddy is the top selling male actor at AEF!"

"Yo, you're something else," he replied as he dried his torso.

"What I'ma be is all over your dick as soon as you get it over here. Are you finished with your dang shower?"

"Yeah, I'm about to get dressed."

"Come naked." Jurnee laughed. "We gonna have you naked the moment you step under this roof, anyway."

"Now you're really talking crazy," he replied. "Is my son asleep?"

"In your dreams. His tail never sleeps! But I love my lil man."

"What he doing right now?" Trevon wrapped the towel around his waist and grabbed the phone off the sink.

"In his crib, looking at Ariana. I just fed him, so he *should* be asleep by the time you get here. And yes, I'll make sure he's on his back when he goes to sleep."

Trevon stepped over Rex and hoped he had the endurance to gratify Jurnee and Ariana. His body was still in recovery mode from his one-on-one coitus with Chelsea. "You, uh, talk to LaToria today?"

"No. But I sent her a text about going shopping with the kids tomorrow. Y'all two still at odds?"

"Yeah, something like that," he replied. "I tried talking to her today, and she said some dumb shit and hung up in my face!"

"You call her back?"

"Hell no!" Trevon replied, discontented.

"You shouldn't be like that."

He frowned. *Always taking LaToria's side, even when she's the one in the wrong!* "Ain't calling her back because I'm tired of her bull-"

"Stop right there, Trevon!"

He shook his head, knowing she was about to get on his ass whenever she used his name.

"She's the mother of your firstborn and you can *never* get tired of her as long as Victoria is in the picture. I know y'all going through a lot of shit, but Victoria needs both of you and that's keeping it one hundred with you."

She's right. Hell, she's always right. "I'll call her in the morning," he grumbled.

"And I'll make sure of it."

Just as Trevon reached for his Gucci briefs on the bed, Rex made a gruff bark and scrambled to his feet. He barked again and bolted out of the bedroom. "Hold on a second," Trevon said as he headed for the door.

"What's wrong? I heard Rex bark."

"Somebody at the front door, I guess. But I didn't hear the doorbell or a knock."

"Might be one of your stalkers," Jurnee kidded.

"Yeah, right," he replied as he hurried down the hall. *Odd. Rex usually barks like crazy when someone is at the*—Trevon came to a halt when he reached the living room. Rex sat at LaToria's feet, licking her hand. "Uh, Jurnee, let me call you back. LaToria here."

"Okay–Just call me back later."

He ended the call. "LaToria?"

She looked up with fresh tears and eyeliner running down her face. Trevon forgot about all their issues and rushed to her side. He took her shivering body in his arms and held her close. She sobbed against his bare chest.

"Baby, what's wrong?" he asked, full of concern. "Talk to me."

"I almost died!" She sobbed. "On m-my way here, I almost g-got hit by this b-big ass truck. I was so sc-scared. All I c-could think about was you and our b-baby and—"

"Shhh. It's okay, LaToria." He closed his eyes and tried not to think of life without her.

"I wanna come back home," she said. "Ple-please, Smooch. I wanna come back home. Don't wanna fi-fight you no more. I can't do th-this no more. I just wanna be with you."

Trevon allayed LaToria's grief until her tears dried on his chest. He held her close, never once removing his strong arms from around her.

"You, okay?" he whispered moments later. "You were shaken up real bad, huh?"

She nodded as she wiped her eyes. "I need to take a shower," she said as Rex licked her ankle. "And then-" She paused to gather herself. "I need to be with you, Smooch." She stood and fought the temptation of pulling his towel off. *No. I gotta wash—scrub the feeling of Conda off before I give myself to Trevon.*

Trevon leaned back on the sectional sofa as LaToria hurried down the hall and back to the bedroom. *What the fuck I'ma do now?* He picked up his phone and called Jurnee. After the first ring, his call went to her voicemail.

"Hiii! You've reached Jurnee D. Cruz—"

"Shit!" Trevon murmured after he ended the call. He tapped the phone on his forehead and waited a few breaths before he tried to reach Jurnee again. Just as he pulled up her number, his phone buzzed with a text.

No need 2 explain. BM1 will always come before BM2. Don't really wanna talk 2 u right now. Let me deal with dis on my own. GN.

"Damn!" He dropped the phone on his lap and shook his head. This was the first sign of any jealousy Jurnee showed toward LaToria. He knew she felt some type of way when she referred to herself as BM2 (Baby Mama #2). In his standpoint, both women were number one, and the same went for his kids. He had to deal with Jurnee differently than he would with LaToria, and that in itself presented a tricky challenge. Two women with two unique breeds of emotions.

~

"HE'S NOT COMING?" Ariana slid her hand gingerly up Jurnee's bare hip as they lay face to face on the plush mattress.

"Not tonight," Jurnee whispered, making a weak effort to conceal her hurt.

"Shoot!" Ariana had her mind set on feeling Trevon's strong erection inside her. "Are you mad about it?"

Jurnee sighed and turned on her back. Her new position slid the sheets off her olive breasts. "A little bit and it's confusing me," she admitted.

Ariana sat up, revealing her undersize breasts. "Don't let it get to you," she whispered as she stroked Jurnee's face with a gentleness that came from the authentic love between them.

Jurnee smiled in the dark bedroom. "I won't." She reached for Ariana's left breast and circled her index finger around her pointy nipple. "I don't know how I'd make it without you in my life."

"Let me make you feel good." Ariana slid the sheets back and lowered her mouth to Jurnee's.

They kissed affectionately, taking turns with each other's tongue inside their mouth. Jurnee stayed on her back as Ariana licked and kissed a path down her excited flesh. She closed her eyes, squirming as Ariana licked softly up the moist length of her throbbing essence.

"Yesss!" Jurnee purred, wishing it was Trevon in secret.

KANDI FELT RENEWED after the lengthy shower. She welcomed all the special memories that filled her head as she wrapped a towel around her body. The first day she met Trevon, she gave him some slow head in the shower until he ejaculated in her mouth. A subtle smile formed when she saw all of her personal hygiene items still under the sink. With her heart settled she took care of her after shower routine with hopes Trevon would be at peace with her presence. When she opened the bathroom door, she nearly tripped over Rex.

"Out!" Trevon ordered from the bed.

Kandi turned the bathroom light off as Rex trotted out of the bedroom. "I see he listens to you now."

"Sometimes." He stood as she crossed the room to close the door. He admired the noticeable shape of her ass under the towel. *Damn! My queen looks so good!*

"Can I stay with you tonight, Smooch?" She faced him with her hands clasped behind her.

Trevon stared at her with the towel still around his waist. "Only if you promise to stay forever."

"We have so much to talk about, Smooch."

He nodded. "I know. But at least we'll be talking and not fussing."

She lowered her sexy green eyes. "I miss you so much!"

"C'mere and stop acting all crazy." He opened his arms.

Her smile widened as she crossed the room and stepped back into his arms. She felt light on her bare feet when he kissed her. She wrapped her arms around his neck as he slid his strong hands under the towel to grip her ass.

Trevon wanted to possess every cell of LaToria. He sucked gently on her spearmint-flavored tongue as he pulled the towel from around her waist. A deep, yearning moan was exchanged between them as his towel fell to the floor. She dropped her left hand from his neck and ringed her soft fingers around his elongated penis. She stroked it with a teasing twist each time her hand reached the tip.

He groaned with his tongue grinding against hers. He squeezed, palmed and rubbed her luscious ass as if it was new to him. He slid his fingertips down the crevasse of her ass until he discovered her lubricious pussy. She panted as his fingers danced in and out of her opening between her thick thighs. She licked cravenly across his lips and pumped her hand faster on his penis. Her whole body shuddered from the need of him.

He fingered her moist furrow as she squeezed his throbbing shaft. He tongued her from collarbone to her jeweled ear. With his free hand, he cupped her breast to his mouth. Her pregnancy had increased her breasts from 36D to 34DD.

"Mmmm. Lick it, Smooch." She threw her head back as he sucked on her nipple. Time seemed to pause for her. His fingers inside her, his mouth on her breast, her hand wrapped around the root of him and her heart beating in synchronization with his. Her breaths raced through her lips as he feasted on her sensitive nipples. His actions left a hickey on each breast. LaToria floated on it, floated on love when her man guided her on the bed. He started from the bottom, kissing her feet, her toes, her ankle, shins, knees and in between her thighs.

There, he paused with his face inches from her moist opening. She squirmed when he slowly shoveled the tip of his tongue up between the slick petals of her labia. "Smooch!" she crooned as she pulled at her nipples. She fed him, gyrating her hips instinctively as he slurped on her hypersensitive clitoris in and out of his mouth. "Ummm! Ohhh, Smooch. It's y-your poo-poo. Always yours, Smooch." She squeezed her thighs against his head when he gently licked her responsive clitoris. "Aahh! Aahh! Sm-Smooch.

Ummm! Don't stop! Don't st-stop! Right there! Right th-there! Umm," she squealed, pinching her nipples as her climatic discharge oozed over his lips, chin and into his mouth.

He crawled up her shivering body as she chanted his name in devotion. He kissed both of her pronged nipples and licked between the swells of her perfumed breasts.

"Smooch!" she moaned and drew her knees up, offering her all to him. "I love you!" Their eyes met as she reached down for his raw penis to guide it inside her wetness. He penetrated her, holding his breath with the aim to make love to the woman below him. LaToria, his Kandi.

5

BUENO PUSSY

Coconut Grove, Florida
Tuesday, July 28th

"Ma!" Kandi held her phone near her face as she stood near the stove having a FaceTime call with her mom. "I know I forgot to call last night and I have a good reason."

"I bet you do. I said to have fun. Not be irresponsible and stay out all night! Don't get me wrong because I don't mind watching Victoria, but you—"

"I'm with Trevon, Ma!" Kandi beamed.

"As in what?"

"You know," she said. "We made up, and I spent the night with him!"

"That's wonderful!"

Kandi walked barefooted toward the refrigerator wearing one of Trevon's button-down shirts. "I'm about to cook my baby daddy some breakfast."

"Love him, feed him...and love his ass some more." Takiyah smiled on the screen.

"Ma, you crazy!" Kandi said as she opened the refrigerator. "What lil Mama up to?"

"On the floor watching a cartoon. Oh, she did a successful potty this morning!"

"Aww, I missed it," Kandi whined. "My baby growing up so fast."

Tahkiyah laughed. "Don't worry, because there will be plenty more. Now, what's up with you and my future son-in-law?"

"Well," Kandi said as she took a carton of eggs out and set them on the counter. "We had a long serious talk this morning and I'm going to stick by him as he completes his contract with AEF. It's a business. However, I told him the *only* time he'll be with any of those AEF girls is when the camera is rolling."

"Are you sure you can handle that?"

Kandi slid a jug of milk aside and grabbed a pack of bacon. "Yeah. I've been in his shoes before. I believe he can draw the line between business and pleasure."

"Just follow your heart is all I can tell you."

"That's what I'm doing," Kandi replied as she dropped the bacon beside the eggs and closed the refrigerator.

"Where is he now?"

"On his way back from Jurnee's crib."

"Hmm. And what's the deal on that?

"We're all one big family, Ma. I'll never ask him to choose between Jurnee and I. She's still my bestie, and we already been through some tough times."

"Are you happy with all this?"

Kandi turned and opened the cabinet above the wall mounted microwave. "Yeah. I realized I wanted everything to be perfect."

"You have to make sacrifices in the name of love and I told you that before Victoria was born, now you see the true meaning of it."

"Yeah, I guess so," Kandi replied as she pulled a box of grits out of the cabinet.

"Are you and Jurnee still going to be doing y'all thang on the side?"

"Ma!" Kandi gasped. "That's TMI," she said, grinning as Rex

trotted into the kitchen and found a spot to lie on the spotless kitchen floor.

"All three of y'all need to go to bed together and just let it all out."

"Change the subject, ma. You tripping for real!" Kandi smiled.

"I'm just saying. But anyway, when are you coming home?"

"Uh, soon after I spend a little more time with Trevon. I'm going shopping with Jurnee today."

"I thought you did that yester—"

"I lied. And before you get upset with me, I promise to explain everything to you when I get home."

"LaToria! I told Trevon what you told me and—"

"Everything is okay, Ma. I told Trevon I told you I went shopping."

"Baby, please don't start a habit of—"

"Ma," Kandi said. "I'm sorry and I won't lie to you again, I promise."

"Good. And stop cutting me off when I'm talking." She frowned.

"Yes, Mother." Kandi rolled her eyes, enjoying the relationship she had with her mom. "What you need is a man."

Tahkiyah sucked her teeth. "Ain't got time for the stress. Besides, I got a darling grandbaby to raise."

"Sure do. And I'ma save a bunch of money by not paying for a babysitter," Kandi joked as Rex jerked his head off the floor. He made a low growl, barked, and bolted for the front door. "Ma," Kandi said as the doorbell chimed. "Let me call you back later, okay?"

"Do that. And I love you."

"Love you too." Kandi laid her phone on the counter and headed for the front door. "Shut up, Rex! Loud ass!" She grabbed his thick leather collar and struggled to pull him from the door. "Rex, sit!" She stepped over him as the doorbell chimed again. "Who is it?" she shouted. "Rex, I'ma put your badass outside! Now move and stop all that loud ass barking!"

Rex lunged for the door, barking aggressively. Kandi gave up and used her head instead of her muscle. She left Rex at the door and marched back to the kitchen. "Rex!" she called out as she stood at the sliding glass backdoor. "Here boy!" She dangled a chicken flavored dog treat.

Rex continued to bark until he caught scent of the treat. Kandi tossed it outside and Rex went right behind it.

"Sorry, Rexy." Kandi slid the glass shut. "I'll let you back in later." Kandi hurried to the front door as the doorbell chimed again. "I'm coming!" she shouted. *I swear it better not be a bitch 'cause I'ma check her ass fo' sure!* Her stomach hit the glossy hardwood floor after she looked at the visitor through the peephole. *What the fuck is this motherfucker doing at my door?!* She slowly stood up, forgetting about how she was underdressed as she disengaged the alarm and locks. She snatched the door open with her beautiful face twisted.

"Hi, Kandi!" Sean Levinson smiled. "I saw your SUV and I—"

"Hold the fuck up!" Kandi held up her hand. "Are you out of your damn mind? What makes you think I'd discuss anything with you at my home? You done bumped yo' motherfucking head!"

He sighed. "I just thought—look, I'm sorry,"

"Damn right you are! And what are you doing here any fucking way?"

He pointed down the street at his glacier white Bentley Continental GT. "I'm visiting a friend from my college days," he explained. "And I saw your—"

"Yeah, yeah, you told me that!" she interrupted.

Sean roamed his eyes up her bare legs and thick thighs. "Did you give my offer more consideration?"

"Find someone else! I'm not interested in being fucked by you or any of your actors."

"Excuse me?" He narrowed his eyes.

Kandi reached back for the door. "What you need to do is excuse your ass out of my fucking face! Don't call me no more and you sure as hell better not step foot in this fucking yard again!"

"I drove all the way from Los Angeles to see you!"

"So fucking what! Yo' ass coulda walked for all I care!" she shouted

He chuckled and slid a hand down his face. "You can't be serious? I'm offering you half a million for two films and you're turning me down? No offense, but you know this offer is rare for a black woman."

"Sean," she said through her teeth. "This is my last time warning you to get the fuck out of my face. Take that money and fuck yourself with it because I don't need shit from you."

"Wait!" He took a step closer. "Just hear me out."

"No!" She frowned. "Ain't no wait because I don't wanna hear shit you got to say!"

"I'll double the offer!"

"See, you think I'm fucking playing!" Kandi spun with the intentions to let Rex out from the backyard. She took two steps when he roughly grabbed her wrist.

TREVON ROUNDED the corner at the same moment to see LaToria struggling at the front door with a white man. His temper rose from 0 to 100 before he took his next breath. He stomped the gas and the Aventador SVJ Roadster leapt forward. Seconds later, he floored the brake pedal and jumped out of the roadster by climbing over the door. Lava burned in his eyes. His fists were forged like hammers as he ran up the driveway.

"You trying to die today!" Trevon raged. "Huh?! Muthafucka!"

"Sir, please! It—I was—" Sean stammered as he retreated from Trevon.

"Who is this muthafucka, LaToria?!" Trevon walked up in Sean's face.

"Smooch!" LaToria ran off the porch towards Trevon. She grabbed his arm and tried to pull him back. "He's not worth it!"

"Who the fuck is he?! And what the fuck he's doing putting his hands on you?!" Trevon yanked his arm free and shoved Sean against LaToria's X7. "You got a problem, muthafucka? Grab me like you grabbed my girl just a second ago!"

"Trevon!" LaToria shouted as Sean cringed against the SUV. "Think about Victoria! Please calm down!"

Trevon grabbed the front of Sean's shirt. "If I *ever* see you near her again, I swear to God I—"

"Trevon don't!" LaToria cried. "Please don't swear on something you'll regret. Just let him go so I c-can talk to you."

Trevon stared at Sean with a burning motive for murder. He shoved him a second time against the SUV and released him. "Say something! And see if I don't knock yo' fuckin head off!"

"Sean, leave!" LaToria reached for Trevon's hand as Sean backed away. Trevon rode the rough waves of his sudden temper as he watched Sean running away.

"Smooch, come in—"

"You fucking that guy!" He got up in her face.

LaToria quickly shook her head. "Don't take it there," she cried softly.

"Fuck you mean? You out here damn near naked wit—" *Wait! I'm tripping.* He closed his eyes, sighed, and circled his arms around her shoulders. "Are you okay? Did he hurt you?"

"I'm fine," she said against his chest. "I just don't wanna see you in no trouble."

"Look, go inside and put some clothes on. Lemme park my car and then I want you to tell me who the fuck that was and what's going on."

She nodded, teary-eyed, with her arms locked around his waist.

Back inside the house, she told him everything about her dealings with Sean.

"He approached me about a month ago on Facebook," LaToria explained, as she sat across Trevon's lap at the dining table. "I was really pissed at you back then because I heard about you and Chelsea having sex on the regular."

He sighed. "And you really thought it would make things even by you going to do porn in Los Angeles?"

She shrugged with her arms around his neck. "I just wanted to make you jealous and get your attention."

"Please tell me you weren't serious about that shit?"

"I was at first. But obviously I changed my mind."

"What I can't get over is that muthafucka putting his hands on you! And what's his name again?"

"Sean Levinson."

He nodded thoughtfully and committed the name and face in memory. "Baby, don't ever put Rex out when you're here by yourself."

Rex sat under the table, gnawing on a chew toy.

"I won't," she said, feeling bad about the whole issue. "Still want me to cook you some breakfast?"

"Nah, I'm good." His agitation seeped through his tone. "I lost my appetite."

"Sure?"

He nodded and slid a hand between her thighs. "You're staying with me tonight?"

She smiled, showing off her sexy dimples. "Yes, Smooch. In fact, you might wanna get some rest because the kids might keep us up tonight."

"Kids?"

She nodded. "I promised Jurnee that I'd watch Tayvon tonight."

"What time y'all going shopping?"

"As soon as I go home and get dressed up. Why, what's up?"

"Didn't I tell you to put some clothes on, huh?" he said when he discovered that she didn't have any panties on.

She giggled and lightly bit his ear. "I don't have any clean underwear to put on."

"Don't tell me you forgot how to wash clothes," he said as he inched his fingers closer to the source of heat between her thighs.

"Mmmmm, you're making me slippery." She giggled and

lightly bit his neck as she opened her legs. "That dick felt bueno last night. I loved how you had my legs up on your shoulders—and that dick was just snaking in and out of my poo-poo."

"Bueno? You speak Spanish now?"

She nodded and sucked in a breath when she felt his finger sliding up and down her slickness. "Si," she panted, nuzzling his neck. "Bueno means good and Jurnee is teaching me."

He kissed her chin and penetrated her moist gash with his middle finger. "Talk Spanish for me."

She shuddered and licked his ear. "My poo-poo is mojada!"

"What does that mean?"

"Aaaah," she moaned against his ear. "It means my poo-poo is wet."

"You wanna cum for me again?"

She moaned. "Si. I wanna do it." She blew against his ear as his erection swelled under the weight of her ass.

He needed to be inside her. What moved him was love not lust. When he removed his slippery fingers from between her thighs, he slid them right into his mouth. Unlike last night, he now had the urge to fuck her. She sensed it when he carried her to the bedroom.

"Oohhh. This feels sooo good!" LaToria later moaned into the pillow as Trevon ate her ass and pussy out from the back. She knew she was in for a thorough fucking when he gave her butt cheeks a good spanking. Without being asked or told, she assumed the position, face-down, ass up.

~

HOURS LATER, Kandi tried to deal with the awkward silence between herself and Jurnee. They were halfway to the mall with the kids in the second-row seats.

"Why are you so quiet?" Kandi asked with both hands on the wheel. The fullsize X7 rode smoothly down the busy freeway.

Nothing your dick blocking ass can understand! "Just got a bunch of stuff on my mind," Jurnee said, with her hazel-brown eyes concealed behind a pair of tinted glasses.

"Wanna talk about it?"

Jurnee stared pensively through the dark tinted window at the heavy flow of traffic. *I wish she would just shut up and drive.* "Not really," Jurnee fought to handle her green-eyed issues toward Kandi.

Kandi took a deep breath and released it through her nose. "This isn't easy, Jurnee. I don't know what's under your skin so we might as well deal with it."

"Ain't nothing under my skin but blood and bones!" Jurnee turned from the window.

"Nope." Kandi smiled as she shook her head. "I'm not gonna argue with you, and I mean that, okay? So, you can straighten your face."

Jurnee sighed. Kandi switched lanes and stole a quick glance back at the babies in the car seats. Victoria was gazing up through the tinted glass roof while Tayvon slobbered on a brown Gucci teething ring. "I'm not gonna stop bugging you until you tell me what's up."

Jurnee settled her temper for the sake of the kids. "Being VP at AEF isn't easy as I thought it would be."

"Is that why you're tripping?"

"Si," Jurnee lied. "I have to find a full-figured girl in two weeks for Trevon to do a film with."

"What happened to the one you had lined up?"

Jurnee glanced at her gold and black, manicured fingernails. "She's pregnant. And Janelle left instructions she wants an amateur to star in the film with Trevon."

"How's the search going?" *Maybe I can help? Because the sooner his contract is done, the sooner we can move on with our lives.*

"Not good. I got Ariana helping me with my search on Instagram, Twitter, and Facebook. I might post a little something on YouTube and see if someone will bite."

"Does she have to be black?"

Jurnee nodded. "Janelle is depending on me to keep AEF running."

Kandi reached for Jurnee's hand across the center console. "Listen, girl, don't stress yourself over this, okay? Hell, I'll help with the search. Oh, yeah! Guess who I ran into today?"

"Who?"

Kandi smiled. "Our talented friend... Conda."

6

KEEP IT ON THE DOWN LOW

Coconut Grove, Florida
Tuesday, July 28th

So sorry I 4got 2 call U last nite.

Trevon read the text from Chelsea as he sat outside lifting weights.

It's all good. BTW I spoke to Jurnee. She'll write a new scene.

Trevon texted back.

Cool! Can't wait to read the new script!

Where are you now?

@ the beach wit my girls. Went 2 Club Honesty last nite! OMG I met Plies!

Take any pics?

A ton! Wish you were there. Pussy was throbbing all nite!

Trevon grinned. *I'm sure U had no trouble finding a man.*

True. But I'm hooked on your dick! Can I get sum 2day?

Let's save our moments 4 the film.

Something wrong?

Trying to work things out with LaToria.

:(:) 4 U at the same time.

Thanks.

Don't B a stranger baby. I will be pulling 4 U & Kandi 2 make it. BUT U know I'll stay down 4 whatever when it cums to U & I. Will be countin days 2 our next film & I promise the kitty will B tight, wet & fresh 4 U :). TTYL

Trevon felt good about keeping it real with LaToria. If he wanted to, he could easily creep over to Chelsea's apartment and sate his needs between her suntanned thighs. He settled back on the deck chair and wondered if his bond with LaToria could hurt his career. Deep down, he wanted her over a lifestyle of porn. Just as he prepared to resume working out, his phone chimed. He frowned at the unlisted number on the screen as Rex trotted toward the shade under the palm tree.

"Hello?" he answered.

"Hmm, I was just thinking about how we had that headboard knocking the wall in that room. And how I sucked your dick, and you ate my pussy from the—"

"Kendra!" Trevon sat up quickly.

"Heyyy, baby! Long time no talk!"

"Damn! What's up with you?"

"Just enjoying life and stuff like that!"

"How's Carmelita doing?"

"Fine, and growing like a stalk. Boo, I'm sooo sorry I missed your birthday and your release from probation party. I know you had a ball because I saw all those pics you posted on Instagram," she said. "And how are your two little ones?"

"Yeah, it was a wild night!" He smiled. "And my kids are good. So, you miss me?"

"Of course, you know I've been supporting your career most definitely. You still doing your thang on film?"

"Yeah. My next film will be another one with Chelsea and after that, I'ma do one with a full-figured woman."

"Wow! About time!" Kendra giggled. "And don't let that blue-eyed bunny turn yo ass out."

Trevon wiped a bead of sweat off his nose. "I'm glad you called. It's been almost eight months since we last spoke."

"I know," she sounded sad. "But seriously, I just needed to get away from everything that reminded me of Miami and...Marcus."

"You doing okay?"

"I'm fine. I finally got myself together, and I lost a few pounds, too!"

"I'm glad to hear that, Kendra and I really mean it."

"I know you do. And you're one of the few people I can call a friend."

"Damn! It's good to hear your voice again."

"Yours too, baby. And I'm sorry I never gave you my new number."

"Don't stress it, okay? Just don't lose touch with me again."

"That's one thing you won't have to worry about, baby. Oh, guess what?" she said excitedly. "Remember my homegirl, Dani, that we did the threesome with?"

"Yeah." *Shit! Ain't no way I'll ever forget that day! BBW lovin at its best.*

"Well, she's getting married next week and I wanna do something super special for her."

"Like what?"

"Well, um, I'd like you to strip for her and a few other girls, and money ain't a problem. Name your fee and it's paid," she said. "Like, I wanna do a wild bachelorette party!"

"Where are you?"

"Don't get mad," she said, "I've been in Miami since last week."

"Stop capping!"

"Word!" She laughed. "I got a room at the Ritz-Carlton. Maybe you could drop by to see me so we can discuss business and catch up on last time, huh?"

The only lost time that mattered to Trevon was having her legs up on his shoulders. His lust for her was too strong to set aside. "You're really in Miami right now?"

"Got no reason to lie or play games, baby. Check your phone, I just sent a pic to it. I'm sure you'll like the new me!"

Trevon glanced at the screen. "Want me to look at it now?"

"That's why I sent it, baby."

"Okay, I'ma check it out now." He tapped the screen and waited two seconds for the picture to appear. "Whoa!" His eyes widen at the nude backshot selfie of Kendra.

"You see it?"

"Hell yeah!" *Damn! That ass is stupid phat! And that small waist!* "Kendra, you know I liked all of you before you lost weight. But real talk, you looking good and I mean *real* good!"

"Good enough for you to come and see a sistah?"

Trevon continued to stare at the *new* Kendra. His mind said *NO!* while his dick said *WHAT'S THE ROOM NUMBER?* "Kendra, you know how our bond is, so I can't keep certain things from you. Me and LaToria are back together and-"

"That's none of my business, baby. Ain't nothing changed with me when it comes to us. I have a *friend* back up in Raleigh, but it's not that special to force me to cut my ties with you."

"Oh, it's like that?"

"You know me, baby. If I want something, I go get it with no regrets. So, what's up? You wanna see and *feel* the new me? You know how I don't play games. Umm, I was just thinking about that one time you hit it raw—had my pussy so wet!"

"What's your room number?"

"How about I meet you at Brittany Baylor's hair salon on South Beach in say, two hours?"

"I say, I'll be there." *Fuck! I shouldn't be doing this.*

"I can't wait to see you. And, Mr. Harrison, I wanna thank you for the attention you gave me when I wasn't happy with myself. It meant a lot to me."

"Wasn't anything wrong with you, Kendra. In my eyes, you were sexy the first day I met your mean ass." He laughed.

"Yeah, I sure was a bitch when we first met!"

"Nah, I won't call you that."

Unexpectedly, Kendra sighed. "Um, if you care to know...the case is still unsolved about Marcus' murder."

Trevon was glad he wasn't on a FaceTime call. "What are they saying about it?" he asked with guilt all over his face.

"Nothing much. A lot of evidence that could help was burned up and—never mind. I don't even know why I'm talking about it."

"You gonna hold it together?"

"Yeah. But I'll be a lot better when I can put my hands on you. You be my secret and I'll be your secret. Deal?"

He stood. "You know I'ma try to beat your back out."

"Ummm! Now you're talking my language, baby!"

"You got my dick hard as hell!"

"Good! Because I got something nice and wet that it can slide up in until it pops. And a deep throat I can taste that dick with."

Damn, she freaky as fuck! "Show me better than you can tell me," he challenged.

"I'll see you at the salon. And don't be late."

"I won't. And hey, thanks for everything you did for me by hooking me up with a laid-back probation officer when you moved to North Carolina."

"You're welcome. You can properly thank me when I get your handsome ass up in this room."

"Say no more. I'll call you back when I get to the salon."

"And I surely look forward to it. Bye, baby!"

"Alright, be safe and I'll get up with you later." Trevon ended the call with a load of guilt straining his conscience. He hit the weights under the blazing sun. *I'ma tear that pussy up!* He envisioned having hardcore sex with Kendra as he got under the 475-pound barbell. *This is the last time I'ma cheat on LaToria.*

~

TREVON TURNED into the parking lot beside the Brittany Baylor's salon at 2:38 p.m. The sun gleamed off the spotless paint of his midnight sapphire blue Lamborghini as he slowed for a speed bump.

"Where you at?" he asked Kendra through the hands-free system.

"I'm parked all the way in the back, baby. I'm looking right at you," Kendra said.

Just as he cleared the speed bump, a horn blew twice on a geyser grey Rolls-Royce Wraith.

Kendra climbed out of the Wraith as Trevon slowed his selfie worthy Lambo to a stop. She had her appearance on point, from her head to her feet. Today, specifically for Trevon, she had squeezed her round ass into a pair of custom-made jeggings that catered to her new waist to hip ratio of 38-44. Her soft and natural 34 D's sat high in the bra that she wore under the low-neck silk blouse. Her chic hairstyle framed her cute face. In all truth, she couldn't help but to be vain about her appearance.

"Hey Trevon!" She rushed into his arms, mashing her softness against his masculine chest. "It's so good to see you again! And damn." She rubbed his big shoulders. "I see you're still working out and looking so damn good!" She wanted to tongue him down on the spot.

He couldn't believe how attractive she looked. "Kendra Paige." He smiled at her. "You look-I don't even know what to say!" *She looks so sexy.*

"Just know what to *do* when we get to my room." Her heart sped up when his strong hands slid down her waist. She circled her arms around his neck, not caring about being in the public. "For all it's worth, I really miss you." She took the moment to take in the full sight of him. She wondered if he had a fashion stylist picking out his clothes. Today he wore a pair of fitted jeans and a colorful fitted shirt that highlighted his muscular build.

"You look like you belong on the cover of a magazine! And this ass!" He grinned. "That's all you?" He squeezed the bottom of her ass. *Shit, soft as hell!*

She smiled. "You'll find out soon enough, baby. Now kiss me."

He kissed her glossy lips before he eased his tongue inside her mouth. His erection throbbed as she sucked gently on his tongue.

"Whew!" She broke the kiss. "I think we better go to my room and talk about business."

"The only business I wanna discuss is how many times I'm gonna make you call my name."

"Mmm." She licked her lips. "That sounds like a plan and I love it!"

"You like it. I love it."

She gazed into his eyes and followed what her flesh yearned for. Like day one, she would hold no regrets having sex with him. "Let's go, baby. We have a lot to make up."

~

"Let me do you first," Trevon said as he later unhooked Kendra's bra and dropped it on her pile of clothes on the floor.

Kendra sat on Trevon's lap, butt naked at the foot of the bed. She bit her bottom lip and lifted her breast to his mouth. "I love feeling your tongue on my nipples!" She began to grind on his erection. "Mmm, that feels good." She threw her head back as his fingers dug into the softness of her ass. Her body came alive with him. "I wanna feel you deep inside me!" She released her breasts and laid her hands on his shoulders.

"Sit on my face." Trevon kissed her nipples and then lay back.

"How about I suck your dick while you do me?"

He reached up and palmed her well-rounded breast. "Whatever makes you happy. Just put that pussy on my face before I get mad."

She licked her lips. "Lift up so I can take your briefs off." She massaged his chest and stomach. *I'ma suck his dick soo good! And then I'll ride it slow and easy.* He complied to her request and moaned when she freed his fully erect penis. They kissed briefly in the center of the bed. She stroked his penis gently until his precum made her fingers slick.

"Let me get under you." She kissed his chest as he rubbed the soft contours of her breasts.

"Anything your heart desires. I'll-"

The mood was interrupted by Trevon's iPhone vibrating on the bedside table. Kendra rolled over and picked it up. She viewed the caller ID before she gave it to him with a flat expression.

"It's the mother of your firstborn."

Trevon accepted the call as Kendra lay her head on his stomach. "Hey, baby. What's up?"

"Some straight up bullshit, Smooch! Today is the fucking worst!"

"What's up?" *Better not be that cracker!*

"A motherfucker stole my BMW!"

"When? Are you okay?!" he inquired. *Oh shit! My kids!* "How are the—"

"Everyone is fine. It was stolen while I was in the mall with Jurnee and the kids. We're stranded, Smooch." LaToria sounded close to tears.

"Relax," he sat up. "I'm on my way, okay? Which mall are you at?"

"Aventura."

"How is Jurnee doing?"

"Mad as hell like me! She's inside the mall with the kids. Smooch, this shit is so fucked up."

"Hold tight, baby. I'm on my way right now."

"Are you home?"

"Yeah."

"Well, call me back—No, I'll call you back because I need to call my insurance company ASAP. Wait! Bring some diapers because most of the baby's stuff was in my ride."

"I got it."

"Okay, I'll see you soon and drive safe. Love you!"

"I will and I love you more." *And yet I'm laid up with another female.* He ended the call with a heavy sigh. "Kendra, I'm sorry, but I have to leave because—"

"I heard." She sat up with him. "And it's crazy because a phone call broke our moment when I had you over my house. Remember that?"

He stared at her and discovered it was impossible not to gaze at her breasts. "I'll never forget any moments with you, Kendra."

She slid up against him and laid her hand on his leg. "You have to go to the Aventura Mall, right?"

He nodded.

"And you told your girl you were home."

"What are you getting at?"

She smiled and eased her fingers around his penis. "Being here with me is half the distance to the mall. If you leave now, you'll get there too soon and you don't need your girl to get any ideas that you lied to her. Sooo..." She stroked his dick a few times as she made her mind up. "I have just enough time to get a taste of you."

"Kendra, I can't. My kids are—"

"Chill, baby. I don't want you to fuck me. All I want to do is suck this bad boy right quick. Please?" She stuck her tongue out and licked his chest. "Mmmm." She flicked her tongue against his nipple as his penis swelled in her hand. "Now lay back and let me give you some of my slow and sloppy head."

Trevon couldn't resist Kendra. The instant his head met the soft pillow, she circled her lips amorously on his thickheaded dick. She knelt beside him and went all in, bobbing her lips and stroking his shaft.

"Kendra! Ohh.... suck it good! Th-that's it! keep going, baby!" he groaned and moaned the entire three and a half minutes until he erupted. I *gotta get back up with her! Even the head is better!* Minutes later, Trevon left the room and bumped into another unexpected face.

7

SPOE & RBYT

Miami, Florida
Tuesday, July 28th

"Trevon!"

Trevon slowed his steps as he neared the elevator. He eyed the slim-waisted, thick-hipped female with a cautious gaze. *What the hell she doing here?*

"Long time no see!" Nashlly fingered a long, reddish curl of fake hair over her shoulder. "You still doing your thang in front of the camera?"

He jabbed the elevator button for the first floor. "Do you know who's on this same floor?" he whispered.

She raised her left eyebrow and crossed her arms. "Who? And why are you talking so low?"

"Kendra!"

A flush of worry crossed her face. "I th-thought she was up in North Carolina?"

"She's just visiting."

Nashlly glanced down the hall behind him. "Um, y'all fucking?"

"That's none of your business!"

"The hell it ain't!" She glared at him. "I know how men get to talking too much when they get in some good pussy. And you can't stand here and say y'all don't be talking 'bout Swagga's unsolved murder!"

Trevon stepped in her face. "You got me mixed up, and it's clear you don't fucking know me. I don't care what you did, and it will stay that way. All I care about is what you did in saving LaToria."

Nashlly met his gaze without blinking. "That's good to hear!" she stated. "Don't nobody know the truth about Swagga but you, your girl, my boy Art and me."

"And it will stay that way."

BING. The elevator doors slid open. To their relief, it was empty.

Nashlly strolled in first, adding an extra swish to her hips. "What's been up with you?" she asked when the elevator began its descent.

"Just taking life day by day. And you?"

She stood in the corner, searching through her purse. "Living with the struggle of life after my five minutes of fame."

"What are you doing here?"

Nashlly found whatever she was looking for and looked up. "Having an affair with a nameless NFL player."

"What happened to that NBA guy you—"

"Had to cut his ass off," she replied as she handed him a business card.

WE TOUCH Massage & Nail parlor
From head to feet
WE TOUCH your stress away.
Stress away.
Open Mon-Fri 8am-10p.m. 1975 Martin Blvd
Wetouch.com Miami Beach, Florida
Call for VIP home visits Nashlly Torain.CEO
305-We-Touch

"This your line of work?" Trevon read the business card.

"Yeah," Nashlly smiled. "I got my own business and I hope you'll show some support. You should since I own all of your films," she fawned.

"I don't see why not." He feigned a smile and slid the business card in his back pocket.

"Ask for me when you call. I'll hook you up with one of our specialties and a big discount." I *hope his fine ass call! He can get all of this pussy fo sure. Mmm, bitches gonna hate if I get some porn star dick.*

BING. The elevator doors slid open and Trevon showed his gentlemen qualities by gesturing Nashlly to exit first.

"Until we meet again." She surprised him outside the elevator with a hug. "Please get up with me," she whispered. "For business or pleasure. You already know you can get it."

Trevon didn't have a large enough net to catch all the pussy that was thrown his way. He couldn't help but stare at Nashlly's strut as she headed across the crowded lobby. By the way her ass bounced, he knew she didn't wear any items under the green stretch miniskirt. When he later slid behind the wheel of his Aventador SVJ, he swallowed his guilt of cheating behind LaToria's back.

"Damn! I gotta go back home and get my Benz!"

~

"CHANGE OF PLANS," LaToria told Trevon as he drove from the front enterance of the mall.

"What's up?" he asked as his son whined in the back seat.

"I have to go to the police station to do a bunch of paperwork on my truck being stolen." She sighed and pushed her fingers through her hair. "Drop me off at home. I'ma get my mom to take me downtown."

"I'll watch Victoria for you," Jurnee volunteered from the back as she attempted to breastfeed Tayvon.

"Thank you!" LaToria turned in the seat to make sure Victoria was properly secured in the new car seat.

"Why y'all ain't buy a new car seat for Tayvon?" Trevon asked.

"Didn't have one in stock for his size," Jurnee winced as Tayvon caught her nipple between his gums. "Facil, Tayvon."

"What that mean?" Trevon asked.

"Facil means easy. Your son be gnawing on me with his hard gums."

He grinned. "Like father. Like son."

LaToria rolled her eyes. "Smooch, shut up!"

Jurnee smiled in light of her stress.

"Aargh!" LaToria slid her hands down her face. "I can't believe some dickhead stole my ride!"

"What was in it?" Trevon asked, as he steered his S580 through an intersection.

"Nothing that can't be replaced. You know I don't be keeping anything personal in my ride."

"What about you, Jurnee?" he asked.

"Just the car seat," Jurnee told him.

"We'll go looking for a new one after we drop LaToria off. That'll work?"

Jurnee nodded. *Perfect. Because I need to get something off my chest.*

"Y'all need to thank God you weren't carjacked," he stressed. "Maybe I need to start taking y'all—"

"No!" Jurnee snapped. "Shit happens and you're not about to shelter us, Trevon."

LaToria nodded in agreement. "She's right, Smooch."

He frowned. "I'll die for every soul in this car!"

"We know that, Smooch." LaToria rubbed his shoulder. "Just calm down."

Trevon settled back in the leather seat and welcomed the new subject of his kids. Jurnee swore on everything that Tayvon's first word would be "mama." She smiled genuinely as she told Trevon and LaToria how Tayvon refused to let anyone pull a pacifier from his tight grip.

Trevon facetiously made jealous comments about his son hogging Jurnee's nipples. LaToria punched him on his arm and told him to stop being nasty. In Trevon's view, nothing but love filled his sleek sedan as he wheeled it to Miami Beach.

~

ARIANA SAT up on the tan leather sofa when she heard the front door open.

"Ariana," Jurnee called out. "Come help us bring all this stuff in."

Ariana smiled. "I'm coming." She met Jurnee in the foyer.

"Trevon is outside," Jurnee said, with Tayvon in her arms. "He's getting Victoria out of the car seat."

"Kay." Ariana adjusted her pink tank top.

"And make sure Trevon doesn't forget my shades. I left'em on the dashboard."

Ariana kissed Tayvon on his chubby cheek and did the same to Jurnee on her lips.

Trevon had Victoria in his arms when Ariana joined him outside. They smiled at each other.

"Hey, handsome! How's my lil princess doing?" Ariana said brightly.

"Sleeping." Trevon replied as Ariana walked up to him. "Take'er for me so I can start bringing everything in."

"Where's Kandi?" Ariana asked as she settled Victoria on her shoulder.

"Should be downtown filing a report with her mom."

Ariana nodded. "Are you gonna chill here for a while?"

All she got on her mind is sex. "Yeah, I'ma spend some time with my kids. What's up?"

She blushed. "No reason," she lied. "But I think Jurnee wants to talk to you about something."

"About what?"

"You'll find out later." She smiled. "Now I'm going in so my lil princess can get out of the sun."

Trevon had no idea what Jurnee had on her mind. *Shit!* He suddenly remembered the slight issue with LaToria popping up last night. He didn't have the chance to speak to Jurnee this morning when he dropped the baby oil and pacifiers off. He made three trips to bring all the items in that Jurnee had bought for their son. On the last trip, he found Jurnee on the sofa with her left prosthetic limb off. The sight didn't draw his attention because he had grown used to her injury.

"Where the little ones at?" He sat next to her and slid his arm around her shoulders.

"Ariana is watching them." She leaned into him.

He tilted his face to hers. "Something on your mind?"

She gave him a quick peck on the lips. "Kandi told me she's gonna try to make things right with you."

"Yeah. We had a long talk about it this morning."

"I'm tired of her taking you through all that drama." She snuggled closer, feeling at peace with him.

"You shouldn't let it get you upset, okay?"

"It's not."

"Yes, it is. What about that 'BM2' mess you threw in my face last night? And then you didn't answer my call."

"I was mad."

"About what, baby?"

Jurnee closed her eyes. "Because I'm getting confused," she replied softly. "None of this was planned to happen."

"But it did, and I sure as hell don't regret anything. Do you?"

She opened her eyes. "No, Papi. I regret nada."

"So, why ain't my baby girl smiling for me?"

Because I think I'm falling in love with you. "Kiss me." She grinned. "Maybe I'll smile."

He leaned toward her as she grabbed his button-down shirt and pushed her tongue into his mouth. Having him now felt so right to her. The kiss progressed as they expressed their unique bond.

"Smiling now?" he whispered against her lips.

She nodded with a wide smile. "I know this isn't easy for you. You love Kandi, and we both know that. And then there's me. A few nights of lust and I got pregnant by you."

"Baby. You know, it's not even close to being like that."

"How do you really feel about me?"

"I care about you, Jurnee. Look at my eyes." He stared at her. "For all it's worth. I knew what I was doing when we had sex."

"What do you mean?"

"I knew you weren't on any birth control. Every time I came inside you, I knew the risk of you getting pregnant."

"And you only did it because Kandi left you. I was your rebound chick and—"

"Don't say that, Jurnee." He reached for her hand. "You're in my life forever. No matter how you view our bond, it's forever, baby girl. You feel what I'm saying?"

"I do now," she whispered with her tears welling. "Just promise me you'll never neglect your son."

"You're talking crazy." He squeezed her hand. "Why would I ever—"

"Promise me, Trevon!"

"Calm down, baby," he said as a tear rolled down her cheek. "I promise, for real. I promise I'll never abandon you or my son.

"Gracias," she whispered as she wiped her eyes.

"What time you got?" he asked. "I need to charge my phone."

She glanced at her watch. "Five after six. You got somewhere to be?" *Please stay.*

He looked at her flawless olive complexion and natural hazel-brown eyes. "Mmm, you look way better than Jennifer Lopez."

Jurnee cracked a smile. "I already know that. Now answer my question. You got somewhere to go?"

"Uh, there's a new club my manager wants me to make an appearance at."

She sucked her teeth and sat up, frowning.

"It's called SPOE."

"Never heard of it," she snapped with a sudden attitude.

"It's downtown on RBYT street."

She stared at him skeptically. "RBYT street? Where the hell is that?" she asked as tears began to fill her eyes again. "On second thought! I don't even care to know. Go to SPOE or whatever and do—"

He grabbed her hand. "SPOE means softest place on earth. And RBYT..." he grinned. "Means, right between your thighs. And that's where I want to be."

Jurnee thought about what he said until it suddenly dawned on her he had toyed with her. She shoved him as he laughed at her folly.

"I fooled you, didn't I?" He held his arms up as she swung the sofa pillow at his head.

"That wasn't funny!"

"Glad to see y'all ain't fussing." Arianna butted in the happy mood as she breezed into the living room. "Now make it perfect and tell me he's staying for dinner." She stopped in front of the wall-mounted HDTV with her arms crossed.

Trevon grinned as Jurnee slid her arms around his neck. "I'll be at the table. And I'm spending the night."

"In that case." Ariana kicked her shoes off. "I'll go set up the baby monitor near the Jacuzzi."

"Good idea." Jurnee licked Trevon's earlobe. "We can try some new things that I might put in Trevon's script."

"Y'all can focus on business." Ariana got straight to the point. "My drive is pleasure and getting my full bisexuality on and poppin! Trevon, you owe us that dick and you ain't leaving till we get it."

Trevon shook his head as Jurnee sucked on his earlobe. Dealing with Jurnee and Ariana at times left Trevon speechless. Lust and emotion. When he had sex with Ariana, he was guided by lust. With Jurnee, each stroke was moved by his emotions for her. Just like day one and every other encounter, sex with Ariana was done in Jurnee's sight. He grew to accept the unique threesomes with Jurnee and her lover. A lover he never had raw sex with. That was Jurnee's main stickler, and Trevon never made an issue of it. The sexual relations between them started when Ariana joined them on the sofa. The women removed Trevon's clothing piece by piece. His button-down shirt and tank top came off first. Ariana licked his chest as soon as his unclothed chest was presented to her. Jurnee kissed each of his stomach muscles while undoing his belt. They took their time with their foreplay. Jurnee peeled her jeans off and her blouse came next. She stuck her tongue in his naval as she pushed her hand down the front of his pants. Trevon released a throaty moan and leaned back on the sofa as Jurnee pulled his erection out.

"Here's what I want." She licked it from the hilt and up to the tip. "Asi grande."

"So big," Ariana translated as she nibbled on Trevon's ear.

Jurnee changed her position and knelt beside Trevon. She grabbed a handful of her long, black hair and moved it away from her face. She wanted him to see how her lips would rise and fall on his dick.

"This is gonna be fun," Ariana said, staring at Jurnee as Trevon slid his hand under her pink tank top.

Jurnee lowered her lips slowly down the length of Trevon's penis with her eyes shut. She lifted her lips with a true adoration to please the man in her mouth. Up and down, she set a nice, smooth tempo that had him moaning her name.

Ariana removed her tank top and fed Trevon her pointy nipples. She couldn't remove her eyes off the erotic sight of Jurnee's mouth slurping on Trevon's penis. She wasn't aware of much else but that one sight.

He rubbed Jurnee's ass and squeezed it through her silk panties. He kept his attention balanced between the two women. He managed to get Ariana fully naked and her shaved pussy in his face. She stood and straddled his face, offering her thin-lipped pussy to his tongue.

"Aaahh! Yesss! Keep licking it just like th-that," Ariana moaned, with Trevon's tongue flicking across her pussy lips.

Jurnee sped up and angled his dick toward her. She slurped and licked every inch, wanting him to cum.

Ariana shivered as she rode Trevon's face. "G-Gonna do it on h-his face!" She purred. She increased her grip on the top edge of the sofa as he palmed her bare ass.

Nasty as they wanted to be. They reached the first of many climaxes via oral sex. Free love was Jurnee's stance, at least for now.

8

ASS ME A QUESTION

Miami, Florida
Tuesday, July 28th

Kandi stood far from the stance of naivete. She realized a ton of heartache laid in her future if she tried to make Trevon choose between herself and Jurnee. She intentionally gave him the time, freedom, and space to spend with Jurnee and his son. Her mind had to accept reality while her heart tried to ignore it. As she left the police station in Tahkiyah's dark silver BMW M850i coupe, she held her tears at bay. She knew Trevon and Jurnee were still sexually involved. That reality of the bond Jurnee shared with Trevon left a spike in Kandi's heart. *This love shit hurts too much.* She thought as she slowed for a red light. She couldn't tear her thoughts from the idea of Jurnee and Trevon having sex at the very moment. *The only reason she got a baby by him is because I ran out on him.* She glanced at the time on the center dash with a frown. 8:15 p.m. *Shit ain't fair! He fucking all these other bitches while I'm raising Victoria. He thinks it's all about his black ass! Aargh! I fucking love him too much!* She squeezed the steering wheel, waiting for the light to turn green. *I just gotta ride this bullshit out until he's done with AEF.* She nodded. *And I might as well keep a fuck buddy on the side until Trevon can commit to me. Nah, I can't give Smooch's pussy away.* When the light turned green, she pondered on the idea of driving up to North Miami. *Fuck it! She can have him for tonight. I'll fall back because what I want with Trevon is forever!*

"Call, Mom." She used the hands-free calling system. *I gotta ask my mom something.*

"What's up?" Tahkiyah's voice filled the BMW.

"Ma, I need to ask you a question." Kandi switched lanes and sped past a city bus.

"About what?"

Here it goes. "It's about love. Like, can a person be in love with somebody and turn around and be with another person sexually?"

"No!" Tahkiyah answered with conviction. "True love won't allow you to give yourself to another man. I know you didn't say you. I'm just making a point. For example, I had a friend that had a husband in a prison. Anyway, she said she had her needs and she couldn't go without sex for three years."

"She cheated?" Kandi asked, knowing the obvious.

"Wasn't even three days after her husband went to prison. She kept preaching to me she loved her husband and that she would hold him down. Letters, visits, and blah, blah, blah. She took care of her needs by sleeping with *other* men."

"Did her husband find out?"

"Eventually she told him."

"And what did he do?"

"He went along with it. She kept his account straight and held him down like she promised. But when he got out, he left her for a young female CO he met in prison."

"So, he was cheating just like her?"

"Yep. And here's the point, baby. True love doesn't work like that. True love is being committed and faithful. My friend, she didn't know the bond she had with her husband. When she gave herself to those other men, that ended the love for her husband."

"But she held him down, Ma."

"That's because she *liked* him. Liking and loving are two

different emotions, baby. I'll never call myself loving a man and turn around and let the next have sex with me."

"Okay, I see your point." *And it makes a lot of sense.*

"I bumped into her ex-husband a few months after he got out. And he told me he didn't cheat on my friend *until* he found out she was cheating. He loved her up until then."

"Love is crazy," Kandi muttered.

"No, baby. It's a challenge that takes two people to be real about it." Tahkiyah knew from experience. "And that effort has to be fifty-fifty, balanced. Anything other than that is unbalanced and will fail. Not forty-sixty or eighty-twenty, it has to be equally divided, LaToria. Love isn't crazy. It's an effort."

Kandi began to see the fault in her ways. *Maybe I'm loving Trevon too hard. I'm at sixty and he's at forty. But at least he's loving me, right? I know I love Trevon, and I won't cheat. I gotta be the stronger half, because two wrongs sure as hell don't make a right.*

"LaToria? You still on the line?" Tahkiyah asked after the prolonged silence.

"Yeah. I—you just opened my eyes to something." Kandi smiled. "In love. If it is meant to be, it will be. And from here on out, I'm loving my half. Fifty."

"That's reality, baby. I told you all that because I love you."

"I know you do. And I love you back."

"Uh, you coming home tonight?"

Kandi sighed. "You know what. That doesn't sound like a bad idea." Kandi made up her mind to shove her insecurities aside. *I just want Trevon to be happy. Even if it's not with me.*

~

"THIS FEELS SO GOOD!" Ariana moaned as she took Trevon's blistering strokes, knelt on all fours. "H-hold my titties!" she groaned as her ass and hips jiggled. "Hurry!"

Trevon pounded Ariana's slim frame, staring at his penis

driving in and out of her. He squeezed her hips as he continued to pump her from behind.

Ariana looked back at Trevon when his hands captured her swinging breasts. "Make me squirt a-again! Fuck me hard! Mmm, beat it up, baby!"

Jurnee sat in the Jacuzzi, watching the compilation between Trevon and Ariana on the floor. She had one hand pulling on her nipple while she rubbed her clit with the other under the warm water. "Make her cum. Fuck her pussy real good. Si, just like that. Umm, long dick her. Look at her sexy ass. Look how it's bouncing. Mmm!" Jurnee lifted her wet breast to her mouth and flicked her tongue across her tight nipple.

"J-Jurnee!" Ariana whined. "He's doing it so good!"

"Pussy so... fuckin' wet!" Trevon squeezed her breasts and continued pumping.

"Don't stop! Fuck m-me just like you're doing! Mm-hm. Mm-hm." She panted as she stared at his face.

He slid to the hilt inside her, enjoying every stroke through the thin condom. Sweat covered every inch of their nude flesh. Their moans and skin clapping was an erotic tune to Jurnee.

"Pound her!" Jurnee leaned out of the Jacuzzi and lightly raked her fingernails down Trevon's sweaty chest.

Trevon released Ariana's breasts and took a handful of her hair. He did it in one sudden move without missing a stroke. He pulled, forcing her sexy face to the ceiling.

"Aahh! Fuck!" Ariana winced, bucking against his fast and deep thrust. "Ugghh! Trevon!"

"Take it!" He slapped her ass.

"I'm taking it! I'm taking it!" Ariana shouted. "It's so big, Trevon! Beat it up! Beat it—"

CLAP. CLAP. CLAP. CLAP. CLAP. He gripped her waist and pumped her methodically.

"This that dick you want?" He yanked her hair. "Huh? Is it!" He sped up.

"Yess!!" she gasped. "I need it!"

Trevon turned his head and kissed Jurnee. *Oh shit! This pussy is fire! Gotta maintain and stay in control.*

"Trevon! Trevon! Baby, please d-don't st-stop! Please don't—" Ariana's eyes rolled as her body triggered a mid-breath climax. "I'm, c-cummin!! Ooohhh! Trevon!" She hollered and threw herself against his ramming dick. In her excited rush, her pussy reached its peak and squirted. "Mmm!" she gasped for the hundredth time. "Ooohhh! Trevon—feels so good!"

Jurnee broke the kiss and turned her attention to Ariana. She slid her hand from Ariana's sweaty shoulder, down her spine and up the soft hill of her ass.

Trevon slowed his strokes as Jurnee rubbed Ariana's ass. When he let go of her hair, she shuddered and dropped to her elbows.

"Pussy bueno ain't it?" Jurnee squeezed Ariana's butt cheek.

He nodded, pumping slowly.

"You had enough, Ariana?" Jurnee asked.

"Si, baby! Si," Ariana replied, out of breath. "I... can't... take it no m-more."

Jurnee slid her hand between Ariana and Trevon and grabbed his dick on an outward stroke. She gave it a hard squeeze. "Let me finish you off." She pushed her tongue back inside his mouth as she pulled his dick out of Ariana. "Fuck me in my ass," she whispered against his lips. "Get behind me and cum in me."

He sucked her bottom lip into his mouth as she removed the slippery condom. When he stood, Ariana turned, reached for his raw dick and spat on the tip. Jurnee had her phat ass facing them as she waited for Trevon. She licked her middle finger and reached back to finger her ass. The threesome moved to another level when Ariana stepped into the Jacuzzi. She slapped Jurnee's ass a few times before she knelt in the water.

Jurnee braced her elbows on the blue padded side and looked back at Ariana. "Lamer mi ass." Jurnee wiggled her ass as Trevon eased into the Jacuzzi.

Ariana kissed Jurnee's ass and spread her cheeks.

"Aaahh! Ariana, ummm!" Jurnee cooed as Ariana nuzzled her

beautiful face between her fleshy butt cheeks. "Eat my ass! Ooohh!"

Trevon stood in the Jacuzzi, slowly stroking his dick to the sight below him.

He watched, fixated at Ariana tonguing Jurnee's ass. He was later added back to the threesome when Ariana reached for his dick. She drooled around his shaft as she sucked him. His dick popped from her wet lips when she stopped.

"I want to see it slide in." Ariana rubbed Jurnee's ass and laid her face on it.

Trevon eased into position behind Jurnee as Ariana spanked Jurnee's ass.

"Aaahhh. Put it in," Jurnee moaned as Ariana spread her cheeks apart.

Trevon slid his dick up the slit of Jurnee's butt and right into Ariana's mouth. She raced her tongue around the tip until he pulled back.

Jurnee shivered when Ariana spat directly on her asshole. Her next breath rushed through her lips when Trevon rubbed his dick-head on her lubricated anus. She wiggled her hips, wanting all of him inside her ass. She had the best of both worlds with Trevon and Ariana. Words couldn't describe the breathless ecstasy that overwhelmed Jurnee. Her body quivered from Trevon's tender, slithering strokes inside her ass. She rocked against his push, losing her breath each time their flesh met.

"Asi hondo. Asi hondo en mi culo!" Jurnee moaned. (So deep. So deep in my ass!)

"Who's ass is it?" Trevon slid his hands up her waist. "Who dis ass belong to?"

"Tuyo! Tuyo, Papi!" (Yours! Yours, Papi!)

Ariana stared at the raw strokes. *Mmm! It looks so good! But I can't take it in my butt like Jurnee.*

"Ooohhh, yesss!" Jurnee shouted as Ariana fiddled her clitoris. "Ariana! Trevon! Please don't stop. Please. Please!" she whined as his dick coasted in the wet grip of her ass. She closed her eyes and drowned in the double sensuality she received. Her ass rolled with Trevon's every stroke as Ariana finger-fucked her throbbing pussy.

Trevon ignored the water sloshing below his waist. His focus stayed firm on the grip of Jurnee's hot and wet ass. "Yeahh! This my ass right here." He continued to stroke in and out, sexing her ass with a purpose.

He allowed himself to cater to every need that Jurnee and Ariana requested. The sex flowed as if a camera filmed their every move. A climax came at Trevon's peak, leaving him spent and lacking the strength to continue. He later took a relaxing bath with the two lovers in the luxury bathroom.

Jurnee cooked and fed Trevon, treating him kingly. When the kids woke up around 10 p. m., Trevon took care of their needs, feeding and changing them.

"Are you spending the night?" Jurnee asked when Trevon strolled into her bedroom.

He yawned. "Yeah."

"Good!" Ariana giggled as she sat up on the bed.

"Did Kandi call you back?" Jurnee asked as Trevon sat at the food of the bed.

"Nah, I guess she got tied up." He took off his tank top and looked over his shoulder.

"What?" Jurnee smiled. "Why are you looking at me like that?"

He admired how sexy her appearance was, even at bedtime. Tonight, she wore a pink camisole and matching panties. Ariana was dressed the same, wearing green and black. "Can I *really* get some sleep? Or do I need to sleep on the sofa?"

Jurnee pulled the sheets back and patting the space between herself and Ariana. "Come to bed." She winked.

"Minus those boxers." Ariana tugged at the hem of her camisole, wondering how he would act if he had the chance to be alone with her.

He joined them under the sheets. He kissed Jurnee briefly as Ariana rubbed his chest. His body needed to recharge. In just two days, he had a carnal rollercoaster of sex. Chelsea, Kandi, Kendra, Ariana and Jurnee. *I gotta save this dick for the camera!*

AT THE SAME TIME, Tahkiyah didn't know how to deal with her perpetual lust toward Trevon. She tossed and turned under the sheets, frustrated that she didn't have the resolve to get over him.

"Shit!" she muttered in the dark bedroom. She sighed and tried her best to think of anything but him. I *know he wants to fuck me again. And it's crazy because I want the same thing.* She closed her eyes and slid her hands slowly over her breasts. *LaToria would die if she ever found out about me and Trevon.* She squeezed her nipples as her mind ran toward Trevon. *That dick! It felt so good sliding in and out of me! What I need right now is to bust a nut.* What she needed was one of her private moments. In secret, she still viewed porn to masturbate. Guilt consumed her because her laptop was loaded with Trevon's DVD with Chelsea. Her craving for him grew with each private viewing of his films. She sat up and checked the time on her phone. The screen showed 11:45 p.m.

Tahkiyah reached under the pillow and pulled out a black vibrator. She turned it on, checking the batteries. It buzzed vibrantly. She set it aside and turned on the nightlight on her phone. "Damn!" She sighed with the light on the empty table. Her laptop was in her car. Tonight she wanted something visual to help with her private moment. With her mind set, she jumped out of the bed and got dressed. To her relief, LaToria was in her bedroom with the door closed. She exited the suite and made a beeline to the elevator. Trevon remained the focal point of her lewd thoughts on the elevator ride down to the garage. In her rush to get the laptop, she didn't take the time to put on any panties. The tight jeans had an intimate closeness with her throbbing essence. Halfway down, she took off her stylish glasses to remove a smudge. *I've got to get over Trevon. I can't keep fantasizing about the man my daughter is in love with. Tonight is my last night looking at any of his films.* BING.

Tahkiyah stepped out of the elevator and nodded at the cute security guard in the booth. *I know he's looking at my ass. Might as well put on a show. She* turned and strutted toward her BMW in the brightly lit garage. As she strolled down the row of parked cars and SUVs, she held up her keyfob. *Maybe I should flirt with that guard? Nah, he might turn into a stalker if I gave him some of my knockout.* She smiled at her silliness as the alarm on her BMW chirped off. She retrieved her laptop from the trunk. *I have to stop leaving my laptop in the car.* Just as she closed the trunk, a horn blew, startling her.

"Didn't mean to scare you."

Tahkiyah's frown instantly went away. *Mmm. Who do we have here?* "It's okay. I just didn't hear you pulling up behind me." She smiled. "Um, I've never seen you here before."

"Just visiting a friend," he told her.

"Lucky her."

"It's a guy. And no, I'm not gay." He chuckled.

Hello! I have to get his number! "How long are you visiting?"

"No time limit at this point."

Damn! He's sexy! No wedding ring and driving a Bentley Continental. "In that case. Maybe we can do brunch?"

"That would be wonderful. By the way, I'm Sean."

Tahkiyah eyed him with lust. "Nice to meet you, Sean. I'm Tahkiyah."

"A lovely name for a radiant woman."

Tahkiyah exchanged numbers and promised Sean they would meet again. She would always have a penchant for white men, and Sean fit the credentials. White, handsome, and possibly rich.

Back up in her bedroom, she indulged in her private moments, lusting fervently over Trevon.

9

MALO & BUENO

Miami, Florida
Friday, July 31st
Three Days Later

"I have malo news. And some bueno news," Jurnee told Trevon as he entered her new AEF office at 11:31a.m. on the 8th floor.

"I assume malo means bad?" Trevon leaned across the desk and gave Jurnee a quick kiss on her pink lips.

"Correcto," she told him as he sat down in front of her desk. "Did your manager send you my email last night?" she asked as the light glimmered off her diamond stick earrings.

He nodded. "I read it this morning before I went to the gym."

"And?"

"Well." He shifted uneasily on the chair. "I'm not too open on the idea of a woman sticking a finger or anything else in my ass," he said, unsmiling.

"Trevon, it won't make you gay," she said as she struggled not to laugh.

"I know that," he replied. "It's just—why did you add that to the script, anyway?"

"Wasn't my idea. Chelsea called me about it, said she wanted to be the first to do that with you on film."

"Oh, she did?" *Now I know why she always be rubbing my ass when she be sucking my dick.*

Jurnee smirked. "Maybe I can show you how it feels?"

"I'll pass on that. And how about we cut the finger up the ass out of the script?" *Wait until I see, Chelsea!*

Jurnee rolled her eyes. "I'll take it out," she said reluctantly. "Now, which do you want to hear first? Malo or bueno news?"

He thought about it for a second. "Malo," he decided.

"I couldn't find a full-figured woman for you to do a film with." She shook her head. "The one girl I did come across, she isn't an amateur. Janelle stressed that issue, so I didn't waste my time on her," she said, disappointed.

"What about that one girl from New York?"

"She has way too many issues."

"Like what?"

Jurnee frowned. "She's a drug dealer! And AEF doesn't need that mess up in here. Hell, she's in jail right now for a drug charge!"

"Well, we still got two months to start filming. So it's not like we have to call this project off."

"I hope not."

I might have someone that would do it. "What's the good—I mean bueno news?"

Sitting back, she lowered the zipper on the front of her burgundy and white jumpsuit. "Stop looking at my titties," she said as the inner swells of her breasts drew his attention.

"I can look at what belongs to me." He grinned.

"True," she said softly. "Now, the bueno news. It has something to do with your future film with an older woman."

"Is she an amateur?"

"Si, but there's something unique between the two of you."

He crossed his large arms. "How?"

"You already know her!" Jurnee said excitedly. "And she'll call you tonight."

"Hmmm. So this is like a surprise, right?"

"Si! And Kandi has something to do with it, too."

Kandi! Oh shit! Tahkiyah? Ain't no way! "W-who is she?"

"Think back to your debut film with Kandi. What happened one night after a day of filming that didn't involve Kandi?"

Trevon blinked, with a faraway look in his eyes. *What the hell is she talking about? An older chick that I already*—"I got it!" He snapped his fingers. "On the second night of filming I, uh...had sex." he grinned.

"Fucked the lady that owned the house," Jurnee said. "If you can't remember her name, it's Linda Rorie."

"Okay, I remember her! So, you saying she's gonna be in my film?"

"Yeah," Jurnee replied as she and reached inside her purse that sat on the desk. "She never had the ambition to do porn until we filmed your scene in her bedroom."

"Uh, isn't she married?"

Jurnee pulled out a stack of pictures. "He passed away a year and a half ago." She handed him the pictures. "She fifty-nine and living her life to the fullest."

Trevon slowly went through the nude pictures of Linda Rorie. He easily recalled the wild one-night stand with her in Opa-locka.

"She had a breast lift and a tummy tuck," she explained as he studied the pictures. "She said she'll do only one film, and it has to be with you."

He paused at one picture that showed Linda face down, ass up. *Pussy phat as hell! Yeah, I wanna tap that ass again!* "What will the theme be?"

"Um... I have a few ideas, but I haven't decided yet. Just know it'll be hot!"

She smirked.

"Is she still in Opa-locka where I did my first film?"

"No. She lives with her niece in North Miami Beach. So, does she still turn you on? Being that she's old enough to be your mom?"

"Did Janelle tell you about that night?" He held up one of the pictures. "All bullshit aside. I tried to knock her back out! So, to answer your question, Si!"

"Bueno!" Jurnee clapped. "Because I already signed her to do the film!"

"When?"

"Well, since we are having the issue with the other film. We can switch the time frame and do it ASAP. Even before your next film with Chelsea."

"So, that will be next month?"

She leaned on the desk. "Correct. And you better stop your little trend of diverting from what's in the script. You did it with Kandi and Chelsea. If I write for you to cum on Linda's ass. That's where I want every drop to land. Do you understand, me Mr. Harrison?"

"Yes, Queen Baby Mama."

She laughed. "Stop being silly! But for real. Stick to the script, okay?"

"I will. Just make sure I get to fuck..."

"Linda?"

"Yeah, make sure I get to sex her in a number of positions."

"She's not a teenager and you can't be bending her all up like you be doing me. Oh, yeah! She agreed to do oral sex but no anal."

He studied another picture of Linda on her back. She had her legs spread wide open, exposing her bushy crotch. "Tell'er to leave the hair." He held up the picture.

"I'm ahead of you." She smiled. "You just make sure your region below is bald. And starting tomorrow, it's no sex for you until we start filming. And eat a bunch of pineapples so your cum will have some flavor."

"Shit, I haven't done anything since I was with you and Ariana."

What! Kandi ain't been on that dick? "Don't tell me Kandi is tripping again?"

He laid the pictures on the desk. "We've been—she just seems more laid-back about everything. I went to see her and Victoria yesterday and it—she just..." He shook his head. *I hope she ain't cheating on me!*

"She just what?"

He sighed. "She just had a different mood about everything. Shit that used to get under her skin, she just blew it off. Like, she spoke in detail about the do's and don't's for my next film. Like, she didn't *care* I'm gonna fuck another female."

Jurnee sat back and crossed her arms. "It's business, Trevon. All she's doing is showing you she can face the fact that you do porn. Didn't you say she's okay with it as long as it's all business?"

He nodded. *She gotta be hiding something from me.* "I guess I'm just tripping."

She chewed her bottom lip. *I have my own problems to deal with.* "Kandi asked me if I ever shared Ariana with you?"

"When?!"

"Yesterday."

He sunk in the seat. "What did you tell'er?"

"I lied," she said with a sad expression. "And I felt like shit. I know Kandi loves you and—"

"What do you want me to do, Jurnee?"

"About what?"

He threw his hands up and dropped them on the arm of the chair. "What advice would you give me? Seriously. Try to work things out with LaToria, or focus on my career?"

"I can't answer that. Don't put me on the spot like that. I forgave Kandi for all that mess she did when she thought the baby wasn't yours. Have you?"

He closed his eyes. "I'm not sure."

"Do you love her?"

He opened his eyes and stared at the desk. "I want to," he replied.

"That's not answering my question."

He stood and paced in front of the desk with his fingers laced on top of his head. "She was my first of everything after fifteen years in prison," he stressed. "My first kiss, a shower, oral sex, anal sex, raw sex, LaToria was my first." He stopped at the edge of the desk and dropped his hands to his sides. "I murdered a man because of her. I risked my everything for her. I—LaToria is a part of me," he said. "I know how I feel. I just don't know *how* to love her."

Jurnee rolled her chair back and stood. "Life is more than who we are. You're lost right now, and you really need to find yourself. It's hard. Life itself is hard. I can't imagine how much of a shock this is to you."

He turned and sat down, dropping his face in his hands. "I don't wanna hurt LaToria."

"Then don't."

He lifted his head. "And what about you?"

She remained on her feet. "I don't know if I'm coming or going when it comes to you. Truth be told, you gave me all I wanted in Tayvon. That bond I have with you will *never* be broken." She smiled. "Some days, I do love you, Trevon. But I can't see us being that happy family. Just being honest with you and myself."

"You, LaToria and my kids are my world."

"I know. I really do." She sat down.

"Hey!" He forced a smile. "You're my BM, boss and mentor."

"Then you need to pay me."

"How much?"

She glanced at the time on the computer monitor. "It's eight minutes till noon and my next meeting isn't for another hour. If you're up to it. I was wondering if you could put that handsome face of yours between my thighs?" she whispered.

"In here?"

She pressed the button to talk to her receptionist. "Buffy, could you hold all my calls, please?" she said. "But take a message from the catering service. Big Diesel's twenty-eighth birthday is coming up."

"Yes, Ms. Cruz," came the prompt reply through the speaker.

Jurnee took her earrings off. "I'ma enjoy this new position." She smiled.

"What? Being the VP at AEF?"

"No." She shook her head. "Bending over my desk with my ass in your face." She rose. "Lick my ass and pussy from the back and you *better* make your BM cum," she said tersely.

~

TAHKIYAH DIDN'T WISH to give LaToria the idea that she was promiscuous. For that main reason, she kept Sean a secret. Ever since that chance encounter with him, she made the effort to call him every day. She knew the game and knew how to hang her bait in front of him without being too eager for attention. At the moment, she had her body soaking in the tub. Her eyes were shut as a new song by Chris Brown played on her phone. At the middle of the song, she received an alert for a new text. She checked the screen, smiled, and grabbed the towel to dry her fingers.

Hello beautiful! Jus thinking of U.

Tahkiyah read the unexpected text from Sean.

Thank U! And how did I fill your thoughts?

Wishin U were here wit me.

Where would dat B?

My suite @ the Marriott

What would U want me there 4?

Want me 2 B blunt?

Yes!

I want 2 taste you.

That sounds nice!

IF U was here it would feel even better.

R U sexting wit me?

Can I?

Tahkiyah bit her lips as her nipples stiffened.

Go 4 it.

MDIH!

????

My Dick Is Hard!

Ohh um, how big?

7 ½ inches

Nice. Real nice! Bet U like 2 put it N me?

YES!

Which position?

U on top.

MPGW!

???

LOL! My pussy gettin wet!

Mmmm! I really want 2 taste you!

Make me cum!

How??

Lick my pussy good! Don't stop till I cum on your lips!

Yes! I'll do it!

Really?

Yes! I'm going back 2 California n morning. Can I see U 2 nite?

Tahkiyah squeezed her thighs together under the warm strawberry scented water.

What time?

Is 8p.m. good 4 U?

It's doable.

I'm in room 725 & I'll B waitin 4 U

I'll cum.

Tahkiyah rubbed her wet breasts and waited for Sean to reply.

If U taste as good as U look. I might not leave

You might as well unpack b/c my pussy is sugary sweet. #putitinmyface. Put it in my face.

See U @ 8. Have 2 go.

Stay beautiful. TTYL

Tahkiyah leaned back and closed her eyes. *Maybe a real tongue on my pussy will get Trevon out of my damn head!* She palmed her breasts.

"Ma," Kandi poked her head inside the bathroom. "Can I use your car for a while? I need to run to the insurance company to sign some more papers and stuff."

"As long as you're back by six."

"I'll be back long before that," Kandi said as Victoria clung to her leg. "Can you watch Lil Mama for me?"

Tahkiyah sat up and smiled at Victoria. "You know I will. And put some gas in the tank for me because it slipped my mind yesterday."

Kandi nodded, thankful for the support and love she got from her mom. On her way out the door, she grabbed her shades and phone. Like every other day of the week, she effortlessly drew a comparison to Nicki Minaj. Today she had her shapely figure poured in a pair of tight denim jeans and a clingy, black bra strap tank top. If her beauty and figure didn't make her the center of attention, the message on the tank top did so. *Stop Hatin' B/C I'm Thicker Than You!*

Kandi had a new thick-skinned view when it came to Trevon. She still loved him, but now she allowed things to be what they would be. When she sat behind the wheel of Tahkiyah's BMW, she sent Trevon a text.

Hey Smooch! Call me later after U handle biz @ AEF. Lov U. MUAH.

Kandi laid her phone on her lap and started the engine. Just as she adjusted the seat, a figure quickly approached the BMW from the rear.

10

BUTTER BUNS

Miami, Florida
Friday, July 31st

"Hey, baby girl, it's me," Trevon said, leaving a voicemail for LaToria. "I got your text, and I just left AEF a few minutes ago. Uh, just hit me back when you can. And call me because I really need to talk to you. Kiss Victoria for me. Talk to you later. Love you." He ended the hands-free call inside his Mercedes-Benz S580. He cruised the streets in Miami in the six-figure sedan with the world on his back. Day by day became his mantra with the issues he faced. He wanted things to work in favor toward his bond with LaToria. As it stood now, he couldn't make it through a single day without thinking of her.

With the setbacks building on his full-figured film, he intentionally arrived at Quovadis Estate's front gate at 2:07p.m. to catch Vanessa getting off work. He gazed at her shapely frame as she walked toward a black Ford Expedition. *It'd take a whole bottle of baby oil to cover that body.* He tapped the horn to get her attention as he wheeled his sedan up to the curb.

Vanessa smiled instantly at the sight of Trevon behind the

wheel. She lifted her shades as he slowed to a stop. "Mr. Harrison," she said, making an effort to stay professional. *This man is too fine!*

"Hey, sexy," he said. "How many times have I told you to call me Trevon?"

Grinning, she fingered a strand of black and blonde highlighted hair out of her face. "I'm not messing with you today."

"You got anything planned for today?"

Her eyebrow raised. "Why?" she asked, trying to figure out his motive. *I know I'm not ugly. But he plays this flirting thing too strong.*

"I'd like to talk to you about a few things."

He wants some pussy. I bet he'd turn it up if he knew I was really single. I gotta play my position and not seem too pressed for his attention. "Um, about what?"

"How would you feel if I asked you to do a film with me?"

OMG! He can't be for real! Wait, I seen that search on AEF site for a full-figured girl! Okay, calm down and don't act stupid. "I'd feel like you were running game on me." She crossed her arms.

"Nah," he said. "Never that."

"Are you for real? Or is this just a routine you use to get in a woman's head?" She looked at him, hoping he wasn't trying to make a fool of her.

"That's not how I move, Vanessa. You know my lifestyle and the last thing I have to do is to run any game for sex.

She nodded. "True. But why me?"

"Why not?" he replied mildly.

Because I'm not a size 0! "You're just messing with my head."

"I'm dead ass serious, Vanessa. True, on a personal level, I've had my eyes on you since you first started working here. And I envy your boyfriend." He grinned, hoping she would at least have an open-minded position.

"I still don't believe you."

"Why not?"

She shrugged. "You can have damn near any woman you want. I see all those urban models and swimsuit models on your Instagram page. Look at me." She held her arms out. "I'm a big girl!" *And a size 16 at that!*

"And that's supposed to change my view of you? When I call you sexy, I mean it."

Vanessa sighed and pushed her fingers through her hair. "What about your girlfriend?"

"What about your boyfriend?"

Damn. He got me on that. "Okay, I'm free for the rest of the day, Mr. Harrison. Now what do you have in mind?"

"Let me take you out for—"

She shook her head. "I can't be seen in public with you. Not trying to be funny."

"I understand." He nodded. "But I have an idea."

"Why am I not surprised?"

"Because you know I'm a driven man."

"Not really," she said. "All I know about you is what I see in your porno films."

"Maybe we can change that by the end of the day?"

She shrugged. "It's possible."

He lowered his eyes to her wide hips and thick thighs. I can't wait to see her naked. "Follow me. I have a spot where we won't be disturbed. Do you trust me?"

She looked at the man that invaded her nightly fantasies. "I will until you give me a reason not to. Hopefully that doesn't happen."

~

"WHOSE BOAT IS THIS?" Vanessa asked as Trevon stopped at the sleek, blue and white 42' Fountain speedboat.

"Janelle's," he replied as he assisted her down into the cockpit. "She loaned it to me while she's on maternity leave."

"Oh, yeah! I read about that in her last blog. She had a baby by that author. What's his name?"

"Victor L. Martin."

"Yeah, that's him," Vanessa said as Trevon untied the lines that held the speedboat in the slip. "Do you know how to drive this thang?" she asked as a bead of sweat trickled down her cleavage. *I need to get out of this hot ass uniform.*

"Of course. And I have my boating license." He climbed into the cockpit and showed her how to strap into the high-back seat. "Aren't you hot in that shirt?"

"Yeah, it's attracting heat like you wouldn't believe!" She already had the top two buttons undone to get some air circulating against her flesh.

"Take it off," he suggested. "What's the big difference between a bikini and a bra?"

"A lot, Mr. Harrison." She tried and failed at holding back an attractive smile.

He glanced at her with his finger on the button to start the speedboat. "I want you to feel relaxed, Vanessa. Hell, you're making me hot just by looking at you in that uniform." He laughed as the speedboat bobbed gently.

"Where are we going?"

He looked around the marina at all the yachts and smaller cabin cruisers. "We can ride down to Key West and find a spot to drop anchor. Enjoy the view and just talk."

Talk my ass. Vanessa thought as she pictured herself getting her nasty on in the cockpit. *This will surely be something to tell my girls about!* "I m-might take my shirt off after we leave the marina." She lusted at the sight of him. "Oh, and that shirt you're wearing is making me hot." She flirted, hoping he would take the hint.

Trevon took off his short-sleeved Versace shirt. She stared at his nude, muscled chest as a flock of sea gulls circled overhead.

"You buckled in?" he asked.

She nodded.

"You won't regret this. You'll enjoy the ride," he told her.

Vanessa settled back in the seat as Trevon pushed the button to start the engine. Her mind didn't hold any thoughts on liking the boat ride or not. In lust, the only ride she wanted to enjoy was the pleasure of Trevon on his back and his dick rooted up far inside her.

"THANKS FOR GIVING ME A RIDE," Conda told Kandi along the drive to Coral Gables. "And I didn't mean to scare you."

She nodded. "Tell me again what happened. And don't talk so damn fast."

Conda rubbed his nose and stole a sidelong glance at Kandi's breasts. "Ah, Heather dropped me off this morning to spend some time with one of her friends."

"Who?"

"Becky Connick. She's a big-time attorney and—"

"She's married," Kandi butted in. "I've seen her commercials. White chick with the fake breasts."

"Yeah, that's her. Well, I was doing my thang with her and her husband popped up!"

Kandi sucked her teeth. "Why y'all didn't go to a room or something?"

"He caught an early flight back from Dallas, Texas. She wasn't expecting him until tomorrow night."

"How did you make it out?" She glanced at him. "You don't look like you were roughed up or anything."

"Shit, I almost *didn't* make it out." He licked his dry lips. "Becky had gone to the kitchen to get some whipped cream when her husband walked in. Word on er'thang, I was scared as fuck!"

"What happened next?"

"Well, Becky acted like she was waiting for him. I was peeking from the bedroom and saw how she greeted him naked with a can of whipped cream. She was like 'surprise honey! Let's do something kinky today!' And damn if she didn't give him some head on the sofa."

"For real?"

"Yep. Anyway, she tried to keep him in the living room, but he wanted to do it on their bed. I hauled ass to the closet when I realized what was up."

"That's some real life trapped in the closet, R. Kelly mess right there," Kandi commented.

"Yeah, and I don't wanna ever experience that shit again!"

"That's whatcha ass get for committing adultery." Kandi giggled. "Okay, what happened while you were in the closet?"

"They fucked for like thirty minutes while I hid in the closet."

"Did you do anything with her before her husband showed up?"

"Yeah." He nodded. "I ate her pussy twice, and she wanted me to lick her ass next."

"Boy, you are crazy," Kandi said. "So how did you get out?"

He sighed. "I had to wait until she convinced him to take a shower. As soon as I saw my chance, I got my black ass up outta there. I was about to call Heather when I saw you."

"How much you getting paid?"

"Huh?"

"I know what you are doing, Conda. Heather is pimping you out because of your tongue."

He dropped his chin. "Did you know I was once nominated for AVN male performer of the year?" he said, avoiding her questions about how *little* he was paid.

Kandi nodded. *And you blew it all away to get high.*

"Those were the good times. Now I'm just a common male prostitute. Licking ass and pussy for a hundred bucks. And don't ask me what Heather makes because she gets the money upfront."

"On an average, how many women does she set you up with in a day?" Kandi asked as she sped through a busy intersection.

He closed his eyes for a few seconds. "On a busy day, I'll say five or six."

"Every day?"

"All but Sunday." He looked out the window. "And on that day, she usually spends an hour or so on my face."

Pathetic! But if he's letting her pimp him, that's on him. "I hope you're saving your money and not wasting it on nothing stupid."

"I'm saving all that I can. And by the way, you got a freebie the other night."

"That's okay because we're even now since I'm going out of my way to take you home."

He snuck another look at her breasts. *So muthafuckin sexy!* "Maybe I can give you another one? You tasted so—"

"I'll pass," Kandi stated. *Nope. Not gonna cheat on Smooch.*

He was shocked. "Really?"

She nodded.

Bitch thinks it's all about her! "I can't even lick your ass?"

"Conda!" she snapped. "I suggest you drop that subject before I drop your ass off at the next bus stop!"

"My bad." *Stupid ho must be on her period.*

~

"HARDER!" Heather shouted beneath Sean with her legs pinned over his shoulders. "Pound your cock in me harder!" She licked her red lips and palmed her fake, tanned breasts.

He raced his thrusts in and out of her. He stared at the wall to avoid having to look at her sun weather-beaten face. Though her looks had faded over the years, her pussy remained Grade-A.

Several minutes later, he sat up against the padded headboard beside Heather. She had a cigarette lit and an ashtray by her hip.

"Do you consider your money well spent, Mr. Levinson?" Heather asked as she caressed his thigh.

"Does it matter?" he quipped. "You don't do refunds."

"Darling," she said. "My pussy has a guarantee of fulfillment. And proof of that is in that condom you wore out while inside me."

"And I can't debate that."

"Good. Now tell me who referred my reputable establishment to you?" She took a slow draw on the thin cigarette.

I followed Kandi the other night. "A friend of a friend," he lied, with no thought of telling the truth. The truth was that he had been following Kandi from the time she left the restaurant up in West Palm Beach back on Monday.

"So, you're sticking to that story?" Heather tapped the cigarette in the ashtray. *Something fishy about him.*

"It's the truth. By word of mouth, I heard of this establishment... as you call it."

She smirked. "Well, you proved to me you're definitely not a cop."

"Yeah. And I had to strip all of my clothes off to show you I didn't have a wire on."

"And I sincerely apologize for that treatment."

Now I have to figure out a way to bring up Kandi. I need to know why she was here. "Do any celebrities visit you?" he asked innocently. "Like... any of your female porn star friends?"

"What happens in HOP, stays in HOP. I'm firm on confidentiality, baby." *He already asked one too many questions.* She glanced at her watch and realized that he had a few minutes left. "Can you get him back up?" She reached for his lax penis.

"With a little help."

"Would you like one or two sets of lips on your cock?" she asked.

"The redhead?"

She nodded as she pressed the cigarette into the ashtray.

Before Sean could reply, a knock rapped on the door and Conda poked his head in.

"Conda!" Heather frowned. "Why are you back so early?"

"Long story. But I just got back."

"Is everything alright?" I *hope he didn't screw things up!*

"Yeah. But I need to talk to you when you're done." Conda

glanced at Sean. "Uh, you driving that white Continental out front?"

Sean pulled the sheets up to cover his nakedness.

"Conda! Please excuse us!" she scolded. "Can't you see I'm with a client!"

He closed the door. Out in the hallway, he tried to figure out why Kandi reacted strange when she parked behind the white Bentley. *Does she know that motherfucker or what? He* made a detour along the way to his room to drop by on the redhead.

"Hey." He grinned, strolling into her room without knocking.

"Learn how to knock!" she complained as she changed the sheets on the canopy bed.

He walked straight up behind her and slid his arms around her slender waist. "You won't believe what happened to me today."

"Can't you see I'm busy? I need to change these sheets before my next client shows up."

"Leave them on." He licked her delicate neck, knowing how to turn her on. "Let me show you a new trick I can do with my tongue."

"I don't have the time." She leaned back in his embrace as his tongue slithered up and down the side of her neck.

"Are you sure?" he whispered, waiting for the cue to take off her bra and panties.

"W-we have to be quick, okay?" she relented.

"Hey, one quick question."

"Hmm?"

"Who's the white guy with the boss lady?" Conda asked as he unlatched her bra.

She shrugged. "First time I've ever seen him here."

"You know his name?"

"Uhh, I think it's Sean. Why are you so—"

"Just thought I knew him." He licked her neck again and slid his hands under the loose bra.

"Mmm," she moaned, poking her ass against his erection. "Let me ride your face. I'll cum faster."

He couldn't push the weirdness of Kandi's reaction of the Bentley out of his mind. With nothing important going on in his life, he would make it his mission to find out what was up between Sean and Kandi. *Bitch wanna shine on me! If she's hiding any secrets I'ma put that ho on front street. And I need to Google Trevon Harrison. See what so special about this motherfucker!*

11

THE BREAST MOMENTS IN LIFE

Key West, Florida
Friday, July 31st

"It's so peaceful out here," Vanessa said as she gazed at the horizon.

"So, what's up?" Trevon said from the back of the speedboat. "Do you believe me now?"

She turned and laid her eyes on him. Due to the stifling temperature, he had stripped down to his tight-fitting briefs in the course of the pleasure cruise. "You really want me to do a porno with you?" She handed him a chilled water bottle from the cooler.

"I wouldn't have you out here if I didn't."

"This is too much to think about right now." She sat across from him with dots of sweat covering her exposed cleavage. She had long since ended her insecure thoughts on how she looked with her uniform top off.

"You're a sexy woman, Vanessa." He twisted the top off the bottle while staring at her heavyweight breasts.

Their knees touched in the tight space of the cockpit.

"Being sexy and being a porn star are miles apart," she said as a bead of sweat ran down the valley of her breasts.

He ogled at the appealing thickness of her thighs from behind his shades. "What turns you on?"

She sat back against the warm seat. "Well, you turn me on."

"How?"

"Your body." She bit her bottom lip.

He took a sip from the bottle and rose to his feet. "Touch the parts of me that turn you on."

Oh, my gosh! I can't believe this! Look at that body! "I c-can't." *He's so ripped!*

"Why not? You look at my films and now you can't touch me in the flesh?"

"What do you want from me, Trevon?" She looked up at him. "All bullshit aside."

"Ain't no bullshit to put aside, Vanessa. I seriously want you to do this film with me."

She squeezed the water bottle, changing its shape. "I have to think about this."

"That's all I'm asking."

She smiled and tightened her grip on the bottle to stop her urge to touch *all* of him. They both looked up when a gleaming white seaplane flew overhead.

"Can I see'em?" he asked as the drone of the seaplane engines faded.

She knew what he wanted to see. "For what?" She relaxed her grip on the bottle.

"Because I've been fantasizing about'em since the first day I met you."

"Even with all those perfect women you've been with?"

He sighed. He tried to think of the right words to crush her load of insecurities. When he came up blank, he relied on the true adage. "*Look* at what you do to me, Vanessa." He reached inside his briefs and pulled his erection out through the slit. It bobbed twice and settled within arm's reach from her. The proverb '*actions* speak *louder than words*' proved true.

She gasped, dropped the bottle and stared fixated at the real-life sight of his renowned penis. Mesmerized, she broke through her shyness and reached for it.

He widened his stance as she lovingly fondled his flesh. "Yeah, that's it, baby." He lowered his hands to her sweaty shoulders and tugged at the straps of her bra. "Is that a part of me that turns you on, huh?"

She nodded, totally absorbed in touching every inch of his long and thick erection. *I got his dick in my hand! Trevon fucking Harrison!*

His penis throbbed and twitched in her hands as he worked her bra loose on the middle of her back. The sun heated their flesh, covering them with a shiny coat of sweat. She remained willing with him as he removed the bra. Lust surfaced between them when her triple D breasts were unleashed from the confines of the bra.

She wanted to cross her arms over her large breasts to hide them. She hated how they sagged and hated the map of stretch marks that covered them. A confused expression crossed her cute face when he stepped back from her hands. She quickly assumed he was turned off by the sight of her bare breasts.

He sat down and couldn't decide on which breast to lick first. Acting on his impulse, he leaned headlong between both of her soft, sweaty breasts and tried to lick every drop of sweat.

She leaned back in the seat, cupping her heavy bosom to his delight. She threw her head back and fed him. His name skipped through her lips as he sucked and licked her dark brown, puckered nipples. She rubbed her left breast against the side of his face as he slurped her right nipple in and out of his mouth. Her body signaled a different thirst of him when her knees drew up his waist. He slid off the seat and to his knees with his face sandwiched between her breasts. She released a sonorous moan and circled her arms around his neck.

He devoured her breasts, nursing on her nipples with the sun beating against his back.

"Ooohhh, my gosh. You're m-making me so fucking wet!" she blurted with her eyes closed.

He licked under the swell of her left breast and then he dropped a hand to her belt. He pulled the strap free of the belt loop and tugged upward to dislodge the pin. He relinquished his hold of her left breast to use both hands to free her of her pants.

"Trevon!" she whined as the awareness of the moment flooded her mind. Her breasts rocked and swayed with the motion of the boat as he tugged her pants and panties down her thick hips and thighs. She uttered a low-pitched, frustrated moan when her pants bunched up at the top of her boots.

He patiently untied them and took them off. She drowned under his desire for her. Her insecurities were suddenly replaced with a rash of confidence. She leaned back in the seat and spread her legs open. She then slid a hand to her fully exposed wetness and shuddered as she rubbed herself.

Trevon slid his briefs off and left them on the pile of clothes. He stared at *all* of Vanessa as she fiddled with her clitoris. He couldn't define the heart pounding urgency that enticed him to be inside her. Nothing stood between them but the humid air and temptation. A fleeting thought of LaToria hurtled through his mind as Vanessa lowered herself to the floor of the cockpit.

What the fuck am I doing? Damn, her ass is so fucking juicy! He grabbed his dick and squeezed it as hard as he could. At his feet, Vanessa positioned herself on her back, legs spread wide open, heels in the air. He knelt between her legs and teased her glistening furrow with the throbbing head of his dick. He prodded the crown of his penis up and down the puckered folds of her sopping wet opening. He teased her for a few seconds before he began to repeatedly slap her juicy mound with his penis.

"Yesss! Whip my pussy!" She held her legs apart, hoping he would shove every inch of his long penis inside her. She didn't weigh the consequences of her lust incited actions. All she sought was feeling his raw penetration again and again and again. An euphoric moan changed the shape of her lips when he lifted her legs over his muscular arms. She grabbed his thick shaft when the tip grazed against her clitoris. She stared up at him, stroking his long erection as he moved on top of her. She dragged his bulbous tip up and down her slippery entrance until her legs settled over his biceps. Her stomach tightened as she guided him inside her.

He showed no indecisiveness as he slid inside her tight wetness. She raked her fingernails up and down his sweaty, broad shoulders. She moaned as she instinctively whirled her hips as his lengthy erection plunged in and out of her extremely slithery opening. Their moans sounded out of tune, one soft, one guttural. His continuous strokes had her panting and quivering beneath him.

"Please, don't stop!" She rubbed his chest, staring at his shiny penis. "I want it! I want it!"

Trevon convulsed as he thrusted in and out of Vanessa's tight moistness.

"Yess, yes, ooohhh...gimme that big...fuckin' dick!" she shrilled as his balls slapped the back of her phat ass. Her healthy breasts heaved with his determined strokes.

He lowered his lips to her nipple while he tirelessly pumped his dick in and out of her.

She caressed his back as he maintained a steady pace that had her moaning his name and her rave about how good he felt inside her.

He moaned and licked her neck. *I need to stop.* He closed his eyes. *This ain't business. It's pleasure and I'm cheating on LaToria.*

She sensed a sudden build up in the pace of his satisfying strokes. She winced, digging her fingernails into his back. "Baby!" she squealed as her legs slipped down his strong arms. "Don't stop! Please don't!"

He slammed into her, pumping with all his raw might. He roughly moved her legs up to his shoulders and used all of his vigor to enjoy her.

"Aaahh! Yesss! Fuuuck me! Beat it, baby!" she panted.

"Take dis dick!"

"Give it to me!"

He could not stop. He stayed on top of her, pumping feverishly.

"Hit it-" she moaned, "-from the back!"

He pounded her for a few more breaths before he slowed to a stop. "Turn over!" He slapped her hip and withdrew his penis. *I need to stop.* He sat back on his haunches as she turned over to her knees and elbows. He rubbed her big, sweaty ass and penetrated her from behind.

"Mmmmmm, I love it like this!" She rocked back against his forward thrusts. Her ass jiggled wavelike and smacked against him. Having him in reality didn't match the sights she saw of him on TV.

"Cum for me, Vanessa!" he moaned as he clutched her waist.

"Ooohh—it's going sooo deep! Just d-don't stop!" she moaned, reveling his deep, unceasing strokes.

"Aahh, this pussy so fucking juicy!"

"Mmm! Spank my ass!" she shouted over her shoulder. "Spank it! Spank my phat ass! Ooohh, shit I'm lovin' this! Lovin' your dick! Uh huh! Uh huh!"

He kept his eyes fixed on her brown ass, bouncing back and forth. Her butt cheeks moved in a rippled wave that held him in a trance. His strokes were no longer patient. They came in a hurry, rushing in and out of her. Their flesh continued to thunder between them. Seconds. Minutes. They swam in their lust, fucking for that climax.

"Feels so good!" She rose up on her arms. "Just keep do-doing it! Please, baby. Oooh, fuck my pussy!"

"Ooohh, Vanessa! Ooohhh... this pussy good!" he moaned.

"I wanna cum! Please, ma-make me cum, Trevon," she whined, twerking her ass.

He squeezed her soft love handles. *I'm fixing to tear dis pussy up! Damn, look at that phat ass!* He sped up. Just to hear the wet slushing coming from her pussy.

Vanessa bit her bottom lip and moaned. Nothing prepared her for this. Her pussy spasmed around his sawing erection. Her large ass cheeks moved like the face of the ocean that surrounded them.

Trevon stayed firm between her silken valley. He croaked her name when he felt her pussy clenching along his length. Suddenly a coolness tapped his back, his neck, shoulder, ass, and then the back of his feet. He slowed his thrusts and looked at the sky.

It started to drizzle and then it started raining. She rocked back on his erection and moaned as it slid all the way in. She dropped to her elbows and begged for him to continue. The rain increased as he pumped his erection gently into her. He massaged the rain into her phat ass as he resumed his fluid thrusting. Her ass heaved back and forth, clapping softly.

"Trevon! Baby, I'm gonna cum!" she gasped and wiggled her ass side to side.

He pumped her through the grip of her sudden climax. Her juices left a creamy foam along his erection. The rain pelted their nude frames as he closed his eyes and tilted his face to the sky. Deep down, he wished the rain had the ability to wash away his sins. His strokes slowed to a stop. Guilt slapped him as he pulled out of her.

Vanessa rolled to her side and saw Trevon sitting behind her with his head to the sky. She crawled over to him and stared at the rain, washing her juices off his dick.

He didn't flinch or open his eyes when he felt her lips sliding down his penis. Her tempo matched the way the speedboat bobbed on the calm ocean. It rained, and she sucked him with a gentleness that left him speechless.

~

"CALL ME TONIGHT," Trevon later told Vanessa as she started up her expedition.

She nodded while trying to deal with her promiscuous actions.

"You, okay?" he asked, standing outside her SUV.

She smiled faintly. "Trust me, I'm fine."

"So, no regrets?"

She thought about it. "Well, maybe next time I can get on top."

He stroked his beard. "I don't see no issue with that. It's not like we had a king-size bed on the floor of that boat."

"I can't believe I actually had sex with you today." She looked down at her lap.

He leaned inside the SUV and tenderly lifted her chin. "Vanessa, what we did was something that's been on my mind for a minute. And if you don't do a film with me-" He paused a second. "-I would still like to see you from time to time. I know you got a man and you know I got a—"

"I get the gist," she said. "And I'm definitely down with that." *Ain't no need to tell'im I'm single. Shoot, all I want is the dick, anyway. FWB with Trevon Harrison!*

"Well, uh, drive safe and remember to call me when you can." He waved as she pulled off. As he strolled toward his Benz, he took note of the time: 6:51 p.m. *Go back to the house and hit the shower. And then go see my kids.* He slid behind the wheel of his sedan and sat for a moment to get his mind right. The guilt of cheating on LaTroria ate at his conscience. *I gotta stop this dumb shit.*

~

KANDI STOOD when Trevon entered the living room. *I have to do this.*

"Hey, Baby Girl," Trevon laid his iPhone on the coffee table. "You get my voicemail?"

"We need to talk, Trevon," she said flatly.

Oh shit. She called me Trevon instead of Smooch. "Something wrong?"

She sighed and sat down. "Look, I...can't do this any longer." She looked at him.

His heart skipped. *Chill. Let'er say what she has to say.* "Okay." He sat beside her, wanting things to be perfect between them. "What's wrong now?"

"Look, I know what I said when I was last over here. But—things can't be like this."

"Like what?"

"Me loving you like I do... in spite of you fucking other women."

He reached for her hand. "Doing porn is—"

"It's more than that, Trevon. I *thought* I could deal with it, but I can't. I can't deal with this." She pointed at her heart. "When it comes to you. Just the sight of you or the sound of your voice makes my heart flutter. It scares me because I know I'm crazy in love with you."

"And...I love you the same. What's the—"

"You *like* me, Trevon. Liking and loving someone isn't the same."

"But—"

"Listen to me, please." She squeezed his hand. "Your actions, Trevon. If you truly loved me with all your heart, you wouldn't desire the need of another woman. Business or pleasure. I just realized this, and it hurts, okay. My heart won't let me stand by and watch you be with someone else. I just can't—won't do it."

"So, what are you saying? You're breaking up with me, *again*?"

"Please don't make it seem like that. What I want with you is too strong to share you with any other woman. I know I called myself in a relationship with Swagga while I was doing porn. I *thought I* loved him, but it was false. I *liked* him and it's the same with us."

"You want me to stop doing porn? Is that what this is about?"

"It's deeper than that," she softly replied. "I need you to be fully in love with me, Trevon. You have to be willing to meet me halfway. Halfway is the point where you can honestly say I'm the only woman for you."

"What are you really trying to tell me?"

"I'm gonna fall back. I love you so much that I want to give you space. Give you space to find out what you want in life. As well as who you want to be with. I will only be pretending that I don't care about you doing porn and that's no good for either of us."

"H-How can you say I don't love you?"

"I don't have to say a word," she answered with tears in her eyes. "Your actions speak too loud, and you don't even see it."

"LaToria, I'll quit—"

"No!" She shook her head. "Finish your contract and get your head together. You're fully free. No more probation. No one to tell you what to do. Enjoy it! Find yourself and find out who makes you happy."

"Baby, I d-don't want you to—"

Kandi stood and gently pulled her hand free. "We will forever be linked by our daughter. But for you and I—it's *all* of you or nothing. Do what makes you happy. Even if it's not with me. I do love you. But your heart isn't the same." She kissed his cheek and left him in tears. Alone.

12

ALONE

Coconut Grove, Florida
Saturday, August 1st

For the sake of his kids, Trevon didn't turn his phone off last night. However, he ignored the calls he received from Chelsea, Vanessa, Kendra, and Linda. He didn't go after LaToria because every word she said was true. The fact that he had sex with Vanessa proved that he simply *liked* LaToria. He couldn't move from the sofa. The heartache of LaToria leaving was a weight he couldn't lift. The ringing of his phone at 10:17a.m. and Rex barking stirred him awake on the sofa. The ringtone and caller ID told him it was BM2..... Jurnee.

"Yeah?" he answered despondently.

"You doing okay?" Jurnee asked, concerned. "I know what's going on between you and Kandi. She called me last night."

"I'm good," he replied.

"That's not true," Jurnee asserted. "And as much as I hate to— No, I won't even say that because I gotta keep it one hundred with you. Kandi is right about everything she told you last night. Now you see what it means by the truth hurts."

"How?" he grumbled.

"That you don't love, Kandi," she stated.

"I'm getting tired of y'all tell me how the fuck I—"

"You can dead that tone of talk with me!" she interrupted. "Kandi is getting her life in order for Victoria, and I have to back her on that."

"And breaking up with me will help what?"

"Do you even know what true love is? If you do, tell me right now!" she demanded. Trevon sighed as Rex trotted into the living room.

"That's what I thought," Jurnee said. "You shouldn't be mad at her."

"I'm not," he said implausibly.

"But it hurts, right?"

"Something like that. But I'll get over it."

"No, you won't. You can tell that lie to somebody else."

"Two against one. I can't win."

"That's your biggest mistake right there. We would-could never be against you!"

"I...didn't mean it like that," he replied. "Uh, what my son doing?"

"Ariana is giving him a bath."

He leaned back, staring blankly across the spacious living room. "What else did LaToria say?"

"A lot. But most important, she doesn't hate you, okay?"

"Meaning?"

"No harsh feelings. She even said you can keep the keycard to her condo."

He yawned. "I don't want it to be like this."

"You can't define your wants until you understand what your needs are."

Makes sense. Just like LaToria made a lot of sense last night. "Any suggestions?"

"Of course, focus on your kids and your career. Complete the films you're under contract to do. And *if* you want to deal with any matters of the heart with Kandi—make sure your heart is in it."

"And what about us? You falling back from me just like Kandi is?"

"Of course not. But I'll say this and I won't explain why. That threesome we did with Ariana was the last."

"Why? What—"

"Didn't you hear what I just said? Just leave it alone!"

He shook his head, wanting no parts of Jurnee's sour side. "What are you doing today?" he asked as the phone vibrated with a new text message.

"I have to go see my doctor about a new fitting for my leg."

"Want me to come?" He opened the text when he saw it was Vanessa.

Morning' Sweetie! Been think bout doin' film wit u. If U were 4 real, I'm down 2 do it. Call me. BTW I'm off all day. TTYL.

"No, because you'll only worry too much about nothing."

He wanted to share the good news about Vanessa. *Nah. I'll wait until I talk to her.* "What time you supposed to go see the doctor?"

"Around four o'clock," she replied. "Oh, before I forget. Have you seen all of Kandi's films?"

"Yeah. I looked at'em one time. But of course, I don't watch'em no more. Why?"

"Did you know Conda is back?"

"Who?"

"Conda. The guy Kandi did her debut film with."

"Dude with the long tongue?"

"Yeah, he was let go from AEF because of his drug habit. And he wasn't all that good on film, if you ask me. Anyway, Kandi said he's back and working as a male prostitute for Heather Cocks."

"I heard about her. She the white chick with the fake breasts, right?"

"Si. And she gives porn a bad name."

"Okay, what about Conda? LaToria hooking back up with him?"

Jurnee giggled. "Hell no! And you are so jealous. But I want you to be on point because a lot of people don't know the *true* reason why Janelle cut ties with Conda."

"I'm listening."

"Promise not to tell *anyone I* told you this!"

"I promise. Now tell me what's up."

She sighed. "Well, remember when you first signed your contract with AEF at that party Janelle had at her mansion?"

"Yeah."

"And you asked me why the security was so deep. Like I said, a year before there was a stalker caught on the grounds—"

"And one of the dogs attacked the stalker. I remember everything you told me that night."

"Good. Because that stalker was Conda. Janelle didn't want any bad media about him and AEF, so she didn't press any charges."

"Didn't he make a film with Janelle?"

"Yeah...but it was just a film of him tongue fucking her. And it's rare as hell because Janelle took it out of distribution. She didn't tell no one about Conda but me."

"So, you saying LaToria is dealing with this mutherfu—"

"No. At least not from what she told me. He's bad news, and I hinted that to Kandi as best as I could."

"And why should I be on point?"

"Just running with my intuition."

"Uh, you know a white dude by the name of Sean Levinson?"

"Uh, no. Should I?"

"He supposed to be some big time porn producer from Cali."

"Sean Levinson? Sorry, never heard of him. Why do you ask?"

"Ah, nothing really. Just saw'im on Facebook," he lied. *LaToria better not be on no bullshit with this dude!*

"Trevon, are you really doing okay?"

"I'm fine. You're right, I really need to just find myself."

"And take it day by day. And like I told you, Kandi isn't *mad.* So don't turn your back on her. Be her friend. I know it sounds crazy but in truth it makes a ton of sense."

Trevon had to make a choice. Focus on his career, or deal with matters of his heart. "I won't act crazy if that's what you're saying?"

"That's exactly what I'm saying," Jurnee replied. "Um, did Linda call you last night?"

"Yeah. But I didn't take the call."

"Why?"

"It was after LaToria had left and I wasn't in the mood to talk. I'll return her call after I get myself together."

"Make sure you do both. Call her *and* get yourself together."

"I promise."

Trevon ended the call minutes later, after he assured Jurnee he would call her tonight. Slumped back on the sofa, he returned Linda Rorie's call. She was overly excited to hear his voice, and she didn't mince her words about wanting to have sex with him *again.* He listened to her expressing candidly about her longing to have sex in front of the cameras. In all, she was in favor of being with him on film as well as in the privacy of her bed.

His next call went unanswered when he called Chelsea. He waited for her voicemail to play through before he left his message. "Hey, sexy. Sorry I missed your call last night. Uh, Jurnee told me about that *funny shit* you wanted to add in the script. Yeah, I need to talk to you about that. And FYI, before you hear it on social media—never mind. Just call me back. I'll holla atcha."

Trevon wanted to share the news about LaToria dumping him. *Fuck it. It don't matter to Chelsea, no way.* Rex jumped on the sofa when he called Kendra.

"Hey! What's up with you, handsome?" Kendra answered after the first ring.

"Nothing much," Trevon replied. "Just returning your call."

"You doing, okay? You don't sound happy at all."

"Just going through some things. But I'm good though."

"Hmm, listen. I've been out of touch since we last saw each other because my boyfriend decided to pop by for a surprise visit."

"Really."

"In the shower. He's going back to North Carolina tomorrow, and I can't wait!"

"Why?"

"So, I can get up with you," she replied. "*And* we still need to talk about you stripping for me and my girls."

"Uh, I *know* we can hook up. But I might not be able to do that party because of my obligations with AEF. My manager said it wouldn't be a good idea."

"Awww. Dani isn't gonna like this news."

"Sorry. But it's business, and I gotta protect my brand."

"I understand. But check this out. I'ma call you back tomorrow when my boyfriend leaves. And I *seriously* hope you can bring yo' ass back up to this room."

Trevon smiled. "I'll be there."

"Good! Now let me go because he's getting out of the shower. Muah!"

He rubbed his eyes and called Vanessa. Thoughts of what they did on the speedboat had him wanting her again. *I can't believe I hit it raw!*

"Hello, Mr. Harrison!" Vanessa answered.

"You got one more time to call me that." Trevon grinned.

"Or what?" She giggled.

"Don't push your luck. But what's up? I got your text. And yes, I'm for real about everything I told you yesterday."

"In that case, what's my next step?"

He told her she would have to meet Jurnee at the AEF office. He explained how she would be interviewed and given a medical examination for any STD's.

"I guess we jumped the gun on that, huh?" she said. "For all it's worth, I'm clean and what I did with you yesterday isn't something that's the norm for me."

He squeezed his erection through his clothes. "Vanessa, I don't know why I did that."

"Did what? Fuck me?"

"No, not that. I wanted to do it so bad! I'm talking about doing it raw."

"We got caught up in the moment, baby. Besides, it's not every day I get to get it on with a famous porn star!"

He vividly remembered every stimulating second of the moments he spent inside her. "Uh, are you on any birth—"

"My tubes are tied. And why are you concerned? You shot all of your stuff on my breasts." She giggled.

"Sorry 'bout that."

"It's okay, baby. Shoot... maybe next time you can do it on my ass."

"What did you enjoy the most?"

"Mmm, it's so hard to pick. That dick was hella good when I was under you."

"That pussy was so fucking wet!"

"That's because your big dick was stroking it so good."

"Where you at?" *I want some more of that!*

"At my cousin's house in Carol City. I'm helping her move."

"Your boyfriend around?"

"He's at home," Vanessa lied. "Why? What's on your mind?"

"I wanna see you again," he said, with his dick straining under his jeans.

Silence.

"Really?" Vanessa asked.

"Yeah. And this time, I'll let you pick where we meet."

"Well, my cousin is going to visit her man in prison today. When she leaves, I'll be here alone for at least three hours."

"What time she's leaving?"

"Around one o'clock."

"You want me to drop by?"

"You already know the answer, baby."

Trevon was eager to get back inside Vanessa. He told himself it was business. He wanted to build a strong sexual connection with her that would flood over to their film. She told him she held no regrets over their actions on the speedboat. Their second meeting of the flesh was agreed upon and he promised he would show up on time.

"I'll have a surprise for you when you get here," Vanessa said before the call ended.

Trevon didn't press her to tell him what the surprise was. Whatever surprise she had for him; he didn't want to spoil it. With visions of pounding her from the back, he took a shower and not once did LaToria slip through his mind.

"THANKS for what you did last night, Ma," Kandi said as she combed Victoria's long hair.

Tahkiyah shrugged. "I couldn't leave you like that." Tahkiyah sat on the sofa with a glass of pineapple juice. "I don't like seeing you crying."

"I'm okay now."

"You sure?"

Kandi nodded. "Who's the new guy?"

"What makes you think there is a new guy?"

Kandi rolled her eyes. "C'mon. You put on all that perfume and—"

"I was going to a bar," Tahkiyah hated to lie. *Damn! I was looking forward to sitting my pussy on Sean's face.*

"Which one?"

"Huh?"

"Which bar were you going to?"

"Which one is downtown by the bank? I can't remember the name of it."

"Butterfly?"

"Yeah, that's it."

Kandi glanced at her mom. "You think I did the right thing with Trevon?"

Tahkiyah crossed her lissome legs. "To some degree, yes."

"What would you have done?" Kandi asked. "Could you be

with a man and stand by and do nothing when he's having sex with other women?"

Tahkiyah shook her head. "Porn and love don't mix. I just don't see how any sane person can draw the line between the business and personal."

"I really thought I could do it."

"At least you tried, LaToria. Now it's up to Trevon to find what he wants out of life."

And I hope it's me, Kandi thought.

~

Sorry 4 last nite. Had a fam issue that I had 2 take care of. Guess U R on your way back 2 Cali. Sorry we never got the chance 2 hook up. :(TTYL

Sean stared at the text from Tahkiyah. His mind was clear, and he showed no disappointment over Tahkiyah's no-show. He deleted the text with no intentions of ever returning her text. He sat alone in a rundown motel in Fort Lauderdale. An empty box of pizza sat on the table beside his laptop. With a finger swipe on the screen, he pulled up the news article of Trevon's conviction for first degree murder. He closed his eyes, sighed, and wondered if he had the motivation to see things through to the end.

13

AKA MR. SEX SCENE

Carol City, Florida
Saturday, August 1st

"Come in." Vanessa gestured Trevon inside her cousin's apartment. *OMG! I can't believe he showed up! And on time, too!*

Trevon took off his shades as he stepped inside the chilly apartment.

"You'll have to excuse all the boxes and stuff." Vanessa closed the door with her heart bouncing. *Look at his arms! And he smells so good!* In her excited state, she forgot to lock the door.

He didn't notice much about the living room because his full attention was stuck on Vanessa. Her sex appeal had him speechless for the moment.

"Would you like something to drink?" she asked as he eased his masculine frame down on the sofa.

"Nah. I'm good," he answered, lusting at the way her ass, thighs and hips stretched the fabric of her black and white leggings. Her large-hipped build appealed to him.

She joined him on the sofa as her breasts joggled enticingly under her white tank top. "What's up?" She slapped her hands on her knees. *My pussy is wet already!*

"You," he replied. "You've been on my mind since we—"

"Rocked the boat," she blurted.

He nodded. "I guess we can be blunt about it, huh?"

"That's a good idea," she agreed.

"Uh, do you want me to set up the meeting with someone at AEF next week?" he asked. "I really want you to be a co-star in an adult film with me."

She nodded. "Will you be there?"

"Do you want me to?"

"I'd really appreciate it." She smiled.

"I'll be there," he said. "Tell me this. How do you plan to do this film when you know your boyfriend will be against it?"

"Let me worry about that," she said.

He shrugged. "Deal. I'll just keep my focus on you and getting you a shot at signing with AEF."

"Can I ask you a serious question? And please be honest with me."

"Sure, what's up?"

"Well, I'd like to know if you are having unprotected sex with any other women?"

"Just the mothers of my kids," he answered in truth.

She tried to read his face. "What about that white girl?"

"It's always safe sex with her. And now you're gonna ask why I didn't wear a condom with you."

"Why wouldn't I?" she said flatly.

"Vanessa, I really can't explain why. I guess it's because I've been wanting you so bad."

She smiled. "That shit was so wild yesterday!"

"Hey. You said your tubes are tied. You have any kids?"

"Yes. I have a daughter that's twenty, and she's in college."

Trevon sat up with a surprised look. "You have a daughter that's twenty! Ain't no way!"

"How old do you think I am?"

"Shit. You can't be no more than thirty-four! I know you're not older than me."

Vanessa slid her hand down his arm. "Thank you for being wrong," she said. "But FYI, I'm forty."

"I don't believe that."

"Believe it. And you better believe everything I tell you about myself." *Everything but my relationship status.*

"Okay. Tell me a few things about yourself."

"Is it really important? I mean, how will we balance the lines of how we act? You do porn for a living, Trevon. This will be all so new to me and I don't wanna get caught up."

"Caught up in what?"

"You." She reached for his hand. "How do you carry your bond with that white girl and any other women in porn you have sex with?"

He had no reason to lie. He told her about his sexual bond with Chelsea and how it was sex without emotions. His career was built on sex and, being honest, he told her it was a challenge to deal with.

"How long do you plan to do porn?" she asked.

He stared in thought at a box on the floor. "I'm not sure right now. Just taking it as it comes to me. What about you? Will you sign up for more than one film?"

She shrugged. "Depends on how I do in the first one with you."

"I think you'll do fine."

"I hope so. And I hope I'll be able to perform in front of a group of people."

"What will your motivation be to do porn? Seriously, why are you open to do this?"

She smiled. "It's my fantasy, Trevon. Every time I look at one of your films, I fantasize about being in the scene with you. You, for real, you won't believe how many times I played with myself while looking at your videos on my phone or computer. You're my fantasy."

"And now I'm your reality." He grinned. "Um, did you tell anyone about what we did yesterday?"

She nodded. "Just my cousin. And she didn't believe a single word."

"Has she seen any of my films?"

"If you were to open that box on the floor by your foot. Do you know what you would find?"

Trevon glanced at the box. "Uh, my films?"

"Bingo! She was the one that put me on to AEF about a year ago and I've been a fan ever since! I got *all* of your films downloaded on my phone and a few by Big Diesel," she said. "Oh, yeah. Why don't you have a porn name like everybody else in the porn business?"

He cleared his throat. "Can you keep a secret?"

"Of course."

"Well, my next film, I'll start a new brand. My porn name will be, Mr. Sex Scene."

She smiled. "I like that! I guess Mr. Marcus better step his game up."

"Nah, I haven't reached that level yet. But before I'm done, I will be known for being the best in this business."

She didn't mind the trivial conversation with him. In truth, she felt more at ease with him as they shared minor details about their life. She listened attentively when he explained why he did 15 years in prison for murder. "I read about it on the internet and to be honest," Vanessa said. "I don't blame you one bit for doing what you did. It's sick how people take advantage of kids. Did that guy have any kids?"

Trevon shrugged. "I'm not sure," he replied as his thoughts jumped back in time. He could still see the shocked expression on Dave Falston's face when he pulled out the rusted .38. *Yellow and blue flowers. A pickup truck, and that poodle. I walked right up to him and shot his-*

"Hey Trevon!" Vanessa reached for his hand. "You spaced out on me."

He blinked a few times to gather his wits. "I'm- Just had something on my mind."

"You wanna change the subject?"

"Yeah. But, I guess I need to talk about it."

"I thought you wanted to change the subject?"

"I did. But maybe I shouldn't keep a lid on it. Like, I never really talked to anyone about why I did it. Well, I did it because he touched my sister!"

"Do you have dreams about it?" Vanessa couldn't imagine the stress of taking another person's life.

"No. Not about that day I killed him. But my bad dreams come from my time in prison."

"Maybe I can give you something good to dream about?" she said softly as she snuggled up against him, mashing her large breasts against his arm.

"Why dream when I have you now?"

She smiled. "You're turning me on, Mr. Sex Scene."

He squeezed her soft thigh. "And you got my dick so-"

Before he got the words out, she grabbed his erection through his pants. "Hard," she whispered. "Wanna make the best of our time?"

I'm supposed to be pussy free until my next film. He nodded, deciding to cater to his want and desire of Vanessa. *She so damn thick!*

"C'mon." She squeezed his lump. "Let's go to the bedroom."

He followed her down the hall with his hands on her waist. Once they reached the unfurnished bedroom, she guided him to a bare queen-sized mattress on the floor. "We took the bed frame down this morning," she explained. "I hope this isn't too ghetto for you?"

"We did it on the *floor* of a boat yesterday," he reminded her. "This mattress looks soft, and I'll have all the room I need to stroke that pussy like I really wanted to."

"Mmmm!" She slid her hands up and down his chest. "That's what I want you to do."

He palmed her wide ass and asked about his surprise. She rubbed his thick beard and told him he would have to wait. Guided by lust, they took their clothes off. Vanessa pulled off the tank top, revealing a white push-up bra. Her brown eyes never left Trevon's face as she boldly removed it. He took off his shirt, shoes, pants and socks and dropped to his knees to assist Vanessa with the snug leggings. She rubbed his muscular shoulders as she slowly stepped out of her leggings and socks. Stripped down to her panties, she bit her bottom lip to subdue her moans. Her legs were prickled with goosebumps as he massaged her ass while kissing her mound through her damp panties. She had showered only minutes before he reached the apartment, so she knew she was fresh. Her face went slack when he tugged the back of her panties down her voluptuous ass. She gasped when he took the front waistband of her panties between his teeth. He slowly removed the pink garments down her juicy thighs and quivering legs. The raw, entrapping scent of her pussy reminded him of a fresh mango.

"Trevon!" She threw her head back when he slid his hand up her inner thighs. She balanced herself on his shoulders as she kicked free of the panties.

Trevon blew against her clitoris as he toyed with her bare ass. He correctly determined Vanessa full-figured measurements that enthralled him... she had 54 inches of ass that he wanted to examine. He teased her grown woman frame by rubbing his nose on her clitoris and spreading and closing her butt cheeks.

Vanessa wasn't a big fan of cunnilingus. What she desired was that elongated extension between Trevon's legs. "Where that dick?" she panted as she slid her bra straps off.

He stood and removed his briefs in one rushed movement. Vanessa seemed to melt down to the mattress when she eyed his manly nudity. She stared at his dick as he joined her on the soft mattress. No instructions were given as he lay on his back. She crawled beside him and merged her voluptuous body with his. She cupped a nipple to his mouth, and then she circled her hand around his solid flesh. He sucked on her nipple as she stroked his dick up and down, staring at it. Their foreplay went on without pause for a minute or two. Her delight rose when she smeared a pearl of precum all over his tip with her thumb. He moaned with a mouthful of her nipple. Up and down, she stroked his shaft as her pussy flowed like a river between her thighs.

"I wanna ride it," she whispered as another pearl of precum seeped from the tip of his penis. She licked his chest as she slid a leg over his waist, lightly kissing around his left nipple when his dick probed the wet folds of her honeypot. Her lips slid up his chest and neck and came to a stop on his ear. "I'm gonna ride your dick until you cum," she whispered against his ear. "You can cum inside me."

He rubbed her soft hips as her pussy juices coated his dick. "Put it in." He squeezed her hips. "Show me you can ride this dick. Show me how bad you want it." He smacked her hip as she sucked his earlobe into her mouth and reached back and around her ass. He moaned as she fumbled with his slippery dick. He felt her shudder when the tip of it slid inside her.

She came up slowly on her arms, sitting back on his raw erection. "Awww fuck! It's sooo long like th-this!" She closed her eyes and moved her hips in a sinuous drag that snaked her pussy up and down. "Mmmm, Trevon!" She kept her eyes shut, gliding herself on the length of him. "Oohh, yeah! Oohh, yeah! Yasss! It's sooo big!" Her breasts swayed as she slid back and forth. "Fuuuck! I love this dick! All up in me!"

He caressed her ass as the sensation of her wet warmth constricted around his dick. He allowed her to set the pace as her soft, appealing moans flowed from her lips. His dick slithered in and out of her gushy hole. "I'm riding your dick!" She winced. "Damn! Aaah. Feels so nice!"

"Pussy wet as hell!" He slapped her hip like a jockey striking a mare along the straightaway. Her next set of actions sunk her clear-coated fingernails into his shoulders. She bounced up and down, clapping her loose ass against his thighs.

"Gimme that pussy!" He lifted up on his elbows, welcoming the feel of her titties hitting him in the face. "That's it! Yeah... twerk it on my dick!"

"Oohh, shit! Trevon! Trevon!" she shouted at the top of her lungs.

He licked her breasts as she twerked on his dick. They fucked hard and steady on the soft mattress. Their moans and dirty talk spurred their actions as they changed positions three times in twenty minutes. She took the dick on her side, throwing her pussy back against his jarring strokes.

"Ready fo' me to beat it up?" he said behind her ear without missing a stroke.

"Yasss! Ooohhh! You're so deep up in me!"

He eased out of her velvety wetness and licked her shoulder. "You got some excellent pussy!" He reached for her leg and ducked under it as he positioned himself between her thick legs and thunder thighs.

She raked her nails up and down his ripped stomach as he hiked her legs over his shoulders. Her pussy leaked its slick fluid down the fleshy valley of her ass cheeks. "Fuck me real hard," she said, out of breath. "I wanna feel your balls smacking my ass!"

He slid his dick up and down the length of her pussy a few times. On the last trip, he pushed forward and eased himself slowly into her. She gasped, digging her nails into his waist.

"Ooohhh, fuck! This pussy is stupid good!" He leaned over her, using his strong arms like a pillar to support himself. He started pumping with full, measured strokes. His long strokes had her moaning and shouting beneath him. He pounded her, slapping his balls on her ass, crashing into her, stroking deep. His strokes came fast, showing no signs of letup. She went delirious under him. She shouted his name and slapped her palms against his chest. She felt him throbbing deep.

He was bent on staying inside her until she climaxed. He couldn't stop his torrid pace, and the fact of it scared him. Pussy wasn't new to him. Since his release from prison. Trevon had been intimate, with a bevy of top-notch women. Excluding LaToria and Jurnee, he couldn't recall being so eager as he was now with Vanessa. His infatuation toward Vanessa and her scrumptious full-figured frame had him wanting to hang her pussy on his dick like an ornament. She dug her fingernails into his back with her feet toward the ceiling. Again, she didn't think of any consequences. All that concerned her was the sensation of having Trevon pumping nonstop until he came inside her.

What the hell? That's Trevon's car! Ariana slowed her Chevy Traverse and snatched off her designer shades. "Sure is!" she muttered to herself, stopping at the stop sign. *Who the hell is he visiting?* She glared suspiciously at the Ford Expedition that sat in front of his S580. The idea of calling Trevon on FaceTime crossed her mind, but she came up with a better idea. Seconds later, she eased to a stop in front of the apartment. She threw her shades back on, quickly primped her hair in place, and grabbed her Gucci bag off the passenger seat. She exited her SUV with her heart thumping. The sun warmed her arms as she strutted up to the front door. She knocked softly. No answer. She waited. She glanced over her shoulder at the four-door Benz. *That's Trevon's car for sure!* She knocked again. No answer. She turned the knob. "Hello?" she softly called out through the door. She peeked inside. Somebody was either moving out or moving in. "Trevon." She opened the door and invited herself inside. She slid her shades up and looked around the living room. Just as she started to call Trevon's name again, she heard another bitch moaning his name down the hall to her left. She snapped and made her way to the bedroom.

14

FUCK ME LIKE THAT

Carol City, Florida
Saturday, August 1st

"Who the fuck is that bitch!" Ariana jabbed a finger at Trevon's chest when he stepped outside.

"Ariana, what are you doing here?" Trevon grabbed her arm and steered her away from the door. She snatched her arm free. "Get the fuck off me!" she said sharply.

"Ariana, you need to calm down, okay?"

"Who is she, Trevon?" Ariana emphatically jumped back in his face.

He glanced back toward the apartment, hoping Vanessa would stay inside. "She's a friend," he said flatly.

Ariana crossed her arms. "That's the best you can come up with?" she said angrily. "I'm a friend too! And you never fucked me like *that* before!"

"What are you talking about?"

"You was all up in that bitch raw!"

Trevon sighed. *Why the fuck she tripping?* "What are you doing here?" he asked again.

"One of my friends stay down the street," she explained. "I just dropped her off, and I was on my way back home until I saw your car!"

"And you figured you'd waltz your happy ass right on inside?"

"I knocked!" she shouted. "Ain't my fault your nasty ass didn't hear it!"

Even in the light of the drama, he couldn't fail to notice how sexy Ariana looked, even when she was pissed. "Okay, what do we do now?" he asked, knowing his actions with Vanessa wouldn't be viewed in favor by LaToria or Jurnee.

Ariana smacked her glossy lips and spitefully rolled her eyes. "You know you wrong," she shouted in his face. "How long have you been fucking her? And who is she?"

Trevon went ahead and took the easy choice by telling Ariana the truth.

"She—" Ariana pointed toward the apartment. "—is gonna be the girl in your full-figured themed film?"

He nodded, hoping like hell his words would satisfy her feisty ass.

"And Jurnee hasn't met her yet?"

"Nope. But I'll set up an interview next week at AEF."

Ariana ran an idea through her mind. "So, what you're telling me is what you got going on in there is *business*?"

"Uh, yeah and no. I mean—"

"Is she gonna be in the damn film or not, Trevon? And you better not lie!"

"From what she told me. She wants to do it. But I'm not so sure after this," he said, troubled

"Don't try to put this shit off on me!" Ariana frowned.

Trevon knew he couldn't stand outside too long, with Vanessa waiting for his return. "Why—I mean, what's up with Jurnee saying we can't do any threesomes no more?"

Ariana flipped her long, curly black hair over her shoulder. "I did something stupid. Something I regret," she intentionally left him hanging on her words.

"You might as well tell me, Ariana. What did you do?"

"I, um...." She dropped her eyes to the ground, "-told Jurnee it would be a power move if we all did a threesome on film."

He looked confused. "She got mad about that?"

Ariana snapped her head up. "I'm not talking about in private. I suggested we do it for AEF."

"Oooh, that's different."

"She blew up. We argued, and she said I was getting too attached to you."

"Are you?"

She smacked her pouty lips. "This isn't about me! It's about you and that girl...whatever her name is."

"Vanessa," he told her again. "And now we're back to my question. What do we do now?"

Ariana saw the opportunity to make a move. She thought about the last time she had a threesome with him. *I saw the way he looked at me when we were alone in the tub. And the way he be eating my pussy! He wanna fuck me without Jurnee around. I just know it!* "I assume you wanna keep this little thang you got going with Vanessa a secret, huh?"

Trevon didn't answer. For the moment, the best response was no response.

"I assume you do," Ariana said. "And since I know I'm right. I have a small, just between us proposition I'd like to run by you. And by the way, aren't you supposed to have that dick on a rest until your next film? I think you do."

He crossed his arms. "What do you want? And yes, I'd like to keep this on the hush."

She grinned. "That's what I thought. Now hear me out because I'll only say this once. Trust me and I'll do the same for you in return."

~

VANESSA GAVE Trevon a stony stare from the sofa when he finally returned back inside.

"Can I explain?" He stood in front of her.

"She one of your girlfriends?" She crossed her arms.

"Yes and no."

Vanessa rolled her eyes. "You best check that girl about walking up in folks' shit without knocking! Who the fuck she think she is? And how did she know you were even here? That's the shit that got me upset! That and the fact that she ruined a good nut I had in the making!"

Trevon again ran with the truth instead of dodging around with a lie. Vanessa's stiff posture relaxed. "She's your baby mama's lover?"

He nodded. "I know it sounds crazy," he said. "But it's the truth. Ain't got no reason to lie to you or play any bullshit games."

"This is some straight up drama." She shook her head. "I thought for sure I had to show out with that girl."

He stared at her for a moment. *I wonder if she's down to finish what we started?*

"Why you looking at me all crazy?" She smiled

"What time is your cousin supposed to get back?"

"About an hour and a half. Why?"

"We got some unfinished things to take care of." He grinned as he laid her hand on his thigh.

Don't look thirsty! Don't look thirsty! She boxed her urge and lust into the corner. "I have to run some errands for my cousin," she lied as she noticed his new erection.

"I hope you're not changing your mind about dealing with me?"

She shook her head. "Not at all, handsome." She unbuttoned his jeans and then she tugged the zipper down. "I wanna give you some head." She pulled his dick out and stroked it.

He lifted his ass off the sofa as she tugged his pants and briefs down. "You wanna do it right here?"

She squeezed his dick as she leaned her face to his penis on the sofa. "Yeah, why not?" She kissed his stomach and turned her face to the object in her hands. She licked the tip a few times before she closed her eyes and started sucking.

LATER, around 5:30p.m., Trevon had returned home, showered, and hit the streets again to spend some time with his daughter. He didn't call ahead, so his visit caught Tahkiyah by surprise.

"Where my daughter?" he asked Tahkiyah as she strolled from the kitchen.

"LaToria took her to see a movie."

"How long ago?"

Tahkiyah came to a stop at the opposite end of the sofa. "About thirty minutes ago. Did you call her to let her know you were dropping by?"

He shook his head and tried to curb his lustful thoughts toward LaToria's mom. The task he faced was a pressing challenge. Even in a simple tee-shirt and solid-colored leggings, Tahkiyah oozed a rich and sophisticated sexiness that was undeniable and appealed to all of his senses.

"LaToria told me what's going on between you two," she said softly.

Damn! She ain't wearing a bra! I can see her nipple prints way over here. "And what do you think about it?"

She removed her glasses and rubbed her eyes. "I'm still on the fence about it," she told him. "But my main concern is how y'all will act around, Victoria." She slid the glasses back on and stared at him with a blank expression.

"I'm cool. Ain't got no smoke with LaToria. In truth, everything she told me last night made a lot of sense. I really need to get my life together."

She nodded thoughtfully. "Are you going to finish your films with AEF?"

"Yeah. I got two kids to think of and I can't leave all that money on the table."

"So, your motivation to do porn is for your kids and not lust?"

Good question. "Will you look down on me if I said both?"

"No. But you can still put your kids first," she said.

He smiled. "I think I can do that."

She returned his smile and gestured toward the sofa. They sat at opposite ends, doing their best to snub the sexual tension between them.

"Hey, did LaToria tell you about an issue she had back on Tuesday? I almost had to fuck this one dude up!"

"Who? What issue?" she asked, concerned.

"Some clown from California. White dude by the name of Sean-what's that motherfucka last name! Uh, yeah—Sean Levinson! She tell you about him?"

Tahkiyah casually took her glasses off. "No, she didn't. But what happened?" she asked, keeping her knowledge of Sean a secret. She was dying to know how LaToria knew Sean. *Something isn't right!* She gave Trevon her full attention as he told her all about the drama that happened last Tuesday. Anger settled in her stomach at the idea of Sean playing a twisted game between herself and LaToria. *I swear to God his cracker ass better not be up to no slick shit! I'm the wrong bitch to fuck with!*

Trevon clashed against the temptation to steal an occasional glance at Tahkiyah's youthful shaped breasts. He told her everything about Sean and the reason LaToria was dealing with him in the first place. Oddly, Tahkiyah's mind was elsewhere after Trevon said what he had to say. Tired of ducking temptation, he stood and told her he had to run some errands for Jurnee and his son.

Tahkiyah's lust toward Trevon was replaced with a drive to see what Sean was trying to do. She paced in the living room with her phone ringing in her hand. "Pick up, pick up the damn—"

"Hello?"

She felt relieved to hear the private investigator's voice that had tracked down LaToria. "Staton. This is—"

"Ms. Tahkiyah Bradford," he interrupted. "I still have you in my caller ID."

She massaged her forehead. "I have a problem."

"You still in Miami?"

"Yes."

"Okay. What's your problem?"

"I need you to check a guy out for me."

"Name?"

"Sean Levinson. I figure he lied to me, so you'll have to start from ground zero."

"You have a number for this Sean? If you do, I have a little system that can hack into his phone and I'll know more about him than his own mother," he boasted.

"When can you start?" she asked impatiently.

"As soon as I'm paid."

"I'll give you half upfront."

"Deal. What's the number? And by the way, my fee hasn't changed, Ms. Bradford."

SEAN YAWNED behind the wheel of a green Dodge Charger after he glanced at the time on his smartphone—5:51 p.m. He picked up a small digital camera off his lap and aimed it across the busy boulevard. The autofocus worked perfectly as he centered the camera on a moonbeam metallic Aston Martin DBX. He took several pictures of the expensive SUV. He sat up in the seat when Jurnee exited the doctor's office, pushing a stroller. *There's my one-legged beauty.* He snapped half a dozen pictures of Jurnee and the baby. The sun glinted off the shiny paint when the DBX pulled out of the parking lot. Sean didn't need to follow Jurnee because he knew where she lived. He sat in silence for another five minutes before he started the engine. As he turned the radio on, he received an unknown call. It chimed four times before he decided to answer.

"Hello?" Sean waited. "Hello?" he asked again as a gap in the flow of traffic opened up. Thinking nothing of it, he ended the call and tossed the smartphone on the passenger seat. With his priority taken care of, he figured he could pay Heather another visit. Sex with no strings was perfect for him. Everything had to be in order before he started his course of actions with Trevon. He drove straight to Coral Gable with his mind set on removing the pedestals that supported Trevon. One by one, he had the intent to ruin him, even if it came to hurting the ones he loved. At the top of his list was Trevon's freedom, followed by his two kids, and then Jurnee and Kandi. He wouldn't show any compassion. None!

TREVON NEEDED some time to unwind by himself. The nightlife on South Beach beckoned him to indulge in its unique ambiance. His ostentations Lamborghini Aventador SVJ Roadster hit the strip a little after eight p.m. Trevon sat behind the steering wheel with a timeless classic by Wu-Tang Clan thumping from the system.

"I bomb atomically, Socrates' philosophies and hypothesis can't define how I be droppin' these mockeries, lyrically perform armed robbery..."

He wheeled the roadster, bobbing to the beat with his left wrist draped on top of the steering wheel. The palm trees swayed along the strip, girls in skimpy bikinis filled the sidewalk, all enjoying the moment. He slowed to a stop for a red light in the Art déco section. An array of neon lights lit up the strip, turning the Miami night into a whirlpool of bold, flashy colors. The neon lights reflected off the Versace glasses that covered his eyes. Freedom. Trevon would never take it for granted, not even the smallest things. He took in the scene with a laid-back poise, playing it cool as he eyed some of the finest women in South Florida. Girls with supermodel looks were bountiful up and down the vibrant strip. He knew the attention his six-figure roadster would draw.

As he sat at the red light behind a Mercedes SUV, a horn blew. He glanced at the rearview mirror and noticed two white girls behind him in a convertible Aston Martin. The cute brunette in the passenger seat waved at him when he looked in her direction.

A breath later, she gestured for him to pull over to the curb. When the light turned green, he cruised through the intersection and slowed to another stop when he found a space to park along the strip.

The white girl found her way inside his Aventador a few seconds later. She did most of the talking, telling him how much she liked his car and that she'd like to get up with him when the time presented itself. He waited for her to ask what he did for a living. He toyed with her curiosity and told her to guess. Professional sports? Drug dealer? Those were her stereotypical ideas for a black man in a Lambo. He showed no harsh feelings. He took the opportunity to gain a new fan and, without showing an ego, he told her about his career in adult films. She thought he was running game until she Googled *Trevon Harrison Porn Star*. Her whole demeanor changed when she realized he was famous. She showed her support by buying all of his films, downloading them on the spot. Before she left, he took a few selfies with her. He added her name and number to his phone, thanked her for her support and told her to spread the word on his films.

Minutes later, he turned into the beachfront park along the strip. Model chicks, looking their best, nodded at him as he steered the 770-horse powered SVJ Roadster through the crowd. The Park was lit by blue and yellow LED lights. They blinked in time with the beats coming from the tower of boxed speakers. Trevon's attention was held for a moment when a fine carmel-skinned female strolled in front of his car in a neon green two-piece bikini. He lowered his frames to admire her well-exposed butt cheeks.

She reminded him of a shorter version of Amber Rose. Just as he started to tap the horn to gain her attention, he saw a familiar car up ahead. He found a spot to park between a white Suburban and a silver Escalade. He slid out of his ride and made his way toward the matte black 1969 Ford Mustang Fastback. The restored 740 horse powered muscle car sat nicely on a set of 22-inch black Giovanna rims. As Trevon neared the old school Mustang from the rear, he noticed smoke floating from the cracked driver and passenger side windows. The Dade County tag on the Mustang read *B Diesel.*

Big Diesel was signed to AEF and Trevon considered him a friend. The two became friends six months ago when Trevon attended a pool party at Big Diesel's lakefront home.

Probably got a chick from King of Diamonds chilling with 'im. Trevon assumed as he tapped on the tinted driver's side window. A billow of potent Indian hemp stung his nose as the window slid down. Trevon fanned the smoke from his face and leaned down to holler at Big Diesel. His words were choked in shock when he locked eyes with Big Diesel's red-faced passenger. One of his BM's!

15

SMOKING BUDDIES

South Beach, Florida
Saturday, August 1st

Trevon simmered over with jealousy as Jurnee stepped out of Big Diesel's Mustang. His jaw turned to iron when he saw how seductively she was dressed. She wore a white and blue bodycon dress that intensified every sensual curve on her body. Even in his sour mood, he noticed how her prosthetic left leg did nothing to lessen how stunning she looked. She held a Gucci clutch bag in one hand and a red plastic cup in the other.

No wonder she ain't answer my fucking call! Trevon thought, as she joined him near the bike rack. "What's up! You fucking Big Diesel?" He got right to the point. "Now I see why you didn't answer my calls."

Jurnee poured her drink in the grass. "No." She looked at him, unruffled. "I'm not fucking him. Never have and never will," she replied, with no desire to argue.

"So, what the fuck y'all got going on!"

"We're just smoking buddies."

"And you gotta dress like that! Just to smoke!"

Jurnee sighed and found a bit of pleasure in Trevon's jealousy. "Why does it matter how I'm dressed? I just told you I'm not doing anything with him."

"How did you get here?"

"Huh?" She blinked, looking unsteady and tipsy.

"I asked you—"

"He picked me up. And no he—"

"Get in the car!" Trevon pointed toward his Aventador.

"Excuse me?"

"Jurnee!" He got in her face. "Get in the car and I'm not playing!"

She stared at him, feeling an odd warmth from his jealous emotions. Big Diesel was all she said he was. A smoking buddy and a rare platonic friend. Not to mention she also viewed herself as his boss. To avoid a scene, mostly for Trevon's benefit, she ended her smoke session with Big Diesel and left with Trevon. In the midst of his bitter anger, he still had the mindful duty to open the door for her. He sped from the South Beach park with a firm grip on the steering wheel. Not a word was traded until they crossed the scenic MacArthur Causeway back to Miami.

"Were you going to hit me?" Jurnee asked softly as she gazed out the tinted window.

Trevon glanced at her. "You must be high as hell to think like that."

She opened her clutch bag and pulled out a box of breath mints. She knew how he disliked kissing her with weed, changing the scent and taste of her mouth. "I didn't do anything with him." She shook two mints into her palm.

"I heard you the first time!" he replied roughly.

"Do you believe me?" She popped the mints in her mouth.

He flexed his grip on the steering wheel.

"Don't ignore me, Trevon. You know how I hate that."

"And you should know how I hate that bullshit you doing!" he blurted.

Before she could reply, Big Diesel called. She answered the call after the second ring and purposely put the call on the speaker.

"What's up?" she asked naturally.

"Ah, I didn't mean to cause no issue, Ms. Cruz. Er'thang good wit' you and Trevon? You know I fucks wit' him and I don't wanna-"

"Everything is fine," Jurnee said. "Put yourself in his shoes."

"Yeah, I feel ya. But real talk, let'im know ain't mean no disrespect."

"He knows that," she said. "And be sure to go over your script with Porsha Lust and let me know how y'all feel about the changes. Anyway, let me go so I can fix things with my baby daddy."

Trevon didn't find any humor in Jurnee's conversation. When she ended the call, she stared at him and said, "Why are you tripping?"

He shot an angry glance at her. "You on some bullshit!"

"And how you figure that?"

"Oh, you think it's cool to ignore my calls to hang out with the next muthafucka!"

"Please stop cursing at me," she said. "And I was wrong not to take your call," she admitted.

"How long y'all two been *smoke buddies*?"

She chewed the mints. "Ever since my accident."

"What! That fucking long! And you telling me y'all never fucked!"

"What part of 'I never fucked him' do you not understand, Trevon!" she shouted.

"The part about you going behind my muthafucking back to be with him! And you better not have him or any other dude around my son!"

"Stop the car, Trevon!" she fumed, wanting to slap the shit out of him. "It's cool for you to fuck around! But now you wanna act all stupid just because I wanna hang out with a friend! You can't treat me like this!"

Trevon had no thoughts of pulling over, and Jurnee knew it. Another wall of tense silence revolved around them as he took her home. Dealing with jealousy scared him, and he didn't know how to control it. Seeing Jurnee in the company of another man pulled up a new set of emotions inside him. He instantly became territorial with Jurnee.

Jurnee left her tears unchecked as she stared out the window. Part of her understood why he reacted as he did. She felt guilty about ignoring his call. She tried to find a way to make peace because having any issues with the father of her son wasn't an item she found favor in. "I'm sorry," she whispered.

Tevon reached across the center console and merged his hand with hers. "So am I," he told her in a calm tone.

She turned in the seat. "I won't do it again."

He nodded. "I just—my mind went crazy when I saw you with him. But on some real shit-"

"Shhh." She squeezed his hand. "Let's drop it. I was in the wrong and I'm really, really sorry."

He smiled. "Okay, it's a dead issue."

She felt better inside, and it showed through her smile. "It's too early to take me home," she said with an alluring pout.

"Whatcha wanna do?"

"Something spontaneous!"

"You're still high?"

She giggled. "You blew it. Now, what's up? We gonna do something spontaneous or not?"

"Uh, it can't deal with sex because I'm—"

"I know about your no-sex until the film. I'm the VP of AEF, remember?"

Bet she would flip fo' real if she knew about Vanessa! "Okay. How about we drive down to Key West?"

She liked the idea. "Let's go," she said. "Hey! Do you remember that day we first met at AEF?"

"Like it was yesterday. You in those tight ass jeans, looking fine as hell!"

"And look at us now."

"Yeah." He smiled. "I never thought we would ever—have a baby between us."

~

HEATHER LOWERED the glass of wine and picked up her ringing phone. She lifted an eyebrow at the sight of Kandi's caller ID on the screen. After the fifth ring, she settled back in the bathtub and answered the call. "Kandi? What can I do for you?"

"Are you busy?"

"Of course not. Just soaking in this bubble bath. It's a slow night, so I'm treating myself to a little R and R," Heather replied. "Now, what's on your mind?"

"The other day, yesterday. Did you get a new client by the name of Sean Levinson?"

Heather lifted her toes out of the water and wiggled them. "It's not a good business practice to speak on any clients."

"This is serious, Heather. I wouldn't be calling you about him if it wasn't."

"Hmm. You sound upset. So, tell me... what's the story about him?"

"So, he was there? I saw his car in the driveway."

"What's this about, Kandi? If there is something I need to know about this guy, I'd appreciate if you told me."

"Honestly, I'm not sure right now. I just don't like how he popped up at your place after I visited you."

"You think he's following you?"

"Maybe. I don't trust him, and you need to have the same stance."

"You said you saw his car yesterday. Why didn't you come in?"

"I never planned to go in. I had to drop Conda off."

"Conda? How did you two cross paths?"

"You should already know that. You're the one that had him

visiting one of your clients at my condo. I had to give'im a ride back to—"

"Hold up a second." Heather sat up. "Did you just say he was at your condo?"

"Yeah. He told me he was doing his thang with Becky Connick until her husband came home early. And then he—"

"That's not true!"

"Huh? I'm just telling you what he told me."

"I'm not doubting that, Kandi. Yes. I had him out to visit a client and I can assure you it wasn't Becky Connick. FYI, she doesn't favor black men, and that's why I know Conda told you a lie."

"So, you saying he wasn't supposed to be at my condo?"

"Positive. He was supposed to be at We Touch massage and nail parlor. I think it's a few blocks from you. Ever heard of it?"

"No. And if what you're saying is true. I *really* wanna know what Conda is up to."

"That makes two of us! And you can bet on that luscious ass of yours that I'm not giving you a curve on this."

"Where is he now?"

"In his room with a client."

Kandi sighed. "Okay. Let me get this straight. Conda *wasn't* supposed to be at my condo, right?"

"Correct. And—wait a second!" Heather recalled the early morning talk she had with the redhead at breakfast. The redhead told her how Conda wanted to know about Sean. Heather told Kandi about Sean's second visit a few hours ago. He made small talk after sex and oddly he asked her if her parents were alive.

"I don't share *nothing* personal with any man!" Heather explained. "One thing for sure and two things for certain. This guy Sean is bad news!"

"What about Conda?"

"I'll handle him. Don't you worry about a thing. I have just the move to trap him in a lie. I need you to do something for me and you'll have to trust me, okay?"

Kandi didn't reply immediately. "Tell me first. And then I'll think about trusting you."

~

TREVON AND JURNEE reached Key West and left their drama back on South Beach. They ended up at a beachfront parking area that offered a photographic view of the North Atlantic Ocean.

"Can you name the seven oceans?" Jurnee asked as she sat on a picnic table beside Trevon.

He picked up a seashell and threw it toward the beach. "I can name three or four," he told the truth. "But I bet you can name all of 'em?"

She smiled. "The Antarctic, Arctic, Indian, North and South Atlantic, North and South Pacific and those are your seven oceans."

"Name the seas."

She laughed. "You must not know how many seas there are?"

He shook his head.

"Guess?" She nudged him.

"Uh, ten or twenty?"

"Not even close. Try fifty-one!"

"For real? How you know so much about oceans and seas?"

She snuggled under his arm and leaned against him. "Well, before I become Honey Drop. I had three years of college for oceanography."

"Seriously! Why you never told me that?"

"Because you never asked." *And I never had a man I wanted to open up to.*

"What happened? I mean...why didn't you finish the class?"

"Lack of money happened. I got behind with my tuition and I started stripping. Dancing is my second love, so it wasn't a big deal to me."

"How old were you?"

"Um, twenty-one, and a long, sad story short. I got into porn a year later. The money, fame and great sex took my head out of my books."

"Do you regret anything?"

She kissed his cheek. "Nope. I couldn't be happier."

"You really mean that?"

She nodded. "I don't waste time in dealing with regret. Maybe you should give it a shot, huh?"

"There is a lot I need to try," he said solemnly. "Starting with learning how to be a man."

"Just take it day by day. I know you're still dealing with all that time you did in prison."

"Yeah, I am. Hey, you said dancing is your second love. What's your first?"

"Back then, it was the ocean. But now it's our son."

He hugged her and kissed her forehead. "What about your family?"

"Can we not talk about that? All I'll say is that most of my family is still in Santo Domingo. And I have a cousin up in New York, but we don't talk. My family now is you and Tayvon."

He lifted her chin and kissed her softly on the lips. "How's that new prosthesis feel?"

"Okay, I guess." She glanced briefly at the object below her left knee.

"I don't know what I would've done had I lost you in that accident."

"Well, you didn't."

Thank God! "Know what I like most about you?"

"Tell me," she said as the white-capped waves broke against the sand.

"It's your honesty. Since day one, you always gave me the truth. Even when I didn't want to hear it."

"Like that time, I told you how I didn't like you having that gun I found."

He remembered like it was yesterday when she flipped out over the gun. "We've been through so much in so little time."

"That's part of this trip called life." She closed her eyes. "Listen to the ocean."

Trevon held Jurnee at his side and listened to the ocean with her.

"It covers more than seventy percent of the earth's surface. But it still can't measure up to the love I have for you and our son." She reached up and rubbed the side of his face.

"What makes you happy?"

"Being alive," she replied. "And finally, being a mother. At one point I was so scared that I would never have a baby."

"It's all behind you. No need to stress that no more."

Jurnee glanced at Trevon's watch. "I'm ready to go home. I asked Ariana to wait up for me tonight."

Upon hearing Ariana's name, Trevon couldn't stop from asking about the issue again. "Uh, you still not gonna tell me why you're cutting the sex off between me and Ariana?" *Let me see if Ariana told me the truth.*

Jurnee sighed and reluctantly told Trevon the reason behind her decision. Her words matched what he was told by Ariana. "I'm *not* getting jealous." *Maybe I am.* "But I just want to cool things down between you two. And she really did piss me off about asking me to come out of retirement. That girl done lost her mind."

Trevon faced his guilt without blinking. *Maybe I should tell her about me and Vanessa? If I don't, Ariana is gonna keep it over my head. And if I do come clean, I'll fuck up the bond she got with Ariana. Damn!*

"Baby." She rubbed his arms. "There's something you need to know, and you better not doubt me. You are the only man I've been with since you put your seed in me. I want you to know that."

~

TREVON ENJOYED his moments with Jurnee, and he promised himself that their bond would grow beyond the aspect of sex. He took her home and checked in on his sleeping son. On his way out the door, Ariana stopped him.

"Don't forget our proposition," she whispered. "I'm keeping my word not to say anything."

He nodded tightlipped and made his exit, hoping he could find a way to end the *proposition*.

16

MOTHER FUCKING

Miami, Florida
Monday, August 10th
Nine Days Later

"We shouldn't be d-doing this, Ms. Carter." Trevon glanced nervously toward the front door of the tiny two-bedroom apartment. "What if your son comes back early?"

"He just left and he'll be at that gym all day," Ms. Carter said. "Besides, I think you knew he wouldn't be here. And you know this will stay between us." She ambled up to him and laid her hands on his hard chest. "I've been noticing how you look at me. And this isn't the first time you came by looking for Big Diesel when you've know he isn't here."

He tensed up as she rubbed his chest.

"Don't let this chance slip us by. I know I can show you a good time. Even at the age of fifty-nine."

He shook his head. "Ms. Carter, I can't do this. Your son is like a br-brother to me."

"I won't let you leave until we handle this. I know you want to do it, just as bad as I do." She tugged at the hem of his fitted tank top.

"It's wrong. We really shouldn't be—"

"Shhh. Just try to relax...okay? Come and sit with me in the living room. She grabbed his hand and guided him to a black and green sofa.

Along the way, he took an eyeful of how her leggings molded her ass. She remained on her feet as he sat down.

"Take that tank top off," she requested softly.

"Ms. Carter, this is wrong. I don't feel good about this."

"For every item you take off. I'll do the same. I'm giving you the chance to stop fantasizing about me," she stated, with her hands on her hips. "Your move."

Trevon slid a hand down his beard and gazed at the woman in front of him. He admired the way her breasts stretched the fabric of her halter. Sighing, he sat up and pulled his tank top off his muscular frame and over his head.

"Nice!" Ms. Carter cooed. "Now it's my turn." She removed the halter and tossed it at him. It landed on his left shoulder. "Like'em?" She brazenly held her arms out and presented a full-frontal display of her bare 32D's.

He nodded and reached for the waistband of his sweatpants. He lifted his ass off the sofa and shoved them down his thighs and legs.

Ms. Carter wasted no time in matching his actions. Her dark-brown breasts joggled erotically as she took off her white leggings. She moaned and dropped to her knees when she laid her eyes on the unmistakable swelling under his briefs. She settled between his legs and grabbed both sides of the slit in his briefs. The fabric ripped apart, revealing his turgid penis.

"Oooo, it's ... so big!" She grabbed his dick and massaged it. "It's beautiful!"

"Ms. Car-Carter!" Trevon leaned back into the sofa. "This is wr-wrong."

She ignored him, keeping her focus on the throbbing, warm pillar of flesh that filled her hands. "Shh. It's just the two of us, baby. And from the looks of what I got in my hands. I know you don't want me to stop. Mmm, it's so... thick and really, really long."

He moaned as she fondled him. His stomach tautens when she took him inside her mouth. She started humming as she slid her mouth slowly down his shaft.

"Swallow it!" He rubbed her shoulder.

She moaned as she commenced a sensual fellatio on his lengthy penis. Her practiced technique caused his tip to pop noisily in and out of her mouth.

"Ms. Carter! Ms. Carter!" he chanted her name as the suction of her lips sent a spasm up and down his penis.

She milked him for his precum and slurped each drop away that seeped up. "You taste so good. I can suck on it all day!" She caressed his dick against her face. "Want me to suck it some more?" She kissed the shaft and licked upward on its side.

"Yesss! Please keep going!" Trevon answered, out of breath.

She spat on the tip. "Open your legs wider." She kissed the tip of his penis and sat up a bit. "I wanna feel it between my breasts while I suck it. Just play with my nipples," she instructed him.

He caressed the smooth and soft contour of her breasts. The erotic sight of her cupping them together made his dick twitch. He toyed gently on her nipples as she started sucking the top half of his erection. Again and again, she popped her lips off and on his dick. She did it slowly, slobbering from her mouth. "I knew you would love this!" she moaned. "Now, I wanna give you what you really want."

Before he could say anything, she rose to her feet and took off her panties.

He slid to the edge of the sofa and kissed her soft stomach. His hands slid up and down her bare hips as she caressed his neck and shoulders.

Ms. Carter shuddered when Trevon instructed her to turn around. She did it timidly, knowing how the moment would develop into a lifelong experience that would evoke uncensored memories. She moaned when she felt him embrace her from behind.

Trevon cradled Ms. Carter's sizable breasts while he nuzzled his lips against the nape of her neck. He pressed his thick erection against her bare ass and squeezed her breasts.

Groaning, he slid his left hand from her breast and skimmed his fingertips down her belly and to her bushy crotch. "What do you want me to do to you, Ms. Carter?"

"I...want you to...fuck me." She whimpered as his fingers combed through the dense growth of hairs between her legs. "Ooohh, baby, I won't tell nobody. Please...just this one time, okay?"

He licked the side of her neck, timing it with the moment when he fingered her moist vulva. "Damn... you're already wet."

Moaning, she whirled her ass against his penis. "Don't make me wait any...longer." She panted. "Cmon, baby. Just gimme some of that big dick before I can't give you my-."

She gasped and squirmed when he penetrated her slick opening with his middle finger. He fingered her and groped her right breast until she reached back and grabbed his penis.

Staying in the living room, they took advantage of the sofa. Ms. Carter climbed up on it as Trevon stood behind her, putting a condom on. Her eyes widened when he positioned himself behind her, rubbing her ass.

He entered her, going in deep, to the hilt.

"Ooohhh, fuck!" she gasped. "I want your dick so bad!"

Pussy so phat! He slapped her hard on the ass and started stroking her before she took her next breath.

"Ummm!" she moaned and winced as he stretched her vulva open. "Yesss! Give it to me! Fuck me...ooohh, my gosh!"

Five... Ten...Fourteen...Eighteen...Twenty-five. The numbers accumulated, stroke by stroke, sending Ms. Carter's soft ass bouncing. She squealed, cursed and rolled her pussy around his deep and hard thrusts. Never in her fifty-nine years on earth had she ever been exposed to such an explicit moment. She gave herself to him, enjoying his thrashing strokes, and how his strong hands gripped her waist... Her moans increased with his jarring pace. Suddenly, a glass shattered on the floor in the kitchen.

"CUT!" the female director shouted with a frown. "Who messed up this take?" She jumped out of her personal director's chair and stomped toward the kitchen.

Vanessa stood at fault in front of the sink. "The glass slipped, and I didn't mean to dr—"

"Put the blame on me," Jurnee said as she entered the kitchen with an empty glass. "I asked her to get me a drink."

The director's temper vanished quickly at the sight of Jurnee. "I didn't know you were here!"

"Then I accomplished what I wanted to do." Jurnee smiled toward the living room. "How's the filming going?"

"Great! I'll be done with the last scene tomorrow," the director replied. "Or later this week."

Jurnee glanced at Vanessa. "Learning anything by being on a live set?"

Vanessa nodded as the film crew took a break in the living room. Five days ago, she had made her first appearance at AEF for an interview with Jurnee. Every second was a nerve-wracking moment that was only manageable because Trevon was at her side.

Trevon broke up the threesome in the kitchen when he strolled up with a robe on.

"Watch that glass," Jurnee warned him.

Trevon was back in his element of being a porn star. The scent of Linda Rorie's pussy clung to him like an expensive cologne. He took a seat at the table as the director helped Vanessa sweep up the broken glass.

"Malo and bueno news again," Jurnee told Trevon, as she joined him at the table.

"I hate malo news," he complained. "But what's up?"

Jurnee took her shades off and laid them on the table. "Malo news first," she said. "We have to find a new location to do your film with Chelsea. The school board backed out of their agreement to let us film at that abandoned school that's going to be demolished. We'll have to build a classroom scene. I already acquired twenty desks for props."

"Sounds like you got it under control."

"I do," she said. "But this will throw the film back a week or two. Chelsea is also aware, and she's okay with the delay. Said it will give her more time at the beach and gym."

"And now the bueno?"

She glanced over her shoulder at Vanessa. "Janella got back with me last night and she wants to offer Vanessa a bigger contract than one film," Jurnee whispered. "She thinks Vanessa can be a big star! No pun intended. Anyway, she wants her debut film to be with you and her second film with Big Diesel and the third and fourth will be left up in the air. Janelle told me to ask you to see if she'll agree to four films instead of one. Since you're like her mentor, maybe it's best coming from you."

He liked the idea. "I'll talk to'er after we finish up with this scene."

"Good. And if you talk to Kandi before I do. Please tell her to call me before the day is over. I need to make sure I got everything for Tahkiyah's birthday party tomorrow."

"I gotcha," he said. "I have to take her to the dealership to pick up her new ride when I leave here."

"Everything cool with you two?" Jurnee asked as Vanessa and the director left the kitchen.

He stared at his hands on the table. "It's kinda weird. She's acting like my best friend. She won't even let me near the subject of having sex with her." He looked at Jurnee. "And the odd thing about it... I'm gaining a newfound stance of respect for her."

"She's growing up."

"Maybe it's time for me to do the same thing?"

By 3:05 p.m., Trevon and Linda completed their scenes for the day. Trevon took a shower immediately after the last take and met Vanessa afterward in the living room. He walked her outside to her expedition and told her about the new offer from Janelle. She was too stunned to speak. He assured her that the offer was real and that he would support whatever decision she made. Because of Ariana, Trevon and Vanessa were able to maintain their sexual bond in secret. Days ago, Vanessa told Trevon the truth about being single.

"Thank you for helping me through this!" She hugged him in the driveway.

"Everything is happening so fast! One day I'm watching your films. And now I'll be making a film with you!" she gushed.

"I told you I wasn't running game and don't think I forgot about that surprise you never gave me."

She giggled. "You still thinking about that?"

"What was it?" he asked as one of the film crew walked back into the apartment.

"I, um..." She bit her bottom lip. "I was gonna let you do my *other* spot."

He slid his hands down to her plump ass. "Talking 'bout your Butter Buns?"

"Uh-huh." She nodded. "We can do it in private and on film if you want to? I know you've been busy with your new film. But I hope you can find some time to see me."

"Just be patient," he said. "And I promise I'll take care of your every need in due time."

She smiled, knowing his attraction to her was for real. "Call me soon," she said with a new high-spirited self-confidence about herself.

~

Trevon left the Airbnb house in his Aventador and drove across the city to Miami Beach. LaToria met him down in the parking garage, looking flawless. She had a new black and blonde extension in her hair that suited her captivating beauty. The clingy, purple and black blouse and painted on looking jeans, all by Juicy Couture, left Trevon in deep desire for her. He settled for a peck on the lips as her fruity scented filled the interior.

"Where are we headed?"

"Up to the GMC car lot in Fort Lauderdale. I'm gonna take your advice and try something new. I'm tired of seeing another X7 like mine at every red light."

"What color and model is it?"

"It's metallic black and one of the new Hummer EV trucks. Wait till you see it! It's fully loaded, and the interior is two-tone white and tan leather! I even found Victoria a new baby seat that match!"

"We still set for the zoo today?"

"Yeah. And my mom said you better not forget her birthday gift."

"Oh...before I forget. Jurnee said to call her so she can talk to you about your mom's party," he informed her as he merged into the light flow of traffic.

"I will." She took off her stylish shades and turn in his direction. "Guess who I saw yesterday?"

"Who?" *Better not be that muthfuckin' Sean! He should be back in Cali, anyway!*

"That girl that killed Swagga!" she whispered.

"Where? And why you whispering and looking all scared for?"

"Because!" She grabbed his arm. "We *know* who killed Swagga and the police are still looking into the case! What if word gets out that we were there when he was ki-"

"LaToria. Calm down and tell me what happened. Don't get yourself stressed out over nothing."

She tried to relax and found the effort taxing on her nerves. "Okay, I'll start from the beginning. Um, last month, I bumped into an old friend down in the parking garage. You remember Conda?"

"Yeah. Dude with the long tongue that you did your debut film with." *And Jurnee already put me up on game.*

"Yeah, that's him. Anyways, he's down on his luck and, to be blunt, he's a prostitute. He's doing his thang with Heather Cocks."

"What was he doing at your condo?"

"He *claimed* he was on call, visiting Becky Connick. I called Heather Cocks and found out that everything he told me was a lie. Oh, and I gave him a ride back to Coral Gables."

"How did he lie?" Trevon hid his displeasure of Latoria giving Conda a ride.

"Motherfucker wasn't supposed to be there! Heather Cocks told me she dropped him off at We Touch massage and nail parlor. It's like... less than a mile from my condo. Anyways, Heather Cocks-"

"LaToria. Do you have to say her whole name?"

She sighed, flustered by his interruption. "Okay, *Heather* asked me to swing by the parlor and holler at the girl Conda was supposed to see. She wasn't in and on my way out, I bumped into Nashlly."

"And what she say?"

LaToria crossed her arms. "Did you know she had that parlor?"

He sped through a busy intersection. He had a split-second to either lie or tell the truth. "I saw her late last month on the same day your truck was stolen."

"And you're just now telling me!" she sounded upset.

"I didn't think it was important. We crossed paths. Said few words and she gave me a business card."

LaToria hoped he was telling the truth. "You should have mentioned it, Trevon."

"My bad. Now tell me what she said."

"Well, she took me to her office and started asking me a bunch of questions. She wanted to know if I spoke to the police or the FBI. Said I owed my life to her, and it would be fucked up if I snitched on her. And then she..." LaToria sighed and started rubbing her knees.

"She what?"

"Never mind. Like you said, it's nothing to stress over."

"Don't hold nothing back from me. If she did something stupid, you need to tell me right now, and I mean it!"

Shit! I should've kept my mouth shut. I know he'll spaz out if I tell'im what that bitch said to me.

"LaToria! Tell me what she said," he demanded.

"She—don't do nothing crazy. But she made a slick comment about me keeping my mouth shut if I wanted to keep my face from being fucked up."

Trevon nodded. *That bitch done stepped on the wrong mutherfuckin' family!* "I'll take care of it."

17

BLACK IN WHITE

Miami Beach, Florida

Monday, August 10th

"Girl, you know you wrong for that!" Nashlly laughed as she neared her crystal green Range Rover Sport. She held the iPhone near her face with a large Chanel bag strapped over her shoulder. "I told you he had a little dick before you started fuckin' with him!" Her voice bounced off the building of her parlor as she crossed the dark, empty parking lot. Like most busy days, she was the last to leave. "Yeah, whatever bitch!" She laughed again as she pulled out the keyless remote for her SUV. "I'm 'bout to carry my black ass home. It's late and I've been on my feet all damn day. Oh, and tell your fine ass cousin to hit me up on Facebook tonight."

The alarm on her SUV was turned off as she got within a few feet.

"Yeah, I hear ya. But keep that to yourself and I'll get up with ya later. Bye girl," Nashlly said as she dropped the iPhone into her bag. Just as she reached for the handle, she was grabbed from behind. Her first reaction was to scream. She took a deep breath at the same moment when her attacker pressed a sweet-smelling, damp cloth against her nose and mouth. Nashlly panicked, dropping the keyless remote as the instinct to fight kicked in. She struggled uselessly, taking another deep breath, inhaling more of the chloroform into her system. Within seconds, her body went limp as she was rendered unconscious.

NASHLLY FROWNED as she came to after her forced period of rest. She shook her head to clear the cobwebs. A sudden fear seized her when she realized she was tied to a metal folding chair in a dark room. *Oh, God! Please let me make it through this!* Her heart banged in her chest as she began to hyperventilate. "Plea-Please! Somebody..." She squeezed her eyes shut to stop from crying. The pitch-black darkness left her blind. "Somebody help me!"

"I know how hard you can go." Trevon turned the lights on inside the windowless room and stared at Nashlly.

"Trevon!" She gasped. "Why are y-you doing—" She lost her voice when he showed her a Glock 17 9mm pistol.

"Like I said. I know you can go hard, and I don't need to mention *that* issue, do I?"

Nashlly blinked and shook her head.

"I owe you so much. In fact, I'm indebted to what you did in saving LaToria. You do remember her, right?"

She nodded. "Trevon," she whispered, with tears sliding down her face. "I didn't mean to—"

"Let me talk! Right now, I'm still trying to figure a way out of this for you." He stepped inside the room and raised the Glock to her head.

"Please don't kill me! Please! Oh God please don't!" She sobbed, begging for her life.

"What part didn't you understand? I *told* you everything was good about *that* issue! You must think shit is sweet with me? Think you can make threats against my girl like you a boss bitch or somethin'?"

"Nooo!" Nashlly cried, frantically shaking her head.

"You don't know shit about me!" He went on, ignoring her tears. "But I'll tell you a fact! I'm not a killer. But I swear to God, I'll murder you if you push me! If I ever... Ever hear you even think about doing anything to anyone I love. I'll body your ass faster—"

"I'm sorry! Please, please, please, don't kill me, Trevon. I... j-just was scared. I pr-promise I'll never say another word to—"

"Stay the fuck away from my family, Nashlly! And the *only* reason I'm letting you live is because of what you did for LaToria." He lowered the gun from her head. "Are we at a clear understanding now?"

"Yes! Yes!" *Thank you, God! Thank you, God!*

He sighed as he clicked the safety on. "This bullshit ends in this room," he stated. "The past, that night, is dead to me and LaToria. We have no business together and don't let there be a next time," he warned, with a motive for murder.

"I understand. I promise to stay away from you and Kandi."

He freed her from the cords. "Your SUV is outside," he told her. "And nothing is missing out of it."

"Wh-where am I?" she asked, rubbing her sore wrist. She welcomed the pain because it meant she was alive.

"Inside an abandoned school in Homestead."

Nashlly remained seated. "Um...did you hear about th-the money put up by Kendra?"

"What are you talking about?"

She wiped her eyes. "Word on the street is she gonna put up half a mil in reward money for anyone that got info on Swagga's murder."

"That don't mean shit to me. What about that dude that was with you? Is he gonna keep his mouth shut?"

She thought about Art for a second. "He's up in North Carolina doing his thang and not in need of any money."

Trevon glanced at his watch. "It's five minutes to nine," he said. "A cab will be here in a few minutes with the keyfob to your Range Rover. Don't ask no questions. Just get your shit and go home and leave me and my family the fuck alone."

CHELSEA LOGGED off Instagram when she saw Trevon jogging across the street. She unlocked the door and started the engine by the time he slid into her Corvette.

"You okay?" she asked as she accelerated from the curb.

"I'm good," he replied evenly.

Chelsea had no idea what was going on. She was watching Netflix at her luxury apartment when Trevon called, asking her with urgency to meet him outside at the front gate. He had jumped into her Corvette and told her to head for Miami Beach. Now she wanted answers.

"Can you tell me what's up, Trevon?" she asked. "You're acting weird. And whose Range Rover were you driving?"

He shifted on the seat. "I had to do a favor for a friend, okay? Can we leave it at that?"

She shrugged. "Guess I don't have a choice, do I?"

"Nope." He leaned back against the headrest and closed his eyes.

"Where to now? Since I don't have a choice," she remarked with a sexy grin.

"You expecting any company tonight?"

She glanced at him. "Maybe. But it can be a definite no if you wanna come up to my apartment."

He smiled. "Yeah."

She reached across the center console and placed her hand on his leg. "Glad you're not still mad at me about that idea I wanted to add to our next film."

"I was never mad." He looked at her. "You just should run things like that through me or my manager first."

"I am so, so sorry." She squeezed his thigh.

"What's the big deal about it?"

"Well, FYI, your prostate gland is like, around your urethra at the bottom. And it controls the flow of your cum when you climax."

"How do you know all that?"

She giggled. "From Google and experience. It's not looked at as gay. Well, a close-minded person will knock it and say it's gay. And to them, I'd say they're full of it. But seriously, baby. You'll *never* cum so strong! I'll be sucking your dick soo good and you'll cum a river down my throat! What's gay about that?"

"Nothing. But you left out the main part of you putting your finger in my ass."

"I'm surprised Kandi or Jurnee haven't done it to you yet."

He shrugged. "I can't miss what I've never tried," he said. "So, who *was* your company for tonight?"

"Nobody special," she said as she moved her hand between his legs. "I miss this." She squeezed his penis through his jeans. "It's been two weeks since we last did it at your place."

"Guess I gotta make it special for ya tonight?"

"I hope so." She rubbed his length. "And I'm so glad we are back on our special terms. But I'm not saying I'm happy that things didn't work in your favor with Kandi."

He couldn't find the correct reply. Luckily his phone chimed. He gestured at Chelsea that he had to answer it. She nodded and placed both hands on the wheel.

"What up?" Trevon answered.

"A lot of bullshit," Kendra complained. "My boyfriend is seriously getting on my last damn nerve! I'm still pissed over his extended stay with me when I was down in Miami. He fucked all of my plans up. And now he had the audacity to ask me to marry his ass! Please! I wish I would... not! Soo, what's up with you?"

"Dealing with my own issues here and there," he replied as Chelsea switched lanes.

"Baby mama related?"

"Mainly. But it's life, so I'll deal with it. You back in North Carolina?"

"Yeah. And it will be a minute before I can make it back down there."

He wanted to question her about the rumor of the reward

money. Common sense told him it was best to leave the subject alone. "Maybe I'll swing by your way when I visit my family."

"That's a plan. And your sister is the bomb! I try to watch her forecast every morning on the news station up here."

"Did you see her this morning?"

Kendra sighed. "No...I had a visit from the police instead."

"What did they want?" Trevon remained calm.

"This is gonna sound ridiculous, but I'll tell you, anyway. They came at me on an angle that I, or one of Marcus' other baby mothers, had him murdered for his life insurance policy. I showed my ass! Told them stupid motherfuckers to get the hell outta my face. Uugghh, they really got under my skin. I didn't ask for any of this bullshit."

"You gonna be okay?"

"I really don't know, Trevon. A part of me hopes they find the person, or people, that's responsible. But on the other hand, I can't take the attention it will bring. And Carmelita is of age now, she understands her dad is..." Her voice gave out as she was overwhelmed with suppressed emotions.

"Kendra?" Trevon said. "Kendra? You gonna—"

"Let me get back with you later. I just—this is getting to be too much."

He ended the call, shaking his head.

"Are we still set for tonight?" Chelsea asked.

"Of course."

"Great!" She looked forward to reviving her private off-screen affair with him.

SEAN DROVE by the front gate of Chelsea's gated apartment complex in the green Charger. Behind him, he saw the royal blue Corvette waiting to drive through the apartment complex checkpoint. The events of tonight deeply intrigued him. He had successfully followed Trevon ever since he picked up Kandi from the condo. He kept the Aventador SVJ in sight on the trip to Fort Lauderdale. His digital camera held several shots of Kandi's new, metallic black Hummer EV. Unfocused thoughts wondered through his head as he followed the pair back to the Miami Beach condo and later to the zoo. His patience was tested. He wanted everything to be in place before he revealed himself officially. For now, he hoped his carelessness of being too bold of bumping into Kandi's mom wouldn't blow up in his face.

"TREVON! TREVON! TREVON!" Chelsea chanted at the peak of her climax. Spent, Chelsea bit the pillow and stayed on her elbows and knees with all of Trevon filling her pussy from behind.

She tried to squirm from his steady strokes. She shivered and pulled at the cotton bedsheet. "Can't take no more," she said, winded, with her face on the pillow. He eased out of her.

"I'm still hard," he whispered against her ear, as he pulled his penis out of her sopping wet pussy. "Can you help me out?"

"You want to cum again?" She wiggled her ass against his erection.

"Bad as hell!" He cuffed her bubble shaped ass cheek.

She rolled to her back. "What time is it?" she asked, out of breath.

He glanced at the digital clock on the nightstand. "Eight minutes to midnight."

"Wow! We've been fucking for a long time." She raised her legs and crossed her ankles over his ass. "Stay with me tonight."

He grinned. "Do I have a choice?"

"No, sir, you don't." She giggled, rubbing his chest.

"Just make sure none of your *friends* show up while I'm here. I've been through too much bullshit in the last few weeks."

"You'll never have to worry about any drama with me," she told him. "I'm that cool ass white chick that you can't do without."

He leaned down and licked both of her pink nipples.

"Tell me something, Trevon. I'm curious about something."

"What's up?"

"Are you doing it with any other white girls?"

"Damn! You know what? You're the first and only white girl I've been with willingly."

"*Willingly*?" She lifted her eyebrows. "Seriously?"

"Uh-huh. Last year this one girl put something in my drink, and what happened afterward was some bullshit."

"Who?"

"You're spoiling the mood."

"Promise to tell me later?"

He thought about it. The memory of that day with Cindy was cloudy, and he wanted to erase it. "Yeah, I'll tell you about it. But right now, I need you to help me reach that finish line."

She rubbed his shoulders as he hooked her legs over his big arms. "How about we change things up a little bit, okay? Take it slow since you'll spend the night *inside* me." She slid a hand between their bodies and wrapped her fingers around his dick. "I wish it could always be like this. Just you and me. I think about it a lot." She took his bottom lip into her mouth and squeezed his penis.

SNAP.

"Oops!" she said against his lips.

Trevon pushed himself up on his hands and looked down at the torn rubber. "You and your rough hands," he joked.

"Damn!" she said. "Let me up. I think there's another one on my dresser."

He rolled from between her sensuous legs and removed the broken item from his penis. He sat up and followed her across the room with his eyes. Every aspect and detail about Chelsea turned him on.

"Shit!" she muttered as she searched the top of the dresser. "I can't find it!"

He leaned to the side of the bed and dropped the torn rubber in the trash bucket as Chelsea picked up her purse.

"I know I got another one in here somewhere." Her tousled blond hair fell over her face as she rummaged through the purse.

Trevon slid across the bed and stared at the large wet spot on the bedsheet. He wasn't finished with her and before it was all said and done, he wanted to add another wet spot, bigger than the first.

"Great!" Chelsea pouted. "That was the last freaking one!" She turned around and said. "Um, I'm on birth control."

Trevon faced a big choice with Chelsea when she rejoined him on the bed. Their lust burned at an insatiable temperature. She crawled toward him with an irresistible, sexy come-hither look. They kissed, longing with their hearts drumming. She fixed her hair in a ponytail and told him to stand beside the bed. She sat nude at the side of the bed and looked up at him as she slurped on his colossal penis. She relished having it inside her mouth, but more than anything, she wanted to have him raw inside her wetness and she wanted him like that until she felt him cumming inside of her. Tonight, she hoped she could become the temptress to heighten his want of her. She went all-out with him inside her mouth, yearning to make this Miami night the start of something meaningful with Trevon.

18

BIRTHDAY GIRL

Miami, Florida
Tuesday, August 11th

Chelsea flopped back on her bed, feeling giddy. She smiled, reminiscing on the passionate moments she shared with Trevon last night. Her desire to have natural sex with him was satiated beyond her obscene imagination. Even now, she rubbed her clitoris, recalling how she bounced on his cock reverse cowgirl style. She squealed his name when he gushed a stream of cum up inside her. They fucked again in the bathroom. She took it from the back, beat over the edge of the tub. His grip on her waist stayed firm until he rammed his second climax inside her. They ended their fling after a bubble bath. She snuggled against his naked body under the clean bed sheets at 3:30 a.m. No regrets filtered through her mind as their night came to an end.

She sat up on the bed, changing her thoughts to the most recent moments with him. She started his morning off by sneaking under the bedsheets and servicing his delicious morning erection with some slow head. By 10:00 a.m. he made his exit after tonguing her against the wall in the living room. That kiss, in addition with the raw sex, meant something to her. She slid off the bed, stark naked with high hopes of him returning for more of her special loving. Her nipples prickled just from the thought of him. When she grabbed her purse off the dresser, she glimpsed the box of condoms. They were partially covered by her yellow hair scarf. The same spot where she hid them with her feign search last night.

~

TAHKIYAH APPEARED happy as she celebrated her fifty-seventh birthday at Janelle's Bal Harbor Island mansion. The small-scale party started at noon, with Kandi and Jurnee jokingly fussing over every detail. They wanted everything perfect for Tahkiyah and they accomplished it as a team. Tahkiyah's deep worry centered on the lack of information that came from the private investigator on Sean. She *knew* there was something fishy about Sean, and she wouldn't rest until she knew everything about him. Her interest in him was incited ever since her calls to him went unanswered. Staton assured her he would do his job and asked her to be patient in matters of such. At the moment, she stood alone under the shade of a palm tree beside the infinity edge pool. Looking good was natural to her. She possessed the rare qualities of looking sexy and sophisticated in the same breath. She adorned her ageless figure with a colorful, low-necked maxi dress that detailed her subtle curves.

"I didn't know Sanaa Lathan was coming to this party!" a familiar voice suspended Tahkiyah's brief solitude.

She smiled and turned around to greet Trevon. "Hey, you!" She welcomed him with a cordial hug. The instant his arms circled her delicate waist, she had a flashback. The explicit, vivid image made her shudder. She blinked, slowly removing her arms from around his neck.

"What's up, birthday girl?" He smiled, doing his best to keep his eyes off her breasts. "Whatcha doing out here by yourself?"

"Just taking a moment to process everything." Her smile was easy. "Where is my gift?"

He grinned. "Inside." He pointed toward the back of the mansion. "And LaToria told me to come and getcha so the cake can be cut."

She eyed him, biting the words she wanted to convey in honesty with him. In truth, she still dealt with restless nights, reliving the erotic moment she had with him. Two nights ago, she masturbated in the tub with salacious thoughts of him triggering her climax.

"Do I look happy, Trevon?" she asked softly.

"Sure! I mean—why wouldn't you be happy? It's your birthday. You have LaToria and Victoria—"

"And Tayvon," she interrupted, in case he didn't mention Victoria's brother.

He smiled at the fact that she loved both of his little ones equally. "Yeah, what's to be sad about?" He crossed his muscular arms.

A lot. But I can't share it with you. She smiled. "You're right. I guess I'm just afraid to face the fact of getting old."

"And you're still beautiful, and you know it," he spoke the truth.

She averted her hazel eyes toward the pool. "When I hugged you. All I thought about was what happened last year. How I hugged your neck-your hands on my ass. And how you had me riding you on the floor. I can't stop thinking about it or you for the matter."

He glanced at the ground. "So much for leaving it in the past, huh?"

"I'm trying, Trevon. Honestly, I am," she said.

"We have to do something about this," he replied. "And to be honest with you... it's been on my mind also."

He's telling the truth. "I love my daughter. The idea of her finding out about what you and I did is unimaginable. She would never forgive either of us and that scares me."

"You ain't said nothing wrong," he said as a breeze pushed her curly hair over her bare shoulder.

"C'mon," she said. "Let's go in before the party dictators come out to drag us in."

TREVON LATER STOOD beside LaToria as the party guests watched Tahkiyah blow out the 57 candles on the cake. The party placed a genuine smile on Tahkiyah's face. She opened her gifts from LaToria, Trevon, Jurnee, Ariana and from her friends that came from DC. After the cake was cut and served, the party moved to the patio.

"Hey, Mr. Sex Scene." Ariana casually sauntered into the kitchen. "Gotta sec?"

Trevon sat the bottle of Hennessy on the kitchen island. "What's up?"

She strolled up to the kitchen island with a drink in her hand. "I finally see you're alone."

"Came in to get another bottle," he said flatly.

"I see," she said. "I also noticed how you kept looking at Kandi when we were all outside. You still got feelings for her?"

"What do you want, Ariana?" he said abruptly.

She smacked her glossy lips. "Just asking a question. You ain't gotta get all hostile about it!" she said with a hand on her waist. "Anyways, I don't blame you because she is so pretty."

"There is more to her than her looks."

"I know that. Question is, do you?" She waited for him to reply. "Okay, new subject. Have you been thinking about that...*proposition* you owe me?"

"Nah, I forgot all about it," he joked.

"Whatever." She rolled her cute eyes.

"Where's Jurnee? I haven't seen her since we cut the cake."

Ariana looked surprised for a moment. "She had to go to the office. She didn't mention it to you?"

"If she did. I wouldn't be asking you where she was, would I?"

"Stop being a smartass, Mr. Harrison," Ariana shot back. "But yeah, she left a few minutes ago, and she left your son with Kandi. And that means I'll be needing a ride home because I came here with Jurnee." She winked.

"Why you telling me?"

"Boy! Don't make it happen up in here!" She giggled.

"Are you wearing a bra?" He couldn't spot any signs of a bra under the blue and yellow bodycon dress.

"Nope," she said. "And I'm not wearing any panties."

"I know that's a lie." His hard stare was incredulous.

"Why would I lie about something like that? And I know it's not a big deal because you've seen my tight little booty so many times."

"Yeah. And Jurnee put an end to all that."

"And I still think it's wrong." She pouted. "How she gonna get me hooked on you and then cut us off like it's cool? That shit ain't right! Don't get it twisted. I love eating and rubbing pussy with Jurnee. But I can't go dick free!"

"You tell Jurnee that?"

"I'm tired of arguing with her over you. I guess this is what I get for being with a bisexual woman."

"Why you say that?"

She sighed. "Jurnee will forever be in the middle. She loves pussy just about the same for some dick. You know I love her and the only man I'm okay with her being with is you. And the only man she's okay with me fucking is your ass."

"And now that's all fucked up because she broke our threesome," Trevon summarized.

"Uh-huh. And just so you know, I told her she was wrong for going out with Big Diesel that night you found her."

He shrugged. "They're just smoking buddies."

Ariana looked like she had something to say. Instead, she took another sip of her drink and stared at Trevon over the rim of the cup.

"Why you looking at me like that?"

She set the cup on the kitchen island and glanced over her shoulder. No one stood behind them, so she was free to speak her mind. "I was just thinking about that night when we first met at the club. And how I ended up in that room with you and Jurnee."

He remembered it vividly. "That was a wild night!"

"Sure was." She smiled. "I was scared as hell to do it with you. But damn...when you got it in, and got it going! Umm, that night was special to me!"

"You know where the guest bathroom is?"

"Un-huh, why?"

"Meet me there in five minutes. If you ain't scared."

She picked up her cup. "Try me." She smiled and turned from the kitchen island. "I'll be there. And you better not be playing no games," she said over her shoulder.

He followed her out to the patio and mingled a few minutes with one of Tahkiyah's homegirls from Maryland. Before he went back inside the mansion, he saw LaToria talking with one of her stripper friends. He felt like shit when he turned and headed off to his rendezvous with Ariana.

At the same time, Tahkiyah sipped at her third glass of Hennessy while tracking Trevon. She couldn't take her eyes off his comely face and his invigorating muscular build. Her hazel eyes zeroed in on the definition of his arms and chest. She lowered the glass from her shiny lips as he strolled back inside the mansion. *I need to thank him for my gift.* She thought as she made her way across the patio. Along the way, she helped herself to *another glass of Hennessy. She downed it where she stood, knowing she was over her limit. To hell with this! It's my birthday!*

"LET ME SEE," Trevon whispered at Ariana as he closed the bathroom door.

"See what?" She crossed her arms.

"What's beneath that dress," he replied as he inhaled her peach scented perfume.

She smiled and shimmied the stretchy hem of the bodycon dress up to her waist. "Happy now?"

He walked up to her and grabbed a handful of her soft hips. "I should bend you over the sink and tear this up!" He slid his hands to her ass and palmed both cheeks. "You got the perfect ass!"

"You wa-wanna do it now?"

He licked her neck as he groped the velvety skin of her bare ass. "Not here. You'll make too much noise."

She licked his ear. "Let me guess. You want me to give you some throat, don'tcha?"

"Uh-huh. How did you know?"

"You ain't shit." She sucked in a breath and moaned when he slid a finger up the split of her ass. "Do that again."

He fulfilled her request. "You wanna feel my dick back there?" he whispered.

"Uh-uh. It's too big for my little booty." She dug her fingernails into his shoulders.

"You ever think about me hittin you raw?"

"Mmm, yesss! All the time, baby. I wanna feel it easing in and out of me. Wanna feel you busting in my pussy! In my mouth. On my breasts. My stomach. Face. Just cum all over me, Trevon!" She swooned against him. "That's how bad I miss that dick!"

He spanked her ass a few times and then he turned her toward the toilet. The moment she sat down, he unbuckled his belt. She showed her penchant to having him inside her mouth by licking her lips.

"Don't play with it." He palmed the top of her head and rubbed his dick across her lips. By the fifth swipe, a string of precum dangled from his tip to her bottom lip.

She stuck her tongue out and teased the tip. She circled her slender hand on the shaft and eased him into her mouth. "Mmmm!" she moaned as she slid her lips back and forth.

"Suck it, Ariana. Work them soft lips. You know how I like it done. Aaahhh, just like that." He closed his eyes as she affectionately sucked on his large dick.

She deliberately slurped noisily at the tip as her pussy throbbed.

"Ooohhh...th-that's how I love it right there!" he said, fighting the urge to push to the back of her throat. He fisted her hair and stared at how she tried to deep throat him.

TAHKIYAH'S BIRTHDAY party concluded at 5:30 p.m. without any incidence. To Ariana's true disappointment, Jurnee returned and so went her plans of getting a ride home with Trevon. For now, she had to settle for the spontaneous encounter she had with him in the bathroom.

Trevon's guilty conscience kept him from being in LaToria and Jurnee's face. As soon as he had the chance to leave, he took it. He drove straight home with the intentions of spending the night alone. He took a shower, minus the shower shoes, without thought of doing it. His thoughts wondered in the direction of LaToria when he stepped over Rex on his way to bed. The screen of his smartphone emitted a soft, greenish illumination of the time; 7:25 p.m. A message at the top of the screen showed 7 new text messages.

Linda = *FYI! I enjoyed the scene yesterday! OMG you're the best! see ya soon.*

Vanessa = *U crossed my mind. Can't wait 2 see u again. Be safe.*

Chelsea = *Hi sexy! Just thinkin of U! MUAH.. TTYL*

Jurnee = *Hope u spoke 2 Vanessa? Going out wit Ariana 2 nite. Kandi has Tayvon.*

Ariana = *Bout 2 go 2 club wit Jurnee on a TUESDAY! Lol. BTW day dick is soo sweet yumm!*

Manager = *Good news! Deal looks good 4 you to B on the cover of Wahida Clark's next book!*

LaToria = *Thank U 4 coming 2 my mom's party 2 day! It meant a lot 2 her. Take care! Love you!*

Out of all the texts, it was LaToria's voice that he wanted to hear. Just as he rolled to his side to call her, he received a call from Tahkiyah. He was inclined not to answer it at all. It chimed a few times before he relented, thinking she might have a message about the kids.

"Hey, birthday girl!"

"Yes, that's me." Her sexy voice flowed into his ear. "I'm just calling to thank you for my gift again! Did LaToria tell you I had my eyes on the new iPhone?"

"She might have mentioned it," he replied, thinking back to how good she looked at the party.

"I know she did," Tahkiyah said, lively. "So, what's up with you?"

"Nothing much," he answered. "Just sitting home and calling it a night."

"Alone?" she whispered.

He smiled. "If you wanna count Rex, I'm not."

"Too bad I can't be your company on this special night in Miami."

Here we go again. "Um, you helping LaToria watch the kids?" He wanted to steer the topic from sex.

"Your kids are fine. I called you because I know what to do."

"About what?"

"I want to—want you to have sex with me again. Just one more time and I promise this will end."

He sighed, hoping he could persuade her from her lustful thoughts. "How much did you drink today?"

She laughed. "Alcohol isn't the motivating factor of what I just said, Trevon. If anything, it made me face reality with my feelings."

"Okay...now what about LaToria?"

"You're good at keeping secrets. We can get another room and release this built up sexual tension between us."

"Tahkiyah, listen to yourself. Think about the risk and the chance we'll be taking."

"I have. I've been thinking about that and more ever since we did it."

"We got too much to lose. And again, it's too much of a risk."

"Funny you should harp on about taking a risk," she said, in control of her emotions. "Hmm...tell me something. Is the ten or so minutes you risked today any different from what I'm asking for?"

"What are you talking about?"

She sighed. "Here's some advice. Next time you go to the bathroom. Make sure no one sees the person that went in before you did. You took a risk with Ariana."

19

DÉJÀ SEX

Miami, Florida
Tuesday, August 11th

Trevon choked with regret over his stupid actions with Ariana. His silence on the phone with Tahkiyah proved his guilt.

"What if LaToria had seen you with Ariana as I did?" Tahkyah pressed. "Can you imagine how much hurt you would've caused her? And on my birthday of all days."

"Listen...things between me and Ariana is—"

"It's none of my business, Trevon," Tahkiyah replied evenly. "I feel like the worse mother in the world to keep it a secret."

He closed his eyes. "So, you won't tell LaToria?"

"It wouldn't make any sense for me to. Not when the secret I have with you is more confounding. Don't you agree?"

"Yeah," he answered dejectedly, staring at the ceiling.

"How lucky did she get?"

He frowned. "Can we drop it?"

"No. I want to know what you did with her."

"She gave me some head, and that was it."

"Mmm, I do envy her." Her voice hit a sluttish note that stirred the flesh between his legs. "Was she better than me?" she whispered.

He squeezed the phone as his flesh disobeyed him. He couldn't admit the truth.

"I'm waiting," she said. "I can take the truth, Trevon. Who sucked your dick the best? Ariana or—"

"You!" he blurted.

"How nice," she went on. "But I still envy her because I bet she did something that I didn't have the pleasure to do with you. And do you know what it is?"

"I have no idea. But I bet you'll let me know."

"I want to make you cum with my mouth."

He slid his hand between his legs. "I can't do this!" He squeezed his erection and tried to block the image of Tahkiyah's pretty face. "This isn't right," he murmured.

"My birthday isn't over, Trevon. And you know what I want."

"We can't keep doing this! What about—"

"Shh. Tonight, it's just you and me, okay? I made my birthday wish and now I want you to make it come true."

"How?"

"I'd like you to meet me at a nice, quiet bar up in West Palm Beach. I'll be out the door and on the road by eight. Whatever plans you had for tonight, cancel them because your time and attention will be on me."

He sat up, knowing he didn't have a choice in the matter. "This has to end tonight and I'm for real."

"It will," she assured him. "I can promise you that."

Trevon reluctantly got dressed. He kept his attire simple, wearing a pair of black jeans, tank top and a black and white Gucci pullover. On his way out the door, Tahkiyah's next message told him the name and location of the bar.

~

"Look who's here." Ariana pointed toward the entrance for the VIP at Club Honesty.

"Who?" Jurnee asked.

Ariana smacked her pink, glossy lips. "Big Diesel."

"Call him over! I need to discuss some business with him."

"Shouldn't even have said anything!" Ariana mumbled, rolling her eyes. She reluctantly waved Big Diesel over to the VIP booth with a bogus smile.

Big Diesel stood 6'2, 220 pounds and kept his hair low with glossy brushed in waves. Like Trevon, Big Diesel had the three tools to be an AEF porn star. Above average looks, a head turning physique and a penis worth dreaming about. Ariana had all 13 of his films on her phone and yet her desire stayed with Trevon, aka Mr. Sex Scene.

"Ladies!" Big Diesel strolled up to their table with his frame dressed down in Versace.

"What are you doing here?" Jurnee smiled.

Big Diesel took off his gold shades. "I gotta be where the honeys at! And I see the finest two in here are right in front of me," he said with his eyes staying on Jurnee.

Jurnee blushed as Ariana sipped her drink with a sidelong glance at Big Diesel.

"Can I join y'all?"

"Sure!" Jurnee slid over and gestured at the space beside her.

Ariana rolled her neck and bit her tongue. She wanted Jurnee to herself. A twinge of suspicion raced through her when Jurnee offered her cheek to Big Diesel for a kiss. She didn't have any beef with him, she just didn't open herself up for any friendship.

"So, what y'all up to tonight?" He settled back on the white leather U-shaped lounge seat with his arm behind Jurnee.

Ariana didn't like the closeness shared by them.

"Just getting our club on," Jurnee replied, making no objection of his arm around her.

He smiled and noticed they didn't have any drinks on the table. "Y'all done sipped all the drank up?"

"Yes!" Ariana blurted, unable to mask her attitude. "We only ordered for two, not three!"

Jurnee cleared her throat and shot a menacing glare at Ariana.

Ariana sighed and stood. "I have to use the restroom." She ignored Jurnee's tug on the hem of her pink, sequined Dolce & Gabbana long-sleeved dress.

"Wait here!" Jurnee told Big Diesel. "I need to check her ass!"

"Chill." He reached for her wrist. "I'll just leave. Maybe this wasn't such a good idea for me to—"

"No!" She shook her head. "You stay your ass right here, and I mean it!"

"You da boss." He held his palms up as she slid out of the VIP booth. From his seat, he admired Jurnee's wide ass and how it bounced under the pink ankle-length pants. He bit his bottom lip, lusting hard toward his boss.

"WHAT THE FUCK is your problem, Ariana?" Jurnee said the moment she entered the spacious restroom.

"You're the one with the problem!" Ariana met Jurnee in the middle of the floor, toe to toe.

"Me?!" Jurnee shouted. "What was all that bullshit about? If you got something to say! Say it!"

Ariana gritted her teeth. "I thought tonight was just for us!"

"It is!" Jurnee shouted.

"I can't tell!" Ariana rolled her neck. "You all up under Big Diesel like it's cool!"

Jurnee sighed with fire in her eyes. "Who are you to define what is and what isn't cool? Huh? Do you got a ring on this fucking finger?" She raised her left hand in Ariana's face. "You don't! And that means I can do whatever the fuck I wanna do!"

"Fine!" Ariana stomped as two white girls hurried toward the exit. "I don't care what you do and we can keep it that way!"

"Keep it *what* way?" Jurnee frowned. "Speak your mind!"

Ariana couldn't believe Jurnee's mood. "You're on some stupid shit!" Ariana yelled.

"What's stupid is you and your childish behavior!"

"I ain't stupid! You're stupid!"

"Watch your mouth, Ariana!"

"Or what? What the fuck yo' one-legged ass gonna do to me?!" Ariana regretted every word and her hurt expression showed it immediately. She covered her mouth. Tears welled instantly.

Jurnee narrowed her eyes as Ariana sobbed and told her she was sorry.

"Bitch!" Jurnee shoved Ariana toward the row of sinks. "Try me!"

Ariana shook her head with tears falling. "No. I don't wanna fi-fight you."

"Why not!" Jurnee's voice bounced off the green and gold walls. "You think I'm a cripple? You think I'm handicap!" She lost her control and slapped Ariana against the sink. "Fight me, bitch!"

Ariana backed away, crying and shaking her head. "No...I.. I won't do it." She sobbed.

Ariana's reluctance to fight back enraged Jurnee. She shoved Ariana again and slapped her harder.

"Fight me, bitch!" Jurnee screamed. "Ain't shit wrong with me! I'm not a cripple! Fight me!" She hauled back to hit Ariana again, but her arm was caught in midswing.

"Whoa! That's enough!" Big Diesel pulled Jurnee into his arms as she broke into a fit of chest heaving sobs.

Jurnee's clouded mind didn't allow her to think clearly. She assumed Ariana didn't fight back because of her prosthetic limb. In truth, it played a part in Ariana's unwillingness to fight. But the deeper hold on Ariana's resistance to fight back was the love she had for Jurnee. A love that was being overlooked and taken for granted.

Ariana ran out of the restroom in tears, leaving the woman she loved in the arms of another.

Jurnee wiped her eyes before she left the restroom minutes

later. "Did she leave?" she asked Big Diesel when she met back up with him in the hall.

"I think so."

Jurnee still looked flawless, and she noticed how Big Diesel roamed his eyes over her. "I can't believe I hit her like that."

"You gonna be alright?"

She shrugged. "I don't know."

"Who drove here?"

"She did. And knowing her, she left me here."

"You should call her," he suggested.

"No." She shook her head. "I'll give her some space." She sighed. "Uh, you have any weed to put up in the air?"

"You know I keep a fresh supply on deck."

"Good! Because I need that in my life."

He reached for her hand. "I gotcha. I hope your baby daddy won't spoil our moment again."

Jurnee felt a sudden attraction toward Big Diesel. She didn't have to wonder about how big his dick was because she had been on the set of his last film. *I can handle it.* She thought as she squeezed his hand. "Let's go to your place," she said, struggling to stay true to Trevon.

She left the club without looking back. Had she done so, she would have seen Ariana's Chevy Traverse pulling from the curb.

Big Diesel read Jurnee's body language as she settled in the passenger seat of his '69 Mustang Fastback. She sat facing him with a sexy grin.

"What time you gotta be home?" he asked.

She turned her phone off. "Who said I'm going home tonight?"

He sped home with the expectations of doing something special with his boss tonight. She gave him further hints of her kinky mood by rubbing his forearm along the trip.

~

"Did you enjoy the meal?" Tahkiyah asked Trevon outside the bar in West Palm Beach.

He nodded. "I thought it was a normal bar." He walked her to her car.

"I forgot to mention it's a bar and grill," she replied softly.

He continued the battle with his attraction toward her. She made it hard by the way her looks deeply appealed to him. Tonight, on her birthday, she wore a black sweater dress, black thigh-high boots and a white leather belt around her smallish waist. His eyes roamed over her sexy figure and the smoothness of her legs. He had to admit that he was caught off-guard by her mood over their hour-long meal. Not once did she stir up the topic of sex.

"You're a very lucky man." She turned toward him. "Hearing all those things you've been through is enough to break a weak man down."

He shrugged. "You've been through a lot as well."

She glanced at the moon. "My birthday isn't over." She pulled him closer by his belt buckle. "I have one more thing I'd like to share with you."

He placed his hands on her hips and felt a charge race to his penis. It was useless to fight the urge to be with her. "I'm listening."

She slid her hand to his crotch and softly rubbed the growth. "It's a secret. You'll have to follow me. And when we get there, we'll share some wine and let whatever happens, happen. Then, after tonight, we'll take a step together and put this behind us. You okay with that?"

He gazed into her beautiful face, knowing he was wrong in every aspect. He moved his hands to the back of the sweater dress.

"Don't!" She smiled. "I'm naked underneath."

He squeezed her ass. "Lead the way."

TREVON SWAM in a pool of déjà vu when he entered the room at the Mondrian Hotel. He followed Tahkiyah to the bed with a stunned expression.

"How did you-This is the same room!"

"I know." She smiled as she took off her gold earrings. "I paid extra for it and I figured you'd like the idea."

He sat at the foot of the bed. "This is so crazy."

She turned and stood in front of him. "It's just the two of us for one last night." She rubbed his shoulders. "And we can let loose and do whatever. Make my birthday special, please?"

He slid his hands up the back of her thighs. She giggled when his fingers slid under the elastic hem of the sweater dress.

"Trevon," she whispered when his fingers tickled the bottom of her bare ass. "Mmm, you can have *all* of me tonight!" She moaned, poking her ass into his massaging hands. "That feels so good. Rubbing my ass like that. Told you I was naked under this outfit."

He didn't need any wine as an excuse to end up inside her. Lust had him drunk, and by no other reason, he had to act on it.

Tahkiyah on the other hand, she couldn't commit the act sober. She stepped back from him and called down for room service. He removed his clothes in front of her as she ordered an expensive bottle of wine. The sight of his nakedness left her open-mouthed and shocked. She fell against him as he pulled the belt from around her waist. A breath later, she felt the sweater dress being pulled up her hips, waist, sides, breasts and over her head. She stood nude.

"Trevon," she cooed, as he kissed the tips of her breasts. "Let's not hold anything back."

He guided her hand below his waist and licked on her nipples. He moaned around her ripe nipple as her tender grip rode up and down his erection. A knock on the door paused their actions. Trevon threw his briefs on and hurried to answer the door. The addition of the wine renewed Tahkiyah's zeal. She ignored the wine glasses and downed the red table wine straight from the bottle. The flavorful, grape tasting wine flowed easily down their throats. Back and forth, they consumed it without pause. When she had the bottle to her lips, he nursed on her nipples. And during his turn at the bottle, she tenderly stroked his erection. On and on they drank and touched and sucked until the bottle was empty.

Trevon welcomed the lightheaded buzz from the wine. He slid to the center of the bed as she elected to add some kinkiness by sliding the thigh-high boots back on.

She pushed him flat on his back and tried to touch every inch of him in one breath. Her heart drummed in a synchronize tempo with her pussy. She grabbed his penis and massaged it in a way that nearly caused a premature climax. Her hazel eyes and flawless light-skinned tone held him in a trance.

Their true start began when she straddled his face. She naturally sat on his face backward, thus giving her the pleasure of sucking him as he licked her.

"Mmm, mmm!" She went to work, slurping up and down.

He tongued her moist furrow with a firm grip on her hips. Her leather boots were clamped against his head. He slurped and wormed his tongue inside her oozing sweetness. Their moans filled the spacious room from wall to wall. Sucking, slurping, licking, they flaunted their lust with oral sex.

She moaned and sat up on his face in the midst of their oral bliss. She threw her head back and palmed her breasts. "Aaahhh. Taste good...doesn't it? Lick it, Tre-Trevon," she gasped as she moved herself against his lips and jabbing tongue.

The raw scent of her ass and pussy drove him feverish. He licked at her wetness with a strong desire to taste her release. Even the feel of her soft ass on his face added to his thirst for her. More. They both wanted more of each other. The wine blurred the time between them. Neither took control, they simply went with the intense hold of their lustful wants and cravings.

She screamed his name when he lightly licked her clitoris. Her orgasm spilled into his mouth. She needed a moment to catch her breath before she leaned down and took him back inside her mouth.

He fingered her as she slowly sucked on his penis. They moved without spoken instructions. Moments later, when she pulled her lips from his glistening erection, she licked his thigh and rolled off to his side and got on her hands and knees.

He sat up and kissed the cute dimples above her ass. "Damn! You look so good!" He moved up behind her, rubbing dainty ass. "Reach ba-back and put it in." He slid his hands up her thighs.

She shivered when he groaned and grabbed a fistful of her hair. She wanted this, and her mind didn't allow any regret. Lust took up every space in her head. She held her breath as she reached back for his bare penis.

"Yeahhh. Put it in your wet, pretty little pussy," he moaned.

She whimpered when she felt him sliding inside her. "It's so... all up in me!" She wiggled her ass. "Ooohhh fuck. It's sooo fucking long!"

He kept a grip of her hair as he started stroking her from behind. She winced each time he rooted his entire length inside her. The sounds between them took on a melodious tune.

"Trevon, Trevon, ooohhh, ooohhh, b-baby!" she crooned. "Keep going!"

He moaned. "Take it! You...asked for this!"

"Fuck me, Trevon. It feels so right! Ooohhh...yes, yesss, Trevon." She gave him all she had to offer. Her second orgasm came several minutes later around his thick column as she rode him.

They ordered a second bottle of wine and shared it just like the first. At one point she sucked his dick impassioned to a climax as he stood at the foot of the bed. In the shower, close to midnight, she expressed her hunger of having him inside her mouth for a third sample. He couldn't put out the fire between her thighs or mouth. He managed a fifth erection and entered her again inside the bathroom. He ignored the sour reality that he was fucking LaToria's mom. Stroke by stroke, he plunged into the best he ever had.

20

ONE-NIGHT SEX

Coconut Grove, Florida
Wednesday, August 12th

Trevon woke up at 10:20 a.m. with a head spinning hangover. Due to his wild actions with Tahkiyah- that didn't end until 4:25a.m.- he wanted a brief respite from sex. He groaned with the pillow over his head when his phone chimed. By the tone, he knew it was his manager.

"Yeah?" Trevon answered as he rolled to his back.

"You sound terrible. What's wrong with you?" Anthony said. "By the way, good morning."

"I feel the same way I sound. I feel like shit to keep it real."

"Can you finish your last scene with Linda today?"

"Nah. See if you can get it pushed back to Friday or Saturday."

"You feeling that bad?"

"Trust me. I won't be any good in front of a camera."

"Alright. I'll call Jurnee to let her know what's up. And before I go, I'm waiting to hear back from Wahida Clark on the concept for her book cover."

"Just keep me posted." Trevon yawned.

"Oh! One more thing. Blac Chyna is throwing a party at Club Honesty and she wants you to be there."

"When?"

"Nothing is official yet, but I'll let you know something as soon as I do."

"Okay." Trevon ended the call and placed the pillow back over his head. Just as he dozed off, Ariana called. "What?" he grumbled.

"We need to talk!" Ariana's voice was filled with hurt.

"Can we talk later? I'm tired as hell right—"

"I had a fight with Jurnee last night!" she blurted.

He threw the pillow aside and sat up. "What happened?"

"She slapped me! Twice!"

"What for? Not saying any reason will warrant it. Just tell me what happened?"

"Well, we went to Club Honesty last night and everything was peachy until you know who showed up!"

He rubbed his eyes. "Big Diesel?"

"Uh-huh, and Jurnee called him over to our VIP booth and I showed my ass."

"Why you do that?"

She smacked her lips. "Because I wanted to be alone with Jurnee. Anyways, you know I gotta fly mouth and I got on my bullshit. Plus, I didn't like how he was all up on her anyway. Straight up disrespecting me!"

"All up on'er, how?"

"Sitting next to her with his arm around her!"

"And Jurnee let that shit fly?!"

"Uh-huh...and I wasn't feeling that shit one bit. So, like I was saying, I showed out and got up to go to the restroom. Jurnee came in and we exchanged some heated words and—" Ariana sighed. "—I said something I didn't mean. Don't ask because I'm not gonna tell you."

"Okay. What happened next?"

"She lost her cool and slapped me. And I didn't even think

about hitting her back. Then, Big Diesel came inside the restroom and broke it up."

"Where Jurnee at?"

"Beats me. I left her ass at the club. Well...uh, that's not entirely the truth."

"I'm listening."

"Well, I went out to my truck and left. But I came back and sat outside the club. A little while later Jurnee comes out with Big Diesel."

"Where did they go?" He stood.

"Trevon. Ain't trying to get no shit started."

"Where!" he shouted.

"She went h-home with him."

"She still over there!"

"Uh, I guess so. She didn't come home last night."

He closed his eyes as his temper rose. *So, she wanna fuck with him behind my back! But how am I any better? I fucked LaToria's mom last night. Okay, she lied to me and-*

"Trevon?" Ariana interrupted.

"Yeah," he murmured. "Uh, where you at?"

"Home. But I'm thinking about packing my shit and going to my friend's house in Carol City."

"Nah. Stay for right now."

"Why?"

"Because you can't leave without talking to Jurnee. You still love her, right?"

She smacked her lips again. "Don't ask me no stupid questions. What I want to know is what are you gonna do about this mess?"

He already knew what his next move would be. "I assume you don't want Jurnee to know you told me about this?"

"Um, I don't see how you can bring it up without bringing up my name."

"You don't have to worry 'bout all that. I just need to make sure that what you told me was the truth."

"It *is* the truth!" she corrected him. "Ain't gotta lie to you about nothing. I'm telling you this because I really like you as a friend. So what are you gonna do?"

He rubbed his forehead. "I'm...gonna calm down first. And then...I'm gonna take a little ride."

"Do I get the silent treatment?" Big Diesel asked Jurnee when she ambled nude out of his bathroom.

"I need a towel," Jurnee said flatly, with her wet breasts on display.

He grinned and rose from the foot of his bed and removed the towel from his waist. "Use mine," he said, knowing her eyes would drop to his slightly erect penis.

"Stop playing!" She glanced at his dick. "I'm late for work."

He walked up to her and playfully took her naked frame in his arms. His mouth went to feast on her luscious breasts as his hands took possession of her wet ass. He couldn't get over the urge to be inside her again. "Lemme lick that pussy one mo' time." He sucked her left nipple into his mouth.

Jurnee moaned as she battled with her emotions. Last night, she had gotten high on weed and drunk on Grey Goose. The combination affected her decision making last night, and the result was a hardcore night of sex with Big Diesel. His oral skills were the element that pushed her to go all the way last night. The only thing that stopped her from getting in bed with him again was her strain of contrite.

"I can't," she whispered as he continued to suck on her tingling nipples.

He reached for her hand and guided it to his dick. "Feel what you're doing to me." He licked the space between her breasts and up her neck.

She reluctantly took him in her hand and softly pulled back and forth.

"One mo' time," he said against her ear. "Lemme hit it one mo' time."

She bit her bottom lip as he kissed her neck and caressed her ass. "Umm," she moaned again, stroking his shaft. "We h-have to hurry!" She released him and turned around to bend over on his dresser.

Big Diesel rushed across the room to grab a condom off the nightstand. Just the mere sight of her bent ass naked over his dresser had him close to busting. He came up behind her and smacked both of her voluptuous butt cheeks.

"And you better make me cum!" she said over her shoulder.

He rolled the purple condom down his erection and rubbed the tip against her pussy lips.

"Ooohhh, Diesel. Don't t-tease like that." She looked back over her shoulder.

"Whose pussy is it?" He squeezed her left ass cheek.

She refused to inflate his ego by suggesting he had ownership. "Stop playing and put it in and—" she gasped when he shoved his entire length in. "Ooohhh! Yesss! Do it, Big Diesel!" She widened her stance and gave herself to him again. "That's how I want it!"

He stroked in and out of her with his hands on her waist. He stared at the way her ass leaped back and forth. "Yeahhh. Ooohhh, fuuuuck. I need this in my life!" he moaned.

Jurnee gasped. "Don't stop! I wanna cum...again."

He took his time, wanting the moment to last. His thrusts were on the gentle side as he took in the account of her prosthetic leg.

"Harder!" she moaned.

He sped up, staring at her bouncy ass. "Mmm. Dis dat can't get enough pussy! It's so wet! Aaahh, I've been wantin dis pussy fo'ever!"

"Diesel!" she shouted as his dick pierced her throbbing folds. "Right there!"

He met her needs by pounding her from the back. He fucked her nonstop for close to five minutes. Though he was a pro at fucking, his infatuation for her caused him to climax before she got hers.

"I got you," he said, out of breath as he slid out of her. "You can get yours on my face again." He leaned over her and kissed her shoulder. "Come on the bed and sit on my face."

She shook her head. "Eat me just like this." She reached back and pulled her ass open. "And lick my ass."

Big Diesel wasn't fazed. "What else?"

"Just—"

BUZZ. BUZZ.

He frowned at the interruption of his doorbell. "Hold on."

"No!" Jurnee snapped to her senses. "I'm ready to go. And I *mean* it this time!" She stepped past him and hurried back to the bathroom.

Big Diesel sighed and snatched his boxers off the bed. Along the way to answer the door, he smelled his fingers, enjoying the scent of Jurnee's private nature. Before he reached the front door, he stopped at the living room window to peek outside. His stomach knotted at the sight of Trevon's Lamborghini in his driveway. He strolled back to his bedroom to relay the news to Jurnee.

"What is he doing here!" She turned the shower off.

"Your guess is good as mine. It's not like I called him over here," Big Diesel replied.

BUZZ. BUZZ.

Jurnee sighed. "Shit! Um, just answer the door and I'll stay back here. Maybe he's here just to see you. Y'all are still friends, right?

"So, you want me to lie about us?"

"*Us*?" She stepped in his face. "This is nothing but a simple one-night stand. Yes, I want you to lie!"

He nodded. "Whatever you say."

TREVON GREETED Big Diesel with a fist bump. "What's up, my dude?"

"Ain't shit." Big Diesel invited Trevon inside. "Want something to drink?" *Damn! That sound silly.*

"Nah. I'm good." Trevon followed Big Diesel into the living room. "My bad for not calling. But I wanted to holla atchu about that little issue we had last month."

They sat down on the sofa.

"Talkin' bout Jurnee?" Big Diesel got to the point.

Trevon nodded. "Yeah. Well, she told me y'all are just friends, and I lost my cool when I saw her with you. My main issue was over her not taking my call."

"I feel ya on that. Hell, you handled it better than I would've. I didn't mean no disrespect."

"I know. But I just wanna let you know I got no beef with you. Real talk, I can't control who she fucks. Just because I got a baby by her don't make her mine. Feel me?"

Big Diesel nodded.

"My issue is that she don't lie to me. If she wanna move on, I'll fall back and just be a father to my son. This shit is new to me, dawg. You got any kids?"

"One," Big Diesel said. "But it's super drama with my BM. I'm paying child support and I haven't seen my son in a year!"

"I didn't know that," Trevon said as he fought to keep his cool. "I guess doing porn helps out with your payments?"

Big Diesel sighed. "Yeah. But my BM is using my career to say I'm a bad role model for my son."

"But yet she has no problem spending the money?" Trevon guessed correctly.

"You hit it dead on point, bruh."

Trevon stole a glance down the hall. "You got company?"

Big Diesel scratched his shoulder. "Uh, just a freak I met off my fan page." He grinned.

Trevon stood. "Yo, can I use the bathroom right quick?"

"G'head" Big Diesel said. "And since we are straight on everything. Maybe we can hit the gym this weekend?"

"Sounds like a plan to me." Trevon strolled down the hall to the guest bathroom. As soon as he closed the door, he pulled out his iPhone.

JURNEE PACED by Big Diesel's bed as her phone vibrated in her hand. She heard every word exchanged between Trevon and Big Diesel. Her heart raced, knowing Trevon was just a few steps down the hall in the guest bathroom, wanting to talk to her. "Shit!" she muttered as the phone continued to vibrate. *He doesn't know I'm here. And if I don't answer, I can come up with a good excuse later.* She ignored his call and breathed a sigh of relief when he didn't leave a voicemail.

TREVON WANTED to call Jurnee again, but his pride obstructed him. He *knew* she was under the same roof. He flushed the toilet and rejoined Big Diesel in the living room.

"How's the film that you're doing now coming along?" Big Diesel asked, as Trevon headed for the front door. "Heard she's a freak!"

"Good." Trevon answered. "I'll do my last scene later this week."

Big Diesel opened the front door and squinted from the beaming afternoon sun.

Trevon stepped outside and glanced across the street at the shimmering face of Silver Blue Lake. *Fuck this bulshit!* "Yo!" Trevon turned around. "Tell that *freak* you got back there a message for me! Tell her I see the new terms we on and I'ma fall back. But I'll remain in full support of our son—"

"Bruh? What are you—"

"Dead the lies, Big Diesel. I know Jurnee is here. The bullshit ends here. I ain't about to fight over no pussy. She wanna be with you, fine. I don't give a fuck no more!"

Big Diesel sighed, knowing there was nothing he could say.

Trevon left, slightly crestfallen over the fact that Jurnee had gone to the next man for sex.

Big Diesel didn't have to relay Trevon's message. She sat against the wall near the guest bathroom in tears. Again, she heard every word spoken by Trevon. Big Diesel tried to console her, but his efforts were rejected.

"Leave me alone!" Jurnee shouted with tears rolling down her face. "Get away from meee!"

Big Diesel had no heartfelt emotions for Jurnee. All he cared about was his career and with Jurnee being the VP of AEF-she could ruin him with one phone call. He flopped down on the sofa as she continued to sob on the floor. Feeling pity for her, he called Ariana. To his relief, she picked up on the first ring.

"What?" Ariana snapped.

Big Diesel shook his head. "Yo, I know you can't stand me and I—"

"Is that Jurnee crying in the background?"

"Yeah. And you might need to come and get'er. Some crazy ass shit just went down and I'm stuck in the middle of it," he explained his side. Before he spoke again, a chime sounded from his phone. Ariana ended the call. "Shit!" he muttered at the idea of being stuck with Jurnee. He figured he would let her calm down before he attempted to offer her any help. From the looks of it, he assumed he would have to call her an Uber. *Fuck! I hope I don't lose my job over this!*

~

ARIANA CALLED Trevon immediately after she hung up on Big Diesel. She confirmed the fact that Jurnee was with him. "I heard her crying in the background."

"Whatcha tellin' me for? She can cry on his shoulder!" Trevon replied, as he sped through an intersection.

Ariana heard the anger in his tone. She too was hurting inside over Jurnee's actions, but that didn't stop her from caring. "Do you hate her, Trevon?"

Trevon's only thought was Big Diesel fucking Jurnee. "Fuck'er! I'm through with it!"

21

FACING REALITY

Raleigh, North Carolina
Wednesday, August 12th

Kendra stared with resentment at the two FBI agents seated across her large outdoor covered patio. The ceiling fan twirled slowly, adding a soft breeze. She remembered the two agents. Agent Parker and Agent Hillman, both white males, and in their late thirties. "I don't have all day." Kendra made no effort to conceal her irritable mood.

Agent Parker cleared his throat. "We would like to apologize for how our meeting went on Monday."

Kendra rolled her eyes and glanced at the third unwelcomed visitor. An attractive black lady. "How do you fit in? You're here to talk about some silly assumptions like these other two?"

"No, ma'am," the pantsuit dressed woman replied. "My name is Jamiese Payne and I'm the lead homicide detective on the Marcus Brooks murder investigation."

Kendra settled back against the orange throw pillow and crossed her arms. "You're from Miami?"

Detective Payne nodded. "And you can blame me for the FBI coming at you the way they did."

"Really?!" Kendra glared. "So, you think I hired someone to murder my daughter's father for money?"

"I'm positive you didn't. But I needed to know for a fact, and not just as an assumption."

"Why are y'all here?" Kendra's patience was tested.

"We have a major break in the case," Detective Payne said.

Kendra closed her eyes to settle her emotions. "Who did it? And why haven't I heard of an arrest being made?" She opened her eyes, staring at Detective Payne.

Detective Payne started from the beginning and told Kendra about two men she'd never heard of. Art and Veto.

"Veto is locked up down in Hollywood, Florida for a pending drug charge. From what I was told by the FBI, he's been in the county jail for two months," Detective Payne explained.

"He murdered Marcus?" Kendra asked, fighting to keep her tears at bay.

"No. But he claims he knows who did," Detective Payne said. "He can't make bond and since the feds picked up his drug case, he's looking for a way out."

"What is he saying?"

"Well, for starters, he said a lot. And if his claims didn't hold any facts, I wouldn't be up here. To begin with, he stated he knew David Reed, aka D-Hot, had a hit out on Marcus Brooks."

Kendra gasped. "Are you serious? D-Hot was his producer!"

"I'm fully aware of that. And I do have one question. Are you aware that it was D-Hot that tipped the U.S. Marshals off? He told them they could find Swagga—I mean, Marcus at the airport."

Kendra shook her head in disbelief.

"It's true, Ms. Paige," Agent Parker said. "The entire case is rather a big circle."

"How?" Kendra asked.

Detective Payne told Kendra the facts. Swagga had gained the knowledge of D-Hot's betrayal and went through his bodyguard Rick to put out a hit on D-Hot. It shocked Kendra, speechless. She also learned how the FBI heard the entire conversation between Rick and Fritz on both occasions.

"So, you want me to believe that Rick hired someone for Swagga to kill D-Hot? And at the same time, D-Hot hired Art and Veto to kill Swagga?" Kendra asked.

"I know this is hard to believe," Detective Payne said. "And what I told you isn't the full picture."

Kendra rubbed her forehead. "Just tell me who killed my daughter's father, please?"

"You really need to hear everything, Ms. Paige. I rather you hear it from me before it breaks on social media." Detective Payne explained softly.

"Just tell me," Kendra said. "And don't lie to me."

Detective Payne nodded. "Okay, back to Art and Veto. Like I mentioned, D-Hot hired them to kill Mar—Swagga. And he also had a secret affair with Jamilah, behind Swagga's back and Art's."

I knew that bitch wasn't shit! "How does she fit into this?"

"She had a deal with Art and Veto."

"What deal?"

"She agreed to share some of the insurance money after Swagga's death."

Kendra jumped to her feet. "That bitch had Swagga murdered?!"

"We're not sure at this point," Detective Payne answered.

"What the fuck you mean? Either she did, or she didn't! Which is it?"

Detective Payne understood Kendra's anger. "From what Veto told us. Jamilah *planned* to have Swagga murdered. But she backed off the idea and moved to Atlanta after Art and Veto's first two attempts failed."

Kendra sat down and apologized for her outburst. "Please continue."

Detective Payne crossed her legs. "The first attempt was the shooting on I-95. Are you aware of that?"

Kendra nodded. "Yes. His SUV was bulletproof."

"Correct. And the second attempt was blown because a third person who was helping Art and Veto didn't do their part. I'll mention her in a moment."

"Just get to the point," Kendra stressed. "I can't take much more of this. Please!"

"Ms. Paige," Agent Hillman finally spoke. "We can't mention our suspect at this point. I know how stressful this is. But we are here to solve this case and nothing more. But, I can tell you this. The FBI will look deeply into the statements made by Veto. Murder for hire is a federal charge and from what I've seen so far, we have enough evidence to issue an arrest warrant for Jamilah and Art."

"I assume the name you won't mention is who supposedly pulled the trigger?" Kendra asked, knowing the answer already. "And this Veto will also want the reward money, huh?"

Both agents nodded.

Kendra frowned, then asked. "And what will that Art guy get out of the deal?"

"We're not at liberty to speak on any possible deals with him," Agent Hillman explained. "Just know that an arrest will be made shortly."

Kendra wiped her eyes and looked at her hands. "They told me Swagga was shot before his body was burned. Please tell me that was the truth?"

Detective Payne assured Kendra it was.

"I have a question." Kendra made eye contact with all three before she spoke again. "Did Veto mention anything about a man named Trevon Harrison?"

~

BACK IN MIAMI, Florida, Trevon was in the mood to take a step back from the drama. His phone was loaded with unread text messages from Jurnee, Tahkiyah, Ariana, Anthony, Linda, Chelsea, and Vanessa. He ignored them all as he drove around Miami. His mind and heart were set on letting go of any emotions that dealt with Jurnee. The fact of his own grimy secrets he held from her forced him to be reasonable about the situation. His actions with Vanessa were no different from what Jurnee had with Big Diesel. When his anger finally settled, he found himself back in his childhood stomping grounds, Liberty City. To his surprise, his Lamborghini wasn't the only high-priced ride in the hood. As he parked behind a dark cashmere Bentley Mulsanne, he saw a familiar face in the crowd. Trevon revved the powerful V-12 engine as onlookers took pictures of his exotic ride.

"Menage!" Trevon called out. "What's up, bruh!"

Menage slid off the hood of his Mulsanne and smiled, exposing his bottom row of platinum teeth as he strolled toward Trevon. "If it ain't Mr. Porn Star himself! Your ass learned how to swim yet?" Menage bumped fist with Trevon's.

"I know how to swim now. But I'm not jumping off a boat again."

"That was a wild fuckin' night! How your girl doin'?"

"She good. But I never got the chance to thank you for what you did that night."

Menage shrugged. "Just another Miami night, my dude. We all alive, so it's all good and you don't owe me nothing."

"You sure about that? I can hook you up with a pair of VIP passes to the first annual SPAV."

"What's that?" Menage asked as an attractive light-skinned female slid inside his expensive sedan.

"Southern Porn Adult Video expo. It's a big event for porn-"

"Say no more." Menage rubbed his hands together. "Anything dealing wit' porn, I'm in!"

Trevon glanced at the female primping her hair in the Mulsanne. "Uh, is that who I think that is?"

Menage looked over his shoulder. "Who? My lady friend in my whip?"

"Yeah," Trevon replied. "She looks familiar."

"Her name is Patrina...my main interest."

Oh Shit! I'm tripping for real! She looks so much like Cardi B. "My bad. I must be seeing ghosts right now."

They chopped it up for nearly half an hour before they exchanged numbers and promised to get up with each other. Trevon rode by his old apartment on 65th Terrace, that he once shared with his mom and sister. Thoughts of them filled his mind. "Siri...Call Mom," he said, activating the hands-free calling system. The ringing tone sounded from his phone as he drove past his childhood school, Holmes Elementary. He took note of the time; 4:50 p.m.

"Hey, son," his mom answered.

"Hey, Ma! Whatcha doing?"

"Nothing much. Just sitting here watching a show on Netflix. What's up?"

"Just calling to see how you're doing. I might come to visit you this month."

"Make sure you bring my grandbabies."

"I will." Trevon slowed for a red light. "Angie home yet?"

"No. She's still at work. You gonna call her tonight?"

"Yeah. Ain't spoke to her all week."

Their casual conversation lasted for a few minutes until his mom had to take a FaceTime from her pastor. Trevon promised he would call his sister and that he would send some new pictures of the kids. He later pulled into a gas station along Miami Avenue. *I need to get back on my grind and deal with love at a later time.* With his focus back on his career, he made a call to his manager after filling up the gas tank.

"Yeah?" Anthony answered after the first ring.

"Hey, let's step things up." Trevon accelerated from the gas station in his SVJ.

"How? I mean—"

"My films. I feel I can do more."

"That's good to hear. And it sounds like you're feeling better."

"I am. And before this month is over, I want to have four new films to release."

"Hmm. That's possible. We can do the film with Vanessa and follow it up with your third film with Chelsea. That will give you a total of five films."

Trevon thought about his costars. *LaToria, Chelsea, Glaze, and Linda.* "Get me a new deal with AEF because I know I can do more films. Matter of fact, I wanna do my last scene with Linda ASAP."

"Consider it done. Uh, what's your new drive?"

Trevon switched lanes and sped past a slow-moving cab. "Ever heard of Shimiken?"

"Sure. It's my job to be up on porn. Worldwide. What about him?"

"I looked him up last month and he *lives* porn!"

Trevon spoke on the top male in Japanese porn. Via Google, he learned Shimiken could earn $23,573 per week.

"True," Anthony replied. "And that's an idea you need to think about. The men in Japanese porn are rare! If you were to move to Tokyo and tap into their $20 billion dollar industry—It would be a major step in your career!"

"You think so?"

"I *know* so, Trevon! You would be unique overseas. Hell, you could take over Shimiken's spot and be king of porn in Japan!"

"How would we make that move?"

"With a plan. First, I want to build your brand over here and then we can take your talent to Japan."

Trevon felt driven again. "Do it. Do whatever it takes because I'm ready!"

"I'm on it. By the way. I couldn't reach Jurnee today, so I called the director to tell her about the film delay. She wasn't too happy about it, so I know she'll jump for joy when I call her back. I'll see if I can get you in front of the camera with Linda tomorrow."

"And make sure they have some ribbed condoms and not that kind I used before."

"Got it. Oh yeah, before I forget. Your Facebook, Instagram and Twitter fans wanna know a big question. If you could date any celebrity, who would she be?"

"Damn! That's a hard one. The last time I answered a question like this was on the *Climaxx Late Night Talk Show*."

"Who did you say?"

"Anansa Sims, who else?! But they really asked it a little differently. Anyway, if I could date someone famous, hmm. I have to say, Uh... I can only pick one person, right?"

"Yeah. And I'll post it on your social sites tonight."

"Okay, I'll go with... damn, this is hard. But, um, I'll have to say... the one and only...Melyssa Ford."

"Excellent, excellent choice!"

"That's because of my good taste in women."

"I can't argue with you on that. But let me go so I can get to work. And I'll text you the word I get on your new time to finish your film with Linda. Be Safe."

Trevon ended the call and pondered on the idea of moving to Japan.

~

AT THE SAME TIME, Tahkiyah sat alone on the foot of the bed with her iPad on her lap. She touched the screen to open the email she received a few minutes ago.

Subject: Sean Levinson
From: PIstaton@Unseen.com
To: Tbradford@BradfordPR.com
Sorry for my delay. The follow points are facts.

- *Sean Levinson (That's not his real name) But still digging.*
- *He has some kind of strong fixation on Trevon Harrison*
- *Has no link to porn. The Facebook profile he had is no longer up.*
- *Came across a bunch of surveillance pictures stored in his phone.*

FYI, he's been following Trevon, your daughter, and a Latino female that drives an Aston Martin SUV.

- *He's been on Google, reading up on all facts related to Trevon's first-*

Degree murder charge when he was 18. Not sure of the connection or why.
• *Currectly still in the Ft. Lauderdale & Miami cell tower range. If you wish for me to implement phase 2, it's your call. I can be on site with 24-hours. I would advise phase 2.*
See attachment file of surveillance pictures from his phone.

Tahkiyah's heart rate increased as she viewed the pictures of Trevon, LaToria and Jurnee. A sense of alarm gripped her when she viewed the pictures of Victoria and Tayvon. She drew the line even deeper for the sake of the kids. With her hands trembling, she typed out her reply email. *Please! Don't let this be too late!*

Subject: Sean Levinson
From: Tbradford@BradfordPR.com
To: PIstaton@Unseen.com
I received your email & pictures. Go to phase 2 w/o delay. Your payment will be wired to your account. Email me when you are on site. When he shits, I want to know when & where!

Tahkiyah tapped the SEND icon and set the iPad aside. "I'm getting too old for this mess," she muttered as she glanced at her black 9-millimeter on the bed. She was adamant on taking the steps to protect those she loved.

~

LATER THAT NIGHT, Trevon ended a FaceTime call with his sister to take Jurnee's call. He figured it was time to deal with their issue after ignoring her calls all day.

"Trevon. Please let me explain this—"

"Just drop it," he said calmly. "You lied to me, and there's nothing to explain. I been thinking about it *all* day and it hurts. But truth told, we're even. We're both in the wrong and it's no need to get into it. If you wanna be with Big Diesel, or anyone else, just do what you feel is right," he said. "Just..." He sighed and went silent.

"Trevon, I'm sooo sorry."

Shaking his head, he sat stressed at the foot of his bed. "Things are different now. I can *never* hate you. But I have to fall back. Gotta put my career first because lately I've been lost."

"Wh-what are you saying?"

"Jurnee. I'm about to leave all the matters of my heart alone. It's all about my kids and my career from here on out."

22

ONE MORE TIME

Miami, Florida
Saturday, August 15th
Three Days Later

Trevon's official day of dick slanging began at 8:30 a.m. He felt strengthened since he had abstained from sex since his tryst with Tahkiyah back on Tuesday. Highly driven, he hit the gym on Thursday and Friday, getting his body in top condition. He ate healthy and took the needed supplements and vitamins to increase his stamina.

"Quiet on the set!" the director ordered as Linda took off her robe. She looked the part from head to toe. A sexy MILF that had a thirst for some young dick.

She paid no attention to the film crew that occupied the bedroom. All she cared about and *wanted* was having Trevon's hard vessel deep-rooted inside her.

She pushed her fingers through her curly, shoulder length hair, waiting for Trevon to make his entrance.

"Turn light number two down a notch," the director said. "And make sure camera three gets a close-up of the penetration. And Linda. No matter how pleasing it feels, be still and let Trevon slide it in. After that, just do what comes naturally." She smiled. "Let's get going so we can wrap up. Scene six. Take one...action!"

Trevon stepped out of the bathroom, looking like a black Adonis with a towel tied around his waist. He strolled up behind Linda and gave her bare ass a firm smack.

She stepped back into his arms, pressing her ass against his midsection. A soft moan flowed through her lips as he gently sucked on the side of her neck. She guided his hands up to her bare breasts, following the script.

The camerawoman on camera 2 had a close-up of Linda's breast.

Linda turned on cue and cupped her right nipple up to Trevon's mouth. Camera 1 had a side view of it, popping in and out of his mouth.

The director crossed her legs when Linda tugged the towel off Trevon's waist. She didn't blink until Linda took his erection in her hand. *Maybe I should get a shot of him? He can get it fo' sure!*

Trevon and Linda stuck to the script as they performed in front of the cameras. She stroked him to his full-length before she sat on the bed. For the next two minutes, she sucked on his penis at a moderate pace. His genuine moans filled her ears, stimulating her desire for him. She slobbered all over his mushroom tip while caressing his shaft.

"CUT!" the director said at the 17-minute mark. "Perfect!" She clapped.

Linda kept Trevon in her mouth for a few seconds. She rubbed his ass as she slowly pulled her sore jaws off his throbbing dick. "You taste so good!" She licked the tip and kissed it.

He wanted her to continue, but he knew the final scene would be the climax. The entire film *Mother Fucking* would run for 45-minutes. The scene on the sofa was 15-minutes, followed by the scene they just filmed. The script called for Trevon to have sex with Linda in a number of positions for the remaining 28-minutes.

"Okay people," the director called out, as she read the script and screenplay on an iPad. "We'll fade-in on a side view of Trevon, entering Linda from behind. I want all angles and make sure we got some tight shots of her breasts swinging and her ass bouncing. We also need a close-up of Trevon's ass."

"Is the first position still set for five minutes?" Trevon asked, as Linda sat across his lap.

"Yep," the director replied. "Five minutes of you doing her from behind, followed by five minutes of her on top, then it's five minutes with her legs hooked in your arms and five minutes with her legs up on your shoulders. That will leave y'all eight minutes. Since I'm in a good mood. Y'all can freestyle a five minute block. But the last three minutes it's back to the script."

Linda smirked. "A sixty-nine with me on top."

"Yep. And I want a good facial," the director emphasized. "Okay y'all... let's wrap this film up."

Linda licked Trevon on the ear and slid off his lap. She reached between his legs and stroked his penis to its fullness. Moments later, she crawled on the bed and got into position. The klieg lights warmed her shapely, lotioned naked ass. This was the moment she had waited for.

"Pussy still wet." Trevon slid a finger up the length of her slippery furrow. *Hope I can last up in her. And I'ma most surely be tapping dis ass on the regular.*

"Trevon, if you feel like you're about to cum. Pull out and we'll fix it with the edits. I need you to stay hard for the next twenty-eight minutes," the director said.

He nodded. "I got this."

"Good. Now put that rubber on and show us why they call you, Mr. Sex Scene."

AT THE SAME TIME, Sean and Conda sat at a corner table inside a Cuban restaurant near Bayside Marketplace.

"You said you had something important to share with me," Sean said. "I do," Conda replied. "And like I said before, I think we have a common interest in a few things." He leaned back in the chair as the waiter ambled away with their orders.

"I doubt it," Sean asserted. "But I'll give you your chance to speak. But it's only because of what you did for me in Coral Gables."

Yeah. Too bad I set it all up to make it look like I found your stolen wallet. "And you're more than welcome. Now to get to the point. How do you know Kandi?"

Sean stared at Conda with a blank, expressionless look.

"The porn star," Conda added. "Black girl, phatass, look like Nicki Minaj and-"

"Why is it important to you?"

Conda sighed. "Because—do you know'er or not? It's a simple question. She gave me a ride home last month. That same day, I walked in on you and Heather. Anyway, she saw your car and started acting all weird."

"I tried to sign her to do an adult film, and it fell through," Sean said. "But it's obvious that you know her better than I do."

Conda nodded. "I was in her debut film."

"You did porn?"

"Yeah. But it's behind me now. Had too many issues with things that took my mind off porn."

"Drugs?"

"Yeah...and now I'm at the HOP and under the guidance of Heather Cocks."

Sean loosened his tie. "Does Kandi visit you often?"

"She don't rock with me like that. She's too special to even look my way!"

"And why would I have a common interest with you?"

Conda looked confused for a moment. "I'm assuming Trevon wouldn't allow Kandi to do any films for you, right?"

Sean cleared his throat. "That might be the case. And if it was true, big deal. She's not the first to turn my offer down."

Conda stared at his glass of tea. "Heather doesn't trust you." He looked up. "Are you aware of that?

Sean frowned. "Doesn't trust me? I'm just a client."

Conda sipped his tea, and he told Sean about the call he overheard between Kandi and Heather. "It was the first of this month. Heather was in the tub when she got a call from Kandi, and Kandi told her about something stupid I did." He sighed and shook his head. "My time at HOP is short."

"Why?" Sean asked.

"Kandi told Heather—I was stalking Kandi, that's the plain truth. And Heather knows it but she doesn't know I know."

"And how do I fit in? Seems to me that your issue has not a thing to do with me."

"Kandi mentioned your name. And Heather told her how you be asking too many questions and that made them suspicious of you."

Sean shifted uneasily in the chair. "What is there to be suspicious of? I'm just a client of Heather's."

"How did you hear about HOP? We both know it's super exclusive and just so you know, Heather isn't fully convinced about your story of a friend of a friend telling you about HOP."

"I'm not the police."

"I know that."

"And how are you so sure?"

"You paid Heather for some pussy, that's how. Now answer my question. How did you find out about HOP?"

Sean leaned on the table. "What is the point of all this?"

"What's the point of you telling me a lie?" Conda countered. "Let's start with that point. And start with telling me why no one has heard about you in the porn industry?"

Sean nodded. "So, you've done your homework?"

"It's called Google," Conda said sarcastically. "Now, let's start over without any bullshit."

Sean saw the look of a man in need across the table. "I'm here to settle something. Something that I've lived with for seventeen years. Tell me, how low have you been in life?"

"I'm living it now," Conda replied. "I made Kandi who she is and now she treats me like dirt!!"

Sean stared at Conda. "Maybe we do have something in common after all?"

"I figured we did. So, what's up with this issue you've been living with for seventeen years?"

"You really want to know?"

Conda crossed his skinny arms. "Enlighten me."

"I'D LIKE TO MAKE A TOAST!" Anthony shouted above the latest hit by DaBaby. He sidestepped and squeezed his way to the center of Trevon's living room.

Tonight, a surprise party was in full swing for Trevon's completion of his latest adult film. The entire film crew, including Linda, Vanessa and Chelsea, were all in attendance. Anthony kept the party small and private by inviting only a few other adult film stars. The no-shows were Kandi, Big Diesel, Jurnee and Ariana.

"Somebody turn the music off for a second!" Anthony raised his glass of Armadale Vodka, looking dapper in a crushed purple and white Gucci suit. "Gotta propose a toast to the man of the hour."

When the music paused, all eyes were on Anthony. He looked confused as he searched the living room for Trevon.

"Hey! Can somebody tell me where Mr. Sex Scene is?" Anthony lowered his glass as a dark-skinned female raised her hand.

"He's, um," she giggled. "In the back with Chelsea, Linda and that new girl."

Kandi had dozed off on the sofa when her phone chimed. She rubbed her eyes and yawned. The caller ID showed Jurnee's name and picture. "What up, girl?" Kandi answered.

"Nothing much. Just calling to see what you're doing?"

"Um, catching some shut-eye on the sofa. I finally sat down to watch *Fifty Shades of Grey* and it ain't all that."

"I could've told you that when it first came out."

"I wish you would've," Jurnee said. "I assume you didn't go to Trevon's party?"

"Nah. I got the email from Anthony but I—I'm just not in the mood for a party. Did you go?"

Jurnee didn't reply right away. "Guess we're in the same mood. I sent Trevon a congratulatory text message though."

Kandi glanced at the time on the screen of her phone, 9:48 p.m. "Who's next for him?"

"Huh?"

"Film number seven. Who will his co-star be?"

"Oh! Right now, it's looking like Vanessa and then his third film with Chelsea."

Kandi wanted to throw the phone across the room. She didn't have the stomach to hear about Trevon's actions with porn. "I'm happy for him."

"You really mean that?"

"Nope."

"That's what I thought."

Kandi sighed and tucked her legs up under her. "Are you happy for him?"

"Si. But it hurts."

"I know the feeling. Trust me on that."

"Uh, did Trevon tell you what happened between us?"

"No," Kandi said.

"Well, I guess I better tell you why I stopped smoking weed."

Jurnee spoke the truth and told Kandi all about the drama with Big Diesel. She spoke on every detail, including the fight with Ariana and how Trevon showed up at Big Diesel's house.

"I wasn't in my right mind when I did what I did with Big Diesel," Jurnee explained in truth. "I know I hurt Trevon's feelings and he's been on some other shit ever since."

"How?"

"Well, for starters. He hasn't touched me at all. When he comes to see his son, he acts like I'm not even there. He speaks to me, but it's different, Kandi. Shit is so messed up right now."

"What's up with you and Ariana?"

"We're okay. She's in the bathroom giving Tayvon a bath."

"And what's the deal with you and Big Diesel?"

"Just a fling. Nothing but a simple one-night stand. One night that I regret so damn much. I'm done getting high."

Kandi felt sorry for Jurnee. "We all make mistakes. You know I've made my share."

"I hear ya, girl. But it really hurts because I don't wanna have any harsh feelings with Trevon. No matter what, I want to raise my son with him."

They spoke freely as true best friends without any bitterness. Kandi stuck to her conscience choice to let Trevon live his life. She told Jurnee to do the same. And she added that her son should always and forever come first.

~

TREVON STOOD in his driveway with his arms around Vanessa. "The longer the wait, the more intense our sex will be," he grinned.

Vanessa smiled. "I still can't believe I'll start my debut film with you so soon!"

"Next Thursday. You and me. And you know I can't wait." He slid his hands down her back and over the hill of her ass.

"I thought we were all gonna do it in your bedroom," Vanessa said. "That would have been wild! Do you think you can handle three women at one time?"

"They don't call me Mr. Sex Scene for nothing. You just keep that pussy on ice until I get back inside it. Can you do that?"

"You know I will. And I'll give you your surprise on film, too. Since you like my big butt so much. I wanna see how you'll act when you get up in it."

"Like a fool!" He squeezed her ass.

She caught him off-guard with a brief tongue kiss. She felt special tonight since he held her back so she could be the last to leave.

"Before you go home, don't forget that you're under a contract now," he reminded her.

"I'm aware of that, Mr. Sex Scene," she said under the full moon.

He opened the door of her SUV. "Send me a text when you make it home."

"I will." She smiled as she climbed inside her SUV. Her decision not to stay was based on her stance of not getting too clingy. In due time, she would get all the dick she wanted from him and more.

Trevon headed back inside, showing no enthusiasm towards the fact that he had just added a new film to his credit. In five days, he would start film #7 with Vanessa, soon to be known as Butter Buns. He figured it was too late to call LaToria or Jurnee since it was 11:52 p.m. Just as he turned the kitchen lights out, the doorbell chimed.

Trevon hurried to the door, hoping Vanessa had changed her mind. Feeling safe, he unlocked the door and opened it without checking to see who it was.

"Congratulations on your new film, Mr Sex Scene." Tahkiyah invited herself inside.

Trevon ran face first into a wall of sensual temptation. Tahkiyah sashayed straight to his bedroom, leaving a scent of jasmine perfume in her wake. He locked the door and hurried back to his bedroom, where he discovered her undressing at the foot of his bed.

23

TAHKIYAH'S FANTASY

Coconut Grove, Florida
Sunday, August 16th

"Ooohh, Trevon! Cum inside me—" Tahkiyah moaned as she laid beneath him, "—don't stop! Don't stop! Ooohh… Trevon!"

He plunged his raw erection in and out of her with no will to fight the temptation.

They were joined on top of the brown sheets in the missionary position. Last night, it was pure lust that drew them together. That same emotion impelled them in the early morning hours to continue.

"Don't stop!" She squirmed as his dick slid easily between her silken essence.

"I won't!" he replied, stroking at a smooth pace.

She closed her eyes as he filled her thoroughly. "Yesss! You feel *so* good up in me like this!" she intoned with a grip on his biceps.

He stayed up on his arms, pumping her without pause. He fell into a trance, staring at her breasts jerking up and down. "Dis my pussy!" He pushed balls deep.

She gasped, digging her nails into his arms. "Yes!" she shouted. "It's yours! It's your pussy! It's your pussy!"

Several minutes later and after two changes of positions, he ejaculated inside her as she rode him. Just to be kinky, she wore a black satin blindfold.

"LaToria thinks I'm with a male friend," Tahkiyah told Trevon after they took a shower together.

Trevon stood at the sink, shaving. "I thought we wouldn't be doing this anymore," he said flatly.

She slid her arms around his naked waist. "I can't get enough of you." She kissed his masculine back. "And not once did you ask me to leave last night."

He laid the razor on the sink. "What would you do if LaToria showed up?"

"Can we not talk about that? I'm not moving on an impulse with you."

"How can you say that?"

"Do you see my car in your driveway? No. Because I was smart enough to call an Uber from where I left my car."

He sighed and dropped his chin. "This is still a big risk."

"I know. But I can't get over you, Trevon," she whispered as she started rubbing his stomach. "I feel so—I just enjoy having you inside me." She licked his back. "And in my mouth."

He gripped the edge of the sink as blood rushed to his groin. "How long will we keep this up?" he asked as she mashed her breasts against his back.

She slid her hands lower. "Turn around," she whispered. "Let me take care of that issue between your legs."

He couldn't look at his reflection in the mirror. He was weak and seemingly powerless to reject her. She kissed him when he turned around and anxiously grabbed his penis. His hands moved to her dainty ass. He squeezed it with an undying itch to seek his pleasure between her legs. They kissed passionately until her gentle stroking produced a drop of precum.

"Let's have our fun in here." She worked her hands up and down his penis.

"I couldn't say no if I wanted to," he admitted.

"Same with me, baby," she said. "Now, I want to tell you about a fantasy of mine that might shock you."

~

AT THE SAME TIME, 10:31 a.m. Chelsea handed her ID card to the male security at the front gate of Quovadis Estates. "I'm here to visit Trevon Harrison," she said behind the wheel of her Corvette.

The guard checked her name on the approved visitors' list before he returned the ID with a smile. "Have a nice day, Ms. Kelliebrew."

"Same to you." Chelsea returned his smile and drove over the speed bump after the rail lifted. She cruised through the upper-class neighborhood, with Trevon consuming her thoughts. A welcomed sigh of relief lifted off her shoulders when she reached the street where he lived. She figured he was home alone since only his S580 and Aventador SVJ were parked in the driveway. *I really need to talk to him*. She turned into his driveway and tapped on the horn. Like every other day, she easily looked her best from head to toe. She wore a pair of Jimmy Choo heels and a yellow pair of ass-hugging leggings and a breast emphasizing tank top. As she strutted up the driveway, she grinned smugly at the way her braless breasts joggled.

By the time she stood at the front door, she had put together what should we say. She knocked instead of pressing the doorbell. She waited with the sun at her back. Almost instantly, she heard Rex barking at the door from inside. Another few seconds went by until Trevon opened the door.

"Hi, handsome!" She removed her shades. "I didn't catch you

at a bad time...did I?" She smiled, enjoying the arousing sight of his bare chest.

"I just got out of the shower." He held a towel around his waist.

"I can see that," she said, eyeing his dick print.

"Uh, come in." He moved Rex out of the way and stepped aside as Chelsea sauntered past him, smelling like cocoa butter. *"Damn! That ass looking good as fuck in those leggings."* He closed the door and joined her in the living room. *"Fuck! I gotta act normal and hope Tahkiyah won't be on no bullshit up in here."*

"Hope you don't mind the surprise visit." She rubbed Rex behind his ear as she sat on the sofa with her legs crossed.

"You're good. But gimme a second to get some clothes on."

"I'm not going anywhere, baby. But don't put on too much. You know how things get between us when we're together." She gazed at him with lust.

Trevon grinned as he made his way back to his bedroom. He was stunned to find Tahkiyah sitting on the foot of his bed, still nude. "I swear I didn't know she was coming over here," he whispered as he locked the bedroom door.

"Relax." She smirked at his nervous state. "I know you share that masterpiece with other women, so I'm not tripping."

He took the towel off and reached for a pair of briefs. "Thanks. And I'll try to see what she wants and—"

"No." Tahkiyah stood. "Just be yourself and act like I'm not here." She closed the space between them and grabbed his lax penis. "I made myself cum so many times by watching those two films you did with Chelsea."

He grabbed her ass. "You 'bout to turn me on!" he said against her ear.

She squeezed his dick. "That's my plan. Now hurry up and get dressed before she gets suspicious."

Trevon added a tank top with the briefs. His attire was the norm around Chelsea, and anything otherwise would be irregular. On his way out, Tahkiyah gestured for him to take his iPhone with him. "And make sure it's on." She kissed him on the lips. "I'll be quiet back here, so don't worry about me."

He palmed her delicate ass and slid out the door. *This is gonna be a crazy ass day!* He strolled into the living room and took Rex outside before he sat next to Chelsea. "Damn! You look good!" he said as she smiled at him.

"Thank you!" She blushed.

"So, what's up?" he asked as her cocoa butter body lotion filled the living room.

She turned sideways to face him. "I came over to make sure you're doing okay."

"Why wouldn't I be?"

"Today is *that* day," she said with a serious expression.

"Uh, what day?"

She laid her hand on his knee. "The day you killed Dave Falston."

He stared at her, shocked that she remembered. "That's why you're here?"

She nodded. "I figured you would need someone to talk to. Like, I don't know how you deal with it. But as a friend, I want to be someone you can talk to."

He sighed, leaned back and slid his hand down his face. "I deal with it by not thinking about it," he said flatly. "But, honestly, I'm glad you came over."

"I was hoping I could spend the night with you last night." She squeezed his knee.

"Why didn't you?"

"Um, I thought, Kandi or Jurnee would show up."

And they didn't. "Nah, I slept alone last night," he lied.

"Too bad. Because I would've loved to do a replay of what we did Monday night and Tuesday morning." She grinned slyly.

He slid an arm around her shoulder. "Why do you care so much about me?"

"Because you're real to me, Trevon. You never judged me on my past and you taught me so much in this business."

"How could I, of all people, judge you, Chelsea?"

She slid up against him and laid her head on his shoulder. "Because I'm no better than you. I have my demons that I deal with, too."

"Like what?"

"Nope." She reached under his tank top and rubbed his stomach. "I'm here to talk about you."

"Well, like I said, I never really think about it. But I'll talk about it."

"That's why I'm here. I don't want you to lose your focus."

"I guess you can be my support for today, huh?"

"I can be here whenever you need me. And I'm serious about that, okay?"

"And it doesn't bother you that I killed someone?"

She shook her head. "If you didn't know... Janelle told me to Google the story about why you went to prison. I had to let her know I wouldn't have any issues with doing a film with you. And from what I read, you didn't do anything wrong."

"My sister told me the truth," Trevon said. "I didn't doubt it then. And I don't doubt it now."

"Is it true that you still have dreams about it? The day you shot him?"

He sighed. "You must have read that interview I did last year?"

She nodded.

~

BACK IN THE BEDROOM, Tahkiyah lay on the bed, staring at the ceiling. Her patience was an item to deal with. Twenty minutes had since passed from the moment Chelsea had interrupted her morning fun with Trevon. She sighed, closed her eyes and slid her hands between her legs. She was moist and warm. *I gotta get over him!* She suddenly jerked up and reached for her phone. She had an idea.

TREVON STOOD at the kitchen counter fixing two glasses of lemonade when he received a text message from Tahkiyah.

Fuck her

The terse text appeared on his screen.

He sighed, hoping Tahkiyah wouldn't start acting stupid. To calm her, he quickly replied to her text before things got out of hand.

Chill! she's about 2 leave

He waited for her to reply.

I want you 2 Fuck HER. I want 2 watch!

AYC?

No, I'm not crazy. Just horny. I watch your film wit her :) Its the same. Do it!

U Buggin

Just do it! I want 2 WATCH U fuck her

He shook his head and glanced toward the living room. Chelsea was still on the sofa, looking good enough to eat.

Okay. I'll do it

Good! And make sure she sucks that cock!

Trevon returned to the living room with his mind set on catering to Tahkiyah's freaky voyeuristic request. "I really appreciate you coming over and letting me vent like I did. What do I owe you?" He handed her the glass of lemonade while admiring the fullness of her large breasts.

"You're more than welcome," she said as her cheeks turned red.

He sat next to her after he set his glass on the cocktail table. "Got any plans for today?"

She fingered a long, curly lock of hair from her face. "I'm going to get my nails manicured later. But you know I can make changes for you," she said. "What about you?"

"Shit, I was just gonna chill and do pretty much nothing. But now that you're here... I gotta be honest and tell you how I've been thinking about how we had natural sex at your place."

Chelsea took a sip of the cool drink and set it on the table. "It's been on my mind too. In fact, I hope we can keep doing it like that." She leaned against him and slid her hand under his tank top again.

"I got a serious question. Who else are you having unprotected sex with?"

"No one," she replied. "And I mean that." She continued to caress his washboard stomach in a way that hinted at sex. "And what about you? Besides, Kandi and Jurnee?"

He stared at her pink, glossy lips and light blue eyes. "Vanessa."

She gasped. "Really!"

He nodded. "And it has to stay between us, okay?"

She smiled. "Maybe the three of us can do a film together? But before that happens, I'd like to do it in private if Vanessa is down to do it."

He shrugged. "Maybe. But, I never thought you would be open to being with another woman."

"I like Vanessa. And if—I mean, *when* I venture into girl-on-girl films, I want to start with her. She's super-hot!" She kissed him on the shoulder and glanced between his legs. "Mmm. Looks like someone wants to be freed."

He leaned back into the arm of the sofa as she stuck her hand through the slit of his briefs. "Let's stay in here," he moaned as she rubbed his flesh.

"Fine by me."

"Take your top off."

Chelsea stroked his dick a few times and released it. She removed her top and tossed it over her shoulder. A second later, she moaned his name when his tongue swiped both of her nipples. Her body quivered in need of him, and she was determined to get her fill. Their foreplay began as she gently moved her hand up and down the length of his thick and long erection.

"I need this inside me," she moaned as he nursed on her nipple.

He groped her breasts as he feasted on her tantalizing nipples.

"I wanna ride this!" She squirmed and squeezed his dick

He reached for the waistband of her leggings. He licked under the roundness of her breasts as he tugged the leggings off her ass and hips.

She helped with the effort by releasing his dick and rising to her feet. She kicked the heels off and shimmied the leggings to her ankles. When she stood before him in a pair of pink thongs, he followed her actions.

At the same moment, Tahkiyah stood in the hall, peeping around the corner at the erotic scene in the living room. She bit her bottom lip when Trevon removed his tank top and briefs. Her pussy throbbed when he slid Chelsea's thong off. Her heart pounded as Chelsea dropped to her knees. She watched them with a burning desire that shocked her. She wanted to join Chelsea. The live sight of Trevon with another woman had Tahkiyah weak in the knees.

Trevon gazed at Chelsea's pink lips, gliding back and forth on his glistening dick. "Ohh! Work it nice and s-slow, baby," he groaned with a hand fisted in her hair.

Chelsea kept both hands at the base of his long dick while she sucked the rest. She moved at a smooth speed, yearning for his precum to marinate in her mouth. Back and forth, she engulfed his penis, popping the tip in and out of her mouth.

Tahkiyah stayed quiet and out of sight as Chelsea's slurps reached her ears. She palmed her breasts and gawked at the fluid motion of Trevon's growth penetrating Chelsea's mouth. Her gaze remained fixed as he pulled back from her sensual lips. She rolled her nipples between her fingers as Trevon sat down on the sofa, pulling Chelsea with him. A wave of pleasure rocked her where she stood as Chelsea straddled Trevon. Her view of them allowed her to admire the shape of Chelsea's heart-shaped backside. Wide-eyed, she witnessed the raw sexual chemistry between Trevon and Chelsea.

Chelsea threw her head back as she reached for his erection. There was no hint of hesitation in her lust. She held his penis in the needed position before she sat down on it. Her body shuddered as she began to ride him.

Tahkiyah fingered her moist furrow as Chelsea's ass bounced on Trevon's lap. She saw the raw sex and shivered at the sight of it. Chelsea was loud and vocal, sliding her pussy up and down.

Trevon gave his all to Chelsea, and with it, he forgot about Tahkiyah. He fucked Chelsea with an intense fortitude to stroke her to her zenith. They changed positions as if a script was written. Their passionate moans stirred Tahkiyah's dripping center.

Fifteen minutes later, Tahkiyah had enough of being a mere voyeur. She stepped into the living room as Trevon was pounding Chelsea from behind on the floor. Engrossed with lust, she made it a threesome.

24

SEX & THREATS

Coconut Grove, Florida
Sunday, August 16th

Chelsea went along with the blindfold that was unexpectedly slipped over her eyes. Braced on her forearms and knees, she waited for Trevon to enter her again.

"Do you trust me?" He asked as he knelt behind her, stroking her soft ass cheeks.

"Yesss!" she gasped, jutting her ass higher in the air. "Please... put it back in."

"Listen to me, okay? If what I'm about to do is too much...just say stop. But whatever happens, Chelsea...you can't take off the blindfold, understood?"

"Trevon, please just put it b-back in." She writhed anxiously to feel him thrusting in and out of her pussy again.

"The blindfold, Chelsea."

"Okay, okay, okay, I won't take off. Now please...put that big, black cock back inside my pussy, baby."

Trevon drew a breath, glanced across the living room, nodded at Tahkiyah, then slid his penis back inside Chelsea's clean-shaven pussy.

She hummed as he wormed his shaft deeper inside her. The blindfold excited her and forced her to focus in on the sounds of raw sex.

Her labored pants were synchronized with the sounds her ass made each time Trevon collided into her.

Just as she reached between her legs to finger her clitoris, she felt a hand stroke her breast. She knew it wasn't Trevon because his strong, big hands were gripping her waist.

Chelsea offered her breast to the stranger and moaned.

Tahkiyah's fantasy became her reality, and she felt no indignity about touching another woman. She stared at Trevon, pumping like an animal behind Chelsea's jiggling ass. Pushed over the edge of her senses, Tahkiyah moved in front of Chelsea and ceased her constant moans by cradling her breasts against her mouth. Chelsea lost her breath when she felt a nipple graze her lips. She didn't have the time to think about it. She sucked the nipple into her mouth like a pacifier.

Trevon slowed his pace and watched excitedly as Chelsea nursed on Tahkiyah's nipple. He wondered how far they were willing to go with each other. Instead of assuming, he made eye contact with Tahkiyah and asked her what she want to do next?

LATER, around noon, Chelsea ambled into the kitchen after her shower. "Still not going to tell me who that other girl was?" She smiled prettily.

Trevon closed the refrigerator. "Nope."

"It doesn't matter because I enjoyed every second," she said with her clothes back on.

"Any regrets?" he asked, turning his phone back on.

"Just one," she said. "We should have done it on film. OMG, that was so wild! Now I know I have to do a film with Vanessa."

"It's possible," he replied. "She's open to doing bisexual films, too."

"Please pull whatever strings you can to make her first girl on girl be with me. And I'm really looking forward to doing a private threesome with you two also. Without the blindfold," she said.

"I'll talk to her and see what's up," he replied. "My next film starts next Thursday with her."

She walked up to him and kissed him on the lips. "Thanks for the good time. And FYI, I'll be on the set next week to watch you and Vanessa in action. And sign me up to keep your dick hard in-between takes. Well, let me go before I miss my nail appointment." After he watched her drive away, he stood beside his S580 and checked the text messages he missed.

Linda = *Hey U! Can't wait 4 our film 2 hit the market! Stay in touch.*

LaToria = *Just thinkin about U*

Jurnee = *Spoke wit you manager. I'll know something soon on your new contract wit AEF. I'm all 4 it. Luv ya.*

Tahkiyah = *I made it home. Speechless about what happened today OMG! Got mixed feelings.*

Glaze = *When I get back from my vacay let's do dinner & discuss doing a second film together. Sorry I missed your bday*

Unknown = *What if you had to pick one pain? (A)Life in prison. (B) Death (C)Kandi's death (D)Your daughter's death (E)Jurnee's death (F)Your sons death. Pick one or I'll pick two!*

Nearly an hour later, Trevon paced in the living room with all eyes on him. With two firm and demanding calls, he now had a houseful.

"Trevon," LaToria said from the sofa. "Will you please tell us what going on? You're starting to scare us."

"I second that," Jurnee expressed as she breastfed Tayvon on the loveseat. "Frankly. We all feel the same."

Ariana and Tahkiyah nodded from the sectional sofa they shared with LaToria. Trevon paused and smiled briefly at Victoria sitting on the floor, playing with Rex. Words couldn't explain his relief to have his loved ones in his sight. He grabbed his phone off the cocktail table and pulled up the unknown text message.

"Here's the deal." He made eye contact with everyone. "I don't know what the fu—" He caught himself from swearing in front of Victoria. "I—I don't know *what* is going on, but I needed you all here ASAP!"

Tahkiyah stared at him. Even now, she still had a hard time facing the reality of what she did with him and Chelsea. Though true, those thoughts of sex and fucking Trevon *again* were erased as he explained what was going on.

He held everyone's attention as he told them about the text message. Being on point, he deleted all the others. LaToria jumped to her feet and snatched the phone from his hand.

"Who sent this!" LaToria shook the phone in his face.

"I don't know, baby," he replied, understanding her fear.

"Is this the first time you got a message like that?" Jurnee asked.

"Yeah," he said. "And I'm taking it serious!" he stated as Victoria came up to him with her tiny arms up in the air. He smiled again and picked her up.

"You think it's f—for real?" LaToria asked.

Trevon slid his arm around her waist. "I'm not taking any chances until I find out who sent it."

Ariana noticed the twinge of jealously that crossed Jurnee's face at the closeness of Trevon and Kandi. She realized Jurnee's bond with Trevon was too strong to be broken. It was a fact she had to live with.

"Do you have any ideas?" Tahkiyah asked. "Anyone you had an issue with in the past few days or weeks?"

He sighed and glanced at Jurnee for a moment. "How is Big Diesel feeling about everything that went down between us?"

Jurnee had to think about it. "Honestly, I have to say he's not tripping. He's doing a new film, and he hasn't shown any harsh feelings."

"What does him doing a new film got to do with this?" he asked.

"I'm just telling you, he hasn't changed his moves. We spoke about what happened and that was it," Jurnee explained, wishing she had never dealt with Big Diesel as she did.

Trevon held LaToria closer, hoping he had a way to settle his fears.

Tahkiyah cleared her throat. "What about that drama you and LaToria had with that guy from California?"

Trevon's face went tight. "I haven't seen him since last month!"

"Same for me," LaToria added.

Tahkiyah crossed her legs and sat back with her arms crossed. She knew she was the only one in the room that knew the truth about Sean. "How did he even know where you lived?"

"He saw my BMW," LaToria said. "And he claimed he was visiting a friend or-"

"I remember his car being parked a few houses down," Trevon said as he handed Victoria to LaToria. "I'ma go down to the house and see if they know this guy."

"Wouldn't his name be on the visitor's list?" Jurnee asked. "Why not get up with Vanessa and see what she can tell us."

"Good thinking," Trevon said, as Victoria started to whine.

"Who is Sean?" Ariana asked as Trevon headed for the front door.

LaToria told Ariana and Jurnee about Sean as Tahkiyah excused herself to the bathroom.

Tahkiyah locked the bathroom door and called the private investigator with her heart pounding.

"Good morning, Ms. Bradford," Staton answered.

Tahkiyah sighed. "Where is that motherfucker?" she whispered. "That bastard sent Trevon a threatening text this morning!"

"Well, first, he's at a motel in Fort Lauderdale. And second, whatever text you're speaking of, he didn't send it from the phone that I hacked. Now calm down and tell me what's going on."

Tahkiyah paced a few steps before she sat on the edge of the tub. A breath later, she quickly told him about the threatening text messages that Trevon received.

Staton assured her again that the text message didn't come from Sean. "But I do have a face I'd like you to look at. He's been meeting with this one fellow since yesterday and I've yet to put a name to this guy. Give me a moment and I'll send the pictures to your phone."

"How is this other guy important?"

"If you know him, I'll need his number. Maybe he sent the text because he just left the motel thirty minutes ago."

"So, you'll be able to hack into his phone like you did with Sean's?"

"All I'll need is his number."

PING. "I just received the pictures," Tahkiyah said as he touched the screen to view the three pictures.

"The first two were taken yesterday morning at a Cuban restaurant in downtown Miami. And the third was taken a few hours ago. Do you know the guy with Sean?"

Tahkiyah gasped. "Yes!" she answered. "His name is Conda, and he was in my daughter's debut film! What is he doing with Sean?"

"I'm not sure."

"And Sean is still in his room?"

"Positive. I have a clear view at his door. Now, back to this second guy. Do you have a number for him?"

Tahkiyah stood. "Not this moment, but I will. But for now, stay on Sean and keep me posted if he moves. I'll talk to my daughter to get Conda's number."

"Text me when you get it."

"I will," Tahkiyah said, and ended the brief call. *I can't keep this a secret.* She reasoned as she left the bathroom.

Back in the living room, LaToria sat with a worried look on her face as Victoria followed Rex around the sofa.

"LaToria, look at these pictures and tell me who you see?" Tahkiyah said.

LaToria frowned the instant she viewed the screen. "How did you- what is-"

"I need Conda's phone number, right now!" Tahkiyah pressed.

"Conda and Sean. But why are they together?" *"OMG! This is my fault!"* LaToria thought.

Before Tahkiyah could explain, Trevon returned, and he relayed the bad news of the people down the street, having no knowledge of anyone named Sean.

Tahkiyah remained on her feet, tired of holding the weight of her secrets. *I have to tell them the truth.* "I have something to share," Tahkiyah said. "And don't stop me until I'm done."

25

FINDING CONDA

Coconut Grove, Florida
Sunday, August 16th

Tahkiyah came clean and told everyone about the private investigator and the possible dangers they faced. A gut-wrenching fear gripped Jurnee and Latoria when they were shown the pictures that were taken of them by Sean.

Trevon took it the hardest after hearing how Sean was focused on his past. It forced him to dig in his past for any memories of Sean. He came up empty. Everyone tried to talk at once when the private investigator returned Tahkiyah's text message. The text was direct and straight to the point. The threatening text came from Conda's phone.

"Everybody shut up!" Trevon shouted as Ariana smartly took the kids to the bedroom. "Ain't nobody leaving this house until I take care of this shit and I mean that!"

Jurnee stood. "I can't stay up in—"

"Ain't shit to talk about, Jurnee," Trevon stated. "I don't know what the fuck is going on, but I'll be damned if I take any chances. No one, and I mean it, no one, is leaving this muthafuckin' house!"

Jurnee sighed and sat down. "So, you expect us to sit here while you go out by yourself?"

"She has a point, Trevon," LaToria added.

"I said it's not up for discussion!"

"How can we help you from here?" Tahkiyah asked, having the sense not to argue.

Trevon slid a hand down his face. "Okay, I'll need your private investigator's number *and* Conda's number. And somebody needs to call Vanessa and send her a picture of Conda and Sean to make sure they don't make it through the gate. And find out how Sean made it through in the first place."

"I'll do it," Jurnee said, wanting to help.

"What else?" Tahkiyah asked.

"Where can I find Conda?"

"Try the HOP in Coral Gables," LaToria said with a worried expression. "Smooch, just call the police and let them handle this."

He shook his head. "We got the upper hand. And besides, they haven't broken any real crimes. I need to talk to Conda one-on-one to see what the fuck is up. And don't try to talk me out of this. That muthafucka done crossed the wrong one!"

"Ma! Talk to him!" LaToria whined.

"He's right, LaToria. Sean doesn't know he's being watched, and Trevon will catch Conda by surprised," Tahkiyah explained.

"There has to be another way," LaToria said with tears in her eyes. "We need you Trevon. Victoria and Tayvon need you in their life and not back in—"

"Don't say it." He took her in his arms. "Let me take care of this, baby. You gotta trust in me. Whoever the fuck this Sean guy really is, I'ma find out today. I'm gonna be okay and I need you to be here when I get back."

She began to sob against his chest.

"And the same for you too, Jurnee," Trevon said.

"I hope you have a plan." Jurnee stood and crossed the room to make his hug with LaToria a threesome. When his arm slid around her waist, she felt loved.

"I always have a plan. Y'all just listen to me, *don't* leave this house, and keep Rex inside!" Trevon stated firmly.

"No one is leaving," Tahkiyah assured him. "Just promise us you won't do anything stupid. Find out what you need to know and come back home. Promise us!"

"CONDA HASN'T BEEN HERE in two days," Heather Cocks told Trevon, as she sat at the foot of her bed with her legs crossed.

"And you have no idea where he's at?" Trevon stood near the dresser with his arms crossed.

She shook her head and tapped the cigarette in the ashtray beside her hip. "I didn't realize he was gone until yesterday."

"How?" Trevon tried his best not to stare at Heather's bare breasts through the red mesh, lace trim camisole.

"All of his clothes are missing, and he didn't show up for breakfast." She took a long pull on the cigarette. "And I'm sure Kandi told you about the issue I have with him."

He nodded. "He lied to her about seeing a client at her condo."

"Exactly," Heather said with smoke billowing from her glossy red lips. "And like I said a moment ago, I believe he's with that Sean character." She uncrossed her shapely legs for the third time, flaunting the fact that she didn't have any panties on.

He caught a glimpse of her hairless pussy as she kept her legs open. "Have you tried to call Conda since he left?"

She nodded. "Unfortunately, he's blocked my number."

Trevon sighed and glanced at his watch; 5:45 p.m. *I gotta find this muthafucka as soon as possible.*

"I'm a big fan of your films," Heather cooed as she eyed Trevon like her next meal. "Too bad my career in porn ended when yours is just taking off," she said.

"If you see or even get word of where Conda is—"

"I'll call you." She stood. "Now, if you'll excuse me. I have some clients to entertain."

Trevon left Heather's bedroom and headed to the front door. He ignored the sounds of sex behind the closed doors that lined the dimly lit hall. Just as he reached the living room, the last bedroom door on his right came open.

"I know you!" the cute redhead said as she stood in the doorway. "You're Trevon Harrison! OMG, what are you doing here?" She stood barefooted in a pair of scanty white panties and a pink tank top.

Trevon sighed. "Just passing through. Had to holler at Heather about something."

"Really?" She blushed. "How can I get lucky like that?" She reached for his hand. "I'm free at the moment. And between us, I can show you a good time and it will—"

"I'm not here for that."

"Oh," she whispered as she released his hand and tugged at the hem of the tank top. "Can I ask why you're here?"

"I'm looking for Conda."

She rolled her eyes. *And I bet I know why. He must have heard about him messing with Kandi.*

"Why you roll your eyes? You gotta problem with him?"

She crossed her arms. "Um...maybe I do."

"I really need to talk to him."

"What did Heather tell you?"

"Said she doesn't know how to find him and that he left two days ago."

"She told you the truth."

"And what about you? Will you tell me the truth?"

"Depends."

"On what?"

"How bad do you need to find him?"

Trevon knew he would have to *give* her something before he got what he wanted. "I didn't get your name?"

"Pam," she told him.

He nodded. "Pam, I really need to talk to Conda and if it's money you need, I'll pay."

She chewed her bottom lip for a few seconds. "Conda stole a ring off my dresser before he left and I'm telling you because I want it back."

"And how do I get it back? You know where he is?"

She nodded. "He's freelancing behind Heather's back with some of her clients."

"Who?"

"I'll give you an address. That's all I can do. He'll be there tonight at eight and if he shows up, tell him I want my ring back."

"You have a deal. Now what's the address?"

"Not so fast," she cooed as she reached for his belt buckle. "That was only one part of the deal. The first part will require about half an hour of your time." She pulled him inside her pineapple-scented bedroom and elbowed the door shut. "You're so big!" She stared up at him as she fumbled with his belt. "I've never been with someone currently doing porn!"

"I need that address."

"I'll give it to you *after* you fuck me," she stated. "And I don't want you to be halfhearted about it."

"You got any condoms?"

"Plenty." She yanked his belt free. "I like to do it with the lights on, and my favorite position is good ole missionary, okay?"

Minutes later, he grudgingly joined Pam at the side of her black and green sheeted canopy bed. She made the most of the limited time she had with him. She sucked his raw penis between her pink lips as he fingered her red hair. She sucked slowly along his length, using both hands, one on his shaft, and one on his balls. The sex came with no emotions, as he later fulfilled her sexual request. Keeping her word, she gave him the address.

~

TREVON SLOWED his S580 to a stop along the curb and turned the lights off. He left the engine running as he stared at the unlit house up the street. The quiet Miami Shores neighborhood was unfamiliar to him. Checking the time: 7:42 p.m., he had no other choice but to wait for Conda to show his face. Just as he lowered the window and turned the engine off, he received a FaceTime call from Tahkiyah.

"What's up?" he answered.

"Nothing much on this end. We're all worried about you."

He sighed. "I'm okay. Everybody still there?" he asked, seeing she stood in his kitchen alone.

"Relax, no one has left. And Vanessa went out of her way to work overtime. She's at the front gate to make sure neither of those two assholes sneaks in."

"That's good to hear."

"I figured you would like to know that," Tahkiyah said. "Now, tell me what's up so I can calm the crew down on this end."

He told her what was up and, of course, he didn't mention anything about his actions with Pam.

"Staton told me to tell you about the rental car Conda is driving," Tahkiyah said, after Trevon brought her up to speed.

"What is it?" he asked as a minivan cruised by.

"He said it's a black Chevy Malibu. A Hertz rental. Need me to text you a picture of it?"

"Yeah. And what's up with Sean?"

"Still in the room. He ordered a pizza two hours ago, and that's it."

"How my kids doing?"

"They're safe. All you need to do is come back home to us."

"I will," he replied.

"Well, I don't wanna be a distraction, so I'll get off this phone. But call me as soon as anything new happens and if I don't hear from you in two hours, I'll call you back."

"Okay, I gotcha."

"Bye."

Trevon looked at the Glock on his lap, hoping he wouldn't have to use it.

AT 7:55P.M. two vehicles pulled into the driveway that Trevon had his eye on. A crystal green Range Rover Sport parked inside the lit garage and a black Chevy Malibu remained in the driveway.

Conda turned the Malibu's engine off and stepped out into the warm, starlit night. He leered lecherously at Nashlly, enjoying how her thickness looked under the tight black and blue wrap dress. He followed her inside her house through the entrance in the garage.

"What are you drinking?" Nashlly asked as she turned the lights on above the kitchen island. "I got some vodka or...?"

"Something light," Conda said.

Nashlly opened the stainless-steel refrigerator. "How about some orange juice?"

He nodded, staring at the plump roundness of her ass and wide hips.

"My homegirl said you're a beast with that tongue," she said as she handed him the drink. "And I watched a few of your old films you made."

"Those days are behind me now."

She took off her gold loop earrings. "Do you want your money upfront? This is my first time paying for something like this."

"Afterward will be fine."

She smiled. "Okay. I guess we can get things started. I, um, got some sheets and pillows laid out on the living room floor." She gestured over her shoulder.

"I'm ready whenever you are."

"I need to change."

"Can I make a suggestion?"

"I'm listening."

"Keep it simple. Just wear your favorite pair of heels and nothing else."

She bit her bottom lip. "I can do that, not a problem. But you do know I'm only paying you for oral sex, right?"

He nodded, hiding his letdown of not being able to get between her thighs. "I'm all about my business. Tonight, it's all about fucking you senseless with this." He stuck his long tongue all the way out and moved it like a snake.

Nashlly gawked at it and squealed. "Oh, my goodness! Damn, that shit is long!"

"You still agree to one hour for one hundred?"

She nodded quickly. *How the hell can he talk with that long ass tongue?!*

He closed the space between them and boldly took a handful of her ass. "I'm in a good mood tonight." He clenched her luscious butt cheeks. "You look like you taste sweet! And if you're down for it, I'll let you feel my tongue in your ass. What's up?"

Nashlly giggled. "Lucky me! And baby, I stay sweet, like a candy store."

He grabbed his drink and followed her buoyant ass into the spacious living room. Tonight, he had intentions on licking his way to change Nashlly's stance of no sex. He assumed he had the skills to get her so excited that she would end up begging for the dick. He stripped down to his boxers while she excused herself to her bedroom to change. With the lights down low, he waited for her to return while hoping she would taste as sweet as Kandi. He grinned, reasoning that would be unlikely.

Nashlly stood nude in the bathroom with her left foot on the edge of the bathtub. She rubbed her clit vigorously with her eyes fixed on the screen of her phone. A 2-minute video of Conda tongue fucking a tiny breasted Asian chick on a sofa held her in a trance. She wanted her pussy to be dripping wet when she gave it to Conda to taste. Just as she slid two fingers between her slick hole, the icon for an incoming call appeared above the film. She froze when the caller ID appeared below the sex scene. *Trevon Harrison*. Despite her apprehension, she answered the call.

"Hello?" she answered with the speakerphone on.

"Are you alone?"

She frowned, caught off-guard by his question. "Um, I got company in the living room. But right now, I'm in the bathroom. Is something wrong?"

"Who's your company?"

She stared at the floor. "Why are you asking all these questions? I've kept my word by staying away from your girl and—"

"I know," he interrupted. "But I'm not calling you about that. Something else has come up and I need your help."

"I find that hard to believe, Trevon. Frankly, I'm scared to death of your ass."

He sighed. "This is serious, Nashlly. And I'm not on no funny shit."

"Can you make it quick? Like I said, I got company waiting in the living room."

"Yeah, I can do that. Now listen up and I'll tell you what type of bullshit your company, Conda, is up to!"

She didn't have the courage to ask him how he knew Conda was in her living room. Common sense told her to simply shut up and listen.

26

TELL ME HIS NAME!

Miami Shores, Florida
Sunday, August 16th

"Hope you didn't count my time in the shower toward my hour with you?" Nashlly cooed as she sashayed into her cozy living room at 8:22 p.m.

"Not at all." Conda stood and took in the revealing sight. "And you look delicious!"

Nashlly rocked a pair of red bottom heels and a white see-through chemise and nothing else.

"I'd like to add some toys." She held up a small blue velvet book.

"What do you have in mind?" he asked as she set the book on the sofa.

"Some bondage." She smiled and opened the book.

To his surprise, the book was hollow and held a pair of pink handcuffs and two condoms. He lost his focus at the sight of the chemise riding up her bare ass. With a few steps, he moved around the coffee table and joined her beside the love seat.

"You like what you see back there?" she asked as he stroked her ass cheeks under the chemise.

"You know I do." He clutched her ass and juicy hips while inhaling the fresh scent of her skin. "And I'm down for whatever, baby. Bondage ain't new to me so let's get this started. I'm ready to get that pussy on my tongue." He licked the side of her neck and patted her soft butt cheek. "And I wanna lick this phat ass too, okay?"

Nashlly shivered with sheer excitement as her body responded to Conda's attention. She played her role and allowed him to grope her ass to his content. Goose bumps formed around her nipples when he slowly removed the chemise.

"Your ass is so soft!" he whispered behind her ear. "Can't wait to taste *all* of you."

She bit her bottom lip and wiggled her ass against his hands. She gasped when he slid his abnormally long tongue from her shoulder to her ear.

"Get on the floor. Face down and put this sweet ass and pussy in the air. That's how I wanna start this off. And bust them cheeks wide open for my tongue so I can get all up in that booty hole."

Nashlly damn near tripped over one of the pillows as she rushed to get down on the floor.

"Do you mind if I take my boxers off?" he asked while he untied his boots.

She moaned into the pillow. "Put the cuffs on first. And if you can make me cum. I *might* let you get some of this wet-wet."

He grinned smugly. "I'll agree to that," he said, cocksure about his talented tongue. He gave her juicy ass another hearty slap and grabbed the cuffs out of the hollow book. "Front or back?"

"Front," she said. "And hurry up. My pussy is about to explode!"

Conda stripped down to his briefs and socks before he put the cuffs on his skinny wrist. He sat sideways behind her with his face level to her appetizing ass. He kissed her juicy ass then stuck his tongue out. He slid it across, then up and down the split of her ass before he went to work. She gulped in a sudden breath when he probed his tongue inside her vagina. "Oh, my goodness!" she said in one breath. "Ooohhh, Yesss! It feels so good!" she moaned.

"Mmm, your pussy is sweet!" He snaked his tongue up and down the length of her wetness until he reached the mental count in his head.

"Stick it in!" Nashlly gasped. "Stick it back inside me."

Conda extended his tongue between her thick thighs and used the tip to massage her clit.

"Aaahhh, ooohh, fuck! Don't stop!" Nashlly shouted with her ass mashed against his face. "Ohhh fuck! Yess! Yess! Ummm...fuck! Yesss, baby. Ooooo, feel so nice."

He continued to wiggle his tongue on her clitoris as he inhaled the strong, stimulating scent of her pussy and ass. Just as he changed the tempo of his flicking tongue, he felt the barrel of a gun against his ear. The raw enjoyment of tasting his new client ended abruptly.

~

AT THE SAME MOMENT, Kendra arrived at the Radisson hotel in Miami. She had driven 11 hours from Raleigh, North Carolina, with a fixed agenda. The past stood in the way of her present and future. In the coming days, an arrest would be made in connection with Swagga's murder and Kendra wanted to see it through.

She felt betrayed by the few she had put her trust in. Swagga had his funny ways, but he didn't deserve to die. She couldn't get over what she was told by the FBI agents and Detective Jamiese Payne. Anger, guilt, disbelief and hurt overwhelmed her when she learned the truth about Swagga's murder. She sat at the edge of the bed with her head down. Trevon consumed her thoughts, and with each breath, a new brick of hatred went up against him. She wanted him to feel her pain and loss, and she wanted to see the look on his face when it happened. Sooner rather than later.

~

"GETCHA BITCH ASS UP on the sofa and do it slow!" Trevon gestured with the Glock at Conda. "Play games and I'll knock your fuckin' face off!"

"What the fuck!" Nashlly screamed, standing across the living room with a believable look of shock written across her face.

Trevon backed up so he could cover them both with the Glock. "You too!" Trevon stared at Nashlly, seeing how she didn't make any effort to cover her tempting nakedness. "Sit beside Conda and stay quiet if you wanna see tomorrow!"

"Shit!" Conda blurted from the sofa. "You're Tre-Trevon!" He suddenly recognized Trevon from his Google search and viewing his debut film with Kandi. "What are you-"

"I ask the questions!" Trevon aimed the Glock at Conda when Nashlly was seated. "Let's go ahead and get that straight."

Conda nodded.

"Where's your phone?" Trevon took a quick glance at Nashlly and saw how she continued to play her role.

"On-on the table behind you," Conda replied. *What the hell is wrong with this dude?*

Trevon looked over his shoulder and saw a thin phone on the coffee table. He snatched it up and turned his attention back to Conda. "You got smoke wit' me?"

"NO!" Conda answered quickly.

Trevon held the Glock steady. "So, I guess you feel you can threaten me and my family just for kicks, huh?"

Conda looked confused. "I-I would never threaten you or—"

"Tonight is the wrong fuckin night to lie to me!"

"Man, I swear to you! Plea-Please man. I don't know what you're talking about!" Conda sunk back in the sofa with his cuffed hands shaking.

Trevon held up the phone. "Too late to play stupid! You already know why I'm here, don'tcha?!"

Conda dropped his hands with his heart beating out of his chest. He licked his dry lips. "It was ju-just one night, man. And I didn't kn-know she was your girl."

"What the fuck are you talking about?" Trevon lowered the phone.

"You're here because of what I did to Kandi, right?"

Trevon rushed toward Conda and jammed the Glock under his chin. "Did what, muthafucka?"

Nashlly shrieked, wide-eyed with a true fear of Trevon losing it.

Conda jerked up on the sofa, thinking his life was over. Trevon yelled at him to explain as he pressed the Glock into his flesh. Conda couldn't control his words as they spewed from his lips. He told Trevon about Kandi's late July visit to HOP and the things that went down in his bedroom.

Nashlly no longer felt a part of Trevon's little scheme. Her terror of him and her loss of life was valid. She sat frozen with her eyes fixed on him. He moved back to the middle of the living room, searching through Conda's phone.

I should have never answered his call! His ass is crazy! Nashlly thought with tears blurring her vision.

"This is why I'm here!" Trevon tossed Conda the phone as he shoved the harsh vision of him with LaToria out of his mind.

Conda picked his phone up from the floor.

"Look at the screen!" Trevon shouted. "Explain it!"

Conda shook so hard that he nearly dropped the phone. Confused, he fumbled with it until he was able to hold it. He stared speechless at the text message.

"I'm waiting!" Trevon shouted.

Conda winced at Trevon's firm tone. "I-I never se-seen this before."

"Isn't that your phone!"

Conda jerked his head up and down.

"So how the fuck you ain't never seen that message and it's your muthafuckin' phone! You think I'm here to play games, huh?" Trevon squeezed the rubber grip of the Glock.

"Man, I swear to-"

"Don't fucking lie to me again!" Trevon raised the gun. "You sent the text this morning while you were with-"

"Sean!" Conda blurted. "I was with him this morning at a motel up in Fort Lauderdale! And, and, and... he must have did it! No, I *know* he did it! Bruh, I don't even know your number. And w-why would I leave something like that in my phone? Think about it, please! I swear to you th-that I didn't send that text message."

Trevon relaxed his grip on the Glock. "What you and Sean got going on?"

Conda glanced at Nashlly and realized he was on his own in facing Trevon. He had a lot going on with Sean and right now, the facts of his dealings could save his life. He had no loyalty for Sean, and Conda wanted Trevon to know that fact.

"I c-can prove I'm telling the truth," Conda said. "Just let me make one-"

"You can't prove shit to me!" Trevon shouted. "You expect me to listen to you when all this proof is right in my face? I know all about your stalking ways, and I should bust your shit open for that little bullshit stunt you played on LaToria!"

Conda's hope for seeing tomorrow began to fade.

"Why were you up in Fort Lauderdale with Sean this morning? You sucking his dick or something!"

"He wanted to g-go over some plans about you," Conda said. "He's like- the man is obsessed with taking everything away from you that you love. I won't lie to you. He used my phone. He had to have done it while I was in the bathroom. That's the only true explanation because I sure as hell didn't send it. I don't know your kids' names, I swear to you!"

Trevon sighed. *Maybe this motherfucker is telling the truth? Sean is the one that's taking pictures and doing all this slick shit*! "You still haven't told me nothing! And what's this 'plans about me' bullshit?"

Conda gulped and licked his dry lips again. "Uh, he asked me to set you up."

"How?"

"Uh, h-he wanted me to plant a large amount of drugs in your car. And then he was gonna tip the police off. He figured you would go down hard and face a lot of time back in prison."

"When were you supposed to do it?"

Conda shifted nervously on the sofa. "Uh, as soon as I could. He gave me your home address and pictures of your cars."

"And your stupid ass agreed to do it, huh?"

"He paid me man. And he-"

"How much?"

"One grand," Conda answered. "He gave me the money upfront and said

I'd get another grand after I did it."

"How did you meet Sean?"

"He made a visit to HOP."

"Why should I believe a word from you?"

"Bruh, please!" Conda stared at the gun. "Just lemme m-make one call to Sean and I'll prove th-that I d-didn't send that text. I swear it's the truth!"

Trevon considered it. "Put the call on speakerphone. And you better not say nothing in code!"

Conda nodded and made the call with only one thought being his motivation to remain breathing.

~

SEAN ANSWERED Conda's call after the second ring. "You got some good news for me?"

"Not y-yet," Conda replied.

Sean paced near the small space at the foot of the bed. "I didn't pay you upfront to tell me, not yet. I need this done as soon as possible. You said you wouldn't have any problems with this."

"It'll get done. I just need to catch him when he's not at home."

Sean sighed and paused near the window. "So, why are you calling?"

"Look man, why did you send this bullshit text from my phone while I was in the bathrooom? What the fuck!"

"Ah, I meant to tell you about that, but it slipped my mind and—"

"Bullshit!"

"Calm down." Sean peeked through the curtains. "I blocked your number out so there's really nothing to be sorry about."

"That ain't th-the point!"

Sean saw nothing in the motels parking lot to cause any worry. "Don't make a big deal out of nothing. How about I add a few more to your fee of taking care of things with Trevon? How does that sound?"

"How much?"

Sean turned from the window. "We'll come up with a number, *after* you take care of the task I've given you."

"Uh...okay."

"Now, tell me when you will be able to move on him?"

"Maybe tomorrow. I'll run with your idea of following him and just wait until a chance pops up."

"It'll work. He'll be focused on his family and not his car. And again, call me as soon as you plant the drugs so I can call in the tip."

"I will. You just have the rest of my money ready when I do this."

"My end is solid. Just stick to the plan and you'll have nothing to worry about. Now if that's all, I'll talk to you later."

"SEE!" Conda said. "I told you I was telling the truth!"

Trevon lowered the gun, shaking his head. "Fuck!"

"Sean is behind all th-this bullshit and he—"

"Shut the fuck up!" Trevon shouted, as he tried to think of his next move. "Why is he after me so bad?"

Conda shrugged. "I don't know, man. I swear I don't know!"

"Bullshit! You holding something back!" Trevon raised the Glock and leveled it at Condo's head. "You haven't told me enough to let your ass live! Last chance! Tell me why that muthafucker is doing all this bullshit!"

"Man, please!" Conda begged. "I, t-told you everything! I'm not holding n-nothing back! I don't wanna die! Please don't k-kill me!"

"Tell me something!" Trevon shouted again as Nashlly inched away from Conda.

"I told you everything!" Conda slid from the sofa and down to his knees. "I swear, bruh! I t-told you the truth. And I—"

"You teamed up on the wrong side!" Trevon thumbed the safety off.

Conda saw death in front of him. Suddenly, he remembered something. "Wait! I fo-forgot something!"

"What?!" Trevon pressed the Glock against Condo's forehead. "What the fuck did you forget?"

"I, um, overheard him on the phone when I was in the bathroom. I know his real name."

27

ON THE RUN

Miami Shores, Florida
Sunday, August 16th

"Are you out of your mind?" Nashlly stood in front of Trevon with her hands on her bare hips. "Why the hell did you just let him go after all that! And who the hell is Scott Falston?"

Trevon slid a hand down his face. "None of your business," he replied from the sofa.

"The hell it ain't!" she shouted. "You done scared the shit out of me when you almost lost it with this little stunt! Coming up in my crib and asking me to play along with this mess and now you—"

"Put some clothes on."

She frowned. "This my muthafuckin' house and I'm not one of your bitches. Besides, you see naked women for a living, so don't act all modest now!"

"I'm leaving." He stood.

She grabbed his wrist. "No." She shook her head. "We need to talk, Trevon. I just did some wild shit for your ass! You can't just up and leave and you know it. What if Conda finds out I was in on this shit? You gonna hang me out like that?"

Trevon couldn't think straight with the knowledge of Scott

Falston making a reappearance. He knew of Scott and why he was, after all, that he loved.

"Please." She pulled him toward the sofa. "Just sit and talk with me for a while. You owe me that." She grinned. "And I'm not putting any clothes back on because I'm not ashamed to be like this in front of you. All I wanna do is talk, okay? C'mon... sit down and chill."

Trevon sighed and for the hell of it, he took an eyeful of her clean-shaven crotch and the appealing width of her hips.

"You trying to take it there with me? You already know you can get it," she said softly. "You don't know shit about me." He stared at her.

"I've *seen* all there is to know." She let go of his wrist and circled her arms around his neck. "You don't remember it, do you?" she asked, pressing her breasts against him.

"Remember what?" he asked, fighting the lure of her nakedness.

"When we first met."

"How could I ever forget that night? I swore up and down that LaToria was-"

She giggled. "We met before that. Actually, it was a phone call a month before."

"How?" He frowned.

"I called in and talked to you on-air when you were on the *Climaxx Late Night Talk Show.*"

"Oh, shit! That was you?"

"Uh-huh... your boy Swagga put me up to it. And that same night, I downloaded your debut film that you made with Kandi."

His entire mood changed at the mention of Swagga. "I forgot all about that little thing you had with him."

"It wasn't shit," she said flatly. "But I'll keep it real and tell ya it was all for the money. But tell me this. Why was he hating on you so bad?"

"I'll tell ya if you answer one question for me?"

"Okay...what do you wanna know?"

"Uh, did you ever have unprotected sex with Swagga?"

"That's TMI."

"Yes, or No?"

She smacked her lips and rolled her eyes. "Yes! I let'im hit it raw a few times with hopes I had a baby by him. And don't trip because plenty of bitches would do it if given the chance," she stated.

He removed her arms from around his neck.

"What?" She frowned. "I know you ain't tripping over something like that?" she said heatedly. "For real, Trevon!" She stared at him with her hands back on her hips.

"You might wanna sit down, okay?"

She snatched her chemise off the arm of the sofa with her face balled up. After she angrily put it back on, she remained standing with her arms crossed. "Say what you gotta say!"

He told her about Swagga's secret with Chyna. He wanted her to know the risks she took with having unprotected sex. His own words forced him to consider the unwise choices he made with Vanessa, Chelsea and Tahkiyah.

To his shock, she admitted that she already knew about it.

"How?" he asked.

Nashlly sat down. "Back when I was staying with Swagga. His baby mama Kendra showed up, and she caught us fucking. Anyways, while I was in the bathrooom, I kept my ear to the door and I heard her confronting him about Chyna."

"And you kept fucking with him even after what you heard?"

She sighed and lowered her eyes to the floor. "At first I didn't believe it," she said. "I was being stupid, and blinded by the money. I sorta just stopped giving it any thought."

"Have you been tested since you had-"

"Uh-huh." She nodded. "After Swagga was gone, I started messing with some other dude and he asked me to take an STD test before we did anything."

He looked at her and waited for her to tell him the test results.

"I'm clean, Trevon. I don't have anything, and I didn't even get pregnant by Swagga after all that stupid bullshit I put myself through." She blew a tress of hair from her face and leaned back.

He couldn't resist the urge to stare at her nakedness under the chemise. "Guess what?" he said.

She looked at him with a flat expression. "What?"

"My gun wasn't even loaded."

She rolled her eyes. "Can we not talk about that shit, okay? I feel like a damn fool for trusting you after what you did to me. But I'ma let it ride."

"Why?"

She shrugged. "I dunno," she answered. "I can't fault you for wanting to protect your family and I was wrong to step to your girl like I did."

"So that means we're good?"

"Yeah, I guess." She smiled and stared at his crotch. "Is that dick loaded?" She giggled.

He nodded and, just as he expected, she reached between his legs to rub his dick print. Their carnal attraction was broken when her iPhone chimed.

"Let me take this call right quick." She squeezed the thick lump under his jeans with freaky aspirations of having sex with him tonight. She purposely leaned over to her side to reach for her iPhone on the end table. The short chemise easily slid up her bare ass, exposing all the goodies that she wanted him to enjoy.

Trevon gazed at Nashlly's heart-shaped ass and her phat pussy lips that seemed to beckon him. He admired her all-natural body while she answered the call using the speakerphone.

"What up, Art? This betta be important, boy."

"Some bullshit! That's what's up!" Art retorted.

"Like what?"

"Our boy is snitching! Shit is about to get real hot for us!"

"Who!"

"Veto! He's in the county jail in Broward singing like a bitch and he-"

"Snitching about what?"

"You already know," Art replied. "Word is that he got knocked wit' some work, and the feds stepped in and broke his ass down. Anyway, he put us on the table for the reward money *and* to save his bitch ass!"

"Are y-you serious!" Nashlly's fingernails dug into the arm of the sofa.

"This chick I rock wit' is a cook at the county jail. She kept seeing Veto going in and out of his block to go and talk to some detectives. Anyway, she knows some of the female jailers and you know how gossip be."

"Oh, shit!" Nashlly gasped. "Are you s-sure this is real?"

"Ain't taking no chances! I'm about to get missing until I find out what the fuck is up. Veto knows everything, so you know how this shit will play out."

Nashlly groaned. "I can't believe this shit!"

"Yo, you better take my advice and get low. If Veto is talking, I seriously doubt either of us will see anymore freedom if we're picked up."

Nashlly knew what she had to do. "Anything else you have to tell me?"

"Not right now, I don't. And the blame is all on me for telling Veto what happened that night. I know, I fucked up."

"No need to stress over the past. But listen, call me back if you hear anything else," she said, knowing Art would never call her again. "And thanks for giving me a heads up."

Trevon saw pure worry on Nashlly's face when she turned toward him. Neither said a word in the next few moments.

Nashlly fidgeted with the hem of the chemise. "I need your help."

Trevon couldn't forget what Nashlly and Art did by saving LaToria from Swagga. Her troubles were her own, and yet he made the choice to help her.

"Why didn't you answer my calls, Trevon!" Tahkiyah blocked Trevon's path with her arms tightly crossed. "Look at the time. It's almost midnight! Everyone close to you was here having a nervous breakdown when you didn't return our calls."

He stood paused in the doorway. "I'm okay." He wasn't in the mood to argue or explain his actions.

"I can see that." she snapped.

"Who's up?"

"Just me. And we need to talk," she stated as she brushed by him and stepped outside.

He closed the door and joined her at the edge of the driveway. He assumed she wanted to speak on the shameful secret they shared.

"Don't you have something to tell me?" she stared at him with the moon reflecting off her stylish glasses. "I got an email from Staton and he sent me a recording of a call between Conda and Sean. So, is it true?"

He nodded. "I think it is. It was Sean that sent the text to my phone."

"Bastard!" Tahkiyah said. "I'll let you listen to-"

"I was there," Trevon interrupted. "I heard everything that was said."

"You found Conda. What did you-"

"He's alive. But, I have no idea where he's at."

Tahkiyah released a sigh of relief. "Tell me what happened."

He told her all the details of how he caught Conda slipping.

"Why do you have a gun? You know you're a felon, Trevon."

"I know what I'm doing."

"Really?" She wasn't convinced. "This shit is serious. Sean is after you for lord knows what/ And you let Conda go free before you got all the-"

"I know what this is all about. And your private investigator allowed a major clue to slip by him."

"What are you talking about?"

He leaned against the trunk of his S580. "This has nothing to do with LaToria, or anyone else."

She stared at him, confused. "Please don't keep anything from me."

"His real name is Scott Falston." He waited a few seconds to see if the name was familiar to her.

"Scott Falston," she repeated the name and shook her head. "I never heard of him."

"I doubt you would," he said. "Scott... he's from my past."

"Uh...prison? You did time with him?"

He shook his head. "No. But, the reason I went to prison... it changed his life and I see he hasn't gotten over it, and frankly I can understand why."

"Who is he? Just tell me who the hell he is and what it is that he wants with you!"

"He's Dave Falston's only son. The man I killed for touching my little sister."

Tahkiyah immediately called Staton to inform him of Sean's true identity. She spoke at a hushed tone as she followed Trevon back inside.

"Where are you sleeping?" Trevon asked quietly in the living room. Tahkiyah pointed toward the sofa as she continued her conversation with the private investigator.

Trevon left Tahkiyah in the living room as he went to his bedroom with the weight of the world on his shoulders. He entered his dark bedroom and discovered a surprising sight. Through all the drama and bullshit, it eased his heart to see LaToria and his kids all in the bed together.

He stood in the doorway, staring at all that he would die for. *I gotta get my life in order.* He thought for the sake and future for his kids.

When his phone chimed, he quickly stepped back into the hall and eased the door shut. He viewed the caller ID and saw Nashlly's name and number on the screen. "What's up?" he asked.

"Um, I'm just calling to make sure you made it home, and to thank you for helping me like you did."

"I'm fine. And it's not a big deal."

"Yes, it is. You didn't have to do what you did for me, Trevon."

"It's been a wild Miami night, and we both got some fucked up issues to deal with."

"You know what? I actually planned for a day like this."

"What do you mean?"

"I got some money stashed," she said. "Enough to disappear and lie low and do all the things I need to have done. And for real, I wouldn't even waste my bread going to court for this mess. I can't do no time."

Trevon couldn't find the right words that would make any sense. After a short period of silence, he sighed. "Just be careful, okay?"

"I will. And thanks again for the ride. And who knows, we just might cross paths again down the line. Keep that in mind, and Trevon. You're a good dude. Take care."

"You do the same." He ended the call, hoping she would stay free and on her feet.

"Why is she calling you?"

Trevon turned and faced LaToria. "Conda went to see her tonight. She helped me set him up so I could find out what's up between him and Sean."

"What happened?"

Trevon decided not to bring up the visit he made to HOP. He had more important issues to deal with, and he planned to keep it that way. "I know why all of this is happening to me."

LaToria glanced down the hall. "Want me to wake Jurnee up? She'll want to know what's going on."

"Nah. Let'er get all the rest she needs," he replied, filled with the desire to embrace her.

"Okay. Tell me what's going on."

Just as he began to explain, Tahkiyah rushed up the hall, wide-eyed and gasping.

"Something is wrong!" Tahkiyah said. "Staton...he's not answering my calls!"

28

COMMON SENSE

Coconut Grove, Florida
Monday, August 17th

The facts of the private investigator's homicide made the morning news. Trevon stood in the living room, watching the report with his daughter in his arms. All eyes were on the 70-inch 3DTV as a motel attendant gave an account of what he witnessed.

"Turn it up a little bit!" Tahkiyah said, as she sat on the edge of the sofa.

Jurnee snatched up the remote and turned the volume up.

-at the front counter when I heard two men shouting at each other. Well, like I told the police, that fellow from room D, he was the guy I saw. Uh, they said I can't say his name. But anyway, those two gents was going at it wit' words and such. And the fellow from room D, he kept shouting "Why are you watching my room? Why are you watching my room?" Seemed really mad about it too! So, I kept my head down and kept my eyes on the situation in case I had to call the law. Well, uh, the big fellow, the one that got shot. He stepped out of his car and that's when it really got out of hand. They kept shouting at each other and then the big fellow said a name. And I can't say it because-

you know, police still working on the case. Anyway, big fellow said a name and POW! Guy from Room D pulled out a gun and shot him right in the face! And then he ran back to his room and-

"Oh, my God!" Tahkiyah covered her mouth as the motel attendant continued to talk in front of the camera. "How did this happen?"

AT THE VERY SAME TIME: 8:31 a.m., Scott, aka Sean, sat on a cheap, brown non-descriptive sofa watching the morning news. For the moment, he felt safe inside the tiny one-bedroom apartment in Carol City.

"Uh, why did you shoot that guy?" Conda asked from the kitchen.

Scott frowned and mumbled. "I don't feel like talking right now!"

Conda pushed the lever down on the toaster and stared at the back of Scott's head. *Stupid muthafucka bringing all his troubles to me! I gotta find a way to get rid of his ass! Got enough bullshit of my own to deal with.* "Does this have something to do with Trevon?"

Scott clenched his jaw, highly irritated by Conda's voice and the reeking odor that seemed to crawl up the walls. "Why do you care?" Scott stood during a commercial break and turned toward the kitchen.

"Don'tcha still want me to plant the drugs on Trevon?" Conda had no intentions to tell Scott about Trevon listening in on their call last night.

"We might need to put that move on hold for a few days," Scott replied as he glanced around the poorly furnished apartment.

Conda shrugged. "Just let me know."

Scott merely nodded as he turned and sat heavily on the sofa. "Do you own a gun?"

"No," Conda replied. "But I know where you can get one."

Scott mulled over how the man he shot knew his real name. As he replayed his actions, he realized he reacted without thought. "I need a favor." Scott turned and stared at Conda.

Conda reached for his car keys. "Let me guess? You need me to go get a gun?"

~

TREVON FELT VULNERABLE, and it showed in his slack posture. He sat at the foot of his bed with his head down. Not knowing Scott's whereabouts had him worried.

"We have to call the police, okay?" LaToria stepped inside the bedroom with Tayvon on her hip. "And you need to get some rest. Jurnee told me you've been up all night."

"How can you expect me to rest when all this bullshit is—"

"You're not going through this alone," LaToria stated as Tayvon reached his tiny arms toward Trevon.

Just as Trevon stood, his phone chimed. To his surprise, he saw the call was from Pam, the redhead from HOP. He answered it before LaToria had a chance to pester him about it.

"Yeah, what up?" Trevon said as LaToria frowned at him.

"Hi. I, um, wasn't sure if you would answer. So, I assume you didn't catch up with Conda since you didn't call me to say anything about my ring."

In truth, Trevon had forgotten all about the ring. "Uh, my bad. Just got a bunch of other shit going on."

"I really want my ring back," she said. "And if you are still wanting to talk to Conda, I might be able to help you."

Trevon's issue resolved around Scott, not Conda. "Pam, I'm in the middle of something real important and I will—"

"Did you see the news this morning?" Pam interrupted. "A guy was shot in a motel parking lot up in Fort Lauderdale. And get this... Conda just sent me a text asking if I could find him a gun for sale. He said he's with the guy that did the shooting. I think he's full of shit and to be honest, I—"

"Wait!" Trevon gripped the phone. "What else did he text? And where is—"

"Calm down," Pam said. "I told him I would make a few calls and that I would get back up with him. I called you because I figured you could still get my ring."

Trevon had an idea. An idea to bring all of his stress to an end. "Pam, listen to me. I promise I'll get your ring back today. But I need you to do something very, very important for me."

"Only on one condition," she whispered. "Can you help me get a shot at getting signed to AEF?"

"Yeah, I can do that," he agreed quickly. "Now listen, and you have to do this just as I tell you." Trevon went on and explained his plan to Pam as Latoria stayed silent.

CONDA LATER SLOWED the Chevy Malibu at a corner store along Martin Luther King Boulevard. He scanned the parking lot, searching for the man with long cornrows and gold teeth. *How the hell does Pam know somebody in the hood?* Conda thought as he parked beside a black Ford Bronco. He knew he was at the right location when a short Jamican suddenly appeared to his left. He kept the engine running as the man made a beeline to the Malibu. With the heavy flow of traffic behind him, He had no reason to be afraid. He slid the window down, squinting from the bright sun.

"You Conda?" the Jamican asked as he neared the Malibu.

Conda nodded. "Pam said you can get me what I need."

"True dat, mon. But me gon need to see dat money first."

Conda unlocked the passenger side door. "Get in."

The Jamican hurried to the passenger side to do business.

TREVON COULDN'T SLOW the pace of his heart as he sat behind the wheel of LaToria's GMC Hummer EV. From his position across the boulevard, he had a clear view of Conda sitting in the Malibu with the Jamaican. He waited with strained patience as the deal went down as planned. Trevon later followed the Malibu through several intersections. All that mattered to him was finding peace. To have that, he would need to face Scott on his own terms. All Trevon thought of were Scott's threats. They drove him to act quickly and without remorse. He couldn't imagine life without his kids, and the two women that made him a father.

A hard choice was in front of Trevon, as he continued to tail Conda. Each second moved him closer to whatever end Conda led him to. As they later drove north on 27th Avenue, Trevon began to show growth in his thoughts. Being rash, he realized he could take matters in his own hands. But those actions would be a repeat of what he did at the age of 18. He thought hard about his kids as he maintained the gap between the Malibu and the Hummer EV. He cringed on the thought of going back to prison. He glanced at the loaded Glock on his lap. He had a sudden realization that made his eyes tear up. He realized that his life had meaning. He was loved and needed by many, and being impulsive was not sitting well with his spirit. *I know what I gotta do. No Justice...No peace!*

"HERE...TAKE THIS," Conda said as he entered his apartment. "I think you'll like what's inside the bag."

Scott set his cup of coffee on the kitchen table and stared at the brown bag in Conda's hand. "What took you so long?" he asked, unsmiling.

"I got lost. Plus, I had to stop for some gas," Conda said as he gently placed the bag on the kitchen table. "Aren't you gonna see what I got with your money?"

Scott tried to read Conda's shifty behavior. "Why are you so inclined to help me?"

"Because you got money and I don't," Conda answered. "And I

figure you'll need me. I'm looking to make a nice piece of change doing whatever."

Scott didn't believe a single word that came out of Conda's mouth. "Have you ever killed someone?"

"Man, I lick pussy for a living."

Scott picked up the brown bag without taking his eyes off Conda. "I'm trying to figure out something. What kind of man allows a wanted murderer to seek shelter under his roof? And a stranger to add."

"Should I be afraid of you?"

Scott opened the bag and pulled out a black 9-millimeter Ruger. "Of course not."

"Good," Conda said as he glanced nervously at the Ruger. "Now, what's your plan? Because I know you don't intend on staying here too long. You'll stand out easy since this is a poor, black neighborhood."

"And it's the last place the authorities will look for me." Scott tested the weight of the Ruger.

"You have a point," Conda agreed.

Scott pulled the slider back on the Ruger, loading a brass round into the chamber.

"Where is your other car?" Conda asked. "That white Bentley?"

"In the storage." Scott made sure the safety was on before he slid the Ruger in the waistband of his pants. "Do you have any food here?"

"Not much. Just a bunch of junk food."

Scott drummed his fingers on the cheap kitchen table. "If you continue to help me. I'll pay you handsomely." Scott glanced around the apartment. "And more than enough to move out of this dump."

"Fine by me," Conda replied, feeling at ease with the gun out of sight.

Scott glanced toward the living room and started to rise from the table until Conda's phone buzzed.

"Let it go to voicemail," Scott said as Conda viewed the caller ID on the screen.

Conda looked stunned. "Uh, you might want me to answer it."

"Who is it?"

"Trevon."

Scott sighed. "Put it on speakerphone."

Conda realized his mistake. *Fuck! What if Trevon speaks on what happened last night?* Seeing no other option, he answered the call. "Uh... Trevon? What's up?"

"I was gonna ask you the same."

Conda shifted uneasily in the chair. "Uh, nothing on my end."

"Let me talk to Scott."

Scott jumped to his feet and snatched the Ruger out. "You told him I was here!" Scott said through his teeth.

Conda shook his head. "No! I didn't tell him noth—"

"Scott!" Trevon's voice came from the speaker. "You want me? You wanna play these games with me and my family?"

Scott held a steady aim across the table. "You killed my father," he said loud enough to be heard.

"Because he touched my sister."

"He was found innocent!" Scott shouted. "And what gave you the right?! The right to take the law in your own hands. Tell me!"

"I knew the truth. The system failed, and they got it wrong. Your father was a piece of shit and he got what he deserved."

Scott stared at the phone. "How did you find out who I really was?"

"Let's just say that I know the right people."

"Are they the right people that'll keep the ones you love alive?" Scott said. "I don't care about the time you did in prison. When I'm done with you, you'll have nothing but pain and sorrow to deal with. I promise you!"

"I doubt it," Trevon said. "See, when I killed your piece of shit father, I was young. Too young to know what I was really doing. In your case, that man you killed last night? ...Bet your dumbass didn't know he's a retired cop from up north and you did your crime as an adult. So, you'll be looking at a life sentence."

Scott kicked his chair against the stove. "Your threats are worthless to me. You can't hide forever behind that little gated property you call home. I could've killed your firstborn just as easy as taking a leak. You hear me, boy!"

"Say it to my face. Face me like I faced your punk ass father. I'll give you your chance, and you'll go down the same way."

"That's tough talk, Trevon. Too bad that all it is."

"Try me. Better yet, why don't we handle this bullshit right now. It's a sunny day to die. Kinda reminds me of the day I laid your father down. Look out the front window."

Scott jerked his head toward the living room window. His eyes were wide. "Get up!" He gestured with the gun at Conda. "Tell me what you see!"

Conda's stomach dropped to his feet when he took a peek through the brown curtain. *How in the fuck?* Conda thought at the sight of Trevon standing in plain view across the street.

"Is he out there!" Scott jammed the pistol against the back of Conda's head.

"He's r-right across the street!" Conda answered quickly.

"I thought you said no one knew you had this place!"

"He must h-have f-followed me or something!" Conda said. "Please don't k-kill me. Please, man. Please!"

Scott had to see for himself. He shoved Conda to the floor and inched the curtains apart. "Shit!" he muttered.

"Face me, Scott!" Trevon's voice jumped from the phone on the table.

Scott squeezed the Ruger and backed up from the window. Nothing made any sense. First, it was the man that knew his true identity, and now this. "Come inside and talk!" Scott shouted across the room. "You found me. Now be a man and come inside and get me!"

No answer.

Scott rushed into the kitchen and confirmed the call had

ended. “Don't you move!” he shouted at Conda. Scott breathed heavily as he tried to think of a way out. He paced in front of the table until he had an idea. At the same moment, his phone chimed with a new text message. He ignored it and ran back into the tiny living room. *Trevon wouldn't dare shoot at me in broad daylight.* Scott reasoned as he grabbed the keyfob to the Dodge Charger off the living room table.

“What is y-you gonna do with me?” Conda asked with his back glued to the wall.

“Shut up!” Scott took a second look out the window, and this time the Ruger fell from his hand. Speechless, he stared as five unmarked police cars lined up behind several officers in a defensive position. His phone buzzed on his hip only seconds before a police helicopter roared overhead.

TREVON USED common sense and took a step back to let the police do their job. He called 911, stating that he knew the location of the gunman wanted for the Fort Lauderdale motel shooting. He made the call while he tailed Conda back to the apartment. When Trevon called Conda, two detectives were already on site. As soon as it was proven that Scott was inside, Trevon was taken off the phone and ushered away from the scene.

Be alert! Be alert! Suspect is exiting front door! Trevon heard over the radio inside a police SUV. *Get on the ground! Hands up!* Trevon wanted to see Scott's face. *Put your hands up! Now! Do it now! Suspect isn't stopping!* Trevon closed his eyes. *Suspect has a-* gunshots went off. *Suspect.... is ... down.*

29

BOY OR GIRL

Miami, Florida
Thursday, August 20th
Three days later

With his troubles behind him, Trevon was back in front of the cameras. He began his day of filming at 10:05 a.m. with a poolside sex scene with his co-star Vanessa, aka Butter Buns. After five hours of filming and six sex scenes, Trevon and Vanessa showed their focus by wrapping up the entire film in one day. The glamour shot came when Trevon ejaculated a stream of semen on her shiny phat ass.

The director applauded Vanessa for her performance in her debut AV (adult video). The film would give Trevon a fan base with full-figured women. His genuine desire toward Vanessa was evident on film. In each of the six scenes, he had his way with her, stroking her to a number of orgasms. His thirst for her didn't go unnoticed by the film crew. In between takes, they would waltz nude to the bathroom and remain inside until the director called for them.

"Congratulations!" Chelsea hugged Vanessa. "You were sooo amazing! And I'm so glad you were okay with me being here."

"Thank you! Those pointers you gave me were helpful."

"Where is Mr. Sex Scene?" Chelsea said as she tugged the hem of her purple dress down her thighs.

"Still in the shower," Vanessa replied as the film crew broke down their equipment in the living room.

Chelsea gazed suggestively at the immense width of Vanessa's hips. "We should celebrate your debut film and the fact that you're an official adult actress with AEF!"

Vanessa smiled and tried to maintain her humility. "That sounds like a good idea," she said. "And by the way, Trevon told me what you said."

Chelsea blushed. "About what?"

"About your idea of doing a film with me."

Vanessa's words hung between them as Chelsea continued to blush. Both had an awkward time dealing with their budding lesbian orientations.

Chelsea broke the silence after she pulled herself together. "So... do you think it would, um, be a good idea?" She smiled charmingly.

"Honestly... the last time I was with another woman was back in high school. And that was a loong time ago," Vanessa said.

"Well, I think we can hit it off," Chelsea said. "Are you game?"

Before Vanessa could reply, Trevon entered the living room.

"Ladies!" He smiled, in a good mood with film number 7 behind him. "Make me the luckiest man in Dade County tonight," he said as he kissed Vanessa and Chelsea respectively on the lips. In his honest view, both women were unique and beautiful.

"How?" Vanessa asked with a hand on his chest.

"By going to a nice spot to eat with me," Trevon responded.

Vanessa rubbed his chest and exchanged a furtive glance at Chelsea. "Um, how about we do something more... shall we say, special?"

"How about special *and* sensual?" Chelsea said as she reached for Trevon's hand.

Trevon had Vanessa on his right and Chelsea on his left.

Having them both was something to think about. "What do you two fine, sexy ladies have in mind?"

"We want to share you," Vanessa said, pressing her breasts against his arm.

Trevon instantly thought of the threesome he did with Chelsea and Tahkiyah. He would never forget the sight of Chelsea licking Tahkiyah to a climax.

"I'm down for something freaky," Chelsea whispered. "Just the three of us would be something hot!"

"I agree," Vanessa said. "So, how do you feel about it, Mr. Sex Scene?"

Trevon figured he had the best of both worlds. Chelsea was the epitome of a badass white chick, while Vanessa met his every need as a sexy BBW. "How about your place?" Trevon asked Chelsea.

Chelsea fingered a strand of hair from her face. "I'm cool with that."

"Good," he said. "How about you and Vanessa get things ready for me, and I'll join y'all later? I have to go see my daughter and drop off some baby items."

"We'll be waiting." Vanessa nibbled on his ear. "And don't be surprised if we start the fun without you."

Trevon later wheeled his Aventador SVJ across the city with his future on his mind. Making adult films seemed to be the foundation he would stand on. His kids wouldn't lack for nothing and with each large payment from his films, he set something aside for them. He could not overlook how lucky he was to have two understanding women in LaToria and Jurnee. In time, he assumed his pride would heal over the actions between Jurnee and Big Diesel. His secrets with Tahkiyah were the chains that kept his temper in check. However, he knew his own wrong was too significant to ignore.

"LaToria!" Trevon called out as he entered her condo. He eased the door shut, expecting his daughter to come running across the living room, screaming with joy. Silence. No TV, no music, no voices. Nothing.

He stepped into the opulent furnished living room. "LaToria," he said again. *I know damn well she ain't gone!* He released a sigh and reached for his phone.

"Hey, Smooch."

He turned and found the mother of his firstborn standing at her open bedroom door. The sight left him utterly speechless as he took in the view.

LaToria met his gaze, rocking a red chiffon negligee and matching colored platform heels. The hem of the negligee circled high on her thick thighs. Her breasts sat full and bare under the sheer fabric.

"It's been a long time since I've heard you call me that." Trevon stared at the woman he wanted to give his all to.

"Twenty-three days," she said. "The last time I called you that was back on the 28th of July."

"You've been counting the days since we last had sex?"

She shifted her stance and placed her hands on her wide hips. "Haven't you? Or maybe you don't care, since you have other women that can take my place?"

"No one can ever take your place," he stated.

"Turn your phone off. I need to be with you tonight. And I need to share something very important with you."

He turned his phone off and laid it on the end of the cocktail table. "Where is my little baby girl?"

"My mom took her over to Jurnee's. She knows I need to talk to you and they won't be back until tomorrow."

"And you set this all up?"

"Uh-huh," she said. "I need to know where we stand."

He grinned as he walked toward her. "You look so good to me... you know that, right?" he said in a low tone.

"I did all this for you, Smooch." She circled her arms around his neck.

"Thank you," he said. "Now what do you wanna talk about?"

"Not now. Right now, I'd like you to push your hands down the back of my panties and rub my ass. Smooch, do I still turn you on? If not, I'll—"

He kissed her, sliding his tongue between her shiny, luscious lips. He held no thoughts of Vanessa or Chelsea as he grabbed a handful of her shapely ass. His desire for her came in waves. With each rushed breath, he found himself wanting to inhale the very essence of her.

She quivered as he molded her fleshy ass while sucking on her tongue. She loved him. She had no doubts of it and tonight she would show it. Piece by piece, she removed his clothes, starting with his shirt. Their tongues fought, their hearts pounding loud in their ears. He groaned when his shirt fell to the floor.

"Smooch!" she moaned, raking her green fingernails down his chest.

"I want you to make love to me… forever!"

"I'm here for you," he said with his hands palming the bottom of her soft ass.

Trevon finally realized the meaning of being drunk in love. With LaToria, he felt whole. He felt new again. In their race to be nude, he ripped the negligee from her sultry body and feasted on her velvety breasts.

She writhed and moaned as his warm tongue raced around her nipple. "Ooohhh, Smooch!" She dug her fingernails into his shoulders.

He stepped out of his briefs and matched her in her nudeness. "Turn around and put your hands on the wall." He gave her ass a firm smack that made it jiggle. His urge to flush his tongue between her red, fleshy cheeks grew with each breath. She rubbed her breasts while staring at the thickness of his dick. She wanted *all* of it inside her. Still in her heels, she turned and assumed the position. "Ass so fucking big!" Trevon grabbed a handful of her left ass cheek, lusting at the dimensions and softness. "You want me up in this?"

"All muthafuckin night!" she answered sexually excited. "Please don't tease me wi-"

She squealed and bit her bottom lip when she felt his penis against the split of her lotioned ass. She pushed her ass back against his penis as his hands slid up to her breasts.

"You got me so hard!" he said against her neck.

"And you got my poo-poo dripping wet," she moaned as her body seemed to lift off the plush carpet.

"I wanna eat that sweet poo-poo." He squeezed her breasts. "I want you to let me lick and suck on it until you bust in my mouth. You like that?"

"Uh-huh!" She nodded as she rolled her ass against his hard-on.

"Want me to lick this juicy butt, too?"

"Yess, Smooch!"

"Yes, what?" He pinched her nipples.

"Ohh!" she moaned. "Yes! I w-want your tongue and your dick in my butt. And I need it so deep in my poo-poo until you cum."

He glanced down at his dick and how it was sandwiched between her warm ass cheeks. What he needed the most was raw oneness with her.

She submitted to him as he guided her into her bedroom.

"I'm gonna take my time with you, baby," he said as he lay beside her on the bed.

She opened her legs as he leaned over and kissed both of her nipples. She shuddered as his fingers slid toward the bald mound between her thighs. High off her emotions, she reached down to touch herself, finding a furrow of slickness. "Smooch!" she whimpered as he positioned his face below her soft belly. She closed her eyes and played with her herself.

He caught her off-guard by turning on some music by voice command. He kissed both regions of her inner thighs as the scent of her wetness released a hint of honey.

"SMOOCH!" She gripped the pillow when he began to lick between her thick thighs.

He licked her nice and slow as their official song, "Damage" by H.E.R. enlivened the occasion.

"Mmmm, mmmm, yesss." She moaned, palming her breasts.

He slurped at her sweet wetness as she writhed from his lethal tongue.

"I love you, Smooch," she said as his tongue jabbed in and out of her gushy hole.

He kept his mouth latched against her moist petals, taking his pleasure in tasting her.

"You miss this poo-poo?" she gasped sharply, rubbing her breasts.

~

"HE'S NOT ANSWERING my call either," Vanessa told Chelsea with a disappointed look.

"I'm not surprised," Chelsea said from the edge of her bed. "He will always have a special bond with Kandi."

"Um, are you mad?" Vanessa asked.

Chelsea thought about it briefly before she shrugged. "Not really. But I sorta had my hopes up high for tonight."

Vanessa thought about sending Trevon a text, but she decided not to. "Are you really attracted to me, Chelsea? Because if you are, we shouldn't let Trevon's absence spoil our night."

Chelsea blushed. "I was hoping you would feel that way." She stood and reached for Vanessa's hand. "Can I kiss you?" she asked.

Vanessa took a deep breath and lightly squeezed Chelsea's hand. "Sure, why not."

~

BACK ON MIAMI BEACH, Kandi lay beneath Trevon, raking her fingernails back and forth across his back. With her legs hooked over his arms, she was able offer him her wet opening. She bit his shoulder when the depth of his slow-paced thrusts gratified her.

He made love to her with his short, jarring strokes. "Dis dat good poo-poo!" he groaned against her neck.

They made the best of love all over the bed. He stayed true to his word by keeping a tight rein of his need of her. Stroke by stroke, he gave his all to that syrupy center between her thighs. Her labored moans and soft whimpers replaced the music, while his heavy breathing provided an erotic background.

"SPEND THE NIGHT WITH ME, SMOOCH," LaToria whispered as she soaked in the tub with Trevon behind her.

"You didn't even have to ask," he replied, rubbing her arms. "And when you wake me up. Do it by putting that sweet poo-poo on my lips."

She leaned back contentedly and turned her head. "I miss being with you."

He kissed her softly on the lips. "I feel the same," he said as she lay her head on his shoulder. "It's just so mixed up because of my career and all the other shit I've put you through. Above everything, I never meant to hurt you."

She made an absent nod and followed it with a troubled sigh.

"Something wrong?" he asked. "Talk to me, baby."

She didn't reply right away. "Three...weeks," she whispered.

"Three weeks?" He frowned. "What's gonna happen in three weeks?"

She wiped her eyes. "Smooch," she said. "I'm three weeks pregnant."

30

KANDI'S REQUEST

Miami Beach, Florida
Thursday, August 20th

"Boy or girl?" Trevon asked LaToria after the initial phase of shock left him.

LaToria stepped out of the tub. "I'm not sure, and plus it's too early to tell," she replied as she grabbed a towel off the sink.

He admired her standing nude in front of the mirrored sink. "Anybody else know?" he asked her as she tied the towel around her wet hair.

"Nope, I wanted to share the news with you first."

"I'm gonna help you through this," he told her.

She smiled. "I know you will, Smooch. Now dry me off and stop staring at my ass."

"Anything for my queen." He got out of the tub.

He dried her off from her shoulders to her sexy, pedicured feet. After he toweled her succulent nudeness, he picked her up and carried her to the bed.

"This is how I want it to be between us," LaToria said a little while later, with Trevon beside her. "And yes, I've been thinking about the fact of you doing porn."

"And your thoughts?" he asked, with her hand resting on his chest.

"Honestly... I'm not really sure, Smooch. All I'm sure about is that I can't be without you."

"You don't have to be," he said, running his fingers through her damp hair.

"What if our roles were reversed? Could you agree with me doing porn and still deal with me in your life as your girl?"

He sighed. "You already know my answer to that, I mean... I couldn't stand to see you with another man."

"And yet you expect me to stand by and see you with other women? How is that fair?"

"I didn't say it was fair, baby. Hell, I know what I'm doing is wrong, but it's the life I live. I have three kids to support and porn is all I got going. How could you be mad at me for that?"

"I'm not mad at you... okay. Do you still love me, Smooch?"

"Of course, I do."

"Good. Now hold me tonight and don't let me go."

"I'll never let you go. In fact, I never planned to," he said as she snuggled up against him.

Everything seemed perfect and in order as he held her in his arms. He thought of Vanessa and Chelsea. How could he love LaToria and yet give himself to other women outside the business aspect of porn?

LaToria closed her eyes and welcomed the sound of Trevon's heartbeat. It relaxed her beyond words. Just as she sat up to kiss him goodnight, the doorbell chimed.

"You expecting company?" Trevon asked, as he sat up and reached for his briefs.

LaToria frowned. "Don't even try to insinuate that I would have another man coming here."

Trevon slid from under the sheets. "I was just asking you a question."

"Uh-huh, I bet," she said as he pulled his briefs up. "And what time is it anyway?"

He grabbed his phone off the night table. "Uh, six minutes after nine."

The doorbell chimed for a second time, prompting Trevon to quicken his pace. He left LaToria in the bed, hoping she had told the truth. The idea of another man stepping foot inside the condo had him ready to get on his bullshit. With a scowl, he unlocked the door without looking through the peephole. With his guard down, he opened the door and regretted his brazen actions in his next breath.

~

"WHAT DO THEY WANT!" LaToria paced at the foot of the bed as Trevon got dressed.

"I don't know," he replied. "But when we go out there, let me do all the talking."

"I'm scared!" LaToria said with her heart about to jump out her chest.

"Stop stressing this. We ain't got shit to worry about, okay?"

LaToria nodded. "I'll try," she said.

Moments later, Trevon and LaToria walked into the living room, holding hands. They sat and faced their two visitors.

Detective Jamiese Payne cleared her throat. "Again, I'm sorry for my timing, however, I have something very important to discuss with you two."

Trevon leered at Detective Payne. "And you expect me to believe that?"

"It's the truth, Mr. Harrison."

"And who are you?" Trevon fixed his stare on the second visitor.

"I'm Homicide Detective Shardasia Loken with the Raleigh Police Department in North Carolina."

Trevon exchanged an untrusting look with both of the African American female detectives.

"You're that detective that solved that case of the state attorney's wife that was murdered," Trevon said. "I saw the coverage about it on *Good Morning America*. Why are you down here?"

"I'm assisting Detective Payne at her request," Detective Loken replied. "And we have reasons to believe that one of the suspects in our murder investigation is on the run up in Raleigh."

"And what investigation would that be?" Trevon asked.

"The high-profile investigation on Marcus Brooks aka Swagga," Detective Payne said with her eyes on LaToria. "Care to speak on it?"

Silence.

Trevon felt Latoria's grip tighten on his hand as she shifted unsettled on the sofa.

"You're a father, Mr. Harrison," Payne said, breaking the silence. "I did my research, and I know all about your past. The fifteen years you spent in prison. Your career... in porn and the birth of your two kids. And I also read the U.S. Marshal's report on that issue you had with Swagga."

Trevon stayed silent.

"We're not here to run any game," Payne continued, looking at Trevon and LaToria. "In fact, this was Loken's idea for us to come here and lay all the cards on the table."

"What cards?" Trevon said. "And don't try that played out good cop, bad cop bullshit!"

"No need to get upset," Payne said. "I'll get to the point of the matter. Okay, for starters, we're fully aware that LaToria was kidnapped by Swagga on the night of his murder, and the fact of you not reporting that crime is a crime itself. But I'm not here to scare you with that fact."

Trevon didn't respond. He simply continued to breathe. *Shit! I guess that heads up Nashlly got had some truth to it.*

"Are you surprised that I have knowledge of that?" Payne asked.

Trevon didn't speak.

"Please cooperate with us, Mr. Harrison," Payne stressed. "You did it just a few days ago with your issue with Scott Falston. We *know* you didn't murder Swagga, but you know who did."

"And what makes you so sure of that?" Trevon broke his silence.

Payne met Trevon's hard stare. "It's my job to be sure of these things. And besides, it would be in your best interest to cooperate with us before you get a visit from the FBI," she warned.

Trevon sighed. "What do you want from us?"

Payne waited a moment. "Do you know Nashlly Torain?"

"Yeah, I know her."

"That's an excellent way to start being honest with me," Payne said.

"We know how she saved LaToria," Loken joined the exchange. "And we know the guy that helped her that night."

"Since y'all *know* everything," Trevon vented, "why are y'all here? I didn't kill Swagga and—so, just get to the point."

"Nashlly Torain and her accomplice; Art, are missing," Payne stated. "We started our surveillance of her, I obtained a search warrant for her home and we found signs of a rushed exit."

Shit! That was close! Trevon thought. "Well, she sure as hell ain't here."

"When was the last time you saw her?" Payne asked.

Trevon yawned. "I have no idea where she is, okay?" he said as he fought to keep his calm for LaToria's sake.

"What about you, LaToria?" Payne asked.

Silence.

Detective Payne sighed. "Guys, don't make this hard, okay? Think about your kid and how it would—"

"Stop it right there," Trevon said. "If you plan to force us to talk about anything, don't mention my kids. Real talk, don't come up here thinking that gun and badge gonna push any fear over us. Matter of fact," he stood, "I think it's time y'all made your exit."

LaToria wanted the truth from Trevon as soon as the police left. She questioned him about Nashlly and he told her the truth about what he did.

"You helped her!" LaToria said. "Didn't you hear what they said before they left? If you're caught helping her and you know she's wanted. You can be charged."

"Relax, baby."

"No," LaToria shouted. "This is serious, Trevon!"

"I know that." He flopped down on the sofa.

"Listen to me." She stood in front of him with her arms crossed. "I know I owe Nashlly a lot for what she did. But we got too much to lose to get mixed up in her drama."

"We're not getting mixed up in anything," Trevon said. "We didn't *see* her do anything, and that's the truth. *If* we have to go to court for this, just tell the truth."

She shook her head and sat back down. "If it ain't one thing, it's another. Why can't we just be at peace?"

He eased his arm around her waist. "We didn't do anything wrong. That's all we need to focus on."

"What do we do now?"

"*You* ain't gonna do nothing but stay beautiful," he said, rubbing her thigh.

She sighed. "My mom is going to trip when I tell her about this."

"Well, I suggest you tell her about the baby *after* you tell her about this mess."

"That makes sense."

They sat quietly, lost in their own thoughts. LaToria wanted things to be simple. She wanted Trevon at her side, permanently.

"Do you remember when we first met?" LaToria asked with her legs tucked underneath her.

"Yeah," he said. "I'll never forget when you came inside Janelle's office. You had on some tight leggings and a tank top, looking good."

She giggled. "I knew we were gonna hit it off."

"Hey, remember the first time we did it raw? That was the night I came back from the club."

"Uh-huh." She smiled. "We did it with that slow song by H.E.R. playing."

"Damage. Yeah, that's our song right there."

"Yep! Man, that night was the bomb."

"I can't front." He chuckled. "You had my nose wide the fuck open from day one. I would've never pictured you wanting to rock with me on a personal level."

"Any regrets?"

"None."

"Good. Because I feel the same. And guess what?"

"What's up?"

She sat up. "I love you, Smooch."

"I love you too, baby," he replied. "I know I don't show it like I need to and I'm sorry for—"

"Shhh." She looked at him. "All that matters to me is now. I got Trevon aka Smooch. Them other bitches can have Mr. Sex Scene, okay?"

31

KENDRA'S MOTIVE

Miami Beach, Florida
Friday, August 21st

"Shit!" Trevon muttered the next morning at 10:43a.m. as he helped LaToria change the bedsheets. "I just thought of something."

"What?" LaToria asked from across the bed.

He went on and explained his thoughts of Kendra now knowing about their involvement in Swagga's murder. "She has a reward out for information, and I'm sure the police are keeping her up on things. Damn... she's not gonna like the fact of me knowing what I know and never telling her."

LaToria shook her head. "I never did like her like that much, to tell you the truth. I just want this mess to be over with." She pouted.

He agreed with her as he lowered his eyes to the white boy shorts that hugged her thick figure. "That ass gonna get bigger with baby number two." He smiled.

"Smooch, shut up before I go upside your head with this pillow." She giggled softly, then asked, "Why haven't you told me about your new film?"

He shrugged. "Figured you didn't care too much to discuss it."

"It's business," she said, with the dirty sheets in her arms. "Besides, I saw a tweet your director posted before you got here last night. Y'all completed the entire film in one day." She turned and crossed the room toward the bathroom. "Maybe I should come out of retirement and do a few films with my Smooch."

He pulled the pillowcase off the pillow. "For real?"

"It's possible," she replied from the bathroom. "And I'll do it without any makeup to hide my stretch marks."

"Uh, let me think about it."

"It's not your choice to make," she stated. "Well... I guess it is because I'll only do a new film with you... or with another girl." She smiled. "Betcha wouldn't mind that, huh?"

"That's different," he said as she grabbed her phone off the night table. "What time is your mom coming back with Victoria?"

"I'm calling her now to find out."

~

Conda jerked up off the bed, startled by the forceful knock on the motel door. He rubbed his eyes, yawned, and kicked the sheets off his skinny legs. Times were hard on him since he wasn't able to offer his talents at HOP. To make matters worse, he was back on drugs. *Hope it ain't the fucking police again.* He hid his bottle of pills under the lumpy mattress and crossed the tiny room to answer the door.

"Who is it?" he shouted. "If it's room service... I'm good. Just come back later."

No reply. Only the rattling sound from the air conditioner unit.

He sighed and took a quick peek through the drab tone curtain. Parked directly in front of the room was a gray Rolls-Royce Wraith. Conda rubbed his eyes again as he unlocked the door. He squinted from the sun and looked at the attractive woman that stood unsmiling in front of his room.

"Are you Doug Higgins aka Conda?" Kendra asked.

"Yeah. And who are you?" He crossed his arms.

"I'm a woman with a lot of money and I believe you can do something for me to get some. And from what I'm looking at… you could use some money."

"You the police, huh?" He frowned. "You working undercover or something? I told y'all everything, okay?"

"I'll pay you $100 just to talk to you about a deal."

"Make it two," Conda countered as he noticed the designer clothes she wore. *This bitch got some serious paper. And she is wearing the fuck outta them jeans!*

"Fine," Kendra replied irritably. "Now can I come in, or not?"

He sighed and stepped aside. "Make yourself at home."

"I doubt it." Kendra rolled her eyes behind a dark pair of shades and stepped inside the room.

"You got my m—"

"Here's your money." She held out a single $100 bill. "You'll get the other one after we talk." She kept her distance and remained standing by the dresser.

He took his fee and sat at the foot of the small bed. "Okay, talk."

"I read that statement you gave the police." She gauged him for his reaction.

"And?" He stared at her.

"Scott wanted you to set Trevon up, and he gave you the drugs to do it."

Conda's stomach growled. "And you said you're *not* the police, huh?"

"I'm not. But I have friends that are, and I'll leave it at that."

"And you came here to repeat what I told the police?"

"I want you to do me a favor, sorta like what you were going to do for Scott."

He tugged at the hem of his tank top. "This some kind of game?"

"No. Why would I come over-"

"Oh, let me guess! Trevon sent you here to see if I'm still a threat to him or not? Y'know what? You can have your money back 'cause I'm not fucking with—"

"I'll pay you ten grand to work for me." She pulled the shades off.

He met her stare. "Ain't killing nobody, okay?"

"You won't need any weapons for what I have in mind. And no one is gonna get hurt."

"I still don't believe any of this shit." He glared at her. "You could still be the police, trying to lock my black ass up. And how do I know you *really* got the bread to pay me that amount of money? For all I know, you could be driving a fucking rental!"

"You have a valid point. So, let's make a deal?"

"What kinda deal?"

"If I can prove to you I'm not the police and I have the money to pay you, you'll agree to work for me and take care of what I need done."

"Whatever."

Kendra was driven by a revengeful purpose as she strolled up to Conda. "You wanna frisk search me for any wires?" She held her arms out.

He looked up at her, not sure what his next move would be. *Okay, this bitch wanna play games.* "Take your top off. You ain't about to trick me into touching you."

She didn't blink as she removed the pullover blouse. "No wire," she said as she held her arms out again as her large breasts spilled over the edges of the bra.

He couldn't pull his eyes off the curvaceous contours of her breasts. "Maybe it's inside your bra."

Kendra rolled her eyes and reached up to the bra straps on her shoulder and pulled them down. She thought of her purpose and freed her breasts from the hold of the bra. Her nipples came to attention when they were exposed to the chilly air.

He unfolded his arms, staring at her enticing, dark nipples.

"Satisfied?" she asked with her arms at her sides.

"Not really." He smirked. "Just because you're topless don't mean you're not the police."

She closed her eyes for a moment. *I have to do this!* She opened her eyes and forced a smile. "Again, you have a point. And if I was the police, I wouldn't be able to offer you this..." She cupped her left breast up to his lips and held it in place.

He didn't move. "Offer me something else," he challenged her.

"We're not having sex!" Kendra frowned. Having her limits and fucking him was numero uno.

"Nah," he shook his head. "That ain't what I'm talking about. You really wanna prove you ain't the police?"

She nodded, holding her composure.

"Drop them jeans and let me show you how I earned my name. Real police wouldn't be able to go that far. Do it, and *then* I'll believe you're not the po-po. Now what's up?"

~

TAHKIYAH RETURNED to the conda at noon with Victoria and; Trevon met them at the door, scooping up his squealing daughter as Tahkiyah smiled and dropped her purse on the sofa.

LaToria came out of her bedroom and her heart smiled at the way Trevon interacted with Victoria. He carried her around the living room above his head.

Tahkiyah stuck her fingers in her ears as Victoria continued to express her joy at the top of her lungs.

"Trevon!" LaToria shouted. "Please put her loud butt down before we all go deaf!"

Trevon landed Victoria on the sofa and started another round of giggles by blowing on her belly. Being with his daughter was a joy he would never tire of.

"What she needs is a trampoline," LaToria said as Victoria started jumping up and down on the sofa.

"Not gonna happen," Trevon stated, as he picked his daughter back up and carried her to her bedroom.

LaToria flopped down on the sofa.

"You're looking happy this morning," Tahkiyah observed. "I hope it will last."

LaToria grabbed the TV remote off the end table. "Well, I owe it all to you."

"How so?" Tahkiyah asked.

"Because it would've been hard to do the nasty with Victoria here," LaToria smiled.

"That's TMI. And you better find a way to get around that. For starters, Victoria needs to start sleeping in her own bed."

LaToria sighed. "Every time I tuck her in her bed, she still ends up in mine in the morning. And she does it without waking me up. Sneaky tail."

Tahkiyah smiled. "She gets me like that, too. I caught her climbing in my bed one night last week. And when I asked her why she doesn't want to sleep in her own bed, guess what her grown tail said?"

"Ain't no telling with her," LaToria turned the TV on.

"I know. But anyways, she said, 'My bed too small' and you and I both know that we're spoiling her."

LaToria turned to the local news channel. "I have to find a job. Better yet, a career is what I need."

Tahkiyah lifted her eyebrows. "And what sparked that?"

LaToria shrugged. "Just facing reality, I guess. And by the way, I'm pregnant." She slipped the news in.

Tahkiyah gasped. "Stop playing!"

"I'm three weeks pregnant, Ma."

~

TREVON CALLED Chelsea and Vanessa and kept it real about his change of plans last night. They understood and held no harsh feelings. Chelsea joked how she knew of the strong BM bond that kept him on a chain. She assured him he didn't stop the fun between Vanessa and herself. Vanessa's mood remained mutual.

She was cool with everything, open to maintaining a firm mix of heavy business and a little pleasure on the side. She figured she was keeping him hooked with the promise of letting him experience anal sex with her. Seconds after he ended his call with Vanessa, he received a call from Kendra.

"I'm sleepy, Daddy." Victoria rubbed her eyes as she sat on the floor.

"Alright, nap time."

"No." She shook her head. "I wanna stay up."

Trevon knew she was sleepy, but she was trying to fight it.

"Uh, come lay on my lap while I talk to my friend, okay?"

She nodded.

Trevon grinned as his phone buzzed again. "Hey what's up?" he answered as Victoria curled up against him.

"Hey stranger! Whatcha doing?"

"Sitting on the floor with my daughter."

"How nice," Kendra said. "Kinda makes me feel bad to be calling with the news I want to share with you. And before you ask, I can't tell you over the phone."

"How else you gonna tell me?"

"Face to face."

Trevon remained calm. He didn't want her to know how much he already knew of the news she wanted to share.

"Uh, are you down here?"

"Yeah. And I really need to see you."

"Okay, well, do you have a spot in mind?" *Better be in public.*

"I'll have to find an excuse to get away from my man," she lied. "But if you would, please meet me for lunch at Dominique Bar & Grill on Collins Avenue."

"What time?"

"How about within the next thirty minutes? Can you make it?"

"Yeah. I'll be there."

"Thanks. Well, I have to get off this phone. I promise to explain everything over lunch."

He ended the call and mulled over how he would approach

Kendra. For starters, he figured it was in his best direction to be honest with her, no matter how much the truth stung.

A tap on the door broke his thoughts. He looked up from the floor as LaToria stuck her head inside. She saw Victoria asleep and smiled.

"I knew her butt was asleep. It was too quiet back here," LaToria whispered.

Trevon smiled. "Can you put her to bed? I have to run home to change and—"

"You're forgetting you still have some clothes in the closet?" She reminded him as she gently picked up Victoria. "And where are you rushing off to?"

"Kendra just called. She wants me to meet her for lunch at Dominique Bar & Grill."

LaToria wasn't in the mood to argue her point of him not going. "I hope you're thinking this through."

He stood. "I am." He reached for her hips. "I'ma call Janelle and tell her what's going on. Just in case we need a lawyer."

"Are you going to tell her what really happened that night?"

He shrugged. "You tell your mom the good and bad news?" he asked.

"Yeah. And it was hard to judge her reaction? But, she said she's gonna help with the baby and that we, meaning you and I, need to get our act together."

"We will. I promise." He kissed Victoria on the cheek. "Let me jump in the shower and get this drama over with."

"Will you come back after your lunch with her?"

"Yeah. And... how about you make some of your cheesy lasagna tonight?"

"I'll think about it," she said. "Look, be careful around that woman, Smooch. I don't trust her, and neither should you," she warned, hoping her words would be taken to heart.

Back at the cheap motel, Kendra squeezed the pillow under her head as Conda worked his tongue in and out of her pussy.

"This feels soooo nice!" she moaned. "Make me cum again."

He pushed his stiff tongue inside her wetness as he rubbed her soft and thick hips. He savored her taste for the second time since she entered the room. Her moans rose and fell as he jabbed her with his tongue.

"Where have you been all my life?!" She gasped as she circled her hips around his face. "Mmm, your tongue is like a d-dick!"

Her pussy gripped the length of his tongue, coating it with her creamy release.

She wanted to use him for every intent to hurt Trevon. After their second scene of oral sex, she told him the plan.

32

LISTEN TO ME

South Beach, Florida
Friday, August 21st

Trevon arrived at Dominique Grill & Bar at 12:46 p.m. He parked his Aventador SVJ between an Acura NSX and a Porsche Panamera. For the moment, he planned to sit and wait for Kendra to arrive. From his position, he had a clear view of the entrance and exit of the parking lot.

A row of palm trees lined the maintained grounds behind his roadster and that provide a bit of shade from the sweltering sun. His attention was distracted easily when two bikini-clad women strolled across the parking lot. He eyed the leggy brunette and how her breasts jiggled with each step. He toyed with the idea of tapping the horn. The brunette was attractive, but she couldn't stand in the same class with LaToria. A minute later, his phone chimed. He answered it on the second tone when he saw it was Janelle returning his call.

"What's up, Boss Lady?" Trevon settled back in the leather seat.

"Hi Trevon. Or do you prefer Mr. Sex Scene?" She laughed.

"I'll stick with Trevon. So, what's up with you and the baby?"

"Everything is fine. I'm so blessed, Trevon, and I mean it. Well, the little one knows how to wake me up at night, but I love it!"

"I can hear it in your voice," Trevon said. "How are things with you and Victor?"

"I love that man and I'm so happy to have him in my life!"

"Damn, your life sounds perfect. Got any tips for me?"

"Yeah, pray."

"Uh, when will you be coming back to Miami?"

"Next month," she replied. "And your manager has kept me posted on your career."

"Yeah, I've been on my grind. I'm ready to put more films out."

"Is that what you called me for?"

He glanced toward the entrance when a black Ferrari turned into the parking lot. "Um, actually, I need to discuss something serious with you. Something I should have never kept from you."

"Okay," her reply carried a tone of worry.

Trevon opened up and told Janelle about what happened to LaToria on the same night Jurnee had her car accident. He went on and brought her up to speed with the facts of Swagga's murder investigation, and his current dealings with Nashlly and Kendra.

"Trevon, listen to me. You obviously called me for advice, right?"

"Yeah," he replied.

"Well, you need to take heed to what I'm about to tell you. Do not meet with Kendra—"

"But she said—"

"Trevon. This is serious, and you and Kandi need to take it as such. Whatever game Kendra is trying to play, don't fall for it. If you want my help, you need to start listening to me."

"You want me to stand her up?"

"Yes!" Janelle stressed. "You and Kandi need to go and see my lawyer! Tell her everything you just told me and tell the truth."

Trevon left South Beach in his rear-view mirrors with his thoughts twisted. Using the speakerphone, he called LaToria and told her what was going on and that she should expect a call from Janelle.

"Where are you going now?" LaToria asked.

"Home. I need to feed Rex, and I have a few other things I need to take care of. And yes, I'm staying with you tonight."

Later, at a red light on 7th Avenue, Trevon made another call after blocking his number. He allowed it to ring five times before he hung up. He waited for the light to change and for his phone to chime. The latter happened first.

"Hey?" Nashlly's voice came through the speakers.

"What's up with you?" Trevon asked, hoping he wouldn't regret calling her.

"Making it. But I never thought I'd ever hear from you again."

"Well, I got some bad news. I got a visit from the police last night. And by now you should already know that your boy Art told you the truth—that other dude is snitching."

"Yeah, I know. My cousin told me about the police and the FBI been popping up at my shop. But like I told you, I ain't turning myself in so fuck what they are talking about."

"Well, your boy told the police about Swagga kidnapping LaToria, so that puts us at the crime scene. But real talk, we ain't see shit and that's what LaToria and myself will stick to."

"I appreciate that."

"Oh yeah, you better be glad you left when you did too because your crib was put under surveillance the next day."

"I heard about that. I'm glad Art gave me a call about it," Nashlly replied. "Are you gonna ask where I'm at?"

"Nope. It's none of my business. As long as you're free, that's all I care about."

Nashlly hesitated. "For real? I mean... I'm shocked to hear that you care."

"You saved LaToria's life... and my firstborn," Trevon said as the light turned green. "I don't wanna see you in prison behind Swagga, and that's just keeping it real."

"I agree with you on that. But, I gotta deal with this shit as it comes."

"Are you gonna be okay?"

"Yeah. I know they want to talk to me about the murder and we know how the cards will fall, so that's a chance I'm unwilling to take. Plus I gotta worry about Art and hope he'll keep his mouth shut if he's caught."

"Shit, he should've kept his mouth shut in the first place!"

"Yeah... but it's too late to bitch about it now."

"Through all this bullshit, I never had the chance to say thank you. If you can remember, Jurnee was in the hospital that night. I could have lost so much that night."

"But you didn't. And by the way, you're welcome."

"Uh, just be careful, okay?"

"Same to you, Trevon. You're a good dude, like I said before, and Kandi is lucky to have you. And since the police know about that night, y'all can go ahead and tell what happened. Ain't no need to get the FBI on your back. Just clear your name, and get on with your life."

"That's snitching."

"Wrong, it's called common sense. And like you said, you didn't see me do a damn thing."

Trevon grinned. "I assume you got a plan to stay free?"

"More like strategy," she replied. "And I'm gonna stick to it."

"You do that."

"Hey...I'll be ditching this prepaid number after today."

"I understand and for all it's worth, my number will remain the same."

"I'll keep that in mind. And one last thing before I go."

"What's up?"

"Um, if we should ever cross paths again. Can you promise me a good time?"

"Yeah, we can make something happen. And real talk, had you not gotten that call from Art. I was planning to give you a sample of some porn star dick."

She giggled. "That makes a sistah feel real good. I'll hold you to that promise, Mr. Sex Scene. And you can best believe I'll continue to support your career."

"Thanks, and be safe, Nashlly."

"I will, and you do the same. TTYL."

Trevon drove through an intersection, hoping Nashlly had the resources to stay free. Halfway home, he grew suspicious toward Kendra and the fact she hadn't called. He felt guilty about the idea of her sitting at the restaurant waiting for him.

"Call Kendra," he said, figuring he could come up with a believable lie. Two seconds later, his phone rung on his thigh. *I'll say I had to take Victoria to the hospital. Nah, that'll be bad karma. Think. I got it! I'll say I was called in to AEF for business.* The ringing continued until Kendra's voicemail kicked in. Trevon ruminated his lie as Kendra's voice emitted from his phone. BEEP.

"Uh, Kendra, what's up? Look, I won't be able to make it. Just got a call from my manager and I have to report to AEF. Uh, gimme a call back so we can talk. And I'm sorry if I screwed up your plans. Just - call me back." Trevon drove straight home and was surprised to see Vanessa at work. She was all smiles as he slowed to a stop at the gate.

"Hey sexy!" he said. "I thought you were giving that job up?"

"I am," she replied. "I gave them my two weeks' notice a few days ago."

"Look, I'm sorry about last night. I didn't mean—"

Vanessa held up her hand. "She's your baby mother, Trevon. You don't have to explain that to me. I thought I made that clear when you called me this morning."

"Yeah. So, we good?"

"Absolutely." She smiled. "And for your information, I really enjoyed yesterday!"

"Same with me. So, are you ready for your next film?"

She nodded. "I have a meeting with Jurnee today at three. And before you ask about me and Chelsea. The answer is yeah, we did our thang last night, and it was so amazing!"

"Really?"

"Uh-huh. And I got you to thank for it."

"What time do you get off?"

"Two o'clock. And I'll be rushing to get home to shower and change so I can be at AEF on time."

"Well, call me and let me know how it goes with Jurnee."

"I will. And don't be a stranger," she said, recalling vividly how his penis looked at its fullness.

"Never that," Trevon said as he revved the engine.

When he made it home, Rex greeted him the moment he stepped inside. He fed him and ended up in his bedroom. All he wanted was a sense of being someone worth loving. He knew his actions behind LaToria's back with her mom was straight up shiesty. Every time Tahkiyah crossed his mind, he drowned with guilt and the throb of lust. Just as he took off his shirt, his phone chimed. The caller ID showed Vanessa's name, picture, and number.

"What's up, Butter Buns?"

"You have a visitor on the way. That's what's up."

"Who?"

"Sorry. I promised not to say a word. And don't even mention this call."

Trevon headed for the front door. "For real, who is it?"

"Nope. I gave my word. You'll find out who it is in just a minute. Bye, handsome."

~

"WHAT THE FUCK are you doing here!" Nashlly glared at Art as she lowered a stainless steel snub-nosed. 44 Bulldog. "And how did you find me?"

Art stepped inside the small apartment and took off the black and blond locks wig. "Don't trip, but your cousin told me how to find you."

"Stupid bitch!" Nashlly fumed. "Wait' till I talk to her dumb ass again!"

"Chill yo. I know you're upset and you get every right to be. It's my fault all this shit has blown up because I should've never told Veto about that night."

"Were you followed?" Nashlly flexed her grip on the pistol.

He shook his head. "I would've never guessed you to be in Atlanta."

"What do you want? If it's money, you came to the wrong place!"

"I don't need any money. I came here to fix this bullshit."

"Fix it how? Veto is gonna turn state on us and he's already snitching!"

"That's his word. His ass is facing a fed case as it is and—"

"I know all that shit!" Nashlly shouted. "The only way to fix this shit is to stay on the run and that's what my black ass is gonna do."

"Just hear me out. If you ain't feelin what I'm saying. I'll leave and it is what it is."

"Talk." she said heatedly.

"Okay, Veto is still in the county jail in Broward," Art said. "And remember, I fucks wit' a chick that cooks meals for the inmates. Well, I got an idea, but it's gonna cost us some bread."

Nashlly shook her head. "I ain't giving you a dime."

"I already figured that. And like I told you, my bread is good. Anyway, I'ma come out of my own pockets to fix this shit."

"Then why did you come here to blow up my spot? I swear to God I will murder yo' ass if you lead the police here! And that's word on er'thang!"

"Don't push it!" He glared back at her. "I respect your gangsta because you made sure I was hit off with that half a mil after you handled your biz. But I think you're forgetting about another player."

"Who?"

"Jamilah."

"Why the fuck is she on your mind?"

"She's the one that hired us to do this shit. I spoke to her last week, and she's sweating bullets. Feds already spoke to her, and she agreed with me on what needs to be done."

"I'm listening," she said, upset.

"Okay. All the police got is hearsay. And if you didn't know, it won't hold no weight in court because it's not admissible as testimony. Veto told the police what he heard from my lips."

"And?"

"And… that means their case is weak as fuck. Veto is our problem. The head of the snake and—"

"Get to the fucking point!"

Art tossed the wig on the sofa. "Jamilah wants to take Veto out."

Nashlly rolled her eyes. "He's in the county jail, remember? How you going to pull that off?"

"CAN I COME IN?" Jurnee asked Trevon when he opened the door.

"Nah. You gotta stand out in the hot ass sun," he replied sarcastically.

Jurnee stepped inside and made her way to the living room. "I'm on my lunch break," she said. "And I won't take up too much of your time."

Trevon sighed. "I told you I'm not tripping over the Big Diesel issue."

"Really, Trevon?" She turned and looked him in the eyes. "You haven't touched me since we had this issue, and every time you've come to visit your son, it's been when I'm not home. Now how is that not tripping?"

"What do you want me to do? How can I just forget that you lied to me to be with another dude? That shit hurts, Jurnee. If I didn't care about you, I wouldn't give a fuck who you slept with."

"You have a funny way of caring for anyone, Trevon!" she

shouted. "You act like you can't forgive me for one damn mistake! Okay, I fucked Big Diesel and I'm woman enough to admit my transgression!" She pointed at herself. "Can you do the same?"

"About what?" He frowned. "What am I wrong about?"

She stared at him, breathing hard. "Why are you hurting me like this? All I ever wanted for you was the best. I always kept it real with you!"

"Do you wanna be with Big Diesel?" he asked brusquely.

"No!" she shouted, close to tears. "And I'm not here to talk about him."

He sat down. "Okay, let's talk," he said.

"Please... tell me it's not true."

"What are you talking about? Just come out and ask me."

She wiped her eyes. "I came to surprise you that night you finished your film with Linda—"

"Why didn't you come?"

"Please tell me the truth," she said. "Tell me why Tahkiyah spent the night with you."

33

MY CONFESSION

Coconut Grove, Florida
Friday, August 21st

Trevon dropped his head in shame and wished he could redo his past. Because of his deepest secret, he now sat without the courage to speak.

"Please tell me you didn't fuck Kandi's mom, Trevon! What was she doing over here so late, and alone with you?" Jurnee glared, seething at him with tears running down her face. "How can you sit there and say nothing? Look at me!" she shouted.

He lifted his head and stared at the wall. He felt there weren't any words to say. *She'll never forgive me.* "It's true," he whispered.

"What's true?" She got in his face. "Man up and tell me!"

He sighed and met her gaze. "Please let me explain. I-"

"Now you want me to listen? Remember that shit you told me when I tried to *explain*? You told me to drop it because there wasn't shit to explain!"

He closed his eyes and took a deep breath. "I'm sorry."

"Damn right you are!" she yelled. "How could you do this to me! And to Kandi?"

"Let me explain, Jurnee."

"Did you fuck her, or not?"

"...Yeah...but it's-"

SMACK. She slapped him without an ounce of forbearance. "You sick motherfucker!"

He didn't move. "I know I'm wrong, and you have every right to be upset."

"Upset!" she raged. "You make me sick! How—"

"Please!" He shot to his feet. "Let me explain and I promise to tell you the truth."

She backed away from him with a disgusted expression. "Don't touch me."

He gave her the space she wanted. *I gotta tell her the truth and just pray that she won't tell LaToria.* "Remember when we first met Tahkiyah and how she lied to us?"

"What the fuck does that have to do with now? Were you fucking her back then, too!"

"Yes...yes, I was."

She covered her mouth in utter disbelief.

"I didn't know she was LaToria's mom, and she didn't know about me and LaToria. I swear it's the truth and—"

"It doesn't matter, Trevon!" she yelled. "You fucked her a few days ago! What's your excuse now? What's your fucking excuse, Trevon!" She left her tears unchecked as her heart raced.

"I fucked up, I understand," he said, defeated.

"Damn right you did! And here at times you had me thinking that Kandi wasn't deserving of you. You ain't shit, asshole! You fucking hear me?" she berated.

Trevon started with the truth. He told Jurnee about Tahkiyah's unannounced visit and the playful bet that led him to her room at the Mondrian. His confession drew a new batch of tears from Jurnee when he revealed a painful fact. On the day and time of her car accident, he had missed her phone call because he was with Tahkiyah.

The truth ran from his lips as he went on about his secret affair with Tahkiyah.

"I don't have an excuse," he admitted. "I don't want to hurt LaToria. You have to believe me, Jurnee. It's just—no excuse…" He sat down. "Are you gonna tell LaToria?"

Jurnee fingered a strand of loose hair behind her ear. "No," she said, feeling numb. "If she knew about this, it would destroy everything she has. And…I hate—I don't like how you took this risk… all for a piece of pussy. And Tahkiyah, she knows she's wrong!"

He leaned back and took in the favorable news. "How can I make this right?"

"End it! You have to stop this shit you're doing with Kandi's mom."

"I've tried. But she—"

"Bullshit!" Jurnee snapped. "She ain't forcing you to fuck her, so don't tell me no lame ass excuse. I mean it, okay? End this bullshit, or I will," she said firmly.

He didn't need to ask what she would do. Above all, he could not let LaToria know about the affair. "I'll do it," he pulled his phone out of his pocket.

"Walk me to my car. I have to get back to work." She headed for the door. "I trust you'll do what you need to do without me having to get involved. And you can tell her I know about everything, and as much as it irks me… I'll stay quiet."

"Do you hate me?"

She looked at him with crossed emotions. In truth, she was able to admit that her initial bond with him was built from lust. "No," she whispered. "You're human, Trevon. In life, you must learn from your mistakes. I know this life is so… twisted for you. You went to prison as a teen and came out into a world that wouldn't slow down for you." She touched his face and stared into his eyes. "Correct your wrong. Think about your kids, and the pain this will put on Kandi's heart."

On the road toward repairing their relationship, they hugged for a brief moment.

"I don't hate you," she said. "But I'm disappointed, and this will take some time to get over."

He kissed her on the forehead and walked her outside. He sincerely told her he was sorry and promised again to end the affair with Tahkiyah.

"I'll call you when I get off work," she said when she got behind the wheel of her Aston Martin DBX. "Oh yeah. What did Kandi surprise you with last night?"

"I'll let her tell you."

"Secrets, huh?"

"Something like that."

"I'll call her later. And hopefully you'll come to see your son while I'm home."

"Bring him over to LaToria's condo tonight. I'd like to have everyone together."

"Okay. And... gimme a kiss."

He leaned inside the SUV and slid his tongue into her mouth. It lasted for a few breaths before Jurnee pulled back with her face flushed.

"If I wasn't mad at you. I'd take you back inside and give you some BM number two loving."

"Stop calling yourself that." He slid the back of his hand down her face.

"It's the truth, and it—never mind. Just handle your business with Tahkiyah and know that I don't hate you."

"Okay, drive safe." Trevon felt the urge to say more.

She waved and blew him a kiss as she put the SUV in reverse. Trevon stood under the beaming midday sun until Jurnee's SUV turned the corner. He sighed and headed back inside. *Here goes nothing.* He thought when he flopped down on the sofa with his phone. *Her day is about to turn upside down.* Trevon dialed Tahkiyah's number and made up his mind to jump straight to the point.

"Ma!" Kandi shouted from the kitchen. "Your phone is ringing!"

"Phone ring! Phone ring!" Victoria yelled with her tiny arms wrapped around Kandi's leg.

Tahkiyah stepped out of her bedroom, frowning. "I thought I turned the ringer off! And why are you back so early from the gym?"

"Too many old men were too busy staring at my butt," Kandi answered as Tahkiyah grabbed her phone off the cocktail table.

Tahkiyah rubbed her tired eyes and hid her surprise when she saw Trevon's caller ID. *Why in the hell is he calling me? Knowing Kandi is around.* "Hello?" she answered as Kandi and Victoria remained in the kitchen.

"I got some bad news."

Tahkiyah sighed. "Hold on a sec. Let me step out on the balcony."

"LaToria nearby? I thought she went to the gym."

"Yeah. She's in the kitchen making a smoothie with Victoria. Said some old men were sweating her instead of sweating in the gym. Now what's the bad news?" she asked when she stepped out onto the balcony. "Geesh, it's hot out here!"

"Jurnee knows about us."

Tahkiyah grabbed the back of a white and blue deck chair to steady herself. "How—"

Trevon ended her worry and calmly told her what was up. Tahkiyah sat stunned on the deck chair, hoping he wouldn't end his words with any talk about Kandi, knowing of their scandalous actions.

"Does Kandi know anything about... us?" she interrupted before he could finish.

"No," Trevon answered. "Jurnee said she won't say anything and—"

"It doesn't matter!" She glanced over her shoulder. "We can't see each other again!"

"Uh, that's what I was going to say."

Tahkiyah took a deep breath. "I can't believe this." She stared at the beach below and tried to conceal her worry.

"It's true, Tahkiyah," Trevon's voice came flat.

She heard Victoria's playful scream from the kitchen behind her. "Are you still coming over here?"

"Yeah."

Tahkiyah rubbed her forehead. "I regret everything," she mumbled. "It's all my fault and I'm serious about things coming to an end between us."

"I agree. But don't try to shoulder all the blame because it wasn't all your fault."

She bit her bottom lip. "I'll get over you Trevon, and I hope we can get through this without any drama. My main focus will be on doing right by Kandi. And for all it's worth, I hope you can do the same."

Tahkiyah said a few more words, mostly assuring Trevon that she had the mindset to avoid having sex with him again. She ended the stressful call only a moment before Kandi and Victoria joined her on the balcony.

"What's wrong with you?" Kandi asked.

This will be my last time telling a lie. Tahkiyah forced a smile. "Just got off the phone with Anthony."

Kandi frowned and sat down on the matching deck chair. "Trevon's manager?"

"My ex from DC," Tahkiyah corrected.

"Oh. Y'all hooking back up?" Kandi asked as Victoria climbed up on Tahkiyah's lap.

"Never," she answered. "But he has other ideas."

Kandi shrugged and took a sip of a banana and orange juice smoothie.

"I'm glad you're done with porn," Tahkiyah adjusted Victoria on her lap.

"What *if* I went back to AEF, but only to make films with Trevon?"

Tahkiyah rolled her eyes. "There's more to you than making sex tapes. Not that I'm downing it—it's not something worth pointing out though."

Kandi thought about her future for a moment. *She has a point. But what can I do? I'm a high school dropout with just a tenth-grade education.* "Ma, I'm in my mid-twenties and I don't even have a GED."

"What's stopping you from getting it?" Tahkiyah asked. "And don't use little mama in my lap as an excuse because you know I'll watch her. Get your GED, baby."

Kandi knew she was capable of earning her GED. *Hell, even Trevon has his GED.* "I'll do it!"

Tahkiyah smiled. "And I know you can—"

Kandi's buzzing phone broke their conversation.

"Oh... shit." Kandi frowned at the caller ID on the screen.

"What's the matter?" Tahkiyah asked, as a strong breeze blew across the balcony.

Kandi smacked her lips and turned the screen in Tahkiyah's direction.

"Why is Conda calling you?" Tahkiyah asked.

"Shoot! I don't know," Kandi replied. "Ain't got nothing to say to him at all!"

Tahkiyah's temper rose. "Gimme the phone. I got an idea."

KENDRA REPLAYED Trevon's voicemail for the third time before she deleted it. She tossed the phone on the bed, sighed, and pushed her fingers through her hair. Five brisk steps carried her across the room and into the bathroom. She welcomed the silence inside the hotel room. Her plan involving Conda was set in motion. All she could do was sit and wait. Part of her was upset over Trevon, standing her up. She wanted to confront him and give him the chance to speak the truth. It troubled her deeply that he had something to do with Swagga's murder. She had no issue admitting the faults that hung over Swagga, but those faults didn't justify his murder. Even now, she was still driven to make Trevon suffer for the pain he had a part in. A pain she was reminded of when she laid eyes on her daughter.

She took her clothes off and jumped in the shower. *So, this is my life?* With revenge in her heart, she wondered how Conda would play his role?

JURNEE NEEDED SOME HARDCORE SEX, and Trevon easily filled her erotic thoughts. She sat alone in her office after ending her 3 p.m. meeting with Vanessa. Her mood was induced by viewing a few unedited sex scenes of the film Vanessa recently made with Trevon. Jurnee kept things on a professional level by critiquing Vanessa on what she did right and wrong in front of the camera. In truth, she was pleased with Vanessa's debut adult film. She assured Vanessa that she had a future at AEF, and they would plan to film her second project within two weeks.

Jurnee squeezed her thighs together and pulled up the unedited video on her laptop. Her favorite sex scene came in the middle of the 45-minute film. It began in a cozy bedroom setting, with Vanessa knelt between Trevon's strong legs. She turned the volume up so she could hear Vanessa breasts slapping against Trevon's body as she moved her natural breasts up and down his penis. Trevon sat at the foot of the bed, naked, and breathing hard as Vanessa's oily breasts sandwiched his penis.

Jurnee wrote the script, so she knew only another minute would slip by before the real action started. She remained fixed at the screen as her nipples tightened under the white fitting blouse. *I miss that dick.* She pinched her nipples and bit back her moan. On the screen, Vanessa kissed the tip of Trevon's dick, a close-up.

"Ms.Cruz," a familiar voice came from the intercom on the desk.

Jurnee paused the video. "Yes, Buffy?" She sat back in her chair and hid her displeasure of the interruption.

"You have a visitor. Well, actually, it's Kandi's mom," Buffy informed. "She said it's sorta urgent that she talk to you and she—"

"Send her in," Jurnee cut her receptionist off. "And hold any calls that might come in while she's in my office."

"Got it," Buffy replied.

Jurnee turned the laptop off and remained seated when a soft knock sounded at the door. "Come in. It's open," Jurnee said as she tried to conceal her resentment.

Tahkiyah entered the office with an impassive expression. She closed the door and took her stylish glasses off. "You know why I'm here."

Better not be to tell me you won't stop fucking Trevon! Jurnee thought as she nodded at the toffee-brown chair in front of her desk. "Where is Kandi?"

Tahkiyah folded her glasses and set them on her lap. "She's home. And I'm hoping we can keep this visit between us?"

Jurnee sat back in the chair and crossed her arms. "Haven't you caused enough drama by keeping things from Kandi?

"I'm not going to argue with you," Tahkiyah struggled to keep her cool.

"Then don't." Jurnee said coldly.

Tahkiyah overlooked Jurnee's attitude. "Everything Trevon told you is true. I came here to let you know to your face that it's over between Trevon and I. But most of all... thank you for not telling LaToria."

Jurnee glared at Tahkiyah, biting the harsh words she wanted to spew. "How could you do it?" She cocked an eyebrow. "And don't tell me no bullshit!"

"I wasn't—I didn't know about Trevon's relationship with Latora when I first met him."

Jurnee rolled her eyes. "Whatever. I'm talking about recently... last Saturday."

"What can I say to you to ease your feelings? Nothing. I did it. I fucked my daughter's man... more than once. I'm not happy about it."

Jurnee sighed and tried to relax. *Being pissed at her isn't going to make things better. Hell, I almost lost my bond with Kandi over Trevon too.* "I hate to admit it. But I understand," Jurnee said, uncrossing her arms.

"Good," Tahkiyah nodded. "Now tell me why I should trust you with this secret?"

34

TODAY AND FOREVER

Coconut Grove, Florida
Friday, August 21st

"How did the meeting go with Jurnee?" Trevon asked Vanessa as he dried off from his shower in the bathroom.

"Great!" Vanessa's voice filled the bathroom. "I'll do my second film with Big Diesel and Shocka Long next week."

Trevon glanced at his smartphone on the sink. "A threesome?" he grinned. "You think you're ready for it?"

She giggled. "I'm a big girl, Mr. Sex Scene," she answered jokingly. "And Shocka has invited me to dinner tonight. I guess he wants to get to know me before we start the film."

"What about Big Diesel?"

"Oh, I met him today. We sat and talked at AEF after I spoke to Jurnee. He seems cool and about his business."

I bet he is. Trevon knew it wouldn't be professional to tell Vanessa about the issue he had with Big Diesel. He believed in Jurnee, and in time he would get over the one-night affair she had with him.

"What are you doing tonight?" she asked, breaking his thoughts.

"Uh, spending some time with my kids. And then I gotta review the new script for my next film with Chelsea," he replied as he toweled off his chest.

"I thought y'all already had it?"

"We did. But Jurnee made a bunch of changes so it's kinda new."

"I pitched the idea to Jurnee about Chelsea and me doing a threesome with you. We wanna get on some bondage shit and tie yo'sexy ass up."

"What did she say?"

"She loved it!" Vanessa's voice jumped from the speakerphone. "Said she would run the idea by your manager."

Trevon smiled. "I'm down with it."

"And one more thing. Jurnee asked me about doing an anal scene with Big Diesel and Shocka Long," she said. "I, um, said yes. However... I want my first anal scene to be with you."

Trevon couldn't stop his ego from swelling. It matched the growth between his legs. "How did she take that?"

"She's cool with it. She suggested we could do it in the threesome film with Chelsea."

"You really want me to tap that ass, huh?"

"Definitely, baby. You know your girl Chelsea done told me how good you can stroke it." She giggled again. "Plus I watched the film y'all did, and I want to see what you can do with my Butter Buns."

"Hmm, that's something I'll be looking forward to."

"I was hoping you would feel that way. And you know I didn't enjoy that condom you had to wear when we did our penetration scenes. You spoiled me with that raw dick. Damn, my pussy is getting hot."

"Where you at?"

"On my way to get my hair and nails done. But if you're wanting to get some private time with me... I'll leave it up to you, baby. I'll text you after my date with Shocka Long and we'll see what we can figure out."

Trevon ended the call and threw on a white and blue Gucci tracksuit. The tank top clung to his muscular upper body, emphasizing his bulging arms and thick forearms. He checked his appearance in the mirror and stepped out the door at 5 p.m.

Being a father taught Trevon there was more to life than large-hipped women and hardcore sex. When he backed out of the driveway, he had his mind set on spending time with his kids. With his guard down, he didn't notice the white Porsche 911 Turbo S parked along the curb down the street. Simply put, it was an ordinary sight to see a six-figure car in the gated community. Again, Trevon didn't give the car a glance as he sped off in his sleek S580. The driver in the Porsche waited behind the tinted windows and didn't pull off until Trevon turned the corner. For now, the 911 kept a distance from the S580. Out of sight, out of mind.

KENDRA SLID a strand of hair from her forehead as she grabbed her ringing phone off the dresser. "Hello?" she answered, wearing only a pair of panties and a bra.

"Hi, Ms. Paige. I hope I'm not calling at a bad time?" Detective Payne asked.

Kendra stepped over her Manolo Blahnik shoes and sat on the edge of the bed. She had to stay on point by not letting the detective know she was in Miami. "What's up? I assume you have some news about the investigation?"

"Indeed, I do. For starters, the FBI has delayed their arrest warrant for Jamilah until we make an arrest on our main suspect."

"And you still won't tell me who that suspect is?"

"It's an ongoing investigation, Ms. Paige. Please be assured that you will be the first to know when an arrest is made. Also, I spoke to Mr. Harrison and to state the least, he wasn't much help. Our next step is to bring him and LaToria in for official questioning about the case."

"When?"

"I'm not absolutely sure because I'm working in step with the FBI."

Kendra looked at the time showing on the phone: 6:48 p.m. "I assume I'll have to pay that guy the reward money *if* what he is saying is the truth. What's his name again?"

"Um, let me check my notes right quick."

Kendra heard the shuffling of papers. *Hurry up bitch.*

"Here it is. It's Vontay Bennett, aka Veto."

"And he's still in the Browned County Jail?"

"At the moment, yes."

"So, the feds haven't officially picked up his case?"

"Not yet. They're waiting to see if he's telling the truth about the murder for hire plot."

Kendra drew a long, deep breath and closed her eyes. "Just keep me posted."

"I intend to do just that, Ms. Paige."

Kendra ended the call. She felt the need to make her own moves. Moves that would supply her with all the answers she wanted. She made a call to an old friend at the Broward County Jail. The line was connected after the third ring.

"Broward County Jail. How may I direct your call?"

"Good evening. I'd like to speak with Chief Jailer, Richard Wheeler, please?"

Kendra lay back on the bed as she was put on hold. *I hope this shit will work.*

"Chief Wheeler, speaking."

Kendra rolled to her side. "Hey, stranger! It's me, Kendra."

"Hey! Long time no hear."

"Put the blame on me."

"It's okay. I've been keeping up on you a little since you left the parole and probation. By the way, I'm sorry for your loss."

Kendra was silent for a brief period. "Thank you."

"What can I do for ya?"

"I need a favor Richard, and I'll be honest with you."

"Okay, what is it?"

"You have a guy locked up by the name Vontay Bennett. I need to visit him, but it can't go on any records. I need to slip in and out without being seen."

"I know all about Mr. Bennett and I'm aware of what's going on, Kendra. You want to talk to him about Swagga's murder case, huh?"

"I already said that I'll be honest, so yeah, it's true."

"Feds are in and out of here, and it wouldn't be a good idea to do this. Let the—"

"I'll pay you," she said. "I must talk to him as soon as possible. Please!"

"I'm sorry. I can't take the—"

"Five grand."

Silence.

She knew he needed the money.

"Can you get here by eight o'clock tonight before my shift ends?"

She sat up. "Yeah."

"Okay, get here as soon as you can and text me when you reach the jail. And if possible, could you have the money in cash?"

"I can do that. And thank you, I really appreciate this."

~

AT THE SAME TIME, Trevon slid back from LaToria's kitchen table. "I'm full!" he said with his third empty plate of lasagna in front of him. LaToria turned from the sink and smiled. "I'm glad you enjoyed it, Smooch."

"What's for dessert?" he asked.

"Me." She giggled as Tahkiyah entered the kitchen with Tayvon in her arms. Trevon stood and glanced toward the living room. "Why is Victoria still up?"

"Because she ain't tired," LaToria replied as she turned back to the sink. Tahkiyah nodded in agreement. "That girl is a mess, for real. LaToria, Jurnee said to fix a bowl of gumbo so she can take home for Ariana."

Trevon exchanged a quick glance at Tahkiyah as she reached inside the stainless-steel refrigerator for Tayvon's bottle. What they shared in secret was dead. A fire that once burned, now had no heat. When Tahkiayh went back to the living room, Trevon cleared the table and helped LaToria with the dishes.

"Uh, why aren't you using the dishwasher?" Trevon asked, as he leaned against the kitchen island.

"This is relaxing," she answered. "I hardly ever use the dishwasher."

"You cooked that lasagna all by yourself?"

"Sure did..."

"Well, it was good."

"Thanks, Smooch."

"Hey, did you tell Jurnee that you're pregnant?"

She shook her head. "Not yet. You know she would've said something about it while we were eating. But, we did speak on some other things while you were giving the kids a bath."

"Like what?"

LaToria set a clean plate in the rack and turned around. "We talked about a lot of things. Important things that we can't ignore." She grabbed a pink towel to dry her hands.

"Are you gonna tell me about it?"

"It's about our present and future."

He strolled around the kitchen island and trapped LaToria between his arms. His hands clutched the edge of the sink. "You, Victoria, Tayvon and Jurnee are my present, and future."

She gazed up at him. "I know, Smooch," she replied softly. "And you know how I feel about you." She smiled for a second and sighed in the next breath.

"What's wrong?"

"Conda called me today. And before you blow up, he called to see if I would ask Janelle to give him another chance at AEF. And I told him to go to hell!"

"I'll call his ass and tell him not to—"

"My mom took care of it. She already warned him not to call me again."

Trevon wasn't satisfied. *I'll pay that muthafucka another visit.*

"Let it go, Smooch. I see it in your eyes," she said. "We already have enough problems as it is with this mess behind Swagga."

"Okay. But, promise to let me know if he calls you again."

"I blocked his number. But I promise to tell you if he calls me from a different number."

"And if he tried—I mean, tries to reach you on Facebook, Twitter, Instagram and any other site."

"I promise," she said. "Now go and brush your teeth because your breath is smelling like lasagna."

He grinned. "I bet it'll smell better if I had your poo-poo on my breath."

"Why bet when you know that's a fact?" She kissed him on his lips. "Do me a favor."

"What's up?" he asked, enjoying the feel of her breasts pressed up against his chest.

"Go and run a bath for me. Make it hot and drop in a few of my peach scented bath salts in the water—"

"And then you'll tell me what—"

"I'm not finished, Smooch." She looked at him. "After you fix my bath. I want you to light some of my vanilla scented candles and then I want you to join me, okay?"

He slid his hands from the sink and down to her hips. "Anything else?"

She smiled faintly and thought about what she had planned for him tonight. "That's all Smooch. Thank you."

He gave her soft, wide hips a gentle squeeze and turned to fulfill her request.

Later, at 7:47 p.m., Trevon had his nude frame soaking in LaToria's oversize bathtub. Everything was set, vanilla scented candles, the soft music by H.E.R. and Trevon's thirst for LaToria. All that was needed was her presence. He had the lights off, leaving the seven candles to provide the light. Tonight, he wanted to show how true his desire stood. He sat up a bit when he heard the bedroom door close. A moment later, LaToria ambled into the bathroom with two wine glasses and a bottle of Armadale Vodka. He was speechless at the sight of her nudeness. The marvel of her in the nude moved him just as it did when they took their first intimate shower together. He gazed at the split of her ass as she set the bottle and glasses on the sink. She stood barefooted, with only a sheen of lotion on her voluptuous redbone figure.

"LaToria—"

"I'm Kandi tonight," she said over her shoulder as she filled the first glass.

He couldn't pull his eyes from her ass. "Baby, I ain't tryna spoil the mood, but I don't think you should be drinking while you're pregnant."

She ignored him and poured the drink into the second glass. "Relax, Smooch. I got this."

"I'm serious... Kandi," he replied tightly.

She turned around and slid her hands up to her heavy 34 DDs. "Stand up." She released a husky moan as she pinched her nipples.

He stared at her breasts as he stood up in the tub. The water dripped off his muscular frame and between his legs stood a jutting erection. Kandi licked her lips as she stared at the length and thickness of it. "Close your eyes so you can experience something really special. And don't open them until I say so."

He closed his eyes. "I know I'm gonna enjoy this."

"I love sucking your dick, Smooch," Kandi purred. "And I love how it feels sliding in my mouth."

He kept his eyes shut and released a throaty moan when a soft hand wrapped around his growth. A breath later, he felt a wet tongue racing around the throbbing tip of his penis. “Yeah.” he moaned, eyes still shut. “Do it nice and s-slow, baby.”

“We will, Smooch,” Kandi answered. “Now look at what you can have today and forever.”

He opened his eyes and was rocked back on his heels from the scene before him.

35

3 + 1= ANOTHER

Miami Beach, Florida
Saturday, August 22nd

Early the next morning at 7:25a.m. a mellifluous moaning repeated itself behind the closed door of LaToria's bedroom.

"Trevon! Mmmm!" Jurnee moaned on her back as he flicked his tongue gently up and down the split of her wet labia. Her body quivered from his tongue and the way it dug inside her sweet hole. She gasped in her next breath as Kandi slurped her left nipple in and out of her mouth. "Don't s-stop!" Jurnee whimpered and reached down to rub Trevon's muscular shoulders.

The threesome moved as one, licking, sucking, rubbing and feeding their needs before the sun rose. Their erotic actions were a continuation from last night. Trevon shared himself evenly between Jurnee and Kandi. Last night marked the first time he had the pleasure of sexing them at the same time. His raw thrusts sealed their unique bond as he mated with his queens. A chorus of moans met his ears when he kissed his way up Jurnee's body. He met Kandi above Jurnee's breasts and shared a passionate kiss, sharing the taste of Jurnee's honey on his lips and tongue.

Jurnee squeezed Kandi's left breast as Trevon hooked her right leg over his arm. His slow insertion robbed her of her breath. "Mmm, gimme all that dick." She gasped as his erection inched deeper inside her pussy. She held her breath until his balls settled on her ass.

"Take that dick, Honey Drop," Kandi whispered in Jurnee's ear.

Trevon began to conquer Jurnee with a series of headlong thrusts. Propped up on his arms, he stared at her olive breasts heaving up and down. He ignored the slight pain of her ivory fingernails digging into his biceps.

Jurnee felt his balls smacking the back of her ass as Kandi sucked on her neck.

Jurnee closed her eyes and submitted herself to her two lovers. She welcomed the strong pounding from Trevon, that took all of her tension away. Stroke by stroke, she became one again with the man inside her.

"Ohh, Trevon! I'm cummin', I'm almost there!" Jurnee announced several minutes later, with Trevon still working inside her pink walls.

He groaned and shortened his strokes to stimulate her G-spot. Her wetness covered his dick entirely and left a white froth around his base.

"Fuck that pussy, Smooch." Kandi slapped Trevon on the ass as she knelt beside him. "Let her cum all over your dick so I can suck it all off." She slapped his tight chocolate ass again and stuck her tongue in his ear.

Trevon sped up, stroking Jurnee with a purpose. He tried to crawl up inside her.

"Trevon!" Jurnee shouted, pushing against his ripped stomach. "I'm cummin'. Oohh, shit you tearing it up!"

"It's my p-pussy!" he roared as Kandi sucked gently on his ear.

Jurnee bit her bottom lip when the tip of her sudden climax exploded. Her breasts continued to heave as Trevon's hard-driving strokes continued. She moaned under him, whimpering her words of high gratification. When she swam through the waves of her orgasm, she turned her focus on him. "Cum inside me!" She slid her hands up to his chest. "Please do it."

He wanted this life. In no form did he see himself having to choose between Kandi or Jurnee. He came in mid breath, losing himself inside Jurnee for the third time, counting from last night.

Kandi stayed true to her words. She threw her leg over Jurnee's face and waited for Trevon to pull his dick out. She took him inside her mouth as soon as his tip emerged from Jurnee's pussy. As she slurped softly back and forth, she enjoyed the teasing licks of Jurnee's tongue cutting through her soaked folds. Kandi kept her lips circled around her man as Jurnee palmed her generous ass and nibbled on her pussy lips.

Trevon remained on his knees, making love to Kandi's warm mouth. He grabbed a handful of her left butt cheek and squeezed it until she started humming around his flesh. Glancing down, he noticed how her lips slid along his span. He wasn't surprised to see her fingers pumping in and out of Jurnee's thoroughly sexed pussy. Today, he came to understand that Kandi wanted the best of both worlds. And the same was expressed by Jurnee. He closed his eyes as Kandi's lips skated back and forth along his engorged penis.

"So y'all two are serious about doing this?" Trevon asked an hour later as he sat with his elbows on the kitchen island.

"Yeah," Kandi answered as she rubbed Jurnee's ass on her way to the freezer.

"It's true," Jurnee added as she searched the refrigerator. "Look up the word ménage à trois."

"I'll tell'im," Kandi said from across the kitchen. "It means a bond between three people living together and fucking," she said. "And sucking," she added.

"And our bond is special," Jurnee turned, leaving her pink

bathrobe open. "We all love each other, and we can share each other."

"Share?" Trevon raised an eyebrow. "Ain't sharing y'all with no fucking body. You can dead all the ideas of swinging and—"

"That's not what I meant. I'm talking about the three of us." Jurnee closed the refrigerator with her elbow. "We'll understand your career in porn. But you will have to live with us." Jurnee smirked.

Trevon glanced at Kandi across the kitchen. All she had on was a pair of purple panties that dug nicely into her fleshy ass. "Let me get this straight... so there won't be any misunderstanding... y'all want to live under one roof? Me, the kids and—"

"Us." Kandi strolled up to Jurnee and kissed her on the lips. "Oh, yeah... and my mom. She'll watch the kids because I'm going back to school." She stood beside Jurnee and waited for Trevon's reaction.

"School? What for?"

"To get my GED. Then I'll..." Kandi shrugged. "I'll think of something."

Trevon sat up and crossed his arms. "Y'all better not be playing any games."

"Baby hush," Jurnee giggled. "We are dead serious about doing this. I love you and Kandi. What's wrong with having you both?"

"And..." Trevon paused as he tried to suppress his grin. "Uh, will we sleep in the same bed? Or will I have to take turns sleeping with y'all?"

Jurnee rolled her eyes. "We'll sleep in the same, but a new, very large bed."

Trevon couldn't believe the lifestyle he lived. "Uh, I gotta think about this."

Kandi sucked her teeth. "Naw the hell you don't," she retorted. "I know your ass is down for it, so stop fronting."

Damn, she knows me too well. Trevon smiled. "Okay, that's all true. But, ain't nobody said a word about Ariana."

A flash of unhappiness changed Jurnee's expression. She

sighed. "To be honest... things have been rocky between us since our fight. It's like she took a step back from me and put up this wall. Anyway, we had a long talk about it, and she wants to go back to school and get her degree."

Kandi consoled Jurnee by easing her arm around her waist. "It's okay, baby."

Trevon knew it would take some time for Jurnee to get over Ariana.

"Can you love us the same, Smooch?" Kandi asked.

Jurnee lifted her head off Kandi's shoulder and said, "Donde seis pueden comer, siete pueden comer."

Trevon shook his head. "What does that mean?"

"Where six can eat, seven can eat," Jurnee explained. "It's a Spanish idiom that's sorta like what you would say in English. There's always room for one more. I know you can love us both."

He moved around the kitchen island wearing a pair of briefs and eased his arms around their waist. The mixture of their perfume filled his nose, strawberry and lemon.

"No more secrets between us," Jurnee said. "And that goes for the both of you. Y'all didn't need to keep that Swagga issue from me."

Kandi sighed. "She's right, Smooch."

Trevon nodded. "We'll go and talk to the lawyer on Monday."

"Good." Jurnee rubbed his chest. "I don't want any stress in our future. Day by day is how we will move, together, but don't expect things to always be peachy."

Kandi glanced at the time on the microwave, 8:18a.m. "My mom will bring the kids back from the hotel in two hours." She grinned seductively and winked at Jurnee. "Are you thinking what I'm thinking, girl?"

Jurnee blushed. "Si." She slid the bathrobe off her bare shoulders. "I don't like it to be uneven."

Trevon knew it was time to please his queens. But he was confused by Jurnee's *uneven remark*. "Uneven?"

"Si. Three is uneven." Jurnee licked her lips. "Make it even and give me another baby."

KENDRA HAD A CHOICE TO MAKE, but time to wasn't on her side. She sat behind the wheel of her idling Rolls-Royce Wraith, drumming her fingernails on the center console. She took in the view of Bayfront Park from the comfort of her air-conditioned coupe. The midday sun had the temperature in the high 90s forcing most to stay in the shade.

"Where the fuck is this fool?" she muttered as she scanned the parking lot. When she didn't see the white Porsche 911 Turbo S, she frowned. As she continued to wait, she thought about her secret visit with Veto last night.

Facing the facts, she realized that all she learned from Veto was what he was told by another. The fact of Veto not being present at Swagga's murder filled Kendra with doubt. *Motherfucker is trying to save his own ass. And the two people he fingered for the murder are missing. How convenient!* Through the midst of her anger, she thought about Trevon's actions. *How can I blame him for anything? Swagga's dumbass should've left Kandi the fuck alone.*

Last night she had grilled Veto for the truth. She learned from him that Nashlly had murdered Swagga, but again his words had come from the next man, Art. *What if he told Veto a lie?* Kendra wasn't firm on a bunch of *"he told me what happened"* bullshit. The more she thought about the entire issue, she felt confused and conflicted toward Trevon. But still, she was extremely upset over the possibility of him knowing key details of Swagga's murder. Again, she had a choice to make. Move forward with her plans for Trevon's downfall, or call Conda off and let the future take care of itself?

At the same time, lunch was being served at the Broward County Jail. Veto remained on his bunk, staring at the ceiling, contemplating the pros and cons about telling the feds about his visit with Kendra. He wanted his freedom and that reward money. *I hope Art ain't tell me no bullshit.* Veto felt like he has been played and was left out of the lick on Swagga's murder. When it was all said and done, Veto received only $10,000 from Art. *And that muthafucka got half a mil! And Nashlly got one point five million! Them greedy muthafuckas ain't-*

"Bennett!" A cute, brown skinned female jailer tapped on the cell door. "You want your lunch tray?"

Veto sat up, hating every breath of being behind bars. "What's on it?"

"Fried fish, cornbread, baked beans and some kind of cake."

Veto sighed. "Yeah," he said, frowning. "And remember to bring me some paper on your next round."

Veto received the plastic tray through a slot on the door. He hated the food, the smell of the jail, the jailers, the inmates, everything! Whatever it took to regain his freedom, he would do it. He had no loyalty to Art, and the same went for Nashlly. *Hell, everybody was snitching.* Veto grinned with high hopes that he would skip any time in prison. The feds and that fine ass detective from Miami had assured him that his information wouldn't go unrewarded. As he popped the lid off the tray, he tried to think of any spots where Art and Nashlly could be hiding. Their arrest would push him one step closer to regaining his freedom.

The smell of the fried fish didn't match how bland it looked. *I gotta get the fuck up out of here!* He took a bite of the fried fish and stared at the floor. Eat, sleep, shit, snitch and masturbate. Veto viewed his days in jail as such. He forced the shitty food down and placed the empty tray near the door. *Fuck this shit. I'ma tell the feds about my heroin connect, too!*

BACK IN MIAMI, Conda felt giddy about his improvised plan that related to Trevon. He had his smartphone turned off, using the silence inside the 911 to maintain his focus. *Kendra gonna bug the fuck out when I call'er ass back with the word on what I'ma do.* He sat low in the leather seat with the tinted windows up. From his position, he had a clear view of the hotel lobby from across the parking lot. His eyes darted from the lobby and landed on the dark silver BMW M850i to this left. A glint off the opening lobby door drew his attention back toward the hotel. He sat up and licked his ashy lips when he saw Kandi's mom exiting the hotel. She wasn't alone, and he figured she would act right in her actions to save Trevon's kids. He eased the door open as Tahkiyah carried Victoria and pushed Tayvon in a covered stroller. He saw the two car seats in the back seat of the BMW and planned to make his move when she was strapping the kids into their seats.

He rubbed his nose, wishing he had another hit of cocaine. His heart drummed in his ears as Tahkiyah reached the BMW. His hand flexed on the rubber grip of a pistol when the BMW was remotely started. *I'ma see if this bitch got some fly shit to say when I put this iron on her back!* He rubbed his nose again and thought about all the tough talk Tahkiyah had spat in his ear over the phone. He took a deep breath and pulled the slide back, racking a round into the chamber. The cocaine had him on his bullshit, and the rush had yet to settle.

TREVON WAS SPENT after his sexual episodes with Jurnee and Kandi.

"Trevon!" Kandi nudged his shoulder. "Wake up!"

He sat up on the sofa, rubbing his eyes. "What's up?"

"Look at the time!" She shoved the screen of her phone in his face.

He frowned, trying to recall if he had promised to do something by a certain time. The digital time showed 12:48 p.m. *What was I supposed to do today?*

"My mom still isn't here. And she's not answering my calls!" Kandi panicked.

He slid a hand down his face. "Relax baby," he said. "Maybe she's on her way and she don't wanna drive and talk on the-"

"She had a hands-free calling system, Trevon."

Before he could reply, Jurnee entered the living room.

"What did the hotel say?" Kandi asked.

Jurnee sighed. "She checked out thirty minutes ago."

"And the hotel is only a six- or ten-minute drive from here," Kandi said. "And we both tried to call and text her, Trevon," she added with tears welling.

Jurnee nodded. "Something isn't right. I just—"

"We all need to calm down," Trevon said. "What time was she supposed to be back?"

Jurnee and Kandi stared at each other.

"Somebody say something!" Trevon demanded.

"Noon," Kandi answered. "We told her to bring the kids back at noon because Tayvon has a checkup today."

Trevon knew he had to maintain his calm. "Give'er one more hour, okay? Hell, she might be on the way up in the elevator right now. Keep calling and—"

Jurnee shook her head. "Something isn't right," she said. "I have—we have to do more."

Trevon closed his eyes. *God. Please let my kids and Tahkiyah be safe. Please!*

36

DOUBLE CROSS

Miami, Florida
Saturday, August 22nd

Two hours later, 3 p.m., Trevon exited the hotel where Tahkiyah had spent the night with the kids. He dreaded the call he had to make to Kandi and Jurnee. He hurried across the parking lot and back to his S580. Once inside, he took a moment to pray. *Dear God. Please let my kids be okay. I know I haven't been in touch with you like I should. But please don't let my kids or Tahkiyah suffer on the account of me. In Jesus' name I pray, Amen.* After a deep, troubled sigh, he grabbed his phone off his lap. Checking his phone, he saw he had three text messages.

Vanessa = *Hey u! sorry I didn't get back wit you last nite. Shocka kept me out all nite. N-E way, I'll make it up 2 u.*

Linda = *Just thinking about u. Call Me soon.*

Kandi = *Call me Asap! My mom still hasnt showed up!*

Trevon had forgotten all about Vanessa. He started the engine and called Kandi with hopes that his prayer would be answered after the first ring. "Is she at the hotel? And why didn't you answer my calls?"

"I left my phone in the car, baby. And no, she's not here. I even went up to the room with the manager and she opened the door for me."

"Something is wrong."

Trevon closed his eyes. "Please don't think like that, okay?"

"Um... Jurnee thinks it's time for us to call the police."

"Do it." He opened his eyes.

"I'm s-scared, Smooch." Kandi's voice broke on the verge of tears.

"I am too, baby. God knows I am."

~

KENDRA RUSHED OUT of the bathroom and grabbed her ringing phone off the bed. She smacked her lips when she saw Conda's caller ID on the screen.

"Where the fuck you been?" she snapped. "I was waiting for your ass at Bayfront Park and you didn't show up! I'm not paying you to—"

"Chill." He cut her off. "I got some good news. Where you at?"

She sighed with a hand on her waist. "I'm back at my room. What's the good news?"

"I, uh, did a major remix on the plan you had for Trevon."

Kendra frowned. "What the fuck did you do?"

"I couldn't catch him slipping. But I caught a few that are dear to him. Matter of fact, I pulled something off that will bring him to his knees."

"Talk!" she snapped.

"I got his kids, and Kandi's mom."

What the fuck! "Uh...say what," she said with her heart hammering. "Tell me you're bullshitting."

"I'm dead ass. I got'er tied up in the back and the kids are in the bathroom."

"Are t-they okay? The kids?" *Oh my god! What have I done?*

"Yeah. I left them some blankets and stuff like that. And—"

"Conda! Listen to me," Kendra said. "Make sure those kids are okay. You need to keep an eye on them at *all* times, you hear me."

"Okay. But you gotta help me with this. Now you can get Trevon to do just about anything you want. And I can—"

"Who knows that you have his kids and Kandi's mom?"

"Uh, just you. Oh, yeah. I left the Porsche at the hotel and jacked Kandi's mom for her ride."

Kendra sat at the foot of the bed. "Where are you?"

"I'm at Fourside Trailer Park near the airport."

"Whose trailer is it?"

"We're good here. Nobody knows I'm here, but you, okay? You can trust me on that. Now, whatcha wanna do now?"

She stood. "Conda… for this to work, you must not change any further plans that are put in place. This is very serious now. Do you understand?"

"Yeah," Conda sighed. "I'll do it. So, what's the next move?"

"We'll show Trevon what true pain is, okay? You did good, okay? And, um, I'll triple the amount I said I would pay you. Now give me the address so I can get over there and get this shit started."

"WHY IS a pretty bitch like yourself packing iron?" Conda sneered at Tahkiyah with her 9-millimeter in his hand. "You tough or something?"

Tahkiyah stared at the floor with tears blurring her eyes.

"Hmm, I wonder if you taste as sweet as Kandi? You know… like mother, like daughter." He laughed.

Tahkiyah's only concern was the kids. She would do whatever he asked, as long as it kept breath inside Victoria and Tayvon. "What do you want from m-me?"

"This ain't about you, baby girl. This beef is behind Trevon. I'm just the man in the middle right now. And when it's all said and done." He smiled. "Trevon ain't gonna be on top no more. We'll see how real he is when he has to pick his fate, yours, or his kids."

Tahkiyah blinked her tears away. "W-what will you do?"

He shrugged. "It ain't on me. But when the time comes. And it will be soon. Our boy Trevon will have to make a choice. His life... yours, or his seeds. Shit, you know the deal, baby girl. Somebody gotta die." He raised the pistol to her head and calmly pulled the trigger.

~

"WHY IS THIS HAPPENING TO US?!" Jurnee sobbed on the sofa with Kandi.

Her heartrending question hung in the air, met with a wall of silence. Trevon sat at the table, staring at his phone, willing it to ring with a call from Tahkiyah. The reality of her unknown whereabouts with his kids was a tough weight to lift. He fought back tears when 7:01 p.m. showed on the screen of his phone. The police had left three hours ago, and their visit only added to his anger and stress. He hated to hear that nothing official could be done until Tahkiyah was missing for 24 hours.

Kandi and Jurnee pleaded for an exception to the rule for the sake of Victoria and Tayvon. When the police posed the question of Tahkiyah kidnapping the kids, Kandi started to cry. In the end, they all agreed to issue an Amber alert with the description of her BMW. *When* she was found, they would settle everything out. Each second was a moment Trevon hated to be away from his kids. The sense of helplessness had him hating the world. When his phone buzzed, he stared unmoved at the sight of Kendra's name on the caller ID. He tapped the ignore icon, sending the call to his voicemail.

~

"SHIT," Kendra muttered as her call to Trevon went unanswered. *I can't take the risk of leaving a voicemail or text. This shit might blow up in my face.* She had to figure something out before it was too late. She switched lanes on I-95 South and made a second call to an old friend at the probation and parole office. *Please be in the office.*

"Hello?"

"Althea! Hey girl, it's me, Kendra."

"Kendra! Heey! What's up?"

"A lot of stress right now. I need a serious favor."

"Name it. And thank you again for helping me out with my money issues."

"That was from my heart, Althea. Okay, you remember that guy, Trevon Harrison, that I had on my case load three years ago when he first got out of prison?"

"How can anyone forget about him? He's the porn star."

"Yeah. Anyway, I need you to pull up his old file and give me his mom's or sister's phone number."

"Girl, that's nothing. Just gimme a second to turn my computer back on because I was just about to walk out the door."

Kendra glanced at her speed and back to the road. *Last thing I need is to be pulled over for speeding.* She slowed the Wraith from 89 to 85 as Althea came back on the line.

"You want both numbers?"

"Yes, please."

~

THIRTY MINUTES LATER, Trevon lifted his head off his folded arms on the dining table. His phone buzzed with a call from his sister.

"What's up, sis?" he said, dejected.

"You doing okay down there?"

He sighed and sat up in the chair. "I'm doing the best I can. Can't say the same for LaToria and Jurnee. They're taking this pretty hard."

Angie cleared her throat. "Are the police still there?"

"Nah."

"Okay, I have something to tell you and I want you to trust me," she said. "I just got a call from some girl that wants you to meet her in front of Perez Art Museum as soon—"

"Sis! My kids are missing! Why would I go and—"

"It's about my niece and nephew, okay?" Angie's voice was firm. "You can't call the police and don't mention this to Kandi or Jurnee."

"Who called you?"

"I don't know. But she claims she knows where my niece and nephew are."

"What about Tahkiyah?" he asked, keeping his voice low.

"She didn't say anything about her."

"Tell me exactly what she said."

"She said for me to tell you that you have no other option but to meet her tonight. You can't call the police and you're to go alone. She said it's in a public area so you have nothing to worry about. And you gotta drive your Mercedes. She said she'll approach you once she is sure that you're alone."

"What about my kids? Are they safe?"

"I asked her. But all she would say was she would tell you. I'm not feeling this at all and I'm scared, Trevon."

"What time do I need to be at Perez Art Museum?"

"You got an hour. I just got off the phone with her. She stressed that you don't call the police."

Trevon glanced toward the living room. "And she didn't ask for any money?" he asked as Kandi and Jurnee sat in stunned silence on the sofa.

"No. And that's what got me having a funny feeling about this."

He stood. "I don't have a choice, sis."

"Yes, you do. We always have a choice."

TREVON HATED the point of keeping Jurnee and LaToria in the dark. He sat inside his Mercedes-Benz with the windows down, waiting for someone to come up to his car. The scene across the street was serene at the well-lit Perez Art Museum. People strolled under the imported date palm trees that lined the sidewalk. From where he sat, he could smell the bay and the different exotic cuisines that were being cooked.

His S580 didn't stand out amongst the Lamborghinis, Ferraris, Porche's and McLarens, it simply blended in with the downtown Miami scene. He shifted in the seat and adjusted the Glock under his left leg. He waited, treating each unknown face that neared his ride as a suspect. All that mattered to him were his kids. Just a fleeting thought of losing them caused his eyes to tear up.

A horn blew down the street behind him. His eyes darted to the rearview mirror. An uber pulled to the curb and picked up a mixed couple. He couldn't relax. He didn't want to. He thought of LaToria and Jurnee, his kids and what they all meant to him. There was no life without them. Just as the Uber drove off, a distinctive set of headlights filled his rearview mirror. A Rolls-Royce. Trevon waited for the headlights to turn off.

A minute went by. The car sat behind him with its engine running. He grew suspicious and eased the Glock from under his leg. He waited, eyes fixed on the rearview mirror.

~

KENDRA STRUGGLED with her next move as she sat behind the wheel of her Wraith. Thinking of what her heart compelled her to do, she turned the engine off. Her heart jumped in her throat when she stepped out of the car and walked up to the driver's side door of the Benz. She took a deep breath, having no idea what to expect from a man she didn't understand.

"Please tell me you're out here for the nightlife, Kendra?" Trevon said, with the window down.

Kendra sighed and fingered her hair from her face. "I called your sister."

"Where are my kids?"

"Safe."

He slid a hand down his face. "Kendra, I don't have the patience to play games with you, okay? Seriously, what the fuck is this bullshit about?"

"I'll explain along the ride to get your kids. But you'll have to ride with me."

"And why should I trust you?!"

"You don't have a choice."

~

CONDA LOWERED the volume on the TV when a beam of headlights brighten the living room window. He jumped up off a tattered cloth sofa and rushed to the window with the .45 held along his leg. He squinted from the bright headlights as he peeked through a slit in the curtains. A moment later, the lights went off, giving the stage back to the moonlight. He stayed posted at the window until Kendra stepped out of the Wraith.

"Did he show up?" Conda asked Kendra as soon as she strolled through the door.

"Yes, and everything is going just as I planned." She closed the door and glanced at the .45 in his hand. "Where are the kids? I told you to keep an eye—"

"In the back room," he said. "They're asleep."

Kendra closed the door. "I got some baby food and diapers out in the car," she said as she walked toward the kitchen.

"Uh, how long are you planning to keep his kids?" Conda turned from the window.

"Until Trevon does what I tell him to."

Conda sighed and dropped the .45 on the sofa. "I hope I won't be stuck with babysitting these kids."

"It was your idea to take them," Kendra reminded him. "Besides, who else can we trust with this?"

"Okay, I get your point."

Kendra glanced at the front door as Conda flopped down on the sofa. "I need you to bring that stuff in from the car, please."

"Can it wait?"

"No," she replied as she pulled a chair from the kitchen table and sat down.

Conda rose with the .45 back in his hand.

"Leave the gun. No need for you to risk being seen with it outside." She looked at him. "And be sure to grab the box of condoms off the passenger seat," she smiled.

"Now that's an item I'll hope we can use." He grinned and laid the .45 on the arm of the sofa and headed toward the door.

She stared at the back of his head as he stepped around the living room table.

Conda unlocked the door and opened it. "Hey, can we order something to eat? I'm-"

Trevon barged inside the trailer and shot Conda twice in the face with a .380 pistol equipped with a silencer.

37

LIGHTS, CAMERA, ACTION

Miami, Florida
Saturday, September 12th
Three Weeks Later

Trevon stared at the peeling paint on the ceiling inside a single-man jail cell. The thin, uncomfortable mat was all that laid between his body and the metal frame that was bolted into the wall. Due to the heat, he lay shirtless and with his hands laced behind his head, clad in a pair of plain white boxers. His muscled stomach, covered with a sheen of sweat, shined under the bright overhead light. A few moments later, the clank of a door opening drew Trevon's attention toward the cell door. He didn't bother to move as the sound of footsteps neared his cell. A scowl changed his expression when a Black female jailer and a white nurse stopped in front of his cell.

"Are you ready to go back to general population?" the jailer asked with a nasty attitude. Trevon ignored her as the timid nurse pushed her glasses up her nose. The jailer smacked her lips and reached for a can of mace on her waist belt. "There ain't no cameras down here. Your size don't mean shit to me."

Trevon sat up and slid his feet into a pair of orange rubber shower shoes. The nurse adjusted the medical bag on her shoulder and tucked a strand of blonde hair behind her ear. "W-what is he charged with?"

"Murder." the jailer spat. "And he's right at home, behind bars."

Trevon stood and made no effort to hide the shape of his penis under his boxers.

"Turn around and submit to the cuffs," the jailer ordered. "I'll only ask you once. I don't want no shit out of you tonight, okay? Nurse Cummings needs to give you an examination and the sooner it's done, the sooner you can go back to doing whatever you were doing. The next move is entirely up to you. So, what's it gonna be?"

Trevon stepped unwillingly toward the bars and turned around. He dropped his head and placed his hands behind his back. His shoulders slumped as the cuffs were secured around his wrists.

"Now step away from the door and sit on your bunk." The jailer slammed the slot shut.

He shuffled back to the bunk and sat down.

"That's a good boy." The jailer removed a brass key from her waist belt to unlock the cell. She strolled inside, throwing her wide hips from coast to coast. "Got any weapons I need to know about? Better tell me now because you'll regret it if I find some kind of shank in my search." She stood in front of him with her arms crossed.

"I don't have any weapons," he replied.

"Stand up," she ordered as the nurse remained at the cell entrance. "I don't believe you, and I'm not in the mood for any bullshit. Now stand up!"

He clenched his jaws and rose to his feet. He towered over her 5'6, full-figured stature, scowling at her.

"Something wrong with your face?" she snapped. "Huh? You got something to say?"

He stared at her and said nothing.

"That's what I thought." The jailor smirked and took in an

eyeful of him, starting from his well-defined chest and down the toned space of his stomach. Brazenly, she tugged the front of his boxers down. The nurse gasped, blushing at the semi-hard growth that hung between his legs.

"It's a damn shame that you're behind bars," the jailer remarked as she shook her head. She bit her bottom lip and turned to smile at the nurse. "Nice, ain't it? You ever seen one that big... even when it ain't even hard yet?"

"We s-shouldnt be doing this," the nurse said, wide-eyed.

"Ain't no cameras down here, remember? And if something were to happen, who would believe this jailbird? Shit, we could practically have our way with him. Ain't that right?" She turned back to Trevon and reached for his dick.

His face went slack.

"He likes this." The jailer eased her grip back and forth, pulling on his flesh. "Come inside and start your examination."

The nurse glanced over her shoulder. "Are you sure no one will—"

"Stop being so scared." the jailer jeered. "Besides, I already heard how you be lusting over some of these inmates. Cmon, girl. You can't tell me you don't want some."

The nurse stepped inside the cell and slipped her medical bag off her shoulder.

"Help me take his boxers off," the jailer whispered, as she continued to stroke the length of Trevon's strength. "Mmm. Look at how thick...and long it's getting. We can make him fuck us. You down with it?"

The nurse bit her bottom lip as she tugged the boxers off his ass and down his built legs.

"Damn, it's still growing," the jailer said, as Trevon stepped free from the boxers. "I have to get some of this dick!"

The nurse tied her hair in a ponytail and kicked off her white tennis shoes. "How much time do we have?" she whispered conspiringly.

"About thirty minutes," the jailer said as the nurse pulled her uniform pants down, revealing a pair of red panties.

Trevon moaned, staring at the nurse as she stepped out of her uniform. She smiled at him and pulled her top off.

The jailer squeezed Trevon's shaft. "I hope you know how to use this big monster. Mmmm, I gotta get some of this."

He groaned as the guard continued to fondle his penis.

"You belong to us," the jailer stated, as the nurse removed her bra. "You're going to fuck both of us, plus you'll lick our pussy until we bust in your mouth." She squeezed his dick and cupped his balls.

"We're wasting time," the nurse said as she sat nude on the bed. "I'll keep him hard while you take off your uniform."

"Good idea," the jailer said softly. "You can suck on his dick to get things started."

AT THE SAME TIME, Jurnee and Kandi were up in Selma, North Carolina, visiting Trevon's mom and sister with their kids. They both needed a break from the fast pace life of Miami.

Jurnee sat on the sofa, breastfeeding Tayvon as Kandi greased Victoria's scalp.

"You heard from Trevon today?" Jurnee asked.

Kandi glanced at her new Apple smartwatch: 5:38 p.m. "He'll be able to call around six."

"I might be in the bed, girl. Tayvon had me up all night. His tail wouldn't be quiet for nothing."

"I heard," Kandi smiled. "I think his teeth are coming in."

Jurnee sighed and rolled her eyes. "Don't remind me because I swear, he gonna bite my nipple off."

Kandi sat back and cracked her fingers. "Whew, I'm done. Go take your new shoes to grandmom, Victoria."

Victoria jumped up from the floor, grabbed her shoes, and skipped down the hall.

"Did you go online and read that story about that guy Veto, that died in jail?" Jurnee asked as Tayvon's sharp fingernails clawed at her breast.

Kandi shook her head. "Trevon told me about it. He said the police can't use his statement in court since he's dead."

"You think somebody killed him?"

Kandi shrugged. "Don't get me to guessing. All I care about is my baby."

"Amen to that."

"And I'm glad my mom found a new man."

"Does she know you're gonna let her have your condo?"

"Yeah. I told'er last night, and she plans to change all the furniture."

"I'm glad she's back to her old self. I know she was out of it a bit from when Conda acted like he was going to shoot her."

"She didn't know the gun wasn't loaded," Kandi opened her eyes. "She told me that all she cared about were the kids. She was willing to die for them, Jurnee."

Jurnee adjusted Tayvon in her arms and reached for Kandi's hand. "That mess is all behind us."

Kandi wiped her eyes. "Are you sure?"

"OOOHHH, fuck! This d-dick feels soooo fucking good!" the jailer moaned as she bounced on top of Trevon. Her ass rippled each time she sat down.

Trevon's groans were muffled by a mouthful of the nurse. She sat on his face, facing the jailer. The smell of sex reeked inside the small jail cell. For the past 15 minutes, the jailer and the nurse took turns fucking and sucking Trevon to their lustful content.

The jailer threw her head back and started grinding on top of Trevon. "Ooohh! This dick is soooo big!" she intoned.

With the handcuffs off, Trevon caressed the nurse's suntanned ass as he slurped at her pussy.

She squirmed on his face, purring through her moments of bliss.

The jailer gasped as she climbed off Trevon's lengthy penis. "Fuck my ass!" she said, with beads of sweat running down her breasts. "I wanna feel your big dick in my butt."

"Aaahhh...mmmhhh!" The nurse jerked her head up. "I'm cummin'!"

"CUT!" the director shouted, as Chelsea stayed seated on Trevon's face.

Vanessa moved behind Chelsea and slid a finger down the split of her tanned ass.

Chelsea dropped to her elbows, offering Vanessa a clear invite to finger-fuck her ass. She licked Trevon's balls as she removed the condom. Her lust for him drove her to suck on his penis.

Two minutes later, Chelsea apologized to the director for her unscripted climax. She assured the director that she would maintain her emotions until the final scene was filmed.

Trevon returned moments later with a raw ambition to add film number 8 to his career. He rejoined Vanessa, the jailer, and Chelsea, the nurse, back on the bunk and in front of the two cameras. Chelsea lay beside Vanessa, sucking gently on her jutting nipple. When he reached for a new condom, Vanessa grabbed his wrist. "Let me put it on," she said. "I... can't believe you're finally gonna put it in my ass."

"Okay, people," the director announced as Vanessa rolled the condom down Trevon's firm penis. "I need six to eight minutes of nonstop anal. Y'all know your positions, so let's get to it."

Chelsea stared at Trevon's erection as she stood beside the bunk. She glanced at the floor to make sure she was behind the tape marker. Her position would give the camera a clear side view of Trevon, easing his dick inside Vanessa's shiny ass. Vanessa was on the mat, on her elbows and knees, leaving her baby oil coated ass high in the air.

"And action!" the director said.

Vanessa stiffened when she felt Chelsea rubbing her slippery ass. She wiggled it as Trevon knelt behind her, slapping her hips.

"Ass so big!" Trevon stared at her asshole, taking his time to relax her.

Vanessa felt so vulnerable. She held her breath when the tip of his dick pushed against her lubricated anus. "Please d-do it," she moaned as Chelsea held her ass cheeks open.

Trevon clutched Vanessa by her fleshy waist and eased slowly into her brown glove box. "Yess!" Vanessa shouted. "Put it in my ass! All of it! I w-want it!" Vanessa bit her bottom lip as her ass stretched around him. "More! Don't stop!"

Trevon maintained himself and gave the director an A-list performance. He found a smooth pace, easing in and out of Vanessa's grippy and glossy ass.

Vanessa chewed on the sheets as Trevon dug her back out. The new pleasure and sensation of having him in her ass left her breathless. Her mind and body submitted with ease to his steady strokes. He felt larger and wider and harder in her ass. She winced from the thickness of him and the depth he pushed inside her. In and out, her ass sucked around him.

"Do it, baby!" Vanessa's moan bounced off the walls as her ass cheeks jerked back and forth. "Fuck my big ass," she said enthusiastically.

He increased his pace, hammering her from behind. He fed her kinky desire, pumping her wet ass with a constant flow of measured thrusts. The flouncing motions of her ass turned into a spectacle. Truth told, her ass was worth the wait.

Vanessa propped herself up on her arms, allowing her breasts to sway. "Oohh my goodness!" she groaned with her eyes closed. "Pound my ass! Pound it!"

The threesome stuck with the script written by Jurnee. Trevon kept his erection up to the eight-minute mark. The money scene ended with him leaning back on the bunk, offering Chelsea and Vanessa his raw erection. They took turns bobbing their lips up and down his thickness until an intense climax shot up between their pursed lips.

~

AN HOUR LATER, Trevon and Chelsea stood outside of the vacant jail by their cars.

"Another film to our name!" Chelsea grinned as she adjusted the shoulder strap of her white and green bodycon dress. "And you know I enjoyed every part of it."

Trevon smiled. "Me too. But I'm in need of a break after four straight days of filming." He glanced across the parking lot and saw the film crew loading the AEF panel truck. "What's taking Vanessa so long? Isn't she riding with you?"

She smiled. "I guess you haven't been paying attention."

"To what?"

"Vanessa and Shocka Long are dating. He picked her up a few minutes ago."

"Nah, I didn't know that."

"Yeah, and she's been staying with him for the past three days," she explained. "I'm happy for her and I wish them the best."

"Y'all still doing your thang on the side?"

She blushed. "Maybe," she replied.

He pulled out his phone and checked the time: 8:10 p.m.

"Is it true what you told me last week?" she asked coyly.

"About what?"

"That you won't have anymore offscreen sex...with me or any other women?"

He thought about his new bond with Jurnee and LaToria. "Yeah, it's true."

"Well, I can't lie and say I'm happy about it," she admitted. "But you know I'll always have a special section in my heart and mind for you."

"Thanks. And you'll always be my first for the *white way*!" He smiled.

Chelsea battled with speaking on the emotions that warped her heart. In all sincerity, she wanted to be in either Kandi or Jurnee's shoes. The emotions weren't envy or hate—she just knew a good man when she saw one. "Well, I guess I better head on home and soak my body in the hot tub." She forced a slight smile. "I think I'll pop a bottle of Chardonnay to relax my mind."

They shared a brief hug before they parted and headed in separate directions. Chelsea had the status that had men lined up to be with her. She refused to be crestfallen over Trevon and to state it bluntly; he wasn't the only man in her eyes that had the tools to satisfy her sexual needs. Later, at a red light on Biscayne Boulevard, she made a FaceTime call.

"Yo, what up sexy?" Big Diesel was shirtless in his living room.

Chelsea needed to flush Trevon from her system. "Hopefully you and me tonight," she said.

"Time and place. That's all I need to hear."

~

TREVON CALLED LaToria along his way back home. He apologized for being late and explained the reason about the retakes with his film.

"I'm glad you called, Smooch. I really needed to hear your voice."

"Everything good up there?" Trevon asked, as he sped through a busy intersection.

"Yeah. And I'm glad I came up here to get my mind right."

Trevon's attention was pulled to the rearview mirror. He frowned as the car behind him flashed the high beams on and off. "Just remember what we agreed on, baby. Everything we do, we do it for the kids."

"Okay, Smooch. I'll let Jurnee know you called... I love you."

"I love you the same. Kiss the kids for me." He ended the call and switched lanes, thinking the car behind him wanted to pass. To his surprise, the car matched his move. *Who the fuck is this?!*

Trevon thought as he slowed his S580 and turned into a gas station. He came to a stop beside the lamppost and eyed the silver Rolls-Royce Ghost with suspicion.

Trevon assumed the Rolls-Royce was following him when it pulled up alongside his S580. He lowered his window when he saw the tinted window on the Ghost doing the same.

"Hey, handsome!" the lovely driver inside the Ghost said. "Or do you prefer to go by Mr Sex Scene? Surprised to see me, huh?"

38

A PROMISE KEPT

South Beach, Florida
Saturday, September 12th

Trevon followed Nashlly's Ghost to the trendy three-story Cibo Wine Bar on South Beach. They grabbed a corner table in the dining room area and held their questions until the waiter left their table with their orders.

"Are you surprised to see me?" Nashlly smirked across the table.

"Of course I am!" Trevon replied. "What—why are you back in the city?"

Her smiled faded. "I know you heard about Veto, right?"

"Uh... I saw it on the news."

"Well, with his unfortunate demise, the state's case is too weak to charge anyone with Swagga's murder. I turned myself in last week and my attorney cleared my name. All that shit Veto was spitting was something he heard from you know who." She paused. "And it helped that you and Kandi didn't mention my name in your statements. Actually, it saved my ass big time."

"So, you're saying this shit is over?"

She reached for her drink. "For me it is," she said. "My

attorney argued that Veto made up a false statement in a desperate attempt to save his own ass." She took a small sip of the wine.

"What's up with the other guy?"

She set her glass down and crossed her comely legs. "He's good. His name is clear and we're both gonna put this shit behind us. But my only issue is with Kendra. I got word that she had a special visit with Veto before he left us," she said as she slid her fingers through her weave.

Trevon thought about the conversation he had with Kendra last week. "Veto told everything. And she knows the truth."

Nashlly sighed. "I figured that already. Now I gotta worry about that bitch putting money out for my head."

"That ain't true," Trevon said.

"And what makes you say that?"

"I need to trust you with something." Trevon paused and waited for a waiter to move out of earshot. "What you saw on the news about my kids and LaToria's mom wasn't true."

Nashlly frowned. "They weren't kidnapped?"

"That part was real. But the whole story of them being found, tied and gagged at that Pompano Beach motel was staged."

"Okay, so tell me what really happened."

"Kendra came down and got up with Conda to try some bullshit that would put me back in prison. She was upset about me never telling her what I knew about Swagga's murder. Anyway, Conda changed the plans and kidnapped my kids and LaToria's mom-"

"For real?" Nashlly asked, wide-eyed.

He nodded. "Kendra didn't agree with his move and she had to play along to keep everyone safe. She came to me and took me to the spot where Conda had my kids..."

"And I guess you weren't in the mood to talk to him?"

Trevon took a deep breath and stared at his untouched glass of wine. "Kendra helped me that night." He blinked and looked at Nashlly. "She said her anger had her mind mixed up. She asked me if I saw who killed Swagga and I told her the truth. Everything that happened, it was because of Swagga being on his bullshit."

"So, you expect me to let my guard down?" she said sharply.

"Kendra is gonna move on with her life. That's all I can tell you."

"And what about you?"

He grinned and thought about his future in porn and being a father. "What I'm gonna do is live my life stroke by stroke and secure a stable future for my kids."

She giggled. "You're so nasty. But I like it."

"What about you? What are your plans since you don't have to go on the run?"

"Go back to living my life. Focus on my business, and maybe I'll settle down with a good man and start a family. I'm learning not to judge a man by his bank account. But don't get it twisted, okay? I still won't fuck wit' no bum or a muthafucka that think he's gonna live off me."

"You won't stay single for long."

She smiled. "Too bad your relationship status is full. I saw the Instagram pictures that your girl Jurnee posted. She's lucky, and I'll say the same for Kandi."

He glanced at her conspicuous nipple prints under the fabric of her blouse.

"See something you'd like to see more of?" she asked softly.

He leaned back in the chair. "I've already seen you naked."

"And did you like what you saw? I know I'm small up top, but I feel I still got a lot to work with."

"Ain't no complaints from my side of the table."

She uncrossed her legs and slid her foot up his calf. "Are you a man of your word?"

"My word is all I got."

"Good," she said as the waiter returned to their table with a tray of appetizers. "I want you to stand by that after we leave. Because if I can recall, you made a promise to me. And since we have crossed plans—I mean paths again. You owe me a good time and I want it tonight, Mr. Sex Scene."

~

"You know I'm good at keeping secrets," Nashlly said when she later led Trevon inside her bedroom.

He laid his keyfob and phone on the dresser as she took off her earrings. "You know you didn't have to tell me that."

"Well, I did. And I want you to know that." She turned to face him. "Trevon, I've been wanting to have sex with you since I viewed your first film on my phone. Real talk, plenty of bitches be fantasizing about getting dick from a porn star."

He pulled her against him by her waist. "What's your fantasy?"

She circled her arms around his neck. "It's me... face down... ass up. And you're behind me... blowing my back out. Make this a special one-night stand that I'll never forget. Can you do all that for me?"

He nodded as he slid the zipper down on the back of her black pencil skirt. He undressed her, peeling her clothes off, until she stood nude in her stylish stilettos.

"I feel like I owe you this." He cuffed her bare ass. "Seriously, if you didn't do what you did, I would have been lost."

"Shhh. Don't spoil the mood. Let's focus on now, can we?" She lowered her hands to his belt and pulled it loose. "I wanna make some sex scenes up in here tonight."

He stared at the dark brown tips of her small nipples. He stroked her soft ass, lifting each cheek in a playful manner. Moments later, his clothes were piled around his feet, leaving him stark naked.

She swiped her tongue up and down his neck as she worked her hands along the intimidating length of his dick. She wanted every inch of him inside her. Sex. Plain and simple, that's all she desired from him.

"Keep those shoes on." He squeezed her hips, grinning.

She nodded and turned toward the bed. Her cute breasts danced side to side as she pulled him along by his erection.

He slid his fingers through her hair when she sat at the foot of the bed. She gazed up at him, stroking his shaft against her cheek. No emotional based words were needed. Only lust joined them on this night. He groaned when she squeezed his shaft while she circled her tongue on the head of his penis.

She kept her eyes open as she began to suck. She didn't rush her actions as she slid her lips back and forth.

"Yeahhh. Nice... and slow." He slid her hair over her shoulder. "Ooohhh... suck dis dick."

She sucked along his shiny shaft at a slow-moving pace. Each time her lips ringed the midpoint, she moaned.

He remained rigid between her soft lips, watching every second of her slurping back and forth. "You having a good time?"

"Hmm—" she slurped harder on his tip while squeezing his shaft.

He pinched her left nipple and fisted his other hand in her hair. "Ooohhh, shiiit! You a beast!" he groaned as she tried to deep throat him.

She kept going, sucking and slurping.

"Ooohhh, Nashlly! That's it right there!" He convulsed when she reached between his legs to fondle his balls.

She unclasped her lips from his dick and wiped her mouth. "I'm ready for you to put this inside me," she said, out of breath.

"You g-got some condoms?" he asked.

"Behind you, on my dresser." She kissed the tip of his dick and slid up further on the bed.

He stared at her clean-shaven pussy. *I'ma fuck the shit outta her!* He turned and crossed the bedroom to the dresser.

"What's your favorite way to do it?" she asked, as she lay on her back, fingering her clit.

"You on your back and your legs hooked over my arms," he replied as he searched for the condoms.

"Look beside the picture frame to your left," she said, staring at his ass. She pushed two fingers inside her pussy to loosen herself up. *My cuzo ain't gonna believe this! Nah I, ain't telling her shit!* She bit her bottom lip and added a third finger. "C'mon, Trevon," she whined as she eased her fingers in and out of her slippery tunnel.

He turned from the dresser with the silver picture frame. He held it up with his brows lifted.

Nashlly smacked her lips. "What?"

"Who are these other two women in this picture?"

She sighed, pulled her fingers from her pussy and wiped them on the bedsheet. She sat up and glanced at the picture. "That's my cousin and her mom."

He looked at the picture again. "What's her name?"

"Who? My aunt or my cousin?"

"Your aunt?"

She hesitated. "What's going on?"

"What's her name?" he asked. "Is it... Andrea-"

"How do you know my aunt?" She frowned and waited for him to answer her question.

He stared at the picture, shaking his head in disbelief. *This can't be true! Ain't no way!*

"What the fuck is going on, Trevon?" She jumped off the bed and snatched up her panties. "You better not tell me you done fucked my aunt!"

"Worse," he replied. "Andrea Harwood is my dad's sister."

Nashlly froze. "You bullshitting!"

"I never knew my father. He was never in my life growing up, but my mom was tight with his sister and she's right here in this picture. I..."

Nashlly covered her mouth. "Oh... shit! That means—"

"We're kin, Nashlly. You're my cousin on my dad's side."

"You gotta be fuckin' kidding me!" She shook her head. "So... My Uncle Tony is your dad?"

He nodded slowly as he picked up his briefs off the floor.

"Uh-uh. I don't believe this bullshit," she said as she shimmied her panties up her legs. "Don't be playing games with me, Trevon!"

He sighed. "Why would I-I can't make this shit up."

"Well, I'm gonna get the truth right now!"

"How?" he asked as he got dressed.

"Just watch." She snatched her new iPhone off the bedside table. "Siri, call Aunt Andrea."

Trevon slid his briefs on and stood at the corner of the bed.

Nashlly put the call on speaker, frowning hard. *Ain't in the mood for this bullshit!*

"Hello?" a soft female voice came from the speaker.

"Hey, Auntie Andrea," she said, masking the sour mood in her voice. "How you doing tonight?"

"Fine. Just sitting here watching TV and resting my knees."

Nashlly shot an angry gaze at Trevon. "Uh, I got a question to ask you about Uncle Tony."

"What did he do this time? Borrow some money and didn't pay you back?"

"Nah, but I need to ask you something about his past."

"Okay, I'm listening."

"Did Uncle Tony father any other kids besides Mia and Travis?"

Silence.

"Where are you?" Andrea asked.

"Home."

"Anybody with you?"

"No," Nashlly lied.

"I guess I need to speak on this," Andrea said. "I didn't agree with the way my brother did his business but... yes, he had a son he turned his back on."

Nashlly's heart skipped a beat. "Why?"

"He was already in a serious relationship at the time and the baby was proof of his cheating ways. He tried to take the easy way out by trying to pay for an abortion," she said. "He was wrong, and I still haven't forgiven him for turning his back on his firstborn."

Nashlly glanced at Trevon, feeling pity for him. "What was—his name?"

"Trevon Harrison. I was at the hospital when he was born. His mom, she was my friend. She was young and fell for your Uncle Tony's false hopes. I was the only one that knew about the baby and his mom wanted me to keep it that way. She didn't need Tony, and she grew to hate him for disowning Trevon."

Nashlly sat down on the bed. "That means Mia and Travis have a brother that they don't even know about."

"I made a promise to Trevon's mom to never tell anyone, and it's a promise I just broke by telling you. Trevon will always be my nephew and I feel so much guilt and regret for the past. He went to prison when he was only eighteen for killing a man that messed with his sister. To this day, he doesn't know that I was the one that sent what little money I could while he was in prison."

Nashlly wiped her eyes. "Where is he now?"

"I'm not sure, honey. I'll admit that I lost my focus on him when I got married and got on with my life. Now tell me how you came to ask me about this."

"I just—" Nashlly's voice broke as a tear rolled her cheek. *Trevon is my cousin!* "Let me call you back. I have to—I'll call you back, okay?"

"You do that. If you intend to break this family secret... I'm on your side and Tony can make all the fuss he wants."

Nashlly threw the phone aside and looked at Trevon. She saw pain on his face. In his hand, he held her blouse. A breath later, she blinked and became aware that she was still topless. "Thanks," she said with her head down. "I sure as hell wasn't expecting this to happen." She put the blouse back on, feeling dirty. "I just sucked my cousin's dick!" she muttered, shaking her head.

Trevon sat beside her. "As I grew older, I never pushed for any info on who my dad was. Why ask questions about a man that didn't give a fuck about me?" he said. "All my life, Father's Day never meant a thing to me. I don't know—"

"Do you want to meet him?"

"No," he replied firmly. "What can he say to me after all these fuckin years?"

She shrugged and stared at the floor. "What about your sister and brother?"

Silence.

He stood. "I have to go home because this is too much for me to take in."

"You can't run from this," she refused to let him take the easy way out. "If you do. You'll be just like your dad."

"Never." He shook his head. "How can I run from something I never had? I never had a father, and I don't need one now."

She wiped her eyes again. "You're my cousin, Trevon." she said. "And it's not my fault that my uncle did that dumb shit—I can't change it," she said.

"I didn't ask you to," he said harshly. "I didn't ask for any of this bullshit!"

"Then leave." She pointed toward the door. "Go ahead and turn your back on this and you'll be just like my Uncle Tony! He made it wrong, but you can make it right."

"Make what right?!" Trevon shouted. "This ain't no fucking reality TV show. This is life. Real fucking life. Tony don't owe me a muthafuckin' thang! I was the one that saw my mom with a broken heart over that... ain't nothing to make right!"

"What am I to you, huh?" she shouted. "You done put a fuckin gun to my head and yo' dick in my mouth! Who am I to you, huh? Blood, or just a dumb ass bitch? I could've bodied your ass when you came running for Kandi that night. But something held me back and now I know why!" she cried. "Please make this right."

Trevon valued the essence of family and tonight he had another choice to make. He shook his head, snatched up his clothes and left Nashlly alone and in tears.

39

#FAMILYFORGIVES

Coconut Grove, Florida
Friday, September 25th
Thirteen Days Later

Trevon viewed the scene in his backyard through a pair of green lenses sunglasses.

The midday barbecue was postcard perfect under the clear and sunny 91-degree temperature. A few battled the heat by jumping in the pool, or relaxing under an eggshell white awning. He saw the whole scene from his bedroom window where he stood with Rex at his side. He grinned when he saw LaToria lifting up her tank top to show her baby bump to a group of friends. His mom, sister and Tahkiyah stood at the far end of the pool, recording videos and taking pictures with their phones. Jurnee sat on the deck chair with Tayvon in her lap and Victoria sitting beside her. He stared at them for a moment.

Life had to change for Trevon. He thought of a life lesson his mom once told him while he was in prison. He would never be the man he wanted to be if he remained the same. All he ever wanted was a family. He had it with LaToria and Victoria, Jurnee and Tayvon. To be a father, he had to change. His will to be a better man was driven by the mistakes he made. By no means did he view himself as perfect and without faults.

"You can't stay back here forever." A soft, familiar voice ended Trevon's private moment.

He turned from the window and smiled at Janelle leaning against the doorsill. "What's up, Boss lady?"

"All of your guests are waiting on the man of the house to step outside."

He pulled the sunglasses off. "I'm just trying to get my mind right before I talk to—"

"Speak from your heart, Trevon. Your mind can play tricks on you. But your heart will always remain true," she said.

"Where is he?"

"In the dining room, waiting on you."

An awkward silence filled the bedroom.

He sighed. "I guess I better get this over with, huh?"

"Yeah, you do." Janelle nodded. "And do yourself a favor and leave all your anger inside this room. I know it hurts. But think about what matters most to you and speak—"

"From my heart," he cut her off.

FIFTY-SIX-YEAR-OLD TONY HARWOOD stood when Trevon entered the dining room. He stared at his son, grappling with finding the right things to say. "I... spoke to your mom." Tony remained on his feet as Trevon stood across the table. "I asked her to forgive me for what I've done. And for all the things I didn't do when it came to you," he said contritely.

Trevon was unmoved by Tony's words. "Did she forgive you?" he asked with his arms crossed.

Tony nodded. "She prayed for me and—"

"Why did you turn your back on me?" Trevon asked, making an honest effort to stay in control of his temper. "You even tried to pay for an abortion?"

"I was young and stupid," Tony admitted. "What I did was wrong and if I were in your shoes. I wouldn't—"

"You'll never be in my shoes," Trevon stated. "You made me. But you didn't raise me. I grew up without you in my life. I never heard another man smile and say 'That's my son!' All I knew was the fact of you being missing."

Tony sighed. "I'm sorry, Trevon. I made a wrong choice."

"Choice?!" Trevon stiffened. "I wasn't a muthafuckin choice! I was your firstborn. You think I have a *choice* to be a part of my kids' life? Fuck no. Every breath I take is for my kids. And you were willing to pay my mom to get rid of me. And now you expect me to welcome you into my life as if this is a fuckin fairy tale?"

"What mistakes have you made?" Tony stared at Trevon. "Are you perfect? Yeah, I fucked up when it came to you. But you know what? I'm human. I can't change the wrong I've done and for all it's worth, God knows I'm sorry. I don't expect anything from you. All I ask is a chance to admit my wrongs. All of them."

"What was my mom to you? Did you even care about her? Or did she run into a true playa? Hell, I might not be the only kid you kicked to the curb and—"

"Now wait a damn minute!" Tony glared and pointed across the table. "I came here to make my peace with you and Sandra, not to be put down like this. People do things that they regret and turning my back on you was one of'em." He paused. "I didn't come here to fight. I understand your anger, and I didn't expect a warm welcome after all this time, okay?" he explained apologetically.

Trevon slid the chair back and sat down. His load of regrets forced him to face his own faults. To begin with, he thought of his regretful actions with Tahkiyah. If LaToria ever got wind of it, he knew there would be no forgiveness.

"Did you ever think about me?" Trevon asked.

Tony sat. "My sister showed me some pictures of you when you were born. And in secret, I gave her some money from time to time to give to Sandra."

Trevon studied the man across the table. Like Trevon, Tony

was tallish and built with a large frame, and it was easily perceived that father and son sat at the table.

"I was already in a serious relationship when I met your mom," Tony continued. "I was twenty at the time and I ran the streets pretty hard back then. Done a lot of dumb stuff that I've left behind. But that's still no excuse when it comes to you."

"Are you with the same girl that—"

"Yeah," Tony said. "I've been with Nisha since high school and we've been married for twenty years."

Trevon glanced to his right and looked toward the backyard. "How did she take the news of all this?"

Tony sighed and slid a hand down his salt-and-pepper goatee. "Pissed at first. She was really mad at me for keeping such a big secret from her and after all this time. My kids took it okay... I think. Anyway, my wife forgave me. And she and my sister, they planned this."

"How old are your kids?"

Tony smiled. "Your brother Travis is thirty and your sister Mia is thirty-three."

Trevon took a few moments to accept the truth. Regardless of the past, he had a larger family to know and love. He thought of his mom and how she was able to forgive Tony. "Do they have any kids of their own?"

"I've been a grandfather for eleven years." He grinned. "Your sister has two kids, twin girls, and your brother has three. And, I've heard you have two kids, too?"

Trevon smiled for the first time. "Yeah, and with one more on the way."

Tony shook his head. "Uh, Nashlly told me that you're in the film business, but she wouldn't tell me all the details. I assume you're doing good to be living like this." He gestured around the large house. "And don't get me started on that Lambo that's in your driveway. Man, that's a nice ride! So, what do you do?"

Trevon had no shame in his career, and he figured it was best to come clean. "I do adult films."

Tony's brows lifted. "As in porn?"

"Yeah, I'm an adult film actor."

"Well, I'll be damned. The boys at the barbershop ain't gonna believe this! My firstborn son is a porn star!" Tony said, thrilled.

Trevon sat dumbfounded at hearing another man mention him as his son. The reality of sitting with his father left him numb. The past of Tony's absence would take time for Trevon to understand. He understood the favors of being levelheaded toward Tony, and it would start today. A strong family was one that offered forgiveness, and Trevon wanted a family.

~

TREVON WAS LATER INTRODUCED to his dad's side of the family. He clicked instantly with Mia and Travis, and everyone, mainly Kandi, made comments on the strong likeness between Trevon and Travis. His sister Mia was slightly built, and she cried when she hugged her new brother. She promised Trevon that she would treat him as blood, and she encouraged everyone else to do the same.

Trevon posted several pictures on his social sites with his two sisters and brother. He added *#2Brosand2Sisters* hashtag to a picture taken by his mom near the pool. He met each of his new aunts and uncles, cousins, nieces and nephews. Peace filled Trevon to a point of tears when his mom led the entire family in a moment of prayer. She spoke on forgiveness and the importance of having a strong bond in the family.

When the food was served, Tony did the honors with Trevon and Travis.

~

"WHAT'S UP, *CUZO*?" Nashlly beamed as she walked up on Trevon. "I see you're all smiles."

Tevon slid the sunglasses up on his head. "Yeah. I guess you were right about me making things right," he said as his brother did a backflip off the diving board.

"Life's crazy, ain't it? Last night I was thinking how our lives crossed and we had no idea we were family," Nashlly said with the sun reflecting off her expensive shades.

"We gotta put that all behind us," Trevon said. "I know we had our awkward moments—"

"And one of'em I'll take to my grave," Nashlly said abruptly.

Trevon shook his head, thinking about how close he came to having sex with his cousin. "I saw you talking to LaToria a minute ago. Y'all cool?"

"Definitely. I asked her to give me a chance at being her friend."

"And what did she say?"

Nashlly grinned. "I had to promise her a family discount at my shop." She laughed. "Trust me, it's all good."

"I'm glad to hear that, and I hope you'll settle down from your fast ways. All bullshit aside, you need to be careful in these streets. We're family now."

"Forever cuzo!" She hugged him and made a mental note to take his words to heart.

The sun stayed on the stage as the barbecue continued. A little while later, Trevon had his shirt off while dancing with Jurnee and Kandi. He enjoyed the smaller things in life that most took for granted. For example, he caught his queens off-guard at different moments by telling them how beautiful they were and how much he was thankful for their love. He played the perfect host by thanking everyone for showing up as they eventually left. His dad was the last to leave. They shared a few private words in the driveway. He welcomed the chance at forgiving Tony, and today was just the beginning.

TREVON CLOSED his bedroom door and paused with his hand on the knob. Living with two women didn't give him much space to call his own. He shook his head, grinning at the sight of Jurnee's panties on the bed. Glancing to his right, he saw LaToria's pink bra on the dresser. Tonight wouldn't be the first nor the last time that his queens would start the fun without him as he strolled toward the bathroom, unfastening his belt. The scent of jasmine and vanilla scented candles met him when he stepped inside the bathroom at 8:25p.m.

"Hey, Smooch." Kandi smiled.

"Hey, Baby Daddy," Jurnee cooed.

His queens greeted him from the tub. He closed the door with his elbow while staring at Jurnee's breasts. They were shiny and wet.

"Are the kids asleep?" Kandi asked as she gently ran a comb through Jurnee's wet hair.

"Trayvon is. But Victoria is watching TV with my mom." Trevon took his pants and briefs off.

He stepped into the jasmine-scented water and shared a passionate kiss with both of his queens.

"What a day!" he said, with LaToria on his right and Jurnee on his left. They snuggled up close, resting their heads on his broad shoulders.

"I'm proud of you." Jurnee rubbed his chest, loving every inch of her Black King.

"Me too," Kandi added.

"Thanks. But what I did today... it needed to be done," he said with his arms around the women he loved.

"How do you feel about all this?" Jurnee asked.

He shrugged. "I guess I'm still taking it in. I know my best move is to just take things slow with getting to know all my family on my dad's side."

Kandi giggled. "Tell'im what happened, Jurnee."

Jurnee blushed. "No, you tell him."

"Hey... one of y'all just come on out and tell me, okay?"

Kandi slid her knee over Trevon's leg under the water. "Don't take this the wrong way, Smooch, but you have a few ratchet cousins on your dad's side."

He grinned. "What happened?"

Kandi told Trevon about one of his male cousins that happened to be a big fan of AEF. "He's on my Instagram and Facebook page." Kandi laughed. "He said he'll never watch my films again since I'm kinda family now. OMG, it was so awkward!"

"I love y'all," Trevon said.

Jurnee smile. "We love you the same, papi."

"Oh!" Kandi sat up. "Jurnee has some good news to tell you."

He looked at Jurnee and kissed her. "Okay... what's up?"

"Well, actually it can be good news for all of us," Jurnee said. "If you're okay with it, I want to get back in front of the camera. And before you say no, it's not for porn."

"Okay, I'm listening," he said as Kandi settled back under his arm.

"Janelle is in talks with a producer out of Atlanta to do a reality show TV series on me. They want to show the world how a former porn star is living. And when they heard how I'm under the same roof and in the same bed with you and Kandi... the producer gave me a serious offer."

Trevon frowned. "A reality series?"

"Yes, Smooch!" Kandi jumped in. "It's gonna be like *Real Housewives of Atlanta* or *Love & Hip Hop*. Hell, we might blow up and get higher ratings than *Keeping Up With The Kardashians!*"

"She's right," Jurnee said. "You know I have a large fan base. I have over four million fans and followers on my social media pages. Seriously, who else is living like us? Men will tune in to see us and the ladies will tune in to see you."

He flexed his chest. "Hmmm, you got a point about that."

Jurnee playfully rolled her eyes. "We all can benefit from this. Please give it some thought because I really think we should make this move. The series will give our fans a true look at porn, and how the business is. And since I'm still the VP at AEF, the company will get a ton of publicity."

"Y'all for real?" he asked, unsmiling.

They nodded.

Trevon sighed. *Am I ready to put my life on display? My baby got a point. Ain't too many men living a lifestyle like me or us.*

"Please, Smooch!" Kandi begged.

Trevon smiled. "Okay, I'm with it."

Jurnee and Kandi squealed and gave each other a high-five.

"What about my contract with AEF?" Trevon asked after his queens settled down.

"It stays the same," Jurnee said. "Matter-of-fact, you can thank Kandi for finding your next co-star for one of your future films."

"Who?" He grinned. "Keyshia Cole?"

"Don't get slapped." Kandi splashed some water in his face.

Jurnee reached for her smartphone. "Ever heard of Lethal Lipps?"

"Thick as hell BBW, with black shoulder length hair and a set of thunder thighs." He grinned at Jurnee. "Yeah, I'ma fan."

"Well, she'll be doing a film with you in the very near future," Jurnee said as she held her phone in the air at arm's length. "Kandi, scoot down some, or cover them big titties. I wanna take a selfie of us right quick."

CLICK.

Jurnee took the selfie, all smiles with her king and lover. A moment later she shared the selfie to Instagram with the message:

@HoneyDrop-#I♥MYKING&KANDI

"Baby," Jurnee said. "I have something else to tell you. Um, we might need a bigger house because... I'm pregnant!"

~

Close to midnight, Kandi muffled her moans by French kissing Jurnee as she rocked herself to a climax on top of Trevon. Her hands were planted on his sweaty chest, giving her the support she needed to gently bounce on his erection. Her body was alive, racing to its second explosion of the night. Jurnee pulled at Kandi's nipples, knowing how hard to tease them.

"Oohh, shit!" Trevon moaned. "Gimme dat good pregnant poo-poo!"

She squeezed his chest. "It's yours, Smooch!" Her breasts heaved as she rode him.

Like a tag team wrestling match, Jurnee jumped on Trevon as soon as Kandi rolled to the side. She rode her king backward, bouncing her ass hard.

Trevon met the strenuous challenge of mating with the women he loved. He didn't believe in the art of seduction. In his view, seduction in itself was an art. Sex. Fucking. Making love, Trevon had it all with LaToria and Jurnee. This was his nude awakening, two wet pussies that held the essence of love. The music moved him. It motivated him. And the tune was musical.

"Trevon! I'm cummin'!"

40

CLOSE YOUR EYES

Miami, Florida
One Year Later

A hush settled over the crowd inside the lobby of the Marriott Marquis World Convention Center Hotel. All eyes turned toward the yellow, blue and white LED lit stage. Under the spotlight, author Wahida Clark stood behind a glass podium, adjusting the mic to her level. A moment later, she waved at the crowd while pushing her stylish glasses up her nose.

"What's up everyone?" Wahida smiled as her cheery voice filled the lobby. "Before I announce the last AV award. I would like to thank Mrs. Janelle Babin-Martin for inviting me and my entire WCP staff to the first SPAV, Southern Porn Adult Videos expo." She paused and pointed at the front row table where Janelle sat with her husband. "This expo is a first of its kind for me, but you best believe that I will be in attendance for next year's expo. I've learned so much behind the scenes and I have so much respect for all of you men and women."

A round of applause filled the laid-back lobby as Wahida's words were taken in.

"Okay," she said after the applause ended. "The last SPAV

award is for the category of AV male actor of the year! This award was hard—" She smiled. "Pun intended, and the votes were fair and tight." She picked up a black and gold card and opened it. "Uh, the men up for this award are Big Diesel, Paul Will, Mr. Marcus, Lex Iron, Mr. Sex Scene and Jake Hammer. All six are here tonight and ladies, I'm sure y'all will agree that all six are all that!" Wahida took her glasses off, wearing a smile from ear to ear. "How y'all feeling this man candy?"

The females in the lobby clapped and voiced their agreement with Wahida. The mood was at peace as the art of sex defined the Miami night.

"And the SPAV male actor of the year is?" Wahida picked up a second card off the podium and held it in the air. A breath later, she used her manicured fingernail to break the seal. She smiled, slid her glasses back on, and paused intentionally to string out the suspense.

A sharp whistle broke the space of silence.

Wahida cleared her throat. "The winner is... Mr. Sex Scene aka Trevon Harrison!"

The crowd erupted with a loud round of applause as a faint gold spotlight held its focus on Trevon's table. On cue, the song '*Tru*' by Lloyd emitted from the speakers as Trevon rose to his feet. He was joined by his queens, Kandi and Jurnee. He circled his arms around their waists.

"You did it!" Jurnee squealed over the applause.

"My Smooch is numero uno!" Kandi said as she adjusted his tie. "We're so proud of you, and we love you so much!"

Trevon kissed his queens, sending the crowd into a louder round of applause. Tonight was his night, and he had many to thank for his accomplishments. He left his queens at the table and made his way toward the stage. All eyes were on Trevon and how he rocked the baby-blue two button jacket and matching trousers, all by Gucci. With the jacket open, he showed off a white jacquard shirt that clung to his masculine chest. The baby-blue suit was Jurnee's idea and Trevon wore it proudly. The moment seemed surreal as he took the steps up the stage. When he reached the podium, Diamond Monroe and La'starya appeared on the stage to present him his award. He greeted both of the ravishing women with a hug and a kiss on the cheek. When he stepped to the microphone, the music faded as the crowd settled down, awaiting his speech.

Trevon took off his shades and held up the rose gold award. "I'm proud of this." He gazed at the crowd and glanced at the statue of a nude man with a towel on.

"I didn't plan or write a speech and, uh, this is... surreal." He sat the award on the podium and took a breath to gather himself. "All I can be... is who I am. True."

"Take your time, papi," Jurnee shouted.

Trevon smiled. "Uh, a true friend once told me to speak from my heart because the mind plays so many tricks. And right now, that's what I'm gonna do. This award means a lot to me. Three years ago, I was released from prison after fifteen years. And at the end of my rope, I took a chance and made a visit to see Janelle at AEF. So, to start out, I'd like to thank Janelle and the entire staff at Amatory Erotic Films. Y'all believed in me from the jump, and I thank you for that. Ah, shouts out to my manager, Anthony Imes. I gotta mention a few lovely and talented costars co-stars that I'm happy to call friends. Pinky, Chelsea, Butter Buns, The Bodyxxx, Misty Stone, Heather Hunter, Chanell Heart, Gemini Love, Lethal Lipps, Sarah Banks, and of course... Cherokee D Ass." He smiled. "Thanks to all that have supported all of my sixty films and a major thank you to all of my LGBT fans. Uh, much love to Wahida Clark that's behind me. I'm proud to announce that I'll be on the cover of her next book, and it was a pleasure doing the photo session with Nuance Art. Shout out to my new personal assistant, Marcenia Waters. You're the best. My social media manager, Nashlly. You proved that I could mix family with business. Uh, how much time I got up here?" He glanced at Wahida.

"Three minutes," she informed.

Trevon didn't want to leave anyone out. "Man, this award is

something special. Okay, a special plug goes to the city of Miami! The porn state is being moved from the state of California to the sunshine state... stroke by stroke."

His comment drew an applause.

"But really y'all, I support porn on a global network," Trevon said. "And to wrap this up. I would like to acknowledge my foundation. My two lovely, and sexy queens, the mothers of my four children, LaToria and Jurnee. Without them, there is no me. I love you both so deep and so true. Y'all know this award is really for you." He raised the award. "Thank you all for your support! Oh, and be sure to watch the next episode of Jurnee's reality TV show, *Nude Awakening!* And yes, y'all, the after-party is at my new spot in Brickell! Y'all be safe. Practice safe sex, get tested and thank you! Thank you so much!"

BACKSTAGE, Trevon posed in several selfies with his celebrity fans. Laverne Cox, Niecy Nash, Lizzo, Winnie Harlow, Sasha Lane, Buffie the Body, Angela Yee, Sinnamon Love, Jazzie Belle, Da Brat, Vivica Fox, Chanel West Coast and many more. His brand, Mr. Sex Scene, was stable, and he carried himself in a businesslike manner in the face of endless, erotic temptation. He faced temptation when K. Michelle stopped him for a selfie. And seconds later, he was starstruck when Tiffany Haddish mentioned she was a fan of his films. He enjoyed the moment without choking on his ego. He didn't pocket any phone numbers of any willing females behind his queen's back. What he had at home kept him fully satisfied and true to the two he loved.

As the expo drew to an end, Trevon returned to the AEF booth to mingle with his fans. He signed countless autographs of his pictures and personally thanked each fan for their support. Janelle smiles at Trevon's reaction when two homosexual men approached him for a selfie. Trevon treated the couple with respect and genuinely thanked them for supporting his career. His actions showed open-minded maturity and a secure stance on his masculinity.

~

TREVON TUGGED his sleeve back and glance at his rose gold timepiece; 10:30p.m. He stood inside his climate-controlled garage with his brother Travis.

"Bruh!" Travis said. "Did you see how phat K. Michelle's ass was?!"

Trevon grinned. "She's something special," he replied as he pulled out a keyless remote from his pocket.

"Where you headed?"

"I gotta make a quick run right quick to handle something." Trevon turned the alarm off his S580 and popped the trunk. "I need you to hold the fort until I get back. And make sure nobody goes up to the second floor," Trevon said as he pulled out a midnight purple Arai motorcycle helmet.

Travis nodded as Trevon walked around his Benz and Lamborghini. "How long you gonna be gone?"

"Not long," Trevon replied as he threw a leg over his midnight purple and blue carbon-fiber Kawasaki Ninja H2R.

"Ride safe, bruh," Travis said as the garage door slid up.

Trevon strapped the helmet on and leaned the H2R upright. He settled in on the seat with a loose grip on the handlebar. A breath later, the powerful 326-hp sportbike popped to life. Trevon revved the engine twice and eased the menacing designed bike out of the garage. An interracial couple stepping out of a BMW i8 paused and stared at the rare $50,000 Kawasaki H2R. Trevon kept the bike tame as he cruised up his curved driveway, revving the ear-splitting engine. As the H2R neared the gate, it slid open by remote. Trevon glanced over his shoulder and saw a small crowd stood with his brother.

Might as well give'em something to post on YouTube. Trevon held the clutch and turned the throttle back, revving the engine up to

10,000 rpm. *Showtime!* He squeezed the front brake and revved the engine up to 11,000 rpm. before he popped the clutch. A heartbeat later, the rear tire fired alive, billowing smoke. Trevon held the H2R, doing a showy burnout under the full moon. In relation to his life, he launched the bike fearlessly, throwing flames from the pipe and doing a wheelie down the street at 88 mph.

~

TEN MINUTES LATER, Trevon slipped inside Tahkiyah's condo as quietly as possible. "Tahkiyah?" he whispered as he closed the door. "Where you—"

"Shh." Tahkiyah tiptoed out of her bedroom wearing a dark purple chemise and matching boy shorts. "Please don't wake the kids," she whispered. "And what took you so long?"

"This is the only time I could get away from LaToria and Jurnee. When I left, they were kicking it with Glaze and Chelsea. Left alone, they'll still be talking about hair weave when I get back." He smirked.

Tahkiyah grinned. "Did you get my text?"

He nodded. "Uh-huh."

"So how does it feel to be the male actor of the year?"

"I'm still me," he replied. "Ain't no way I'll let this change me and I mean that."

"That's good to hear and I'm proud of you!" She smiled. "Now what's up? Do you really want to do this tonight?" she asked, hoping he would stick to his word.

He glanced down the hall. "I'm already here and I don't have any doubts about it. And besides, I know you're the best at keeping secrets." He reached for her hand.

~

KANDI AND JURNEE left the after-party downstairs and met up in the bedroom after receiving an identical text from Trevon.

"Do you know what this is about?" Jurnee asked Kandi.

Kandi shrugged. "I didn't even know he was gone!"

Jurnee glanced at the screen of her smartwatch and read the text again.

My Queen. Go to our bedroom asap & stay put. TTYL

Kandi sat on the blue and black sheeted bed and took off her pearl necklace. "I assume you called him and he didn't answer?"

Jurnee nodded as the gold and green sequin dress hugged her sensual curves. "When did you last see him?" she asked. "We've been up here for almost ten minutes!" she complained.

Kandi thought. "Uh, out by the pool talking to his brother."

Jurnee smacked her glossy lips and tried to figure out what Trevon was up to. "He needs to hurry up because I want to talk to Uncle Luke and—"

Trevon entered the bedroom with a crooked grin, clutching a bottle of Tanqueray No. Ten in one hand, and two goblets in the other. He closed the door with his foot.

Jurnee threw her hands on her hips. "What is this text about? And how are we hosting a party when we're all up here?"

"Chill, Queen," Trevon said, handing the glasses out. "Travis and Anthony will hold the party down."

Kandi took the drinking glass from Trevon. "You're up to something."

He ignored the comment as he turned to lock the door.

Jurnee frowned. "Baby, what are you—"

"Trust in your king," Trevon said. "I need you to chill for a minute and sit down next to LaToria."

Jurnee flicked her raven black hair over her shoulder and flopped down on the bed. "Okay. I'm sitting. Now what?"

He opened the bottle of chilled Tanqueray and filled each glass.

Kandi giggled, "Yeah, he's definitely up to something, that's for sure."

Trevon took a few gulps straight from the bottle before he turned and set in on the black and royal blue dresser. Next, he hurried across the room and slid open the tinted glass door of the walk-in closet. The lights inside the closet came on automatically when he entered the sizable closet.

"Y'all close your eyes right quick," he said from the closet.

Kandi took a sip of her drink. "Mmm, a surprise!" She closed her eyes.

Jurnee pouted. "Do we really—"

"Just do it, Jurnee." He paused. "Don't make me spank dat ass tonight."

Jurnee smiled. "Hmmm, you know I'll enjoy that."

"Just close your eyes, please?"

His request was met by his queens as they sat at the foot of the bed. Kandi enjoyed being surprised, so she didn't spoil it when she heard the bedroom door open. A few moments later, the door closed.

"Okay, y'all can open your eyes now!" Trevon announced.

Kandi and Jurnee were shocked by two sights. Trevon stood before them with an armful of roses and to his left stood the film crew for Jurnee's reality TV show.

Trevon handed Jurnee and Kandi a dozen roses each. "Let me talk. Y'all just listen. Tonight, I'm breaking the rule by letting the world into our bedroom. Tonight is special and I want to make things official with the two women that I love." He took their glasses back and set them on the floor.

Jurnee primped her hair in place, wanting to look her best at all times. She was used to the film crew in the house since they were filming a new season for *Nude Awakening*.

Trevon took a deep breath while trying to ignore the film crew. "My Queens." He looked at them. "We've been in this unique bond for a while, and we've had our share of ups and downs. But most of it has been good. I know I'm the luckiest man alive because I have two of the baddest Queens at my side. I love the both of you the same and tonight I want to show it deeper by my actions. What I feel for y'all isn't something you can doubt. Not today, not tomorrow... never!" He paused again and went down to one knee.

Jurnee covered her mouth.

Kandi gasped.

"Legally, I can't marry y'all both," Trevon said as he pulled out an oversized black felt ring box. "But ain't nothing gonna stop me from making my vows to y'all and doing my all to keep y'all hearts forever smiling."

Tears welled in his queens' eyes.

"Jurnee, LaToria," He opened the box, revealing a matching set of 5-carat chocolate diamond rings. "Will y'all be my queens, forever?"

"Si, Si!" Jurnee said with wet eyes.

"Yes, Smooch!" Kandi gushed.

Thanks to Tahkiyah, she had secretly gotten the rings sized for Kandi and Jurnee. Trevon had snuck out to visit Tahkiyah to pick up the rings. She was the first to get a FaceTime call from LaToria about the good news.

Trevon promptly shoved the film crew back out of the bedroom and turned his attention to LaToria and Jurnee. His awakening was spending time with the ones he loved and day by day, stroke by stroke... he enjoyed the fruits of life with his eyes open and his mind and body free.

"Smooch," LaToria whispered innocently as she rubbed his chest. "Turn the lights off."

Trevon moaned while Jurnee amorously slurped on his penis. He came up on his elbow and took pleasure in looking at what Jurnee was doing to him before he said, "Hey, Google, turn the bedroom lights off."

CLICK

The End

WHAT COULD BE MORE heartbreaking than to live and die... and never experience the joy and emotions of being loved and in love?

~Victor L. Martin

ABOUT THE AUTHOR

Victor L. Martin began his writing career back in 2003. His path to earning the title "author" was achieved while he was incarcerated. Born in Richmond, Virginia and raised in Selma, North Carolina and Miami, Florida, Victor used his life events to mix with fiction with the dose of reality to write his unique tales. Single, with no kids and set to make Atlanta, Georgia his new home will launch Victor to the pinnacle of his career in writing and his journey into filmmaking.

Photo by Dominique A. Covington

ALSO BY VICTOR L. MARTIN

The Game of Deception

Miami Nights

Miami Nights 2: Still Naked

Miami Nights 3: The Climax

Pretty Boy Hustlerz

Pretty Boy Hustlerz 2

CLASSIC
STREET LIT
S-E-R-I-E-S
FROM WAHIDA CLARK PRESENTS
INNOVATIVE PUBLISHING
WAHIDA CLARK PRESENTS
PRETTY BOY
HUSTLERZ
VICTOR L. MARTIN
WAHIDA CLARK PRESENTS
PRETTY BOY
HUSTLERZ
2
VICTOR L. MARTIN
WAHIDA CLARK
PRESENTS
INNOVATIVE PUBLISHING

NEW SCI-FI FANTASY
FROM WAHIDA CLARK PRESENTS INNOVATIVE PUBLISHING
LONERS
DB BRAY & WAHIDA CLARK
EMPERORS ASSASSINS
RESURRECTION
BOOK ONE IN THE KINDRED SERIES
ZED AMADEO
DEBRA RENEE BYRD
THE ROAD TO RESISTANCE
FIRST BOOK OF THE VANGUARD I
CHASE BOLLING
THE ROAD TO RESISTANCE
FIRST BOOK OF THE VANGUARD I
CHASE BOLLING
MAKE
CHASE BOLLING
SCIENCE FICTION FANTASY
FOR THE CULTURE
W. CLARK PUBLISHING
WAHIDA CLARK
PRESENTS
INNOVATIVE PUBLISHING

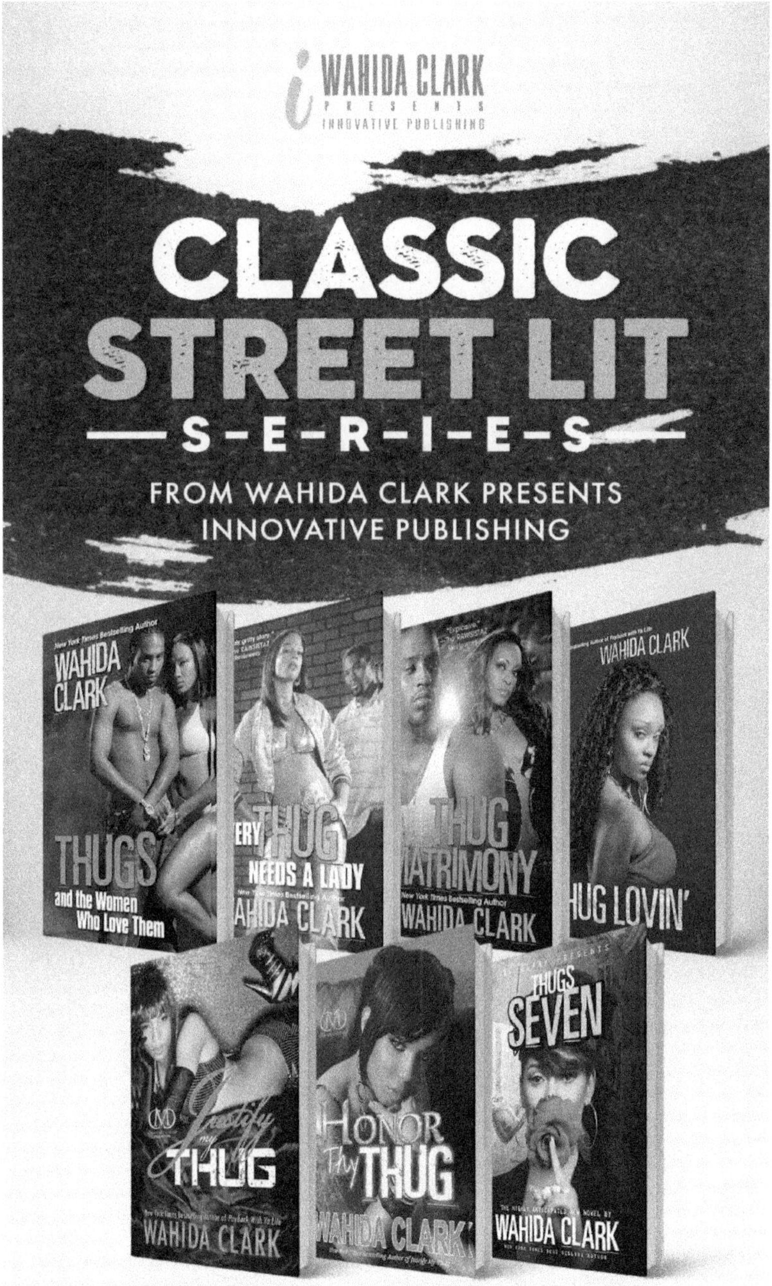
WAHIDA CLARK PRESENTS INNOVATIVE PUBLISHING
CLASSIC STREET LIT
S-E-R-I-E-S
FROM WAHIDA CLARK PRESENTS INNOVATIVE PUBLISHING
WAHIDA CLARK
THUGS and the Women Who Love Them
NEEDS A LADY
THUG MATRIMONY
THUG LOVIN'
THUG
HONOR Thy THUG
THUGS SEVEN

www.ingramcontent.com/pod-product-compliance
Lightning Source LLC
Chambersburg PA
CBHW070736190726
48292CB00002B/295
9781954161450